GOLDEN P

by
PETER WYLLIE SHILLAN

Two young men from entirely different backgrounds are subjected to brutal beatings by their peers in their early teenage years.

One is an extrovert, blond-haired mother's darling, living deep in the glens of Perthshire. The other is a black-haired, scar-faced introvert, brought to manhood in the crucible of the Gorbals in Glasgow.

Donald, the blond, is trained in martial arts by the Asian manservant of Lord Cruachan. Donald's father has a farm tenancy on Cruachan Estate and agrees to his son being trained by Chi Li, the sensei, in several disciplines.

Tammy, the introvert, is trained by a Chinese father and son who have also experienced the full weight of racial prejudice. If you see a Chinky, kick it, being the general theme in the environment in which they exist.

The two young men meet for the first time in Ulster, where the British Government unashamedly exploit the unusual talents of the two young warriors. They are both used as underground agents to uncover and destroy, where necessary, materials and armament being brought into the province to supply a new organisation called the Irish Republican Army.

This embryo minority faction is determined to use the bomb and the bullet to rid Ulster shores of the hated British, their sole aim being that Ireland should be forever Ireland entirely, and only for the Irish.

Donald and Tammy meet the cousins they will eventually marry, but their path of life is difficult, littered with hardship and pain before they achieve their happy unions.

The Yin and Yang philosophy that Chi Li has taught Donald proves itself yet again to Donald, who was initially most sceptical about its application.

Folklore and countrylore threads itself through the tangle of politics with horse breeding and training being the vehicle that carries the story to its culmination.

GOLDEN BOY

by

PETER WYLLIE SHILLAN

*To Diane & Jerry
Kindest Regards
RC Shillan*

HORSESHOE PUBLICATIONS . WARRINGTON . CHESHIRE

British Library Cataloguing in Publication Data

A Catalogue Record for this book is available from the British Library

ISBN 1 899310.16.9

First published 1997 by
HORSESHOE PUBLICATIONS
Box 37, Kingsley, Warrington,
Cheshire WA6 8DR

Book cover designed and illustrated
by Cheshire artist David Nolan

Printed in Great Britain by
Redwood Books Ltd
Trowbridge, Wilts

Chapter One

The south facing aspect of Bhein na Dhubb is precipitous and forbidding. Sheer faces with ugly slabs sticking out at impossible angles, providing a multitude of nooks and crevices, making ideal nesting places for many different kinds of birdlife.

A pair of golden eagles had laid claim to a spacious ledge two thirds of the way up the face of the mountain, ruling in arrogant dominance over all the other birds indigenous to the area.

The male eagle floated on the warm thermals rising from the rocks beneath, occasionally calling to his mate at the eyrie on the ledge. She answered his calls, but was obviously disturbed, even agitated by a presence on the cliff face directly beneath the nest. She shuffled her feathers and hopped from foot to foot showing her displeasure.

Chi Li, personal servant to Lord Cruachan, was aware of the eagle, and its agitation, but the awareness was only on the periphery of his concentration, as he was aware of all things around him, at one and part of his environment

Sitting in the lotus position he was motionless, concentrating on a tableau being enacted far below. His demeanour altered perceptibly as a herd of red deer came into view, led by a magnificent stag.

The stag looked ill at ease, frequently testing the wind, shaking his supremely antlered head as if frustrated by a will of the wisp feeling. He gave a coughing grunt, urinated copiously, then went down on his knees and rubbed his head, neck and chest in the aromatic discharge. Finally he dropped his head to feed.

A hundred yards downwind of the herd an eighteen year old youth called Donald melted into the heather each time the stag lifted its head.

Donald had been stalking for quite some time now. A time consuming ordeal that was coming to fruition. He knew full well that one whiff of his scent, and the deer would be off at a run, scattering to the winds.

Now it was a matter of progress by inches. To successfully merge into the landscape and be a part of it would mean the difference between achieving his goal or dismal failure.

Donald wore only a pair of grey linen shorts, a catapult was stuck down the back of the waistband. His golden tan merged with the dried grasses and bracken, but his blond yellow hair was a problem, making his advance more difficult, as it would be quickly spotted by a wary stag.

The stag and hinds moved to the lee of a granite cairn, a huge pile of boulders that seemed to have been dropped carelessly by some giant hand in a pre-age, but were in fact back spill from glaciation. Whatever, they somehow looked out of place in the otherwise level grassy area.

The hinds lay down to chew the cud, but the stag refused to rest. Unmercifully he thrashed a nearby gorse bush in his frustration, and, whilst he was thus employed, Donald prepared for the final thrust.

The light feather of wind blowing in his face would now alter dramatically. Warm air would rise from the rocks and suck in air from the surrounding area, which in turn would bring Donald's scent to the herd.

Donald brought his feet beneath him like a cougar prepared to spring, then left his position like a sprinter from starting blocks, making for the rear end of the stag, who was still thrashing away at the innocent gorse bush.

He covered the distance in the breath of a second and slapped the stag beneath the tail.

"Lord of the Glen, I salute you," he exulted.

The stag leapt the gorse bush in shock and amazement, then, contrary to the widespread belief, instead of fleeing he pivoted around, bugling his indignation,, and charged towards Donald. Head high, he emitted a staccato grunting cough, harsh and menacing.

Donald, who had been standing smiling in self congratulation at his incredible success, this had never been done before, now had a serious problem to confront.

Fight or flee, but the choice was easy for Donald. He ran towards the stag, everything now a blur of motion. He knew the head would come down to do serious business, he'd seen it so often with fighting stags, and now his life depended on that knowledge being correct.

When the head dropped Donald leapt high into the air, projecting himself forward over the antlers, emulating the ancient bull jumpers of Crete, his hands landing halfway along the stag's back, absorbing the shock on slightly bend arms; he thrust upwards to complete the forward somersault, and such was the power of his momentum he landed on the ground several feet behind the stag, this time with his knees bent to give thrust for a final forward rolling breakfall which brought him to his feet, already at speed to dash for the safety of the cairn of rocks.

The hinds had scattered like chaff in the wind, but the stag made one last attempt to reach his tormentor. Failing in this endeavour, he urinated copiously, spraying his belly and legs, whilst Donald teased him from the top of the cairn.

"Away ye old stinker, go and play with your girls, else I'll have to smack your bottie again," and gurgled with laughter as the stag replied by strutting around on stiff legs and grunting insanely.

Donald waited till the stag at last lost interest and set off after the hinds which were disappearing in the early morning mist.

'Well,' thought Donald, 'that had all been a bit of fun, but now he had another phase of his test to complete. He had to scale the sheer face of Bhein na Dhubb and locate his sensei, Chi Li, nicknamed Chilli by the locals.'

This next test would call for skill, daring and total application of mind and body. The climb would be hard enough, but locating Chi Li would also present a problem, for he could virtually disappear off the face of the earth.

Donald pursed his lips; the long bittersweet ululation of the whaup floated heart-rendingly doleful on the morning air. This was the signal to Chi Li that Donald was commencing with the next phase of the test.

Donald had practised bird and animal sounds from his youngest days and had built up an amazing repertoire, he also could imitate any accent to perfection.

He dropped down from his perch, and taking a slab of brackenbread from his pocket, started to break his fast. Brackenbread consists of oatmeal, wild berries, chopped onions and bacon bound by beaten egg, then cooked in bacon fat in a slow oven. When cooled, it makes a very nutritious cake. Travelling herdsmen in days of yore had used such sustenance in their long travels, a very satisfying repast which could be eaten on the move.

Munching contentedly, Donald proceeded towards the base of Bhein na Dhubb in the near distance. He paused to drink the peaty water from a burn, regretting that he hadn't time to linger awhile and do some guddling for the fine speckled trout he saw lying in the shadows of the bank. A fine Highland sport of tickling a trout until the forefinger and thumb could sink into the gills and heave it free onto the bank.

As he approached the base of the rockface he shuddered at the sheer ugliness of the granite mass confronting him, malevolent and threatening, with vicious jagged teeth sticking out at every angle, some of them obviously loose in their sockets due to the effect of the elements.

Directly beneath the face it didn't look any better. It would take all his determination to climb the tortuous mass. His early morning exertions and excitement would pale into insignificance by comparison to this new ordeal

A fluid tensing of the muscles, and the climb began. Easy the first few feet or so, but increasingly it became much more difficult, the strain on fingers and toes became more intense, but he persevered onwards and upwards.

At last there was a chance of a small respite. Just as well, for the next move was fraught with danger. The fingers of his left hand had purchase on a minute ledge, his right hand he had clubbed in a crevice so that rock pressure on his fist held him secure. His bare toes were spread and curled like a treecreeper's, giving tenuous purchase on a very narrow ledge.

He now had to traverse to the left slightly. To do this he had to release his right hand and bring it across to his left, then reach for a fresh hold with his right hand. The strain on his toes and the fingers of his left hand would be enormous, and the flakiness at the fingertips of his left hand meant that his grip at that particular point was none too secure.

Digging in more fiercely with his toes he unclenched his right hand and, with a tremor of anxiety, realised his trunk would have to sway back to allow his arm to pass between his body and the rockface. Thought of the danger of this move raised the hair on the back of his neck, and a fresh flood of sweat broke over him; however, to make progress he was bound to make the attempt.

An eternity seemed to pass as he clung grimly, exerting maximum willpower to force his muscles, which were burning with over-exertion, to keep him in contact with the rockface. With the perspiration flowing freely, he felt the onset of cramp in his forearms and calf muscles. He was bound to take action or he would surely plunge to his death.

Suddenly, through the mist of pain, he became aware of something digging into the base of his stomach. His right hand, almost of its own accord, sought and found the protruding jagged edge of rock.

Gasping with relief, he adjusted his body to allow his right hand to absorb his weight and ease the incredible pressure off his toes and left hand.

The relief was immediate, and as fortune smiled, he found that from there on there was a sufficiency of hand and footholds to enable him to reach a vertical ledge wide enough for him to take a well earned rest.

Donald surveyed the situation from his temporary haven. The only part that should give him any trouble was an area about eight feet short of his desired goal. At this point a great slab of rock stood out and away from the sheer face like some suburban carport roof.

Breathing restored, and muscles somewhat eased, Donald renewed his attack on the rock face, and, after twenty minutes of determined effort, he reached the overhang.

The perpendicular face on first appraisal was a nightmare to behold. Covered with moss, slick with moisture as water trickled from tiny fissures, it would be extremely difficult to get any kind of a purchase, and worse still, how would he ever be able to traverse the underside of the overhang?

Donald felt tiredness creeping in, and with it came an insidious feeling of defeatism. Was it really all necessary? It was madness to put himself through this. Why bother!

Recognising this erosion of willpower, Donald immediately clamped down on it. Intoning a mantra, he transcended into Theta. A haven of tranquillity, refreshing mind and body.

Something nudged at his sensibilities. A promise! Fragile and elusive as a butterfly hovering tantalisingly, but not quite within grasp. Then, like an Alpen bell tinkling in the distance, intermittent, insistent, then becoming crystal clear, he remembered the teaching of his sensei, Chi Li.

Observation is an acquired art. Appraise in depth. See what you are looking at, not what you think you see.

Donald reappraised the rockface and new information flooded into his brain. He realised that where the water seeped through the fissures it had kept a small area free of moss and the cracks were on a horizontal plane giving reasonable hand holds. Yes! the climb would be difficult, but it was possible.

Right! thought Donald, I can reach to where the roof meets the vertical face, but, where do I go from there? His eyes quartered back and forth across the face. His straining eyes suddenly noted what looked like a dark shadow. He started and gave an exclamation of surprise, for suddenly a jackdaw appeared within the shadow. A fleeting glimpse and it was gone.

This was stimulus enough to get Donald climbing again, for that jackdaw had not alighted from this side, so it meant there was an escape avenue to the other side.

Grimly he made progress up the sheer face. As his fingers entered the fissure it blocked off the water for an instant, then escaped in little spurts, showering him with icy freshness.

His head hit the overhang and he paused to assess the situation. Where had he spotted the jackdaw? Yes! now he had it! From this position, the dark shadow was now a light plane. In that instant a shadow passed across it. The jackdaw again? Perhaps!

He moved a fraction to his left and saw that he was faced with what looked to be the entrance to a small tunnel. He got purchase and pulled himself forward into the mouth of the tunnel and realised his breadth of shoulder was going to be a problem.

He adopted the 'melt bones' technique Chi Li had taught him. This is total relaxation of the muscles to such a degree the bones seem to melt into the flesh. A few wriggles and Donald was free.

He emerged from the tunnel at the great slab of rock that Chi Li had used as a back rest whilst watching Donald and the stag at play. He sat down for a moment of respite, noticing that he had lost quite a bit of skin on his climb up the rockface.

Now he had to locate his sensei. This would not be easy. Humming a mantra and expanding his aura, he stood immobile, listening and looking, even testing the air with his nostrils.

He gave all the signs of having shed the mantle of civilisation, resembling a hunter predator of the jungle. He was functioning in a totally primal way, using archaic ancestral natural talents that had been rediscovered and honed to perfection.

He sensed the nearness of Chi Li, but as that feeling was muted he decided that Chi Li had literally 'gone to ground'. He searched around, led by the nose, for he could smell the light herbal oils that Chi Li used in his toilette.

An upside down 'L' shaped slab of rock gave access down into what looked like a small foyer-like cave with light streaming in from both sides. He paused on the grey granite dust that covered the floor, and spotted the entrance to a larger cave to his right.

His first clue to Chi Li's whereabouts was the dust on the floor which had been lightly brushed over, finishing at the entrance to the larger cave.

His second clue was the distinct aroma of the herbal wash beloved of his sensei.

Donald edged to the mouth of the cave, walking on the outer edges of his bare feet. He was now stalking the most elusive and difficult of prey, man!

Donald went through the opening in a forward rolling breakfall of bewildering speed, taking him deep into the larger cave. He came to his feet, and whirled into the crouched stance of self defence, perfectly balanced with one foot slightly wide and to the rear, arms held loosely but at the ready, waist high.

Even then, he was almost too late as Chi Li hurtled towards him, seemingly out of a void. Three feet away from Donald he stopped, spun in a pirouette and his right foot came scything forward in the dreaded triple kick, aimed at the groin, end of the sternum or jugular, each lethal if delivered on target.

Donald swayed with an economy of movement, and the sublime grace of a trained ballet dancer, avoiding the advancing foot as he thrust forward to meet the attack.

His mouth opened, emitting an eerie, awesome coughing thrum. The warrior's song. A violent vibration, intimidating and nerve sapping, paralysing the nervous system of an opponent.

His left hand rose with the speed of a striking cobra, middle and index fingers extended and rigid, his thumb held between the first joints to avoid bursting Chi Li's eyeballs, as he executed the snakebite; a dreadful and demoralising gouging of the eyes that would immediately undermine the confidence of any combatant.

In the same instant his right hand rose, and with infinite accuracy found the carotid nerve, digging a rigid middle finger deep into its source.

Chi Li collapsed, 'hors de combat'. Quickly Donald applied the recovery technique and jumped clear and took up the defence stance again. Perhaps the battle was not yet over?

Chi Li sat up and focused on Donald, then smiled with calm satisfaction. "Neh! Little one! You have indeed become a warrior," he said, with pride glowing on his face.

He stood up and bowed to his student, who would never be a student again. 'Yes!' he thought with quiet satisfaction, 'I have taught him self sufficiency, he will never be brutalised again.'

Chi Li unwound a length of plaited cotton from around his waist. On one end was a black tassel, on the other a red. He came over to Donald and with his own hands wound the cord around Donald's waist, tying it with a special knot.

He produced a thin silver ring, emblazoned with a dragon and sword motif, and placed it on the fifth finger of Donald's left hand.

When Donald had faced multi-confrontation, and passed successfully, the red tassel would be replaced by a black, and the ring would be worn on his right hand, then he would truly be a sensei in his own right.

Chi Li bowed again, then in ceremonial tones counselled Donald in the code of honour of the true warrior.

"   *Be humble at all times.*

Be generous of spirit.

Treat all men as equals.

Avoid trouble, mentally and physically.

Forever be known as a gentle man.

I charge you with these rules, and you must abide by them. Never use your ability and knowledge for self satisfaction."

Donald's head was full to bursting point, and the lump in his throat was a pain of suffocation. Emotion flowed through him in waves of nerve-searing heat.

Exercising immense willpower his face remained a frozen mask, revealing nothing of the tumult within.

He bowed deeply and stated with a dignity beyond his years, "I see you, sensei, and I give my solemn oath."

Donald stepped forward and held up both hands, fingers splayed apart facing Chi Li, who came to meet him doing likewise. Their palms struck, fingers sliding between fingers, interlocking and squeezing in a warrior's salutation.

Later Chi Li would remember that Donald's fifth finger on each hand had been on the outside, the position of strength and superiority. In truth he would have expected nothing less.

Chi Li went over to a ledge in the cave and returned with a small bundle wrapped in a piece of goatskin,, yellow with age. He unwrapped it and produced a knife about eight inches long, including the handle which had been bound with copper wire that gleamed with a warm golden glow.

Almost shyly, he handed the knife to Donald, saying it had been meant for the son he would now never have, and would Donald do him the honour of accepting this unworthy gift. Donald mutely accepted it with a nod, then whirled and dashed from the cave. He did not want his mentor to see the tears in his eyes.

Chi Li was not disturbed by the abrupt departure of Donald, he well knew the strong emotions that would be holding his young warrior in thrall.

He made himself a sweet herbal tea, and sitting drinking it he recalled in his mind how it had all started, this training of Donald.

He had been returning from the market in Perth with his master, the Lord Cruachan, when a premonition had caused him concern. As they proceeded along the narrow glen road the feeling changed to anxiety. Suddenly Chi Li asked the laird to stop and was out and running before the Landrover could come to a complete halt.

He ran along the edge of a burn, then came to a horrified stop, gasping in sheer disbelief at what he was seeing.

Two well-built lads were holding a struggling youth, whilst another, bigger and stronger-looking than his accomplices, was whipping the exposed back with a length of barbed wire. Laying on with full strength, sadistic delight on his face as he screamed obscenities.

"Stinkin' teuchter. Mealy mouthed arsehole. This'll teach ye, ye posh moothed wee bastard. Ye're yella like yer hair. Tak that, an' that." Each phrase was punctuated by a grunt of exertion as the wire found its mark.

Chi Li was among them like a she bear protecting cubs, as he threw them one after the other onto the rocks in the burn. The youths quickly scrambled up the bank and made off as if the devil of hell was on their tail.

Gently as a mother with her new born babe, Chi Li lifted the slight figure from the rock he'd been spreadeagled across, to find it was Donald, the only son of his friend Stuart Macdonald, the tenant farmer of Craigburn.

Donald made not a murmur, even though the pain must have been excruciating, nor had the bullies had the pleasure of hearing him whimper during the beating.

Chi Li had an extensive knowledge of herbs and their qualities in healing, and always carried a small doeskin wallet containing various lotions and potions. When he had cleaned the wounds on Donald's back he applied the salve that would heal and ease the pain. The laird stood by, pronouncing to the world that he would see the Macmillan brothers one day would get their comeuppance for this dreadful assault.

When the salve had been applied, Donald rolled over and with almost superhuman strength rose to his feet. Chi Li instinctively moved to assist him, but Donald imperiously withdrew from any contact.

Standing erect, the laird and Chi Li saw that he had been subjected to a systematic beating . Apart from the damage to his back, his lips were a mangled mess, his left eye was closing and large bruises covered his chest and insides of his legs, testifying to the judicious footwork of the bullies.

Donald looked at his rescuers in turn. "Thank you," he mumbled through his swollen, damaged mouth, "I'll be fine now, thanks again," and turned to walk away. Half a step and he dropped like a log, but, before he could hit the ground, Chi Li caught him and gathered him up into his arms.

The laird and his manservant were having great difficulty in containing their emotions. Both fighting men of high calibre, having seen many atrocities in various theatres of war, this cowardly act left them morally and physically sickened; beyond that, they could not help but be impressed by the sheer courage and raw guts that had been displayed by the boy being carried gently to the Landrover.

Thankfully Donald, being unconscious, was not aware of the journey to the 'big house', as the locals called the home of the laird. Chi Li held him tenderly each time the vehicle hit a pothole or bounced in the ruts of which there were many.

Quickly, Donald was carried up to a bedroom on the first floor of the mansion house. Doctor Fergusson was called and a messenger sent to bring the Macdonalds.

Chi Li placed Donald in the recovery position in an effort to avoid contact of the most traumatised areas, and as Lady Cruachan entered and saw the extent of the damage she blanched and grabbed a dresser, so great was the shock.

"What animal did this?" she whispered brokenly.

The laird looked across at her. "Don't insult our innocent animals," he growled, "this is the handiwork of the three Macmillan boys, and by God they will sorely rue this day's handiwork."

The laird wheeled and left the bedroom, descended the stairs, advising the housekeeper, Mrs Macgillvery, as he passed her, that he would be in his study, and on no account was the Macdonald to see his son until he, the laird, had spoken to him first. He well knew that when Stuart arrived and saw what had happened to his only child, it would take all his diplomatic skills to avoid a further tragedy occurring.

He heaved a sigh of relief, as the first glimmerings of an idea came to him, and the more he mulled it over the clearer it became. Now all he had to do was sell it to the Macdonald.

Doctor Fergusson arrived and on examining Donald discovered two broken ribs on the left side, which he would leave to mend naturally. He noted the bruising on the groin and inner thighs. Tenderly he lifted the scrotum sac to look for damage to the testes, but found only an empty sac.

He asked everyone to leave the room except Chi Li, and almost stuttered as he asked Donald the burning question. "Donald, what in God's name happened to your testes. I know you had them, for I delivered you myself, and had the privilege of telling the Macdonald that his firstborn was a boy, so what happened lad?"

Donald's eyes fixed on a point behind the doctor's head. "I, well, I, um, I drew them up into myself," he confessed. The doctor looked at his young patient in astonishment.

"Laddie, laddie, it's a physical impossibility. Ach you're all confused with yourself. I cannot for the life of me accept what you have told me."

Seeing Donald's consternation, Chi Li quickly intervened. "Excuse me, please, good doctor," he offered apologetically, "it is possible to do this thing of which Donald speaks. In the eastern countries it is impossible for martial arts warriors to obtain the ultimate rank if they cannot master this technique. I have this expertise, and if it will save Donald from embarrassment, I will gladly demonstrate for you."

Donald looked gratefully in Chi Li's direction, both for the intervention and for the knowledge that he was not unique in this strange ability.

The old doctor looked at them both, then smiled at Donald and winked as he remarked that, due to this unusual ability, Donald was lucky in the circumstances, and would still provide grandchildren for the old Macdonald yet.

The doctor left Donald under the care of Chi Li and went down and joined the laird in his study, accepting with alacrity the ten year old malt whisky he was offered.

The laird advised the doctor that the Macdonald would soon be arriving, and outlined his plan to keep Donald at the manor house until he was better, and then to have the Macdonald agree to Donald being trained by Chi Li in martial arts, so a recurrence could never happen, and would the doctor be good enough to give him support.

Readily Dr Fergusson agreed, and not before time. Coming through the quiet of the gloaming could be heard the sound of the pibroch. The stirring march of 'Donald Dhu' was being played, aye, and at competition standard too, the laird was sure.

The laird smiled across the room at Ewan Fergusson, and observed wryly, "The Macdonald announces his approach in a style that is all his own."

As the laird reached the front door Macdonald was marching along the red pebble drive. Reaching the wide steps, he finished with a fine flourish and mounted the steps with an easy grace and proud bearing.

"A fine evening, is it not, your Lordship?" he teased, with a disarming smile, which disappeared when he saw the grave look on the laird's face.

"Come away in Stuart," the laird replied, "I have a nice ten year old malt that would be the better for your tasting." Giving Stuart no chance to reply, the laird wheeled about and returned to the study.

Stuart entered the study, and frowned with apprehension when he saw the old doctor sitting sipping whisky. "Sit down Stuart," the laird invited as he handed over a large malt, "I have a wee story to tell you, and I want a full undertaking from you that you will hear me out before you say or do anything. Trust me, as we have trusted each other over these long years together. I give my pledge to you, that what I propose is for the best."

The Macdonald was now on the edge of the chair, the drink forgotten, and that was a measure of his concern for he was partial to a dram.

Briefly the laird explained what had happened and what his proposal was. He took a large gulp of his drink, and waited for the explosion. It never happened.

Quietly the Macdonald rose to his feet and carefully placed the whisky glass on a nearby table, the drink untouched.

"Perhaps I have missed something," he forced out through clenched teeth, "or am I to understand that the perpetrators of this cowardly attack meet no justice? Is that what you want me to accept?"

He made for the door, "A doot ye know me not at all," he ground out, "a reckoning is due, and I must exercise my right to claim it. I bid you goodnight, gentlemen."

He reached the door to find his exit barred by Lady Cruachan.

"Good evening Stuart, would you be kind enough to give me a minute of your time?" Gently, but firmly, she took him by his brawny arm and drew him back into the study, lifted the abandoned drink and placed it firmly into his reluctant hand.

"I give you a toast," she announced in a no-nonsense manner, "a toast to a remarkable young lad called Donald Macdonald, who has shown great courage and forbearance in the face of adversity and humiliation, without a murmur of complaint; but, it would be further indignity were he not allowed attrition in full measure by his own hand. He must surely have the right to exact his own retribution, or is that a mere woman's point of view?"

Four glasses lifted as one as the toast was drunk. Stuart again listened to the plans for Donald and agreed it was the best solution, albeit he still bubbled inside with deep seated anger.

Mari Macdonald arrived, and together they went up to see the only child they would ever produce between them. Together they cried at the bedside of their sleeping son, then wearily went home, leaving Donald in the care of their slightly built Asian friend.

Chi Li checked to make sure the sleeping draught he had given Donald was still taking effect, then quietly left the room to seek out the laird. He knew where he would find him.

In the study, the laird was now sitting on his own. He waved Chi Li to a chair, but didn't offer a drink, knowing it would be refused. He explained to Chi Li that he wanted him to take charge of Donald's education in the martial arts, and that they would virtually be exiled to the hunting lodge in upper Glencruachan.

The laird would provide the basic staples for survival, but hunting and fishing would be required by the two to supplement and provide the necessary protein intake.

Always one to learn, Chi Li asked the laird what a teuchter was, he'd heard the oldest Macmillan use the word when he was beating Donald. The laird paused for a while, then looked at Chi Li and explained that it was a parochial word. In

Scotland, the common plover, or lapwing, or peewit, was also called a teuchat, and young farm boys used to collect their eggs and sell them to station masters, who transported them to the high class restaurants in London. It was a way of getting a bit of extra income, but the teuchters were also conservationists, in that they would take only two eggs at a time, but then would leave the clutch to be hatched, knowing that they mustn't kill the goose that laid the golden egg, or in this case, the providing teuchat.

He could only imagine that to be called a teuchter in a derogatory way meant that anyone who would stoop to making money from wild birds' eggs showed that he would go to any lengths to make money, but having said all that, he doubted that John Macmillan understood the principles of it all.

Chi Li thanked the laird and returned to the bedroom for his nightlong vigil beside Donald's bed. He would seldom be absent from his self-imposed task, but he looked forward immensely to this new project the laird had set him.

He had felt he was becoming somewhat lethargic of late and this now would allow him to re-hone his own skills. He had always liked Donald, who had ever been respectful and polite, and Chi Li felt sure that the knowledge he would give to Donald would never ever be used in the wrong way.

Chapter Two

By the time Donald reached the top of the middle glen of Cruachan he had regained his composure. He gave a call sign to his Arab mare, he knew she would be close to where he had left her when he started to stalk the stag.

The peculiar fluting whistle he used was unique to him and the mare. Three notes, rising in scale, cut off by hitting the back of his teeth with his tongue, then three notes down the scale; the part in the middle sounded like the dirl of a grace note on the bagpipes. He doubted if anyone would be able to emulate the callsign.

The mare came into view in immediate response to his whistle, her beautiful dished head appearing over the bracken as she raced towards him. She nibbled at him, expecting, and receiving, a tidbit, even though it was only a very badly squashed piece of brackenbread.

The Arab mare had been a gift from the laird to Donald on the occasion of his sixteenth birthday. She had originally been meant for the laird's daughter, but sadly the daughter had died, a victim of poliomyelitis, so the little mare had been running wild for three years. She was high spirited, unhandled, and would not yield to the brutal handlings meted out to the Garron ponies that were used throughout the estate.

The laird remembered Donald's amazing ability and rapport with animals and decided that the two would well suit each other. This proved to be the case, for when the head groom arrived with the fractious, bad tempered looking pony, her tail was lashing from side to side like a berserkers whip, her teeth kept flashing ominously as she kicked and skittered around.

Quietly Donald approached her, holding out his hand palm up, the small gathering watching with bated breath. Donald invaded the filly's space a little deeper. He pursed his lips and produced a sound similar to that a foal would make to its mother, a gentle plaintive whicker.

The filly stopped dancing around, and moved towards Donald, who repeated the sound. Again the filly edged forward, then sniffed at the extended open palm. Donald leant forward slightly and blew gently into her nostrils. He took the finals step up close to her, then ever so gently, like a butterfly landing on a flower, he rested his hand on her silken nose, and again blew into the delicate trumpets of her nostrils.

She exhaled small, snorting gusts, then nibbled at the fingers of the hand beneath her velvety nose.

Donald slowly lifted his hand, rubbed her forehead, then caught the flickering ears, pulling and caressing gently as he crooned a wordless lullaby.

Finally he placed his hand behind her slim jawbone, and exerting a slight pressure, spoke clearly for the first time.

"Come with me, sweet girl. I'll look after you. We'll be good friends, you'll see. Come on! Gently does it. Away with Donald."

To the astonishment of the onlookers, they moved away together, as if it was the most natural thing in the world.

The head groom turned to the laird, shaking his head in wonderment at what had occurred. "I've been amongst horses all my life," gasped in disbelief, "but I have never seen anything like it. She was a vicious wee monster and turned into a veritable lamb. Had I not seen it with my own eyes I would never have believed it." He shook his head and continued, "I have heard of the gift, the horseman's telling word it is called, but I never gave it any credence. In fact I still think I am dreaming. What about having him join the grooms, sir? He'd be worth his weight in gold in the stables."

The laird smiled and shook his head in the negative. "No! I think not. Donald has just returned from exile and is now keen to help his father, Stuart, on the farm at Craigburn, and that is how it should be."

Donald led the filly up the winding narrow glen road towards Craigburn, never rushing her, crooning and talking to her all the time. It was then that he decided to train her in a totally different way to that used on the hardy Garron ponies of the estate.

Falling off a Garron's back meant you were left without a ride, but Donald's idea was, that if a horse enjoyed your company and trusted you, then it would be likely to wait while you picked yourself up and remounted. This in fact proved to be the case on several occasions to come.

Because the mare was unhappy with bridle or saddle it was a challenge to overcome. Patience, kindness and infinite repetition brought the required results, as time eventually proved.

He taught the mare to come to the whistle by always having a tidbit for her as a reward, but eventually she only had to get wind of his scent and she would race towards him.

Patiently he handled her, rubbing first with his hands, then currycomb and dandy brush, but whatever he used he let her see them and sniff them, never making sudden moves, and all the time crooning softly to her. Eventually he could wash and groom her, clean and pare her hooves and clean her delicate nostrils, and in general do any of the tasks allied to good horse management. Her coat gleamed like oiled silk, her eyes were clear and bright with intelligence, with her ears flickering in attentiveness. A truly delightful little mare in every way.

The rapport was firmly established between Donald and the mare now, so gradually he started leaning across her back, and when she tolerated this with no fuss, he increased the weight by lifting his feet clear off the ground.

He brought a three-legged milking stool into the loosebox, and let her get used to its presence. Next, he stood up on it, letting her see him towering above her. The next move was to slide his leg across her back and let his weight settle. He felt her tense, muscles quivering. He skin seemed to shiver like the windblown surface of a loch. He crooned softly to her, gently pulling at her ears, and stroking the quivering flesh.

The beautiful dished head turned and she sniffed his right leg, then, to his surprise and delight, she walked forward to the hayrack and started nibbling at the hay.

Donald continued this exercise many times, even in the paddock, where she could have charged away. He nudged her with his heels and she moved forward, then to get her to turn right he squeezed with his right heel and pushed his left toes behind her front left leg. Obediently she turned, and did the same to go left when he reversed the tactic.

He leaned back and pulled on her mane, making a shush sound, and was delighted when she came to a halt. He brought his left leg across and slid to the ground. Immediately he hit the ground he took hold of a handful of mane, and again putting his left hand on her back, he leapt astride again.

Donald continued this kind of training, always praising her and giving her tidbits, until it all became quite commonplace. Pressure of both heels set her forward, lean back to stop. Lean forward meant go fast, and this she certainly could do.

To Donald, used to the bumpy ride of the short-coupled Garron, her speed, and the sublime smoothness of it, was a wonderful exhilarating experience.

What a reward for patience and perseverance, kindness and consideration. Donald gave no thought to his own part in the culmination of his training, or his own understanding of animals, his natural gift and affinity with them.

Perhaps what transpired during the following weeks was unusual, for quite quickly the rapport that developed was almost uncanny, it seemed that he had only to think of a change in direction and she would immediately carry out that manoeuvre.

Maybe it was an unconscious movement of his body posture that conveyed his intentions, but whatever it was, a coordinated thought process seemed to exist so that there was no physical appearance of control.

Soon Donald was carrying out his duties on the farm, always using the little mare when he required a mount, and the glen folk soon got used to seeing the pair racing around, for all the world looking like a Centaur of Greek mythology.

Often Donald's thoughts would return to the time he spent in exile at the hunting lodge, where Chi Li had honed his already proficient skills of tracking and stalking.

He was taught how to use ordinary house utensils as lethal weapons, either for offence of defence.

His observation was taken in hand, for as far as Chi Li was concerned, Donald was almost blind.

Chi Li started the exercise by putting several articles on a tray, allowing Donald to observe them. Next he would remove certain articles and ask Donald to name the missing articles.

This was advanced to rearranging the items and getting Donald to replace them in their original order. When Donald had mastered this technique, Chi Li took him outdoors and a whole new world evolved before Donald's eyes.

He was taught the advantages of peripheral sight as well as direct vision. He learned to use his nose in a way that has been forgotten by modern society, but also learned how to merge with his environment and become a part of it.

It was during this time that he also developed close proximity presence and could discern whether that presence was danger from the source, or if it was a large or small presence.

He had kept up his practice with the catapult and used it to supply the stewpot in the lodge. He soon scorned a sitting target and would take a bird on the wing or a running rabbit.

During his stay at the lodge he had worn only a pair of shorts, and always he ran unshod. At first this had seemed a strange request by his sensei, but he quickly discovered that the tactility of his feet enhanced to such an extent that, should his foot land on a twig that might snap and betray his presence, almost of its own accord his foot would curl and muffle the sound, or glide over to firmer ground.

The cruel winter months presented different kinds of problems for Donald and Chi Li. Sometimes they were confined to the lodge for days on end, but Chi Li, with great imagination, forestalled any kind of cabin fever that could have disrupted their rapport, by inventing all kinds of exercises, games and techniques that further enhanced Donald's skills as a warrior.

At the end of two years, Donald was a self-assured and competent warrior in every sense of the word, but still had retained his innate politeness and civility, a credit to the careful attention of his sensei.

Occasionally Donald would think of the Macmillan trio, but not with any apprehension now that his training was completed. Time in itself would bring the inevitable confrontation.

On the way home from giving Donald the brutal beating, the Macmillans carried out another vile piece of thuggery. At the junction of the main road and the lane leading up to their home stood a little cottage, where widow Stewart lived with her tabby cat for company.

The widow was standing at the garden gate talking to the roadman, and turned and greeted the lads with a friendly smile.

The friendly cat came running out and rubbed itself against John's leg. Impatiently and roughly he pushed it aside. Perversely it returned to continue its greeting.

"Get aff o' me ye bloody thing," he growled in irritation. The cat returned with arched back and waving tail.

Mrs Stewart had moved back along the path, intending to go and fetch something for the boys, she paused and turned round to see what the commotion was.

In the meantime, John bent down, picked up the offending animal and dropkicked it over the gate. The cat landed with its back feet on widow Stewart's ample bosom, the front feet on her cheeks. The bared talons sliced through to the bone, narrowly missing her startled eyes. Fractions from blindness.

The force and shock threw her onto her back with the cat still screeching and tearing at her. The horrified roadman broke the inertia which had rooted him to the spot, dashed through the gate and pulled the demented cat clear of the havoc it was doing to the face and chest of its owner.

Throwing the cat clear, he gently lifted the widow to her feet and, recognising that she was in deep shock, started to guide her along the garden path towards the house.

"Aye! Get yersel inside, afore a kick yer arse as weel," shouted the delighted John to the roadman, then, laughing loudly in chorus with his brothers, continued on their way home.

They were met at their home-steading with curses from their choleric, prancing, furious father, a brutal foulmouthed man who ruled his little empire with boot and fist. He lashed around trying to land a telling blow to vent his ever ready anger, but his sons were well used to this and scattered like chaff in strong wind.

They finished the chores that had been waiting for them, then had to run the gauntlet of kicks and cuffs from their still disgruntled father before they could sit down to the evening meal.

Mary, their sister, watched the onslaught of her family trenching, whilst she delicately picked at her own food. She marvelled at the copious amounts they could devour, and at their total disregard of any kind of table manners.

No pleasant conversation attended this family gathering. It was purely and simply a voracious attack, accompanied by slurps and grunts and deep belly belches. Arms stretching out and grabbing, the main aim to get as much down as possible in the shortest possible time. Not a pretty sight whatever.

When the meal was finished, old Macmillan detailed out the evening's chores. No time to sit back and allow a period to digest the food, that kind of thing was only for gentry folk who had nothing better to do anyhow.

They all departed from the house to attend to their various assignments. John gave Mary a scowl as he roughly barged past her, deliberately knocking her against the passage wall, as he whispered an obscenity to her.

He hurried through his tasks, giving little heed to what he was doing. His thoughts were on how to exercise his spite on Mary, who, in his warped mind had gotten him into trouble when he returned from meeting his brothers from the school bus, so that they could give that Macdonald whelp his much deserved beating. He felt she had cliped to his father, letting him know that John was not at his work in the fields where he should have been.

He kept looking out of the rear door of the stable, watching for Mary to finish her task of closing the poultry houses for the night. He saw her close the last coop, and went to the doorway.

Forcing a worried look onto his face he shouted urgently. "Hey! Mary! Quick! Come and see this." Mary made no move to respond to his bidding. She had no rapport with her eldest brother, had he not already this evening displayed his contempt for her.

"What is it John," she enquired suspiciously, "what trick are you up to now?"

"It's no trick, for God's sake," he blasphemed, "it's your favourite old tabby, there's somethin' the matter wi' her. Ah think ye'ed better hae a look at her." Well he knew his sister and her love of animals, particularly her old pet tabby.

Mary, still unsure, approached cautiously but steadily. "If you have done something to her John, you'll be sorry, now what's the matter? Where is she?" she queried, reaching the door.

John moved aside to let his sister enter the stable. "Over in the corner, on that heap o' straw," he answered, as he slammed the stable door shut and rattled in the bars.

Mary had reached halfway to the pile of straw and stopped, realising she had been duped. She knew with deep-seated intuition that her sibling was up to no good.

She turned like a cornered tigress, ready to fight her way out, but she was too late. John grabbed the upraised arms, he knew the damage those long nails, on fingers clawed to strike, could cause and he wanted none of that.

Brutally crossing the slender wrists he wrapped them in his huge workhardened left hand, while his right grabbed her hair, cruelly twisting a handful of the sleek black tresses, close to the roots.

Mary, with maniacal strength, tried to drive her knee deep into his crotch, but he read her intention and easily avoided the desperate attempt.

"Noo then ye wee clipe," he exulted, "ye got me intae trouble wi' the auld yin, din't ye, an' oh! dear me! hae ye got trouble noo. Ye're like that wee arsehole o' a boyfreen, ye think ye're better than yer ain family, wi' yer posh weys an' dainty habits."

"Ah saw the wey ye watched us at oor denner. We disgust ye, don't we? Weel, am gon' tae disgust ye a wee bit mair. Gie ye a taste o' whit we gaed that shite o' a Macdonald."

During his rantings, as spittle flew from his distorted mouth, he had been alternatively twisting and screwing her hair, whilst the fingers of his left hand exerted ever more pressure on the slim wrists they held, to such an extent he had restricted the blood flow.

He completely lost control, his mind in a red mist of temper. He caught hold of the neck of her blouse and reft it asunder, any future punishment from his father that might ensue became of no consequence.

His eyes fell on the naked, budding breasts, already filling out to promising beauty, and the insanity became complete. An explosion of sexual lust devoured him in an all-consuming violent thunder.

He seized a nipple, stiffened by fear, between finger and thumb, squeezing with satanic pleasure. Leaning forward, he gripped the other between his teeth, biting and sucking as low animal noises escaped from deep in his throat.

Mary fought in silent fury at this indecent assault, but was no match to the bestial strength that opposed her, it was like a flea wrestling with a peanut.

Her brother, by now fully tumescent, had released his erection from the confines of his britches, and was now ripping off her delicate panties, as he had already done with her tweed skirt. He was intent only on satisfying his primeval needs.

He threw Mary backwards onto a bale of straw and forced her legs wide with his powerful thighs. He stabbed repeatedly at her with the pulsating, gorged instrument, purple headed and menacing.

Mary kept pushing her bottom into the straw bale, her only means of defiant defence against her brother's maniacal strength. Refusing to be thwarted, or defeated, John grabbed first one leg then the other and positioned them over his shoulders, then, by using his weight, he pushed forward and leant down, effectively trapping the legs and turning Mary's vagina upwards.

The angle was now perfect for penetration, and this John did with a ferocious thrust, totally unconcerned that the unreceptive passage was without lubrication for sexual intercourse, or that his little sister was a virgin.

Mary tried to scream with the violent ripping asunder of the hymen, but her mouth was full of her own arm, which John had used as a gag. She felt as if her insides were being rifled out with a red hot poker, the intensity of the pain exploding continuously.

The suppressed screams preventing a natural release for the horrified emotions burning through her tortured body, she prayed she would faint and so escape this living nightmare, but, in accompaniment with bestial grunts and groans, it continued.

Suddenly, with a sound like that of a tyre deflating, John collapsed heavily onto her, and she felt the flaccid penis fall out. Her brother lay like a poleaxed steer for a time, then with a sob, he raised himself up on his arms and looked at his victim, his own sister. His face was ashen.

"Whit hae a done?" he wailed, like a lost child. "Oh God forgie me, whit hae a done? Mary! Mary! Ah'm sorry lass, really sorry."

Mary rolled from beneath him. "I'll tell you what you have done," she answered in a voice loaded with contempt and disgust. "You despicable bastard! You have just raped your virgin sister. God may forgive you, but I never shall! You are utterly decadent, a filthy, disgusting corruption of the human race."

"You are the perpetrator of an act that not even an animal would consider. May all that happens in your life, from this day forward, stink and rot, and may happiness ever be denied to you."

"I don't know how, but I feel sure that retribution will catch up with you, your Nemesis will find you, and if it were in my gift, I would dearly love to be an audience to that spectacle. Now! Get out of my sight and let me get cleaned up before I have to return to the house, for bad as they are, I couldn't let them know how depraved and disgusting you really are."

John stumbled from the stable like a man in a drunken stupor. With eyes that were blind he sought an escape avenue from his latest degrading act. Like a hunted animal he headed for a stand of pines on a knoll half a mile away and, reaching it, disappeared within the doubtful sanctuary.

Mary, still trembling in the aftermath of shock and horror, crossed to the water butt in the corner of the stable. With a rag of hessian and a bar of rough soap she tried to scrub herself clean of the defilement.

Shuddering with revulsion, and stopping frequently to heave and wretch, she scrubbed furiously at her private parts until she was red raw with her endeavours. She felt she would never feel clean again, as she sobbed with frustration and anger at the brutal injustice of it all.

The sanctuary that John had fled to was subconsciously the haven he had used as a child when his brutal father had thrashed him, and this was a common occurrence. His flight ended at the edge of a deep ravine, where a huge jagged rock jutted across the river twenty feet below. Here he collapsed from trembling legs.

Looking down at the raging torrent below, it seemed to be in accord with his own tumultuous thoughts. The unbridled violence of the raging cataract as it hissed and frothed and leapt unchecked, sweeping everything in its path, was a perfect illustration of his own volatile character.

Indifferent and uncaring parents had produced a wayward, wilful, undisciplined savage, who would brook no denial in his selfish pursuits. Within the large frame was a suppurating pit of violence waiting to erupt at the merest provocation.

Time passed and his emotional storm subsided. In a few moments more his tortured mind convinced him that all who had suffered at his hands that day had thoroughly deserved it.

It was at this moment of his life that he decided the time had come to depose the old bull of the herd. He would be subservient no longer. He would take over the authority from old Macmillan, even if he had to half kill the old swine.

Little did John realise, as he rose from his rocky perch, that, although only sixteen years of age, he left childhood behind him that eventful night.

His mind remained untutored, motivated by animal cunning rather than reasoned approach, and, because of this, he was at all times unpredictable and potentially dangerous.

It was from that same day that Mary's health started to decline. She lost what appetite she had and became listless and easily tired. Her mother berated her for laziness, and failed to see the unhealthy pallor that had developed in her daughter's face.

Covertly Mary observed John, realising that in some strange way he had achieved a more confident assurance that verged on cockiness. With a shudder of apprehension she prepared herself for the brutal onslaught that was bound to happen, for she was certain that John meant to wrest the reins of authority from her father.

One evening, after the meal, old Macmillan was giving the orders for the following day's tasks, and John deliberately contradicted what was being said. With an oath old Macmillan thrust savagely back from the table.

"It's no a bloody discussion we're havin' here. A'm tellin' ye what is what. Now shut yer bletherin' trap an' get yer arse aff o' that bloody chair an' on aboot yer work, else ah'll sink this boot so far intae yer arse ye'll think yer shittin' leather."

John leapt to his feet, and was round the table so fast, his father leapt back in shocked surprise, and hard on its heels came the first twinge of fluttering fear.

Looking into the eyes of his firstborn was a bruising encounter of its own, for in the feral depths was a clear promise of death, cold and clear as fresh snow on a dry stone wall.

The involuntary step backwards was a defeat, plain and simple. The demented youth drove forward, and in a voice laced with venom, and a stiffened finger jabbing for emphasis, he threatened viciously.

"Ye'll never kick me again my wee mannie, and that is a damned fact. If ye even look at me sideways, an' ah don't like it, ah'll split ye open frae arse tae elbow. Is that clear, ye auld shite?" With another vicious dig of his finger into his father's chest, he turned and stormed from the kitchen.

For a moment it seemed that old Macmillan would suffer a stroke. He went bright purple and the veins in his neck jumped out like ships hawsers. Then the colour drained away, leaving him a dirty pasty shade that was more frightening to observe.

He reached out and gripped the edge of the table as if afraid he might fall, his chest rising and falling like a windblown horse. A few moments elapsed, then his natural truculence took over and he berated his family for not being out at their work.

The morning after the confrontation at Highbrae was crisp and fresh, with the scent of bog myrtle and ling heather hanging like a bouquet in the air. Skylarks rose ever higher as their songs cascaded in joyous chorus. Not to be outdone, the lapwings, or teuchats, danced their crazy aerial frolics, vying with each other to be the most daring as they tumbled around the sky.

Muted and morose, the ever plaintive weeping of the whaup would be heard above the staccato chatter of oyster catchers and the booming of the blackcocks at the display lecks.

Old Macmillan was unaware of this pastoral testimonial, he was bent on a desperate attempt to reassert his authority. He had watched John enter the stable. Like a thief in the night, he slid through the stable door and, seeing John with his back to him, found a desperate courage. He raised his heavy hawthorn stick, meaning to brain this upstart son.

At that moment John, sensing movement behind him, whirled and jumped to the side, the stick missing him by inches. In a trice he grabbed a pitchfork and had it at his father's throat, a tang on either side.

With a delighted malicious grin on his face, he pushed his father backwards until he was pinned against the wooden wall of the barn. Savagely he exerted more pressure until the tangs pierced the wall on either side of the neck, that was now tight with new-found fear.

"So! Ye cowardly auld bastard. Ye want tae fight me frae the back dae ye? Weel that's aboot ye're style. Noo! Ye listen tae me! A've jist aboot had a gutful o' ye, an' this is yer very last warnin'. Ony nonsense frae noo on, an' ye're a deid man. Got it?"

He wrenched the pitchfork free and, ere his father could move, the tangs were against his chest at heart level. A sharp thrust and the tangs pierced quivering flesh. Old Macmillan gave a strangled groan and, despite the pressure of the pitchfork, started to slide towards the ground.

John gave a snort of contempt as he pulled the fork free, then threw it like a javelin at the far wall. His father opened his eyes and saw the fork quivering in the wall and realised what power had been exercised in the throw to bury it so deeply.

He knew, without a doubt, that his days as patriarch were behind him, but, worst of all, he knew that he had sired a killer.

Chapter Three

Mary would look back on the events of the night of her rape as being the beginning of a part of her life that grew steadily worse as time passed. She didn't become pregnant, but that was the only crumb of comfort she was to enjoy for two and a half long years.

On leaving school at the same time as her brother Tom and Donald, she lost contact with the young love of her life. He who had been her champion and companion during those halcyon days.

She had learned from her younger brother, Ewart, about the terrible beating Donald had received from her brothers. Try as she might, she failed to obtain information as to his whereabouts, although she made endless enquiries, no-one seemed to know exactly where he was or when he would return, if ever.

When she met Cruachan people and asked about Donald, a blankness would drop over them. They would become evasive and noncommittal, then find excuses to be somewhere else. After all, was not she the sister of those terrible brothers who had caused Donald to be out of circulation.

The brothers carried on terrorising the neighbourhood, one foul deed after another would follow in their wake. Their parents ignored them and the parochial inhabitants despised and avoided them.

They tried with great endeavour to find the whereabouts of Donald. Not because of care or concern, but to enable them to carry on their persecution and harassment.

They were doomed to failure. It was as if he had ceased to exist, their extensive enquiries and investigations proved fruitless.

It is doubtful if they had found out what was happening to Donald, if it would have had any effect on their lives, for they felt themselves totally invincible, fearing no man, or anything in their narrow little world.

They had long been inured to the beatings of their father, and in John's case, that had long since stopped, for old Macmillan would never forget what he had seen in the savage eyes of his eldest son on the last occasion he had tried to trounce him.

John mercilessly and maliciously imposed his will on the rest of his family, exulting in his recently acquired power, but, for some strange reason, almost ignored his sister. Perhaps he lived with a subconscious dread of the black curse she had contracted on his evil head the night he had raped her.

Somehow he felt that a day of reckoning would have to be faced for his outrageous attack and violation of her dignity and virginity. Whatever it was, he still harboured a deep uneasy feeling about that incident in his life.

Tom and Ewart had lost one brutal master only to fall into the thrall of one more callous and unrelenting than the previous one. John ruled with an iron fist, bereft of any kid glove to mask it. He was completely autocratic and used boot and fist with wild abandon when he felt it was needed, and that was generally on a daily basis.

He quickly ran the farm into a state of disrepair, even worse than it had been under his father's administration. His previous sloppy attitudes quickly manifested themselves in a deterioration of everything he controlled. Any transaction with tradesmen or suppliers was always on a cash only basis, for it soon became general knowledge that a Macmillan was not to be trusted.

Mary watched the deterioration of the farm and livestock, and the depravity of her sibling, with heavy heart and consternation. She was of course incapable of exercising any control over events.

Her father had retreated into a world of his own, and seemed to have no interest, her mother never ever had any, so her eldest brother just suited himself, never listening to advice, and certainly never seeking any.

It was around this time that Mary's health started to decline. She seemed to lose her zest for life, becoming listless and introvert. It now took her much longer to carry out her chores around the farm, having to stop and rest at frequent intervals, but this was taken as laziness by her uncaring mother, who chivvied her mercilessly.

Mary dragged on through her miserable existence, mourning the loss of Donald. She suffered with a keenness that knifed her heart. Now she was without a confidant, therefore the loss was all the more acute, and, bravely though she bore it, the pain was unrelenting.

Donald was well aware that he required training in an ability to take care of himself. To pay court to Mary in the face of her brothers' animosity would prove no mean task. Without the ability he was about to learn he would be constantly brutalised and defiled by the sadistic trio. He therefore gritted his teeth and pursued his goal with determination, and in the beginning, promised himself that it would be one more score that would be paid for in full.

During the long winter nights in the lodge, Chi Li taught him techniques of defence and offence. He learned how to use everyday items to attack and incapacitate opponents. The secrets of self-defence in different circumstances, but, also how to develop the unexpected offensive. The ability to completely demoralise any opponent with the ferocity and extraordinary alien behaviour of a unique warrior.

He was not to know that these newly acquired abilities would have far reaching effects much later in his life, and not just the licence it would give him to woo his bonny Mary.

Two years had now elapsed since the horrible beating of Donald at the hands of the Macmillan brothers, and, during that time, Chi Li had transformed him into a well-developed young man.

He now stood five foot eight inches tall, and although he had developed muscles he had previously not known existed, he was not bulky or muscle bound. Each muscle stood out in clear definition. His stomach resembled a washboard, whilst his pectorals were square slabs of rubbery hardness, elastic and durable. Deltoids, biceps, triceps, calf and thigh muscles, all cleanly defined but without the restriction of bulk.

Chi Li was of the opinion, and who was to dispute it, that bulk and weight slowed a warrior down, and robbed him of valuable reaction time. This could not be tolerated, and that was the reason that Donald enjoyed a perfectly proportioned physique, with fluidity of movement.

Chi Li developed Donald's body to a degree that would have delighted Michaelangelo, for with his golden locks and sculptured body glowing with a healthy burnished tan, he was the complete representation of a statuesque Greek God. A glowing Golden Boy.

He moved with an economy of effort, lithe and tigerish, portraying the grace of a trained ballet dancer. His eyes had developed a piercing directness through which the determination of will blazed with searing impact. His aura of self-sufficiency was almost tangible, but he carried it without arrogance, having enhanced his natural politeness and kindness under Chi Li's careful tuition. The end product being a courteous, even humble, person, of stable temperament.

Stamina had gradually been built up by mountain running, first on sheep or deer tracks which was comparatively easy compared to the later, gruelling, muscle burning hell of heather, gorse and bracken leaping, which was completed at the same speed as track running.

Rest periods consisted of sit-ups, and press-ups, for a ten minute spell. A change is as good as a rest, is it not? Chi Li believed so! After the 'rest' a trot down to the loch, swim across and back, then a slow canter back to the lodge.

Rock climbing was introduced into the regimen as it developed character and tenacity of will, in addition to this, it created an aptitude for assessing and planning progress in dangerous situations. It also developed strength in the fingers and toes, and since these extremities were used in martial arts as weapons, it was infinitely necessary that they would not be a weakness in combat.

Whenever Donald sat down at the table in the cabin he would whistle a Scottish jig or reel and keep time by hitting the table with the outer edges of his hands. The outer edges of his feet would be bouncing off the legs of the table in accompaniment. This exercise developed a hard ridge of horny callous along these edges with which he could chop with frightening devastation.

It says much for the natural intelligence of Donald that he could cope with such a varied and comprehensive amount of concentrated instruction.

One to one tuition, of course, played a very important part in his development and in all the demands placed upon him; nevertheless he did not succumb to mental or physical fatigue, or even falter in the total application of mind and body. His integrity of purpose remained resolute for the full two years, which seemed to pass so very quickly.

Donald had heard that, at sixteen years of age, John Macmillan had usurped the position of authority at Highbrae Farm with the inevitable catastrophic results, but his only sympathy rested with Mary, who had to live with the God-forsaken lot.

He well remembered the brutal assertive strength of John, therefore it came as no surprise that he had deposed his father. Always in the back of Donald's mind was the unavoidable confrontation that would ensue when he and John would meet again in the future.

Donald never discussed this particular thought with Chi Li, and, as time passed, he became sure in his mind that he would be the one to prevail. Not only had he become strong in body during his training, he had also developed a confident mental attitude, and, as his mentor repeatedly asserted and assured him, a man's will is his best weapon. By force of will it is possible to back down the most determined bully.

Six months had elapsed since Donald had finished his martial arts course under the direct tutelage of Chi Li. In that period of time, Donald had concentrated on the full training of the Arab mare. Considering the type of training he had exercised on her, it was a remarkable achievement, worthy of the best versed horsemaster, to have completed the task in such a short time.

Since leaving the confines of the upper glen, Donald had kept up his training with Chi Li, to retain his sharpness, and hone his reflexes and reactions to an even higher proficiency.

To help him, Chi Li played his part to perfection. He would spring from concealment and attack with frightening ferocity. A peaceful walk down the glen could be instantly turned into a desperate struggle for survival. Chi Li asked no quarter, and certainly gave none.

The estate workers were at first astonished, and then alarmed, at the sight of two combatants each trying their best to kill one another, or so it appeared, but as they got used to the spectacle, they would shake their heads in amused tolerance and go on about their own business, smiling wryly.

Knowing he would soon have to face his final challenge, Donald trained with furious application and dedicated perseverance. He would have no warning, but this gave him no cause for concern. He felt confident in his own competence.

The path of life is devious, and littered with misfortune, but Chi Li had trained Donald to face life squarely and honestly. He had also introduced the Asian philosophy of Yin and Yang, an ideology of two parts making a whole.

Male and female, essential for reproduction, being one simile! The need of two hands to clap, another. Suffering and pain could be endured because, in the manner of the universe, the cycle would turn, and comfort and ease would take their place. This gave balance to life and hope to the afflicted.

When Donald was introduced to meditation, he failed to reach the state of Theta that Chi Li urged him towards. He could not empty his mind and hold it in that state of void. Chi Li introduced the repetitive Mantra, chanting aloud which brought about the desired state, but it was the second winter in the upper glen before Donald had completely mastered the technique, and then he understood why Chi Li had persisted, for he now had the ability to recharge his entire system which was without parallel.

Habitually Donald would rise before cockcrow and go for a long run, across open fields, ploughed acreages, and do some heather and bracken leaping, followed by a slow canter through deciduous woodland, before returning to Craigburn, always finishing with a lungbursting sprint for the last mile.

Autumn heralded its approach with a frosty freshness that snapped and crackled. Breath escaped from the mouth in rhythmic puffs of billowy mist.

Red deer stags belled and bugled competitively on the surrounding mist covered mountains. The rutting season is not a peaceful time. Hearing them in full clamour, and often the rattles of the antlers that sounded like staccato bursts of gunfire, Donald paused to wonder how the stag he had smacked on the derriere was performing, and silently wished him well.

Nature's bountiful gifts hung in profusion, hazel nuts in abundant clusters, bramble, blaeberry and beechmast, challenging the alternatives of hip and haw, or the sloe from the blackthorn trees, not forgetting the wild rowan berries and the seeds from many different kinds of grass.

Time to stock up the caches and larders, to put on fat against the onset of winter, the following season of peril and hardship. Woe betide those ill-prepared for it, be it man or beast.

Donald always had awareness wrapped round him like a warm plaid, at one with his environment and part of it. He noted the white scut of a startled rabbit, the brush of a disappearing tardy fox, and the droppings of roe deer where they had wandered the tracks.

He heard the dulcet cooings of the indigenous wood pigeon, overlaid by the harsh chatter of magpie and jay. In the distance would be the sardonic laughter of a mallard drake, and always the raucous coughing battlecry of an arrogant cock pheasant would shatter the peace of the woodlands, as he called his dominance over his harem.

All these natural sounds, and his observation of them, provided a wealth of knowledge that everything in his environment was normal, and because of this, anything unusual would be noted immediately.

On a morning crisp and clear and crackling fresh, with the hoar frost shrouding everything with a ghostly veil, Donald was pushing hard towards a grassy clearing what would be the outer reach of his run. He had already covered five miles but his breathing was easy and controlled. Muscles flowed with a rhythmic easy grace, fluid and flexible.

As he reached the ancient huge beech tree that dominated the otherwise clear area, he came to a halt.

A jackdaw screeched an alarm. Without conscious thought Donald dropped and whirled away from the tree trunk as an object came spinning through the air and buried itself into the bole of the beech tree.

A sideways glance was sufficient to show him that it was a 'shaken', a circular throwing device used by martial warriors. A forward rolling breakfall took him rapidly in the direction from whence the missile had come.

Rapid reassessment exploded in his brain in a screaming awareness that this was the wrong thing to do. As he rose from the breakfall, he immediately threw himself into a series of backward 'flic-flacs', then three cartwheels brought him back to the wide bole of the great beech tree he had left ten seconds before. He darted into the haven of its broad bole and, leaping upwards, pulled himself onto the lowest of the wide sweeping branches.

As he had started his backward manoeuvre he caught a glimpse of a figure rising from concealment, hooded and dressed in loose fitting, all black apparel. It was the second clue, and he needed no more to know that his multi-confrontation was upon him. He exulted in the challenge. Adrenaline pumped through him in an exhilarating intoxication, as his mind became crystal clear and icily controlled.

He knelt on the bow of the tree and waited in ambush like a jaguar of the forest. From another direction entirely there appeared a second figure, clad exactly as the first, running crouched over and covering ground rapidly.

Donald decided that this threat would have to be dealt with first. Grabbing his catapult, he loaded and fired in a blur of speed that was a tribute to his lightening reflexive reaction.

The projected missile hit the running target on the side of the temple, dropping him like a poleaxed steer. Donald now directed his concentration towards the first assailant, who had not seen his colleague brought down.

He stood under the branch where Donald had taken refuge. The puzzled look on his face turned to consternation when trouble fell on him from above.

Donald dropped squarely onto the shoulders of his adversary. As he landed his left leg whipped around the neck of his confused quarry. The neck was encircled and held firm in the hollow of Donald's knee. Donald's right leg went straight down the back of his opponent and the toes of his left foot found anchorage in the hollow of his own right leg.

It was a dreadful hold, if exercised fully the neck could be snapped like the proverbial twig. Donald threw his weight forward and the body beneath him fell flat, face forward on the ground.

The bested assailant screamed in sheer agony, as the pressure increased, and furiously beat the ground with his open palm, three times rapidly. This is the signal amongst martial warriors of total surrender, and, if accepted by the opponent, a declaration of honour to take no further action.

Donald released his hold and jumped clear. Not a second too soon, for the scream had acted as a homing device for a third attacker who exploded into action as he reached the scene.

Despite Donald's speed of release, only his mercurial reactions saved him from two dreadfully punishing kites aimed in rapid succession at either side of his neck.

Rolling clear, he whirled to face his opponent, who attacked with feet and hands in a whirling furious assault. He was highly skilled, with a great variety of moves, rapid and well-directed.

Donald retreated before the barrage of potentially lethal deliveries. His mind was ice-cold and calculating, as he waited for the first opening to turn the tables and become the aggressor.

Calmly and confidently he parried and defended each move with enduring patience, as he circled within the green sward. As he repelled each thrust, he observed his opponent with measures concentration, seeking a flaw or weakness in the techniques employed against him.

At last he found it! After every four hand movements his challenger would scythe forward his right leg, aiming to land a groin kick. Donald required no further indications or clues, the avenue was exposed to turning the contest into a two-sided affair.

Patiently waiting his chance, Donald counted the hand moves. As expected the foot came surging powerfully forward. Instead of retreating, he jumped up and forwards across the extended leg, and trapped it between his thighs, throwing his weight slightly to the right. With a calculated intense jerk he swung violently to his left, dislocating the joint with an obscene sucking sound.

His opponent was totally disconcerted by this entirely unorthodox attack. He screamed chokingly through gritted teeth in the explosion of pain from his ruptured knee joint, but the assault was not finished.

Donald reached down behind him with his left hand and grabbed the ankle of the leg trapped between his thighs. In the same instant he released the thigh hold to get his legs together on the inside. In a flicker of movement he bent and, when he arose the damaged knee was across his left shoulder.

With a robust thrust of his buttocks he swung the body out and away from him, and as it swung back, as positively as a pendulum following its path, he shifted his stance to allow the trunk to come through between his legs. He then dropped his weight onto the lumbar area of his opponent's back. As soon as his full weight settled, his feet shot forward, across the shoulders and alongside the neck of the unfortunate casualty of combat.

The large toe of each foot sought and found purchase under the chin of the victim, then, using his calf muscles and the shoulders of the recumbent figure as a fulcrum, he forced his toes upwards. The signal of surrender came before he had a chance to exert the pressure that would have broken the neck.

As Donald bounded clear, he was immediately concerned with the appearance of another threat approaching at speed, and dropped into the defensive stance ready to commit himself to battle yet again.

It was Chi Li who was approaching, and as he came near, he stopped and held his hands high, palms forward. He smiled with satisfaction, and regard for his student was a warm glow in his eyes.

"Shall we assist the wounded warriors, Donald?" he enquired, with respect and admiration strumming through his voice. "They have been worthy opponents, and deserve the best of aid, which we have the knowledge to provide. I have brought a few items that I felt might be required."

Chi Li had already administered to the needs of the first two who had succumbed to Donald's attentions and, as he looked down at the third victim, he could see the knee was beginning to swell, and must be causing a lot of pain, not that it was evident from the face of the recumbent warrior. Pain was a private thing, not to be shared by all and sundry.

Donald went across to the casualty, and gave him a respectful bow. "I'm sorry for the suffering I have inflicted upon you," he offered. "The only thing I can offer by way of recompense is to point out a flaw in your technique which afforded me the chance to take advantage."

The stricken warrior smiled through his pain, respect in his eyes, "I would appreciate that very much," he gasped, trying to sit up and bow. "You are a very skilled fighter, a warrior par excellence, and a credit to your sensei. I would be honoured to take whatever advice or instruction you could offer."

Chi Li knelt beside the warrior and, with a casual assurance, dug deep into the fallen soldier's neck with a questing thumb, rendering his patient instantly unconscious. Advising Donald where to hold the afflicted leg he quickly relocated the knee joint and bandaged it to hold it immobile.

Having completed his administrations, he brought his patient quickly back to consciousness and made him a drink from a small phial. It was a potent painkiller. The patient was soon sitting smiling and joking with his colleagues.

Donald was introduced to the three Gurkhas, and a meeting was arranged for the following evening. Then, with a bow and a cheery wave, Donald set off for Craigburn, satisfied that he had given a good account of himself, and that he would now receive the final black tassel to his belt.

Chapter Four

The village of Ardrochan provided the main amenities for the surrounding countryfolk, with a post-office cum general store, a country pub called The Ardrochan Rest, a kirk and a village hall, centred within a few local stone built cottages.

The hall was an extension of the kirk's dominion, jealously guarded against non-churchgoers. Only members of the kirk were made welcome, which could dramatically restrict social intercourse if one was not within that membership.

This is where Donald had decided to make his first social appearance since he returned from the hunting lodge. Saturday night is traditionally the night of relaxation and recreation for the hardworking countryfolk, and the pub and the village hall were the two main venues.

Stuart and Mari set off in the pony and trap to attend the Scottish Country Dance which would be held in the hall. Stuart would meet a few friends in the pub and then join his wife after a few drinks and a chat.

Donald declined to join his parents, saying he would see them at the hall later. He was excited and happy to be seeing his bonny Mary once again and trembled with anticipation at the thought of holding her in his arms during an old time waltz, with perhaps even a stolen kiss if he were lucky.

At Highbrae, Mary had decided to accompany her parents to the monthly dance, but reckoned it would probably be her last visit. She didn't much like watching the drunken antics of her brothers and father, and since the person she most hoped to see was never there, there was not much point in attending the functions.

She entered the hall quietly with her mother; her father and brothers would not show their faces in the hall until they had filled up in the inn.

John, as usual, brazenly handed out drinks to his brothers who were not yet old enough to enter the pub, this would be the ignition for their atrocities as the night progressed. It was a case of God help somebody, somewhere, for they were evil enough without the aid of alcoholic stimulants.

Donald was in no need of stimulants as he came swinging down the narrow glen road. His chin was on high as he sang his favourite lovesong, Bonnie Mary o' Argyle.

The high clear tenor voice cleft through the gloaming with the clarity of best crystal, and the two Englishmen, who had composed this best loved Scottish lovesong would have been well pleased with his rendering, for it was sung from the heart.

He was well into the second verse and going strong when he passed Cruachan house. The laird and his wife were sitting chatting to Chi Li and they looked at each other and smiled indulgently. 'Ah, young love, and did not the boy deserve his share.'

It was that night that the laird broached the subject that he had been thinking about for some time, and was delighted when he got wholehearted approval from his good wife.

It was that same evening that Chi Li asked the laird to arrange for three Gurkhas to visit, with a view to Donald facing his multi-confrontation test. The laird agreed and said he would make the necessary arrangements.

Chi Li noted that Lady Cruachan seemed to become quite upset, and hastened to reassure her, telling her that he would be observing, not for Donald's sake, but to ensure the Gurkhas came to no harm, for Donald was as elusive as a moonbeam and faster than the proverbial quicksilver.

Chi Li then excused himself, saying he felt he would like to go down to Ardrossen and listen to the dance music.

Lady Cruachan looked at her husband with a puzzled frown. Her husband smiled tolerantly and explained that Chi Li still didn't like Scottish dance music, he was in fact going down to keep his eye on things, being a little anxious about anyone who offered Donald violence.

Donald entered the village hall where a 'Gay Gordon' was in progress, with his favourite tune being played, 'Donald Dhu'. It made him feel quite welcome. He had noted the two younger Macmillans cackling like demented hyenas outside the pub door, obviously well oiled up, and knew there would be trouble ere the night ended.

Mary was sitting against the far wall, an aloof looking wallflower, but to his hungry eyes, the most beautiful thing in the whole world.

Swiftly he glided to her side, and asked for the pleasure of the dance. She whirled and gasped in disbelief, he caught her before she hit the floor.

Quickly he carried her to a nearby chair. His mother, who had watched the meeting, arrived at his elbow with a cup of hot sweet tea. Mary, who had not completely fainted, was encouraged to drink the reviving beverage, and was soon sitting hanging onto Donald, asking question after question.

The entrance door to the hall exploded inwards, rattling like gunfire as it bounced repeatedly off the wall. Heads turned in unison, to witness the arrival of the Macmillan menfolk. Well into their cups, brains in neutral, and legs disjointed, eyes as wide as rabid wolves.

They were an unpleasant and unwanted sight, obviously in search of some unsavoury sport, their language would have blistered the ears of a marble statue.

Arrogantly they rubberlegged a blasphemous path through the middle of the floor up to the serving area at the far end of the hall. John, being the self-appointed leader, hammered with his large calloused fist on the counter.

"Right you!" he snarled menacingly at the nearest woman behind the service bar, "Gi'e us some o' that slop ye ca' refreshment. Rattle yer hocks, ah'm in nae mood tae be kept hangin' aroon."

He took a half bottle of whisky from his inside jacket pocket, and drank deeply and noisily, finishing with a loud extended belch, blowing the whisky fumes and his bad breath directly over the recipient of his verbal attack.

John had made a terrible mistake. He was just about to realise it, and was in for a humiliating lesson.

It was Mari Macdonald that he had insulted and she accepted slight from no person on God's earth. In the space of a heartbeat she grabbed a meatknife that had been used in food preparation earlier, and, in a flicker of movement that certainly defied the bleary, whisky-misted eyes of her aggressor, sank the tip an eighth of an inch into the dewlap beneath John's chin, lifting him onto his toes with a startled screech of pain, as he hung on the blade like a hooked salmon.

"How dare you speak to me like that, you despicable, disgusting piece of filth?" she berated him. "The likes of you will never intimidate me. You think yourself a man, do you? Let me assure you, you are the scum of the earth, not fit to cohabit with the lowest form of animal life."

"When I remove this blade, you will leave this hall and the decent people within it. Never come back, ever! Is that clear in your feeble brain? I would gladly give you a permanent smile beneath your chin, then lay bare your backbone through your belly. Now go, before I change my mind!"

She gave the knife a parting half twist, then released the white faced, totally demoralised and humiliated bully. He slumped with a groan onto the serving counter, shivering and shaking like the beaten coward he was.

He had never had to face a person such as this in all his days of terrorising people. The fiery temper of an Irish Kelly is a formidable encounter, and he had just experienced the rough end of it in a most degrading confrontation.

He levered himself off the counter and wheeled about, almost tangling in his own legs that quite suddenly seemed to have lost their strength.

He beckoned with his arm, and made for the door, with his father and brothers trailing after him. Everybody in the hall gave a great cheer as the whipped dogs dragged their tails out through the exit.

The Macmillans had been totally unaware of Donald's presence in the hall. Not so Mrs Macmillan, who stopped in front of her daughter, who was hanging onto Donald for dear life.

"Ah hope ye hae a hame tae gang tae," she spat venomously at Mary, "fer it'll no be Highbrae. Ye're feenished there. Ah never want tae see hide nor hair o' ye ever again. Ye're a slack-arsed wee bitch onyway, an' winna be missed. Rot ye in Hell, ye treacherous wee bitch."

With righteous indignation and idiotic wrath, she stamped her way out of the hall in the wake of her demeaned menfolk. Through a complete lack of intelligence, or consideration, she had failed to see that her only daughter was ailing, thinking rather that she was pulling a fast one, so that she would have less work to do on the farm.

Big Stuart and his friends entered the dance hall, like a breath of fresh air, greeting everyone with a smile and a cheery wave. Stuart grabbed a young lass and dropped straight into the old-fashioned waltz that was being played, singing the well-known words in his deep baritone voice. When the girl recovered her aplomb and joined in, so did the rest of the dancers.

Donald held Mary close to him and sang directly to her. There was no better way to proclaim his love than by the words of a bygone master, Rabbie Burns.

"Oh, I would love you still my dear, till the sands o' time run dry."

Having made his entrance in the grand style, Stuart went up to the serving counter, and reaching across swept his Mari forward and kissed her soundly. Strange as it may seem, this time Mari was completely flustered, going bright red and pummelling the broad, firm chest. Stuart's joyous laugh rang loud and clear. Holding her tight, he gave her another resounding kiss before releasing her.

"What about a nice cup of tea sweet girl?" he asked, with a smile on his face, "and don't look so disconcerted, dearheart, everybody knows I love you, and it was my sincere pleasure to demonstrate that truth, which I would not hide from anyone."

"Now then, are you going to sit with me for a moment, and then we'll have a dance, for I am fair raring to go?" he said, adding softly for her ears only, "in more ways than one."

Mari's bright eyes declared her love for this often outrageous man of hers. Colour still high, she quickly organised tea for them both, then went to sit with her husband, telling him what had occurred before he arrived.

She expressed concern for Mary Macmillan being exiled from Highbrae, but he quietened her fears, saying, sure there were more rooms at Craigburn than they knew what to do with. Mary was more than welcome to come there, for indeed he had been thinking for some time that Mari needed a wee bit of help now and again, and this was just the remedy.

When Mari for once forgot her innate modesty and gave him a heartfelt kiss, he put his arm around her and remarked, "She'll have a far better home with us than she has had all her life, I fancy, but I tell you what, one of the first things we are going to do is have the doctor give her a thorough medical. Just look at her! I'm sure she is far from well."

Mari looked across to where Donald and Mary sat close together, frowned and said in a worried voice, "I thought she was just a wee bit shocked at the sudden appearance of Donald, but I can see what you mean. That white peaky face, with those big brown eyes standing out like peaty pools in a snow scene. Good heavens above! Now that I look at her, I can see that she's as thin as a rake. Poor wee mite! I'll soon get some meat on those bones, you wait and see if I don't!"

Mari Macdonald had made a prophecy that she would never fulfil. There was no way she could have suspected that the young girl, who filled her with compassionate love, would ever be able to respond to the care and attention that would be lavished on her by all the members of her new home.

Life is not fair, but then, nobody ever promised that it would be. Without hardship and sorrow it would be difficult to define happiness and comfort. Chi Li had used these words to Donald, and so did his father, in an effort to console him quite some time later.

In the back of the ponytrap Mary clung to Donald as if her life depended on it. She listened to Mari and Stuart singing the old traditional songs, the rich deep contralto and the baritone a wealth of perfect harmony. It didn't seem strange to her, when Donald joined in, that he had a clear tenor voice, but she knew, without doubt, that the three of them could have trodden the boards in any of the best venues in the world.

When they reached Craigburn, it was all hustle and bustle, with Mari unashamedly ordering her menfolk around, whilst she organised one of the best bedrooms for her newfound daughter, for that is how she saw this gift from heaven. The fact that Mari would never be able to have another child of her own had turned her into a mother of the world. She would have liked to have had a large family, being herself an only child, who had missed not having siblings during her childhood.

Mary's happiness was complete, for the first time in her life she was being smothered with motherlove. Her champion and lover was close at hand, and the room that had been allotted to her was a veritable palace in contrast to the poky hole she had occupied at Highbrae.

Sunday tasks on a farm are kept to the minimum, and within an hour Stuart and Donald were back in the warm kitchen ready for breakfast.

Mari sent Donald upstairs to waken Mary. He knocked on the door, then opened it and peeked in. Seeing Mary was covered up to her chin, he eased in quietly and kissed the pale cheek with loving tenderness.

Holding the covers to her chin, Mary sat up. For an instant she looked confused, then, as realisation swept over her, the tears sprang to her eyes. It was not unhappiness that brought these tears to her large brown eyes.

With a sob, she grabbed Donald, who, putting his arms around her, realised how thin she was, and reflected how much happiness it would give his mother to put some meat on her bones, he could almost hear her saying it.

Mary entered the kitchen and was greeted with three warm smiles. She crossed to Mari, kissed her on the cheek then hugged her almost with ferocity, then turning to Stuart she did likewise.

She sat down at her appointed place at the table, took a deep breath, then said quietly but firmly, "Two things I want to say before I break my fast. I am most grateful to all of you for taking me into your home. I quite honestly don't know what I would have done without you coming to my aid."

"The second point is, I have been very spoiled this morning, being left in bed when there is work to be done. Normally I am not a lie-abed. The only reason I can think why I did so this morning is that I have never slept in such a comfortable bed in all my life. However, I insist that I must be allowed to do my share of the work, and I would like you all to agree to that."

Mari, on one side of her, and Stuart, on the other, each reached across and took each a small frail hand in theirs. Stuart's basso profundo rang out, "Lassie! Lassie, as they say in the vernacular, 'dinna fash yersel'. There was no need to disturb you when we arose. Heavens above, we were only out there for half an hour. There was little to do."

"Aye, of course you'll be allowed to do your share, for we want you to feel you are part of our family, and I mean that with all my heart. Now then! Let's get into this fine breakfast, for I am absolutely famished."

A farmhouse breakfast at Craigburn was a hearty meal, eaten at leisure. Thick rashers of bacon, cut from the joint that hung from the ceiling, black pudding, fresh eggs, mushrooms and crisp fried homebaked bread, with toast and homemade marmalade to follow if required.

Time and again Mary was encouraged to eat up, but, try as she did, she could only peck at her food. She looked across the table at Mari and said, "Such a lovely spread, and I've done no justice to it whatsoever. I'm sorry Mari, but perhaps my appetite will improve. I've just been off colour for a few days, but I'm sure that will alter before long as well."

The response to this was typical of the deeply caring family she had come to live with. "Think nothing of it," she was advised by Mari, "we probably eat too much anyhow, but, having said that, we tend to burn off the calories with hard manual work. As you say, my lovely one, you need time to adjust and, heavens above, there is no rush whatsoever."

After breakfast it was time to get ready for the first service at the village kirk. Mary had to wear the outfit she had worn to the dance the evening before, but Mari decided that it would be the very last time the wee girl would be embarrassed by lack of suitable clothing, and the following morning she arranged for herself, Mary and Lady Cruachan to attend a ladies outfitters in Dunkeld, and, as Stuart said afterwards, the two old sisters who owned the small shop must have thought all their birthdays had come at once, with the amount of clothes that were purchased that morning.

When the family returned from the kirk on Sunday, Donald took his sweetheart for a stroll around the steading, and Mary couldn't help but see the vast difference between Craigburn and Highbrae. Everything here was in good order, even the farm machinery had been cleaned after use. The buildings were all in good repair, with no peeling paint anywhere in evidence.

They returned to the kitchen when Donald noticed that Mary was tiring, and found Stuart with his bagpipes in pieces, giving them what he called a service. Although they were an ancient set, having been handed down from father to son through the ages as was the custom, they were in pristine condition, although the ivory parts were yellow with age.

This particular set had been played at the battle of Culloden, and would be played by Donald's greatgrandchildren, Stuart was convinced of this.

Stuart looked up as they entered, stopped whistling a strathspey, and informed them that Mari was off somewhere attending to a birth. Mari helped out the district nurse from time to time, being a fully qualified midwife in her own right.

"Now then! I am an old sweet tooth, and love hot chocolate," confessed Stuart, "shall we pamper an old man's whim and have one?" Mary smiled brightly and responded with alacrity.

"What a good idea! If you'll tell me where things are kept, I'll prepare some now. Do you both take it with hot milk?" and when Stuart replied, "och aye, it's the only way", they were soon sitting round the table enjoying the sweet drink.

Mari returned with her friend, the Lady Cruachan, and shooed the menfolk out, saying "us girls are going to have a nice blether". Stuart knew that what was going to happen was that the elder ladies were going to prepare Mary gently for a visit from Dr Fergusson. He decided that this was probably a good time to point out to Donald that perhaps Mary was not in good health.

Donald and his father beat a hasty retreat, seeking sanctuary in the large kitchen garden at the rear of the house. It was a peaceful haven, the large stone wall keeping it free of the prevailing westerly winds.

A profusion of birdsong greeted them with a variety of melodies, sweet and pure. The drone of the honey bees from the two hives at the far end of the garden added a relaxing feeling to the setting that was as sleep-inducing as the gentlest of lullabies.

They sat quietly relaxing, enjoying the warmth of the Indian Summer sun, and the pastoral peace that engulfed them.

Donald was close to nodding off when Stuart murmured drowsily, "you do know that wee Mary is not at all well, Donald, don't you? She's as thin as a rake, and the colour of putty. Your mother and I have decided to get our old friend, Dr Ewan Fergusson, to come and give her a thorough medical."

Donald came upright, as if he had been jabbed with the tangs of a fork.

"What did you say, dad?" he exclaimed, as a sudden rush of fear scalded through his veins, "oh no! Are you sure? Och of course you are, or you wouldn't ask Ewan to call. Oh dad! Maybe she is just a wee bit run down. Oh no! My poor wee Mary. I was really hoping that this would be a nice fresh start in her life, away from that brutal uncaring family she has suffered so long."

Drowsiness shed from Stuart, like water from a mallard's back.

"Now then, son" he admonished gently, "don't let us cross bridges before we reach them. Just let us wait and see what Ewan has to say. Perhaps all the wee lass needs is a bit of rest and a tonic. I just mentioned it to you, so you wouldn't inadvertently tire her out going riding around your favourite haunts and so on. She has come into our care, and so we must do it properly, don't you agree?"

Without a word of answer, Donald rose from the lounger and strode almost angrily down towards the bottom of the garden. This Eden had lost its appeal, once again the serpent had shown its forked tongue of evil. His mind was in a turmoil, fear engulfed him, knowing that he was powerless to do anything for his sweetheart if she was seriously ill. He dropped into the lotus position and whispered a mantra with increasing fervour, deliberately blocking out the frightening theme running amok within his brain.

A few minutes passed then he stood up, heaved a great shuddering sigh, then turned and walked back to where his father waited. Looking down, he managed a small sad smile, but his voice was firm as he said, "Thanks for the advice dad. It must have been hard for you to tell me. I must admit, I was just so glad to see Mary here at home with us that I never really looked at her properly, although I remember looking at her this morning and thinking how thin she had become."

They sat in empathetic silence for a while, then Donald stood up and said he would go and see his wee mare. Stuart knew that he would secure a certain amount of solace from the other love of his life and made no effort to detain him. He was conscious of the fact that his son had suffered a severe shock, but he did not regret having brought the subject up, for it had been done through kindness, albeit an unpleasant task.

Some time passed as Stuart sat and dozed pleasantly in the warmth of the sun, to be roused by a call from Mari. He rose and strolled up through the garden, whistling a soft Scottish lilt as he ambled through the bouquet of the heavily scented rose.

He reached the kitchen door as Lady Cruachan was leaving, she smiled and had a soft word in passing. Donald came round the corner of the byre and waved goodbye to his mother's friend, and entered the house at his father's heels.

Half an hour later Mari wrapped her protege in a warm plaid and followed the men out to do the evening's chores. With loving concern she made sure that Mary was involved, but the tasks assigned to her were not in any way arduous.

Mari had already decided that, until Ewan Fergusson had given Mary a thorough going over, her tasks would be light and interesting, with no great physical demands placed on her.

It had been a Sunday that they would all remember, for different reasons, and, as Mary knelt at her prayers during evensong service, her thanks were heartfelt and long.

She asked a second blessing, that she would become strong again, so that she could in some measure thank these good people, by being able to contribute her share of the hard work that is ever the part of farming folk.

Chapter Five

At Highbrae the Macmillans gave no thought to the daughter they had abandoned so ruthlessly. Life went on in its normal blasphemous way, everybody cursing and blaming everyone else, with care or consideration an unknown quality of life, something beyond their ken. Each strove with vicious intent to achieve their own selfish ends. The battle was continuous and determined, no quarter asked or given, with John in brutal autocratic control, which he exercised with mindless savagery.

Three weeks after the expulsion of Mary from the family home, again on a Saturday night, the four Macmillans decided to give Dunkeld the pleasure of their company. As for the auld hen, well, she could stay home, and good enough for her!

They arrived at a pub called The Herders, which was frequented mainly by farm workers and estate workers from the surrounding area, who enjoyed a pint with their fellow peers.

The main lounge had subdued lighting, whilst at each end a cheery log and peat fire created a comfortable atmosphere, much appreciated by the regular customers.

John burst in through the door in his usual arrogant fashion and roughly elbowed his way to the long bar. Thumping the bar with a clenched fist he demanded two double whiskies and two pints of ale. As usual the beer would be passed out to the waiting brothers.

Sitting by the fire on the south wall were two of the local lads. One of them was the local police sergeant's son, Billy Thompson, who was celebrating his eighteenth birthday by having his first pint in a pub, being now old enough to frequent licensed premises, and exercising that right.

He remarked to his friend that they would finish their drinks and leave as he was sure there would be trouble before the night was out, and he wanted no part of it.

Billy and his pal downed the last of their drinks and quietly rose and made their way to the exit, but the contrariness of life manifested itself with consummate nonchalance and devastating quickness.

John was returning from a second visit to his brothers and met Billy at the door. Roughly he grabbed the youngster by the neck and thrust him savagely against the rough granite wall, unmindful of the damage that occurred.

"Whit's the matter wi' ye" he grated through clenched teeth, "is my company no' guid enough fer ye? Weel a canna remember gie'in ye permission tae leave, so ye'll jist have tae have a wee skelp tae remin' ye wha the boss is hereabouts, so tak that an' here's a wee bit mair."

When Billy's head hit the wall on the second occasion it had fractured the skull, such had been the force of the contact.

John got fully into his stride, sinking his great fist into Billy's stomach and then banging his head in alternating barbarity. Tiring of this, he threw the defenceless lad on the ground and proceeded to lay the boot into the prostrate body with undiminished fury.

Billy's pal left the scene like a scalded cat, but he was not wilfully deserting his friend. He raced round the corner to the police station, a matter of yards away, entered, and then collapsed on the reception counter, white-faced and shaking.

"Quick! Quick!" he screamed frantically, "Big John Macmillan is killing Billy at the Herders."

Duncan Macrae, a special policeman who was on duty, spent no time asking questions. He came round the desk with bewildering speed for such a huge man and was on his way to the scene of the disturbance, shouting to the young man to get the doctor as quickly as possible.

Arriving at the pub, he found Billy lying in a pool of blood, ashen white, his breathing very shallow and, thankfully, he was unconscious.

Remembering his first aid training he made no move to alter the position of the traumatised youth, trying only to stem the flow of blood. He shouted for somebody to bring blankets, but his cries went unheard. He was horrified at the amount of blood on the courtyard cobbles, and he could see that Billy had been badly worked over in addition to the damaged head.

Billy's pal and the doctor came racing round the corner. Efficiently, the old doctor took charge. Swiftly he bandaged the head, then carried out a preliminary investigation before asking Duncan to carry Billy round to the surgery, which was opposite the police station.

When Duncan had done all he could to help the doctor, he left the surgery and quietly strolled back towards The Herders. It was now his duty to take John into custody, to be charged with assault and battery. He would be lucky to escape a murder charge, only the next few days would determine what the indictment would be.

Duncan was a bachelor who gave much of his spare time to special police duty and he enjoyed a quiet respect from the townspeople he served. He was uncommonly well-suited for his voluntary work, standing six foot four in his stockinged feet, with a huge barrel of a chest, and arms that would have made excellent legs for a horse.

He moved with a deceptive grace, most people walking beside him had to do a semi-trot to keep apace, for he covered ground rapidly, although from a distance it appeared as if he was merely ambling along.

Reaching The Herders, he quietly pushed through the door and paused just inside to survey the scene and try to establish the location of his quarry.

He had never in his life leapt before he looked and, knowing the reputation of John Macmillan, he certainly wouldn't leave anything to chance.

Catching sight of the culprit at the far end of the bar, he pushed his way through the drinkers, many of whom were totally unaware of what had transpired outside the pub.

Stopping a few feet away from the bully, who was loudmouthing everyone around in a berating, scathing voice, Duncan raised his voice slightly above the hubbub and announced clearly, "John Macmillan, you will accompany me to the police station, where you will be charged with assault and battery on Billy Thompson."

A hush descended like a smothering blanket, as every eye in the place focused on Duncan. John turned and leant nonchalantly on the bar with one elbow, arrogant and disdainful.

Contemptuously he looked Duncan up and down, then snarled, "Oh aye, is that a fact? Have ye brought an army wi' ye, auld man. That wee shite got whit he deserved. He thinks that because his faither is the sergeant o' police that he rules the roost aroon' here. Weel I showed him a wee bit different. Noo he kens fine wha the boss is. Noo, ye rattle yer hocks and bugger off oot o' here if ye ken whits guid fer ye. I'm busy wi' this thirst o' mine an dinna hiv time fer an auld hasbeen like ye."

Duncan smiled and took a step nearer. Calculatingly he prodded the volatile ego of John.

"Now then, my wee mannie, come away you quietly, else I'll have to give you a wee smack, and you know you would wet your nappy if I did that."

John lunged from the bar, quivering with the intensity of ungovernable rage. A volcanic fury bubbling inside him screamed for release. His left fist, the size of a granite boulder, came hurtling forward as if steam driven, generally a right lead is expected in these circumstances. It stopped, as if it had hit a wall.

Almost lazily, Duncan's right hand had risen, palm forward. As the fist landed within his own huge hand, he curled his fingers and exerted tremendous excruciating pressure.

John's face went puce coloured, his mouth a rictus of agony as the relentless pressure on the knuckles increased, bone and cartilage collapsed beneath the implacable onslaught.

Still holding John within his sustained vicelike grip, Duncan slapped him open-handedly across the side of the face. The sound of bone breaking was like a gunshot, clear and decisive.

As the hand travelled backwards it made contact again, this time the nose cartilage was fractured. A high-pitched scream rent the air, erupting from the broken mouth of John. But his ordeal was not yet over.

Deliberately Duncan released the damaged hand, then quite brutally pistoned his right fist deep into the left hand ribs of John, the sound of them breaking suggestive of a butcher's cleaver going through meat.

Quietly Duncan repeated his request for John to accompany him to the police station and telling him his rights.

Old Macmillan stepped into the fray as his eldest son collapsed on the sawdust on the floor. He had slightly recovered from the unbelievable events, someone besting his son. In a moment of sheer madness he aimed a punch at Duncan, only to find that he had missed completely, and then his world collapsed as Duncan's fist collided with the side of his head. He dropped unconscious to the floor, beside his mewling son.

The old doctor who had attended to Billy, and now had him in intensive care in the local cottage hospital, entered the pub for his evening dram. He looked at the two recumbent figures and sighed deeply, paused, and then decided he would still have his dram, he felt he needed it. As he sipped his whisky he turned and smiled at Duncan and then, giving a grimace, asked him if in future he would be a good lad and not slap quite so hard.

John Macmillan was unceremoniously hoisted to his feet, whilst old Macmillan had a glass of water thrown in his face to bring him round, then rudely evicted and told never to return. Outside he discovered that the two younger sons had deserted him and he was now faced with the long walk back to Highbrae on his own.

At the police station John was formally charged with assault and battery, occasioning actual bodily harm and attempted manslaughter. This could all be superseded by a charge of first degree murder if Billy succumbed to the serious head injuries that had been inflicted on him.

The saying goes that the devil looks after his own, and this may well be the case, for it transpired that John was very lucky in several instances.

The on-duty surgeon at the cottage hospital recognised the serious nature of the head wounds, and Billy's deteriorating condition, and had him immediately conveyed to the neurosurgical ward in Perth Infirmary.

A visiting consultant in that discipline happened to be there on a training semester for other surgeons and was engaged in a late night lecture when Billy arrived. He decided that a demonstration was worth a thousand lectures or any great oratory, so proceeded to carry out the necessary repair work to the badly damaged head of Billy.

The result was that the patient ended up with a silver plate in his skull and a slight speech impediment that would stay with him until he went to his grave.

The third piece of luck for John was the fact that he was arraigned in the Law Courts in Perth. The presiding judge took into consideration that it was John's first offence and accepted a plea of contrition and remorse, which resulted in a sentence of two years on Perth Jail, but to undergo psychiatric counselling whilst serving his sentence.

This, of course, was gladly accepted by defending council, who strongly advised John to agree to the conditions laid down, adding in an undertone that John was indeed a fortunate fellow, for he had found out during his investigations just what a nasty character he had been obliged to defend.

At Perth prison, John settled into the system quite quickly. Coming from farming stock he was gainfully employed in the kitchen gardens and grounds, which meant he was not confined to a cell like a battery hen, in fact he enjoyed a form of freedom.

The food he received was much better than the indifferent slop he was used to at home, so, with good food, light work and a modicum of freedom, the stay in prison promised to be more in the nature of a holiday than a punishment.

The other inmates of the prison gave him no trouble, particularly when he brutalised a hard man from Glasgow who had tried to intimidate him in the showers.

The prison warders had conveniently turned a blind eye on the incident, agreeing that the troublemaker from the big city had received his comeuppance, and it had been long overdue. Soon John ruled the roost, and his slightly submerged arrogance resurfaced to the detriment of all around him. He was nevertheless careful in the sight of authority, hoping for early release for good behaviour.

At Highbrae, old Macmillan had taken over the reins of authority again, and was already plotting ways to retain them when John returned. He developed a habit of carrying a steel bar wherever he went. It was thirty inches long and about an inch in diameter, and his pet name for it was 'the leveller'. It was a deadly piece of equipment, capable of inflicting dreadful damage on any unfortunate on which it was used. He had given it a couple of playful little tries on Tom when he made a takeover bid. It had certainly stopped him in his tracks.

The Factor of Glen Avro paid a visit to Highbrae to advise Macmillan that the laird had returned and was not at all happy about the condition of Highbrae steading or the quality of the land. If things did not improve, there would be serious thought given to the re-tenure when it fell due in two years time.

Incensed by this interference, as he saw it, old Macmillan whipped the end of the steel bar under the Factor's nose. "Listen you," he screeched, spittle flying from his distorted mouth. "This is my land and ye're tresspassin' ye uppity bastard get yer arse oot o' here afore I gie ye a wee tickle wi' this." Viciously he jabbed the end of the bar into the chest of the unsuspecting victim.

White faced and shaken to the core, the Factor sprang back and retreated to his mount, a Connemara Grey, who had been grazing nearby. So upset was he that he could hardly get himself into the saddle, his trembling legs being virtually useless.

His humiliation was further compounded by the raucous insane laughter behind him, but what frightened him more was the sound of hysteria threading through it. He was convinced that the evil little man was on the threshold of madness.

Getting astride the mare, stimulated by his candid fear, he gave her a cut with the whip which sent her hurtling through the gates of the stockyard already at the gallop. To say that the mare was astonished at the use of the whip would be an understatement, for the Factor was a lover of animals, usually treading them all with kindness and consideration. His only excuse for this uncharacteristic digression could be laid firmly at the hands of old Macmillan, who had frightened him near to death.

With the steading of Highbrae behind them, the Factor quietly slowed the mare from her careering flight and gave her a caressing stroke as he soothed her with compassion.

"Sorry old girl, I'm sorry. I was not very nice to you, I'm afraid. That man really frightened me, and I took it out on you. Forgive me old thing. That man is demented. He should never be tenant of a farm. I promise myself this; I will do all in my power to ensure he is ousted at the earliest opportunity, for truth to say, he is ruining that nice wee farm."

The mare flickered her ears and nodded her head up and down as if in agreement, she was well used to the Factor thinking his thoughts aloud whilst he rode around the estate he governed for a landlord who was most often absent.

Old Macmillan gave no thought to having made an enemy of the one man on the estate who could have him evicted. His unbelievable arrogance denied the possibility of anybody getting the better of him.

With the confrontation behind him, he conducted himself exactly as he had before. To hell with that pansy bastard, he wouldn't come back for a second dose, of that he was sure. He was firmly entrenched at Highbrae, it was his farm and he would be here until the day he died, and curse them all.

When the Factor reached Avro House, he handed the mare over to a groom and hurried towards his office. He had urgent business to attend to, which, in his opinion, couldn't wait. Going to the filing cabinet he pulled out the Highbrae file and, sitting down, he started to peruse it with profound satisfaction.

Half an hour later he sat back with a satisfied smile on his face. The rights of tenancy showed quite clearly that the farm had to be kept in good order, which included the buildings and the land. Failure to do so could result in the tenure being terminated.

The only drawback was that a period of two years was to be allowed after a formal warning had been given, to enable the tenant to make good and bring the farm up to an acceptable standard.

The Factor called his secretary and dictated the letter of intent. Sealing it in one of the official envelopes with the estate crest on it, he called the farm manager and asked him to personally deliver the missive to old Macmillan at Highbrae, but he was to take two of his strongest farm workers with him in case of trouble. He explained what had happened during his earlier visit, and his thoughts as to the man's instability.

The farm manager assured him that he would do as directed, it would give him great pleasure to present the important communication safely into the hands of old Macmillan. Hopefully he would create a commotion that would require strong physical action to control and conclude satisfactorily.

The manager was due for disappointment, for when he found Macmillan out in the fields, he quietly accepted the letter and, after reading the contents, stuck it carelessly in the back pocket of his overalls.

He grinned wolfishly and then snarled as his eyes took on a dangerous glitter.

"Guid o' the mannie tae provide me with the wherewithal tae wipe ma arse, fer that's whit a'll be daein' wi' this bit o' garbage. Ye kin tell him frae me that he's a spineless wee fart, that he hadnae the guts tae deliver it hissel. Aye an' anither thing. Tell him tae be awfy carefu' if he gangs oot on his lanesome, parteeclarly on a dark nicht. Ye never ken, p'raps somthin' could fa' on his heid."

The foreman listened to this monologue and when it was finished smiled menacingly and growled through clenched teeth.

"Take heed of what I say to you, you ugly minded pig. Hope you, that the Factor never so much as hurts his thumb from now on, because, if he does, I'll believe that you have caused him harm, and that will be to your eternal regret. I will find you tho' you hide in hell, and when I do, may God help you, for nobody else will ever be able to. That is a pledge taken in front of witnesses, and one I shall keep. It is a pleasure I look forward to, and I hope you are stupid enough to disregard what I have said to you. I believe you are that right enough."

The manager lifted his cap in a derisory salute, wheeled about and returned to his waiting mount, held by one of the workers who had accompanied him on this errand.

The three envoys left the scene with quiet dignity. Behind them, old Macmillan stood in a froth of conflicting emotions. His natural truculence demanded instant action against the upstart who had dared to address him so on his own land, but, like all bullies when faced, the bubble of fear drew caution over him like a protective blanket, effectively smothering what he knew would be a grave error to offer violence in the existing circumstances.

Mindless rage suffused him, but craven fear restrained him, so he stood twitching and shivering as passion devoured him.

On the way back to Avro House the three men discussed old Macmillan. They were all in accord that he was losing his mind, and wondered idly how a man could get himself in such a state when, in fact, he should be enjoying the fruits of his labour and his loins. Three well-built grown up boys and a good wee farm that only needed a bit of work on it to make it productive and profitable. Ah well, he had always been a hard, uncaring sort of a swine, so he was probably getting his just rewards.

Mrs Macmillan had watched the interchange between the men from the dairy window, and, although she heard not a word, the stance of her husband foretold a nasty evening in store for all of them at Highbrae when the old man returned from the fields. Sighing wearily she mentally prepared herself for the worst, and for the first time since Mary had been banished, gave some thought to the expulsion of her daughter.

It appeared that, from that time, everything had started to deteriorate rapidly at Highbrae. Her work had doubled of course, John was now in jail, and, if she had read the signs right, another problem was on the horizon, she could feel it in her weary bones.

Old Macmillan was strangely quiet when he entered for the evening meal, merely pointing at whatever he wanted passing to him. When he had stuffed himself to repletion he pushed back from the table and lit up his evil-smelling briar pipe.

Taking a couple of deep, lungbursting sucks, he at last looked around at the waiting faces and pronounced in a voice laced with venom, "So they want us oot o' Highbrae do they? Weel I hope they are satisfied wi' what is left, for I'll burn it tae the ground afore I just meekly walk away. I'll have naethin'! Neither will they! Hooever we hae twa year yet afore they can kick us oot, so we'll see whit happens in that wee while, shall we not?"

Mrs Macmillan's face went white with shock. "Oh no!" she wailed, "whit will happen tae us, where'll we live, what in the name o' God will we do?"

"Shut yer screechin' face woman, or ye'll get the back o' ma haund," snapped her husband, raising his fist to emphasise the point. "I've looked after ye weel enough for a' these years, an I'm sure that I'll manage fine for a while yet, sae nae mair tantrums oot o' ye, thank ye kindly. Noo shut yer mouth an' let me ponder, in fact, get the hell oot o' here the lot o' ye an' get the evenin's wark done."

Thankfully they all scampered off, glad to be out of the menacing atmosphere that filled the kitchen like an evil stench. They wondered what depraved schemes would emerge from the vicious and tortured mind that was constantly filled with evil intent.

None of them would dare to ask what plans were devised, or have the temerity to suggest any. When old Macmillan felt the time was ripe he would, in his own crude fashion, advise those he felt had a need to know.

Until then, it would be carry on as normal, if such a phrase could be applicable within the bounds of Highbrae.

Chapter Six

The week following Mary's arrival at Craigburn, Doctor Fergusson called to give her a complete medical examination, chaperoned by Mari, who hovered anxiously in the background.

Calmly he went through the procedures that would provide him with a prognosis. By careful and gentle questioning he elicited quite an amazing amount of information from his patient. How she felt tired all the time, always feeling weak, and an inability to concentrate for any length of time.

During his internal examination he noted that Mary had lost her virginity, and that there was some slight damage. He was also aware that she winced and stiffened fearfully at his gently questing fingers.

Palpitation of the abdominal area seemed to provoke distress and her breathing was quite shallow. The skeletal quality of the girl's body was quite pronounced, and the skin showed little elasticity and was of a poor colour.

Finally he was through, and still talking quietly and soothingly he advised Mary to get dressed, and would Mari be so good as to make them all a nice cup of tea. Leaving Mary to get dressed, saying, "there's no hurry, dear girl," he and Mari went down into the kitchen.

Mari's face showed all the concern she felt for her nursling, and Ewan sympathetically responded quickly to the mute appeal, saying as kindly as possible.

"Mari! Unfortunately Stuart was quite right. The wee lass is certainly not in good health. Now then! I know this just diverts the devil, but as I cannot be a hundred per cent sure of what I suspect, I am going to arrange for her to be taken into hospital so that a series of tests can be carried out."

"I rather fear that she is poorly indeed. Without the confirmation of blood tests and so on, I cannot give a final prognosis, but I think she has cancer, and, as you well know, we have not yet in the medical field got the beating of this particular nasty."

"The thing is, do we tell her of my suspicions, or leave it until we have confirmation one way or the other from the hospital authorities? That is the big question at the moment."

Mari gulped breath deep into her lungs that had been starved as she listened to the doctor speaking. Her beautiful big Irish eyes flooded with tears, then spilled down her face in a glistening cascade of sorrow.

"Oh my poor wee bairn," she husked mournfully. "Oh, please don't let us tell her anything for the moment. Let me spoil her and love her and try to build her up a wee bit first. You never know, perhaps a spell in loving care will bring about a recession of the disease, if that is what it is. At least let me try. Please!"

"Of course, of course," Ewan soothed, "we don't know for sure yet. I could be entirely wrong, though I must add, I doubt it. At any rate, let's wait and then we can make a decision when we have all the relevant facts. Just one more thing. Let us not tell Donald either. Let them have a wee bit of happiness until they have to be told."

Mutely Mari nodded her acquiescence, as she desperately fought to regain control and composure before Mary rejoined them. Hastily she erupted into a frenzy of activity, after absent-mindedly wiping her face with a wet dishcloth.

When Mary entered the cosy kitchen, the doctor was sitting at the table sipping his tea, whilst Mari, with iron hard resolve, was making sure she didn't rattle her teacup in the saucer and betray the turmoil that raged within her.

Quietly the old doctor advised Mary that she was quite run down, and he wanted some tests to be carried out at the hospital, just to be on the safe side, did she understand?

Mary looked from one to the other, then nodded her agreement, then, like a homing pigeon, she crossed to Mari in a mute appeal to be held. Scalding tears that had been held in the grip of an iron will escaped at last, unchecked and copious, as Mari opened her arms and enfolded Mary to her throbbing troubled heart.

"My love! My love!" she crooned softly, as she kissed the dark tresses beneath her chin, "we'll soon have you better, never fear. We'll feed you up till you're like a wee dumpling. In no time at all you'll be as fit as a flea."

When the old doctor left Mari wrapped her ward in a warm woollen coat and took her for a walk around the steading. There was a newborn calf to be admired, and six border collie pups that were always ready for a bit of fussing, but, in truth, it was all a diversion to take Mary's mind off the doctor's visit.

As the gloaming laid its soft mantle across the pastoral scene, and the shadows melted, evensong caressed their ears in peaceful harmony, they turned and made their way back to the farmhouse to prepare the evening meal.

Two weeks later the summons to the hospital arrived, advising Mary that she would be kept there for an entire week. Mari and the laird's wife attended to all the arrangements, each vying with the other to make things easy for Mary.

It was during this week of Mary's absence that Donald had his multi-confrontation with the three Gurkhas. The evening of the following day he attended a very select presentation ceremony at Chi Li's self-contained flat within Cruachan House.

He was delighted to receive the second black tassel for his belt, and to have the warrior's ring officially transferred to the fifth finger of his right hand.

The entire proceedings were conducted in a very formal manner. Donald felt like shouting aloud his joy but not a glimmer of emotion was visible on his face. A true warrior is always in icy control.

That is not to say that the three Gurkhas and Chi Li were unaware of what Donald was feeling, they knew well enough, but respected the iron control he maintained throughout the emotive formalities.

He was hard pressed, however, to sustain his composure when each of his former adversaries insisted on giving him a small gift to demonstrate their esteem for such a worthy convert to the sensei ranks. To them it had been an honour to have contributed to the occasion, even though they had been at considerable risk.

The first gift was the 'shaken' that had thudded into the tree trunk by his head, that had been the signal for the start of the contest. This piece of armament is a hundred millimetres in diameter, a complete circle of cutting blades. It is so designed that when it meets resistance its spinning action pulls it deeper into the target. It is a lethal contrivance that requires long hours of practice to be able to deliver it towards the target without damage to the thrower.

The second offering was a pair of short throwing clubs, intricately carved and lead weighted at the impact end. They were exactly twelve inches long and made of hard ebony wood with ivory inlays, however their true value lay in their extreme accuracy in flight.

Donald started to itch with impatience, wanting to be practising straight away, but already the third Gurkha was stepping forward with his present, which was perhaps the most unusual gift of the three, having many uses.

At first glance it looked like a length of ribbon with a wooden toggle at each end. In this mode it could be used as a multi-coloured headband, a tourniquet, or a deadly garotte.

It could be released into a twelve foot length of extremely strong cord, and when the toggles were pressed in a certain way, they became miniature grappling irons.

The Gurkha who presented this remarkable piece of equipment spent half an hour with Donald, versing him in its many uses and teaching him some unusual knots that increased the versatility of the gift.

To be accepted as a warrior by these seasoned fighters was thanks enough for Donald, but to receive these carefully considered gifts in addition, without outward show of emotion, was almost more than he could contend with.

An iron will exercised its influence and prevented him from losing face, but it was a tremendous inner battle. It flashed through his mind that he would rather face them all again in conflict than experience this tumult that was fast eroding his composure skills.

At last the ceremony was complete, all that was left now was to share a warriors' meal. In this, as in all things, Chi Li had excelled. The meal was a worthy finale to any ceremony. The base ingredient was the ubiquitous rice, the staple of all Eastern diets, and the sauces were masterpieces on their own.

There were chicken dishes, pork, game, fish and vegetable dishes, flavoured with herbs and spices that titillated the palate with often indefinable tastes and textures.

No true warrior ever drinks to excess, and that was respected on this occasion, but there were offerings of rice wine and herbal teas and fruit juices to calm the tastebuds between the courses. Yes! It was a night Donald would long remember.

Mary returned from the hospital. The results of the tests would be forwarded to Dr Fergusson in due course, when all had been collated and confirmed.

The Macdonalds unashamedly spoiled and pampered Mary, with light pleasant tasks during the days. In the evenings Mari would play the piano and sing in her rich contralto voice, then Stuart and Donald would perform their party pieces, singing, piping or step dancing. Mary had never felt so happy in her life.

Three weeks after Mary's return from the hospital Dr Fergusson arrived at the steading one evening. Although he bore ill tidings his face divulged nothing of the sorrow he felt. With the charm of a caring diplomat he smiled and greeted everyone with courteous bonhomie.

"Yes, yes, indeed! He would be delighted to have a cup of tea, and yes, if he must, a wee snifter would be quite in order. Was it not a beautiful, clear, frosty night? How did the parochial saying go? Ah, yes! He had it. It's a braw, bricht, moonlicht nicht, the nicht, Mrs Richt, can a walk oot yer dochter?"

He looked around at the amused faces and continued in his old world charming voice, saying it was a real pleasure to drive up the glen on such an evening.

The smiles he had encouraged were but fleeting glimpses of courtesy, and soon replaced by anxiety. Not for the first time in his life as a doctor he felt like the harbinger of death. He glanced at the anxious faces and ceased his procrastinations.

"The news is not as good as it could be," he approached the subject, still with a trace of reluctance. "It has been established that Mary is extremely anaemic, which means that she suffers from a deficiency of red corpuscles in her blood. What she needs is a carefully controlled diet to correct the ailment. Now, I am quite sure that in her new environment this will be easily attended to, so it is just a case of time and patience, and we should soon see an improvement."

Looking round the relieved faces, he felt like a traitor. He had not divulged the entire truth. The reason for the diversion was simply that he wanted to speak to Mari and Stuart on their own, but of course he could not do this with the two youngsters in attendance.

He had been forced to say something in their presence, for had he asked them to excuse themselves in the first instance they would surely have suspected something was seriously wrong.

Mari intuitively understood that the doctor was caught in a cleft stick, and a deep foreboding within her very bones warned her that there was bad news still to come.

Escape action was called for. She hustled and bustled around the kitchen, chattering like a magpie as she set out cups and saucers. The whisky bottle landed on the table with a welcome thump, for yes, it was the perfect night for a nip, to match the nip in the air.

Mari showed her organising skills when everyone had finished drinking their tea. Donald was to take Mary round the livestock in the steading for the final nightly check. It was a duty that she knew Mary delighted in. Was there not that wee calf in sore need of a cuddle, and of course the collie puppies to say goodnight to.

Mari herself would have to take some instructions from the doctor regarding Mary's new diet, so the sweethearts wouldn't need to hurry, for it would be boring old talk for a while.

The teenagers departed arm in arm, and were scarcely out of the door before Mari had turned to her friend the doctor with questions bubbling on her lips, which quivered with apprehension.

Ewan lifted his hand to stay the torrent that was sure to come, but with infinite compassion launched into the true state of affairs. He knew that excuses for his hitherto prevarications would be superfluous, so came directly to the point.

Mary was suffering from cancer of the blood, the medical term being leukaemia i.e. an excess of white corpuscles in the blood. Although he had said virtually the same thing in his first statement, the difference is that anaemia can be cured, whereas leukaemia would require a gift from God, in other words a miracle, to effect a cure.

Mari uttered a deep, impassioned groan of despair as she collapsed on the old leather sofa beside her husband. She sank her head on his chest and wailed in her utter grief. Great sobs racked her body as she writhed and twisted in total surrender to her heartbreaking anguish.

Stuart held her tenderly, but made no effort to stem the storm of emotion that engulfed his wife. He knew that nature's safety valve was operating, and its therapeutic essence would enable Mari to overcome this devastating blow and allow her to come to terms with her grief.

Slowly Mari quietened, the sobs subsided, but for a few more moments she clung to Stuart. Giving a long lingering hug to her protector, she rose, sniffed mightily and went across to Ewan and took his hand in hers.

"That must have been very hard for you to do, my friend," she husked, the thread of pain still evident in her voice. "The things you have to do, and the burdens you have to bear in the name of your profession. I thank you for being so considerate in reserving the bad news until we were alone."

"Now we must decide what to tell our two little ones. My immediate thoughts are to leave them both with the knowledge they have. Do you both agree?"

Stuart and Ewan were already nodding their heads in agreement. They both started to speak at the same time, then both stopped in deference to the other. Ewan signalled to Stuart to continue and he nodded in acceptance.

Stuart took a deep breath to steady himself, and his voice, for he was also deeply affected by the sad news, and husked in a subdued timbre that lacked its usual vibrancy.

"I agree! But with certain reservations. I firmly believe Donald should be made aware of the true facts eventually, but I will choose the time and place, and furthermore I will be the one to tell him. I do insist he has to know, however hard the pill is to swallow."

Ewan glanced at Mari with concern, unsure how she would react to this assertion by her husband, she had ever been a tigress in protection of her loved ones, but he felt that Stuart was totally correct in his declarations, and decided to add his professional voice to the proposal.

"I have to agree wholeheartedly with that, Stuart. We must treat him as an adult in this matter. Truth to say, he is more mature than many grown up people of my acquaintance. However, it will not be an easy task, and I don't envy you, Stuart. All I can say is, that if I can be of any assistance when the time comes, you have only to mention it. Now then good friends, I am afraid that, having completely ruined your evening, I must be on my travels for I have quite a few calls to make before bedtime. I bid you both goodnight."

The door closed behind the doctor, and Mari and Stuart came together in a comforting embrace. Mari gently disengaged and murmured in self disparagement, "Look at the state of me! I must clean up this old face of mine before the youngsters come in from the steading or else our subterfuge will be disassembled before we start."

With brisk determination she set about the task of recovery, and reverting to her normal style, directed Stuart to tidy the table and then stoke up the Raeburn fire for the night.

Donald and Mary returned from their evening walk, the calf had been loved to distraction, the Arab mare had enjoyed her usual tidbits and caresses, and all the other animals had been checked to ensure that all was well.

Mary went across to Stuart and gave him the customary goodnight kiss. Turning to Mari she snuggled into the welcoming cocoon of love. She pressed her face into the curve of Mari's neck and whispered softly.

"I love you so much it frightens me. You are the best mother anyone could have in the world. I just want you to know that."

Withdrawing from the embrace, she returned to Donald and, seeking the shelter of his arms for a moment, kissed him goodnight, then quietly departed to her bedroom.

Mari was standing with tears flooding from her eyes, she looked across at her son and choked out, "God, she is so beautiful, Donald! No wonder you love her. May God in heaven give you the maximum time He can to enjoy such love."

Stuart's basso profundo interceded almost indecently at this point.

"Come on, you two, it won't be this in the morning. Remember the old adage, early to bed etc." In truth he was just a little scared that Mari would blurt out the true nature of Mary's affliction in her very emotional condition, although thinking about it later he reflected that she had too much strength of character to ever allow that to happen.

Cruel winter laid its icy grip across the glen, at times creating arctic isolation as the narrow glen roads filled with drifting snow.

To the Macdonalds this proved to be no great hardship, being well inured to the seasonal changes, and as ever, properly prepared for each in its turn. The stock were safe and snug in the sturdy stone buildings, and the sheep were in the lower sheltered fields and could forage successfully between the storms.

As was usual, the garron ponies made their way down the glen to easier pickings, and, with their traditional hardiness, would fare well enough on their own.

During the winter months Mary seemed to gain in strength and a hint of colour seemed to dusk her face. Stuart, who covertly monitored her condition, decided it was a false declaration, not a natural glow of health, and he mourned quietly for her and his son.

He knew that soon he must apprise Donald of the true state of affairs, and his heart quelled at the thought of it. He would not sidestep the issue, or the responsibility, but he knew deep in his soul that it would be one of the most unpleasant tasks he would ever have to perform.

The end of spring chased summer into the breech, and it was to prove one of the best summers for many years. Taking advantage of this halcyon benediction, Donald would bring round the Arab mare to the garden gate. With Mary sitting astride, they would wend their way quietly up through the glen to a favourite location that Donald had used on so many occasions as he learned to emulate the wildlife sounds around him.

It was a completely round circle of sward, surrounded by gorse and bracken, totally private. He called it his fairy glen, and it did seem to hold a feeling of enchantment.

He entertained his sweetheart, going through his repertoire, and she exclaimed with delight as one bird after another would answer and come to investigate the source of an intruder or possible mate.

Tiring of the game eventually, they lay like contented seals basking in the sun. Donald, as usual at this time of year, was in shorts, and although his tan was fractionally light at the start of summer, he never really lost his dusky hue and certainly would not suffer with being sunburned. He was acutely aware that Mary would, however, and would periodically sit up and check that his ward was not suffering unpleasantness. Mari, as usual, had given him strict instructions, even if not needed, in regards to his responsibilities for Mary's welfare.

It was on one such day that Mary sat up and adjusted her widebrimmed sunbonnet. Pulling her knees up to her chin, she folded her arms across them and leant her chin on her arms.

"Donald," she sighed, with a quiver in her voice, "I have something to tell you that will make you very unhappy, maybe even angry. I must tell you however for it festers within me like rotting garbage or a foul cancer."

"I feel sure that you know that my dream was to come to you as a virgin bride. That cannot be, I'm afraid, because I have been robbed of that precious dowry in the most horrible circumstances. So much have I regretted what happened that I have even contemplated suicide, however I didn't have the strength to carry it out. Please forgive me, Donald, for something that I was powerless to prevent, although needless to say I tried desperately."

Donald listened with increasing horror as the story unfolded. Gently he gathered the distressed lass into his arms, his first thought to comfort her and ease the pain she so obviously still felt. The tears fell freely from her large brown eyes, and sobs racked the frail body as she relived in her mind's eye that dreadful violation.

"There! There!" he soothed, "to think you have lived with this on your own grieves me, my darling. Why on earth have you never told me before? Don't you know a trouble shared is a trouble halved? Did you honestly think that because you are not a virgin I would love you less? Darling, I am not a collector of maiden veils, believe me, it makes not the slightest difference in the world. To me you are the only girl I would ever want to marry, so think no more about it. Try to erase this evil thing that happened to you from your mind."

"Mary," he continued, "there is only one thing I want most in the world, that is for you to get well, to regain your health. That is the most important thing at the moment, my dearest love, so forget this nonsense about being a disappointment to me, for you could never be that."

With a flash of insight, he realised that she felt she was tarnished goods and somehow unworthy of their love.

"Listen my heart," he breathed in her ear, "as you are at this moment, you are perfect, in every way, but I will get angry if you denigrate yourself, because, don't you see, if you do you besmirch and defile this wonderful love we have, and I couldn't ever let anyone do that."

"Let us enjoy our love, my darling, for it is a pure and clean gift from our Maker. Hush now, sweetheart, no more tears, no more sorrow. Life will never be perfect, so let us take what comes, savour the good times and grin and bear it through the hard times."

Quietly he held her until her emotional storm abated. She would never really know the murderous feeling that swept through him like a searing flame through tinder-dry grass.

That someone had violated his Mary was a despicable act he could barely contemplate, but the fact that the perpetrator of this heinous crime had been her own brother was almost beyond his comprehension. He would seek the most serious redress, of this he was determined, and only his iron will kept him in balance, and gave him the control to carry out what was most necessary at the moment, and that was to comfort and reassure his love.

Lying back on the springy grass, he pulled Mary close to him and crooned a wordless lullaby, rocking her gently in his arms as a mother would a fractious child.

So they lay in comforting embrace, full of innocence and sweet young love, which already the harshness of life had tarnished slightly.

The warmth of the sun and the droning of the ever-busy pollen gatherers soothed the senses and the fairy circle regained its enchantment, creating a pastoral sanctuary for the young lovers.

As if in harmony with the rustic scenario a lark, high in the heavens, poured forth a virtuoso musical serenade of unparalleled exuberance.

Not to be outdone a mavis, or songthrush, on a nearby rowan tree, lifted its head skywards, giving rich contralto to the dulcet soprano of the skylark.

The cooing of wood pigeons played a bass accompaniment, and in the near distance the harsh chatter of a magpie crashed like castanets. Pastoral perfection, from God's own hand, free as the air they breathed, a performance of exquisite simplicity.

Donald came to with a start. Anxiously he surveyed the tender skin of Mary. If there was one blemish his mother would be outraged, and that was something not to be faced lightly. With a sigh of relief his searching eyes told him all was well. Gently he roused his sweetheart, and suggested that perhaps they had better start back towards home. They could then take it nice and easy and have time to look around as they proceeded through the countryside that offered a profusion of flora and fauna worth seeing.

Mary enjoyed country walks with Donald for, although she was a country girl with a natural ability to observe wild life as she passed along, she lacked Donald's trained observation and he would point out things that surprised and delighted her - a mallard's nest, a swooping hawk, the scat of a travelling fox, a rabbit's run, where roe deer had fed the previous evening, and occasionally a fawn lying within its own camouflage.

His country knowledge astounded her, such as the reason a wild duck, if forced from its clutch of eggs, on the instant of leaving them would spatter them with excreta that carried such a foul smell that egg eating animals would pass them by, leaving them untouched. Many wild birds would feign a broken wing to draw danger away from their nests, endangering their own lives in the process with total disregard.

He had observed on one occasion a rabbit doe actually face up to her traditional enemy, the stoat, in an effort to protect her young, and stranger still, she had succeeded.

Rooks were notorious for divebombing the mighty golden eagle as he arrogantly sailed through their territory, and would continue to harass him, to such an extent that he would depart for more peaceful surroundings.

The wonder of nature that most enchanted Donald was the aerial mating dance of the peewit, or teuchat as it was called parochially. Its tumbling aerobatics accompanied by the flump, flump of its square ended wings, surpassed anything else of nature's bounties, in his opinion.

There was always a touch of comedy attached to the display, turning and tumbling with the insane pee-wheep, pee-wheep which seemed a ludicrous supplement to such an outstanding exhibition of death defying feats. Often it would appear that the performing artiste must surely hit the ground, so involved he would appear to be in his efforts to impress his mate, sitting on her scrape of a nest on the ground beneath him.

Donald would explain to Mary about the common eel being spawned in the local burns, then swimming to the Sargasso Sea to grow to maturity, only to return to the same burn to procreate in turn.

The royal salmon achieved a similar phenomenon, and Donald was quite sure that their navigational proficiency was still an enigma to mankind.

Stories such as these, with little personal anecdotes, utterly captivated Mary, and certainly on this occasion cleared her mind of less pleasant things, so that by the time they reached Craigburn she was laughing with carefree abandon.

They stabled the mare and ambled casually towards the welcoming smell of the evening meal. Mary declared she was starving, however the meal that she did eat was a stark reminder to those watching that her appetite was sorely depleted.

Life at Craigburn followed its regular pattern, as season followed season, and the traditional tasks for these periods were dealt with in regulated order.

Farm work is unending, but not necessarily tedious, and where an affinity with the land and the animals it supports is involved, it can be, and often is, a labour of love.

Mari was unrelenting in her efforts to keep Mary in good cheer, and to make sure that she was never given a task that would tire her or cause distress in any way.

She guarded her ward with the ferocity of a tigress protecting cubs, and was untiring in her endeavours to make Mary feel wanted and cared for.

Two years after Mary joined the Macdonald family at Craigburn the large farmhouse kitchen underwent a structural alteration. A deep double-doored cupboard in the south facing wall was turned into a bed in the wall.

It was a snug little nest and Mary could lie within the draught-free sanctuary and still be close to the ones she loved so dearly. She now had to spend a lot of time resting, so the new arrangements made sound sense, and meant she was not isolated upstairs.

The residents of the glen would call on the slightest pretext, bringing with them small gifts of delicacies to tempt her failing appetite.

Lady Cruachan was a regular visitor and spent hours chatting on various topics. Being well travelled and most articulate, she brought the essence of distant shores to the wee lass, who had now become a prisoner of her immediate environment.

Mary would never enjoy the experiences and sights that were described to her so fluently by this gracious matron. She realised she was not getting any better and was struggling with the need to bring the matter up for discussion with Mari, but somehow she couldn't quite find the courage.

Stuart decided that Donald now had to be made aware of how seriously ill Mary was, although he shrank mentally from the task. He arranged it quite simply by delaying Donald one evening after milking was finished and the final clean up had been attended to.

At the rear of the byre was a boarded window seat and leading Donald to it, he said, "Let's sit down a minute, I want to have a wee chat with you." As they settled he put his arm around his son's shoulders and, giving them a quick squeeze to demonstrate his love and support, he continued.

"I feel quite sure, Donald, that I don't need to tell you that our wee Mary is not getting any better. In fact she grows steadily weaker, and of course is now confined to bed."

Miserably Donald nodded his head in agreement, as his father continued, "the truth of the matter is, that your mother and I decided not to tell you or Mary that she was diagnosed as having leukaemia, and not anaemia as you were told. In effect Mary is slowly dying, there is no cure within the medical world at this time. You must know how sorry I am lad. We didn't tell you because we wanted you both to have as happy a time together as was possible in the short time left for

Mary. I plead for your understanding, son, but I'm sure you realise it was done out of love."

Donald laid his head against his father's chest as the acid bite of scalding pain engulfed him. Unashamedly he wept with deep racking sobs, hanging on to the platform of his father's strength. Shuddering hiccups of searing agony convulsed his wiry frame as the storm of grief raged through him.

As he had done with the mother, so he did with his son. Stuart quietly held his son whilst the tempest raged, knowing that it was the best thing to do in the circumstances.

Paradoxically he was glad that the grief had an avenue of escape. It was less likely to stay within and fester into bitterness that would twist the character and destroy reason.

Gradually Donald quietened, but still he clung to the safety of his father's embrace. When at last he turned to look at Stuart he discovered that tears were running unchecked down his father's face, which was haggard and drawn with suppressed pain.

With a convulsive shudder, he hugged his father fiercely and cried.

"Oh, Dad! How selfish I am. You and Mum must have gone through hell these past two years keeping such a secret and allowing us the tranquillity of ignorance. I will never be able to thank you enough for that. My God, but you are wonderful parents, and, believe me, I have always thought that. Oh! My dear, dear Dad."

They both arose from the window seat and Stuart pulled the Hunter fob watch from the bib pocket of his overalls, and pulled a face as he hurriedly returned it to his pocket.

"Come on, lad," he entreated, "let's get our faces into the horse trough and get sluiced down. It's time for the evening meal, and you know the penalty for tardiness."

Donald nodded his head, then catching his father by the arm he suggested pleadingly, "Dad, just one thing! Please don't let us tell Mary, let us give her our love and support until she departs this earth."

Although his voice thickened again with his plea, Donald now took firm hold of his emotions and, after a few minutes of deep breathing, had regained his equanimity.

A couple of months later, after the evening meal, Mary asked Donald to lie beside her on the bed in the wall. He complied with alacrity and when he had comfortably settled on his back, Mary turned to him and, cuddling her face into the hollow of his neck, whispered, "Sing our song for me Donald, it always gives me such a warm feeling, and somehow I feel a wee bit low spirited tonight."

Donald wriggled himself a little higher on the pillows, and looking across to his mother asked her to accompany him on the old upright piano. Mari went across and seating herself played the introduction to Mary of Argyle, knowing full well that was the song in question.

Stuart brought a chair over to the bedside and hummed the opening bars in his deep resonant bass, then stopped and looked at Donald in surprise when he missed the opening and Mari started the introduction again.

Donald had just experienced a heart-juddering premonition. A brief flash, like a jolt of electricity, and then it was gone. Taking a deep breath, he waited for the cue, and this time came in right on time.

"I have heard the mavis singing,
It's love song to the morn."

The clear young tenor voice rose and soared with searing intensity, his heart and soul as naked as an unsheathed blade, as the beautiful words poured forth.

So intense was the feeling that quivered through the room like a living wraith, that Mari and Stuart felt the very hairs on the backs of their necks stand out in a vibration of primordial stimulus.

"It was you, my gently Mary, and your warm and winsome smile,
That has made my life an Eden, Bonny Mary o' Argyle."

The last lines of the song rose and fell with the high notes clear and distinct, and then, utter silence.

Mary gripped Donald tightly, but it was the spasmodic embrace of farewell, and the death rattle signalled its utter finality.

Donald turned in shock and disbelief, he pressed the still warm body close to him in an instinctive attempt to re-animate his lifeless sweetheart. The tortured wail of despair keened out in cadence with his mother's, who knew the significance of the sound she had just heard, and had come running over to embrace Donald and Mary.

Stuart joined them, and for countless moments they held each other in silent desolation. They all realised their love for this beautiful young woman had not been able to avert her destiny.

Later they would draw comfort from knowing that they had done all in their power to make life a pleasant and happy time for her during her time at Craigburn.

Mary was laid to rest in the Macdonald plot in the pleasantly sheltered graveyard in Ardochan. Not one of her natural family attended although they had been advised of Mary's passing. In many ways it had been expected, it was typical of their uncaring attitude.

Most of the mourners were from Glencruachan, although there were a few from Glenavro who had known Mary and appreciated that she was unfortunate in being a member of the family into which she had been born. Despite this handicap she had always conducted herself in a pleasant and courteous manner, and would be fondly remembered for those qualities.

Life goes on, and as the time passes the pain of bereavement eases, but for the Macdonalds it was a slow process of recovery. They did not indulge in an excess of self pity, or wallow in their grief. They knew the big hearted girl who had left them would not have wanted a demonstration of continual mourning to blight their lives. Rather she would have wanted them to remember her as having had the most wonderful years of her short life during her time with them, and to be happy for what they had shared.

For John Macmillan time also passed, and five weeks after the demise of Mary he was released from Perth prison. Residents of Glenavro and Glencruachan would have been astonished to learn that he had been released a few months early for good behaviour. The other inmates of the prison had caustically remarked that he had enjoyed the good fortune of not having been caught in any misdemeanours.

As time had progressed his natural aggression had firmly reasserted itself, much to the detriment of his prison colleagues. He had quickly established a brutal reign within the prison and did not relinquish his barbaric hold until the day he walked through the prison gates, a free man.

Chapter Seven

Mist swirled like a diaphanous veil, partially shrouding the solitary figure that tramped wearily along the glen road. Hobnailed boots beat a disconsolate tattoo, as large hands clenched and unclenched, like tortured crabs in a macabre dance. The left hand had a grotesque twist in three of the fingers, embellishing the eccentricity of their activity.

Perhaps it was a clear indication of a deranged mind that conceived demented plans, then discarded them for something more fiendish as the twisted thoughts ebbed and flowed.

The spell in jail had done nothing to quell the murderous rages he was prone to. Mindless rage possessed him now, as he measured out the long miles towards Highbrae. In his irrational judgement he had many scores to settle and his first port of call, when he had reasserted his authority at home, would be a visit to Craigburn. The visit would not be to the liking of that little arsehole, Macdonald. Oh no! It would be no social calling for a cup of tea, that was a bloody fact.

Next in line would be a certain special policeman down in Dunkeld. Now he had a very special surprise for him! He certainly wouldn't be thinking all his birthdays had come at once when he, John, had finished with the aggravating bastard.

These were the thoughts that kept John's mind active as he tramped out the long miles from the country bus stop, this maelstrom of murderous intent increasing as each dreary mile followed the next.

When he reached Widow Stewart's garden gate, he paused long enough to kick the gate to matchwood in a fit of vandalism. The poor old lady peered anxiously from behind the net curtains, praying that this destructive moron would not seek to gain entry to the house itself. She felt vulnerable, and very much afraid. She still bore the scars of her cat's claws, when this dreadful man had kicked her pet over the garden gate onto her chest.

She felt that locked doors would be of little avail to prevent entry against this powerful, evil being. In this she was absolutely correct, for locks will only deter the entry of honest, trustworthy people, and this threatening presence was in neither category.

Luck and prayers must have prevailed for John turned away from the destruction of the gate with a satisfied smirk on his face, to continue his journey homewards.

Hunger growled in his belly, violence roiled in his head and his jaws ached with the continual clenching of his teeth. This frightening apparition was a veritable bomb waiting to explode.

He was also thoroughly disenchanted with the long walk that had been forced on him, so somebody would suffer the consequences of that. To his mind it was just another indignity that he had to bear. In all his innocence, the world and its people seemed determined to always give him hassle and strife. He could handle it though, he was a fighter and he would show all who crossed him that it was a foolish venture indeed to oppose or defy his desires.

In this frame of mind he arrived at his home, unheralded, unannounced and bubbling like a volcano about to erupt. With callous disregard he kicked the door off its hinges and exploded into the smoky smelling kitchen.

Four shocked faces turned in disbelief. Had it been the devil himself, they couldn't have been more appalled or horrified. Each of the four knew, without the least shadow of a doubt, that trouble personified had just fallen on them.

Old Macmillan rose from his chair with an angry bellow, his tickling rod, as he called it, firmly gripped in his hand, as if it were a life saver.

"What the hell dae ye think yer da'en," he snarled, "an hoo the hell hiv they let an eejit like ye oot o' jile?" He brandished the steel bar in John's face in an attempt to intimidate his brutish son, and thus retain control and authority in his own home.

The gesture was the only stimulus John required, a touch paper to gunpowder. He stepped forward and wrenched the bar from his father's hand as if he was taking a lollipop from a child.

He swiped his father across the ribs, smiling fiendishly as he heard bones break, and, as the old man bent over in agony, he callously crashed the bar across his shoulders with such power it drove the old man to the floor.

"Noo then, ye auld shite!" crowed John, waving the bar like some new won trophy. "Are ye convinced noo that a'm the gaffer. Or wid there be ony body else want tae hae a wee go?" The total silence was answer enough.

Old Macmillan groggily rose and went to sit in his usual chair by the fire. His haunches had barely touched the seat when a large misshapen fist grabbed the front of his overalls and violently threw him across the room.

"Ye still haven't got it, have ye? That's no yer seat ony ma'er. Ye hae jist conceded the right tae me. Noo, ye jist watch yer manners frae noo on, fer ah'll no be loth tae gie ye a wee reminder if it proves necessary."

He bounced the bar off the table, scowled at this mother and growled through clenched teeth.

"Ye get off yer arse an' get me fed, an' quick aboot it or ye'll be in line fer a wee tickle forbye." Mrs Macmillan jumped like a scalded cat and darted out to the pantry, glad to be out of sight of this frightening monster she had brought into the world.

Fear lending speed to her efforts, she quickly produced a huge platter of fried leftovers from dinner time and placed them carefully on the table in front of her son. She returned to the larder and brought a jug of buttermilk and a large mug, and placed them within reach of John, who was wolfing down the unappetising mess that was his belated dinner. She then beat a hasty retreat to her bedroom, glad to be away from the menacing atmosphere.

Perhaps if the two younger brothers had taken up cudgels on their father's behalf and made a concerted effort to overpower their sibling, the cruel usurpation of power could have been avoided, but they had sat unmoving throughout the violent exchange.

Their elder brother had held them in thrall ever since they could remember, and they well knew his reactions to anyone who would say him nay; so as far as they were concerned life would probably be more interesting now that John had returned and regained control.

When John found out about their imminent eviction from the farm it evoked neither consideration nor concern. What filled his mind like a festering sore was revenge on those who had caused him humiliation or grief.

First on the agenda would be that upstart Macdonald, he would pay the price for his mother's treatment of John in the village hall at Ardochan. Secondly, that overgrown swine of a policeman who had damaged his hand, then, if he had time, he would devise a wee something for that uppity fart of a factor.

Two weeks after he had returned home John had decided what he was going to do at Craigburn. It would be a most covert assignation, the witching hour the ideal time to commit the foul deed.

With his two brothers sticking to him like shadows, they set off on their odyssey. A full moon shone with a clear hard brilliance, illuminating the surrounding countryside with ethereal delicacy. Hoar frost festooned the trees in ghostly magnificence and sparkled on the grass like scattered diamonds.

A Christmas setting, as depicted by artists, but there was nothing Christian in the hearts of the marauders that brazenly marched across the fields.

That there was so much light bothered the two younger brothers, but when they mentioned it, very carefully, to John, he assured them it was exactly right for what he had in mind. He wanted to see, and be seen. He was due this redress and was certainly going to procure his God-given right, so would they shut their mouths and stay close.

Entering the central cobbled area of the Craigburn steading they nosed around like scavenging hyenas. The little Arab mare hung her head over the half stable door to see what was happening. Her high intelligence had forever made her curious about what was going on around her.

John's breath exploded with satisfaction. Ah yes! He had heard about this little treasure. Well, fine, she would do for a start to the evening's entertainment.

Spitting on the palm of his hand and taking a firm grip of the tickling stick he had wrested from his father, he strode across to the loosebox door. The short steel bar glinted evilly in the moonlight with a malevolent glitter. The mare snorted in alarm and backed away from the door, animal instinct warning her that danger was imminent.

In his bedroom, Donald awoke. Neither breathing nor posture changed until his senses attuned themselves to his surroundings. His eyes opened and a feeling of inexplicable foreboding galvanised him into explosive action.

He was out of bed, into his shorts and running for the door within a heartbeat of time. As he passed his parents' bedroom door he shouted to alert his father.

Passing through the garden gate, he heard the Arab mare snort with fear, and he accelerated like a spur-driven colt.

John heaved open the stable door. The frightened mare reared in alarm, forefeet clawing the air in front of her. With berserk strength John brought the steel bar across one of her weaving legs. The snap of the bone sounded as clear as a rifle shot.

The mare dropped with a scream of pain, and her attacker hit her again with brutal sadistic delight. The bar hit the mare right between the ears on the top of the beautiful dished head. This final blow, although it was not meant to be, was a kindness to the mare, for such was the force of it she died instantly, and was immediately freed from her pain.

A horrifying thrumming sound filled John's ears as he turned and stepped clear of the stable.

The intimidating, awe-inspiring thrum seemed to fog his mind, and so terrifying was the sound he could only stand and look with consternation at the apparition that filled his vision.

A veritable whirlwind of violence exploded in his midriff, the snakebite, delivered perfectly, blinded him. He screamed in agony and lifted the steel bar to strike out at his adversary.

He felt his wrist gripped in a band of steel as the offending arm was jerked up behind him. The hand lost sensation and the bar clattered onto the cobbles. The arm was hoisted even higher until the ball and socket parted company.

John screamed for his brothers to help, but they stood transfixed.

A pair of heels landed in the hollows of his knees, followed by a pair of kites to either side of his neck, dropping him to the ground, powerless to participate any further.

Donald grabbed the bar, rolled John over with his foot, and brought the bar crashing down on the right kneecap of the recumbent figure, who screamed anew at the excruciating agony.

Recovering slightly from his petrified state, John's brother Tom grabbed a pitchfork and, levelling it like a pikestaff, he ran towards Donald, intent on skewering him on the tangs.

Donald had been aware of the potential danger from the younger brothers but on the periphery of his concentration, confident enough to know he could control them if the need arose.

Instead of retreating from the threat, Donald darted forward, swaying only sufficiently to clear the tangs on his left side. His left hand took purchase at the juncture of the shaft and gave a quick jerking forward tug, assisting Tom's movement towards him.

Bending the first and second knuckles of his right hand, Donald drove it directly into the base of Tom's nose, virtually ripping the cartilage off the face. At the same instant his knee rose and sank deep into the solar plexus, with such force that ribs could be heard breaking as the power of the blow carried up through the apex of its travel.

Donald threw the second opponent aside and leapt towards the third brother, who dropped to the ground and covered his head with his hands. Ewart had seen and heard enough to give him nightmares for years to come. He wanted the ground to open and swallow him. Anything in fact that would remove him from the sight of this awesome avenging figure.

Donald stopped before the cowering creature, and post battle revulsion deluged him with shame. He had used a mallet to kill a flea. It had been a totally one-sided contest, and now he felt that he had used the exercise to expiate the latent anger at life that Mary's death had left burning within him.

Taking a deep breath, he addressed the quaking youth at his feet.

"Get these brothers of yours out of here. I don't care how. Give my apologies to your parents, and to your brothers, but please do not ever come back near our steading. You were trespassing in every sense of the word, and may God forgive your trespasses, for I cannot."

He whirled away and ran to the loosebox, where his father knelt beside the dead mare. Stuart looked up as Donald entered the stable and sadly offered his son consolation.

"She would not have suffered for more than a second, son, the second blow made sure of that. Now you and I will bury her at the bottom of the orchard, she will not go to the knackers and be used as dog food. We'll do the right thing by her. What do you say?"

Mutely Donald nodded as he sank to his knees and cradled the once proud little head. Laying his head against hers, he wept bitter tears in this, his second bereavement in such a short time.

Rocking back and forth in a paroxysm of grief, he railed against the world for being so unfair. It was then that Stuart advised him that nobody had ever promised that life would be fair.

Quietly he sat beside his son, knowing that his strength of character would see him through this terrible time, and, to gently bring him away from the vale of tears, he opened a discussion about the affray he had just witnessed.

"You know that noise you were making, Donald," he inquired hesitatingly, "how do you do that? I have never heard anything so chilling and fear-inspiring in my life. I have served with Chi Li in the armed forces, and been involved in many hand to hand encounters, but I have never heard him use that facility, yet you must have learned it from him."

For a brief moment Stuart thought that Donald was too immersed in his suffering and grief to respond, then Donald looked at him with eyes like glazed cherries in a bed of aspic.

He blinked furiously, like a sleepwalker coming awake. Briskly he rubbed his face and eyes and, with a voice hoarse and drawn with pain, he replied to his dad's question.

"It is just another instrument of aggression, dad, if it is used correctly it is supposed to attack the central nervous system of one's opponent and render him semi-paralysed, therefore making it easier to incapacitate him. It takes a long time to learn because it is a combination of larynx and diaphragmatic control, and yes, Chi Li can do it, but once I had got the rudiments of it and had practised it for a while, Chi Li said I was better than he."

Standing up he took a few agitated steps around the loosebox, then turned and looked at his dad.

"Dad! Can we bury my wee mare now?" he pleaded, a false brightness in his eyes, that were tear heavy, "we'll just have time before the milking has to start. I would rather it was over and done with. Can we, dad?"

Stuart promptly agreed and using Meg the Garron mare to pull her former stable mate to the bottom of the orchard, they applied themselves to the grisly task, Donald finding some relief in the manual exertion.

When the wee mare was finally interred in her last resting place, Stuart left his son on his own to make his final farewell and returned to the house to make them a cup of tea before starting the milking.

He poured a generous measure of whisky into each mug, feeling that it would cheer them up a little, it had been one hell of a night. 'Thank God Mari isn't here' Stuart thought to himself, but he must have transmitted his thought to his son, for that was the first remark Donald made when he came into the warm kitchen.

Since Mary had died Mari had taken to assisting Dr Fergusson in the capacity of midwife, and had been called away to a pending delivery, prior to Donald and his father retiring for the night.

Which reminded Stuart, he would have to tell the foreman that his wife would have to attend to the dairy, one of the tasks that Mari usually undertook in the course of her daily chores.

It had been Dr Fergusson who had suggested to Stuart that Mari could be better diverted from her grief by being presented with a new interest, and what better way than bringing new life into the world?

Stuart had readily agreed, and it was true to say that Mari had responded in a very positive manner.

This diversion had turned out to be a double blessing in as much as she had missed the violent death of the mare, and seeing her son in what would have been a very distressing scene for her.

Life at the farm had returned to its normal routine, but for Donald the sheer enjoyment of life was missing. There was no sparkle to the days, although he didn't mope around. He continued to practice his martial arts with Chi Li, and he ran consistently each morning, but it had all become dull routine. He really needed a challenge to shake him into fresh awareness, to stimulate his zest for life and living.

The laird grieved for his young protege, and conferred with his wife and Chi Li as to the best course of action to improve things for Donald.

They came to the conclusion that a new Arab mare could be the answer, but when the laird suggested this to Donald it was almost brusquely rejected. The answer being that he had not been able to look after the one he had properly, and that he really didn't have the time now to train a horse to the same standard he had with his first Arab.

A week later the laird got Stuart's permission to have Donald start training in estate management under the factor of Glencruachan. Stuart did wonder why this kind of training had been suggested as it really wouldn't be of much practical value to Donald, but he held his peace, believing that the new interest would have therapeutic value to his son.

Stuart was not to know that this training was part of a long term plan that had been evolving in the laird's head for quite some time now. In fact, this was a golden opportunity to put the first phase into action without giving an inkling of what he had planned for the future.

Donald had lost his first young love, which is always difficult to accept, but he had also lost another love that had been important to him. The pain of these two losses ground away at him with a ceaseless ache, persistent and aggravating as a thorn in the flesh.

Standing on the side of a hill one cold blustery morning, with the sleet driving into his face like pygmy arrows, he looked around and thought, 'I must get away from here, from this glen, if only for a while. There is a whole big world out there and I've seen nothing of it. I am a prisoner of my present environment. I need to get free. Oh God, how do I accomplish that?'

At Highbrae, the Macmillans had been duly evicted. Old Macmillan had been unable to burn the steading as he had threatened to do, primarily because Mrs Macmillan had managed to warn the Factor of his intent. This was not done out of any sense of civic duty, but because she feared that her husband would land in jail.

The Glenavro Factor had expected something of the sort, but he accepted the warning and took the necessary measures to prevent any destruction being exercised on the property.

The Macmillan sons had been strangely quiet of late. Nobody seemed to know what had in effect pulled their teeth but, whatever it was, the local populace were just glad the terrorism was not in evidence any more.

John's vision was greatly impaired although he was not completely blind, but it was sufficient a handicap to affect his lifestyle, keeping him confined within his immediate family environment.

He walked with the aid of a stick, and his damaged right shoulder gave him almost constant pain, however, the biggest change was in his attitude to life.

Gone was the swaggering aggressive bully, left in its place was a self-pitying whining wreck clinging to his mother's skirts till he almost drove her to distraction.

Strangely enough, this dependency, this new feeling of being needed was the catalyst for a change in her character that made her become almost pleasant.

Old Macmillan appeared to have been completely demoralised at losing the farm, and had turned into a complete introvert, losing all his aggressive drive, allowing himself to be directed by his wife, who at one time had been the family skivvy to all the menfolk.

Tom and Ewart had become frightened of their own shadows, always seeming to be looking over their shoulders, and were well satisfied that they were leaving the area for pastures new.

The outcome of the circumstances that had occurred at Craigburn had affected the entire Macmillan family, leaving it now in matriarchal dominance.

They left the Highbrae steading without a farewell. The general consensus seemed to be good riddance to bad rubbish. They had done nothing to endear themselves to any of the local inhabitants, so fond farewells were sadly not in evidence.

They travelled westwards in a horsedrawn four-wheeled wagon and eventually reached the west coast of Sunderland, taking up residence on a waste piece of land close to the sea that no-one seemed to begrudge them.

The father, Tom and Ewart did jobbing work where they could find it, supplementing this with poaching or stealing when the opportunity presented itself.

John, in the main, stayed close to his mother, or wandered the shore like a lost waif, ostensibly beachcombing or searching for firewood, but with his poor vision he was not very successful in either endeavour.

It was all a far cry from being farm tenants and Mrs Macmillan looked back with many regrets that her menfolk had not had the good sense and integrity of purpose to maintain the status they had enjoyed at Highbrae.

Two years after the departure of the Macmillans, Donald had still not escaped from the environs of his native glen, but he was to realise that this enforced delay enabled him to successfully complete his training in estate management, and that he would be pleased that he had accomplished this in the years to come.

The tragedy of his first love left him wary of any involvement with the opposite sex. Now a young man of twentyone years of age he had avoided, yes! with infinite courtesy, interested approaches from local maidens.

His father and mother both tried to play the matchmaker, but he stubbornly avoided involvement. The laird and his wife had also played their part, but Donald remained aloof to all offers.

The philosophy of Chi Li was again going to be proven. The yin and yang of life, the eternal circle of balance, would once more turn the wheel.

Donald, who had accepted this philosophy, still found it hard to believe that it would be applicable to himself, but his path of life was indeed going off at a tangent that would alter his whole life.

A telephone call from Mari's aging parents in Ireland created a state of flux in the Macdonald's family life. Quite simply, they wanted Stuart, Mari and Donald to leave Scotland and take up residence in Ulster at the Barranbarrach Estate, which was becoming a bit too much for old Kelly to cope with, as each short year followed the next, which always seemed shorter still.

The Barranbarrach Stud would be Mari's inheritance, the argument had continued, so why should they not come and take over now and allow the parents to enjoy a pleasant and leisurely period in their autumn years?

Donald's heart quickened for the first time in years. As far as he was concerned it was the diversion he had been wanting. Ireland was perhaps not the world, but at least it was somewhere. It was a move from his existing environment, and he hoped with all his heart that his parents would accept the offer.

The family discussed it, and discussed it again. Finally it was decided, the overriding factor being that it would be Donald's inheritance one day and it was only right that they should claim it, and why not now, rather than later.

Lord and Lady Cruachan had been friends of the Kellys for many years, and when they heard the news they were delighted for the Macdonald family, even though they would be very sorry to lose these fine people. As the laird pointed out to his wife, owning is better than tenancy, no matter how pleasant that tenure may be.

To assist them in the transition he insisted on a neutral evaluator being brought in to assess the value of the stock and farm machinery. He then bought the entire lot and said it would make it easier for a new tenant to come into a farm that was already a going concern, rather than having to build up from scratch.

Stuart was in no way fooled by these blithe assertions, he knew full well that it was as good a parting gift as this excellent laird could come up with. He felt a great sadness at the imminent parting, for they had been friends for many years and had shared many confidences whilst enjoying a dram.

Their friendship had been forged in the crucible of war in Burma, where they had met Chi Li, and Stuart's future father-in-law, Kelly of Barranbarrach. It was in this same foreign field that Stuart had met Mari, who was nursing in Singapore, although her father had tried very hard to dissuade her of the idea.

Although sad to be leaving, Stuart was acutely aware that it would be the best thing that could happen for Mari and Donald, to get away from Craigburn. He had been particularly concerned of late with the restlessness that Donald could not completely hide. This way they could still be together as a family, and that had been the final persuasion in Stuart's mind.

On the day of departure it seemed the whole glen had turned out, everyone in Sunday best, with smiles and tears and wishes of good luck.

Pipers vied with each other to play the most intricate pieces, wanting desperately to impress the man who had for so long coached them and who was now leaving.

The previous year's champion marched forward and presented his bagpipes to Stuart, with a request for him to play 'The Shepherds' Crook' as a farewell. This particular tune asked for was a competition compilation of immense difficulty, but none could beat the Macdonald in his mastery of the demanding techniques.

Through a mist of tears, and a sudden fear that his constricted diaphragm might deny him his usual natural flair at this important occasion, Stuart drew himself erect, took a deep, steadying breath and started to play.

A hush descended on the gathered company as the demanding intricacy of the piece was fingered by a master.

The fingers twittered and danced in a blur of movement, slurs and grace notes glacial sharp and crystal clear, the full range of chanter, the drones sobbing their cadence in the background.

The crowd stood enthralled and enrapt, knowing they would never again hear piping at this standard. Not a dry eye was in sight, the women wept openly, the men discreetly, but none felt shame. What they did feel was privileged to have been audience to this virtuoso performance.

When the last note died away there was a cathedral hush. The laird marched forward and, passing the pipes to their owner, he took hold of Stuart's hand and, with tears running unchecked, he pulled Stuart to him and embraced him like a brother.

The applause burst around them, clapping and shouting until throats protested and hands stung. It gave the moment of respite the laird required to get his voice working.

"Farewell, my friend, may God's hand guide and protect you. I give you our Scottish valediction. Haste ye back."

The laird whirled and went across to his wife, gently disentangling her from the arms of Mari. Hurriedly he kissed Mari, then, with almost indecent haste, he dragged his wife over to the Landrover and, getting in, drove off without a backward glance.

Donald had been standing apart looking very dejected, his eyes kept searching the crowd obviously without success. A slight figure materialised as if from nowhere. It was exactly what his eyes had searched for, Chi Li his sensei. For the first time in his life he saw tears in the eyes of this man who would normally die before losing face.

Donald stepped forward and grabbed his mentor in a fierce clasp, to hell with face he thought, as he kissed both the wrinkled cheeks.

"Father of my spirit, hold me ever in your thoughts, for you will ever be in mine," he choked out, sobs sticking in his throat. Stepping back, he held up his hands, inviting the warriors salute. Their hands gripped and knuckles cracked, one last embrace and Chi Li stepped away and virtually disappeared before Donald's eyes.

The laird returned to the scene, got out of the Landrover and picked his way through the crowd until he reached Donald.

"Donald, I almost forgot," he cried, slapping his forehead. "I know you are sailing from the Isle of Whithorn. Now then, when you arrive there you will be advised that there is some merchandise for you to take with you to your new home. Be kind enough to let me know that it was available, and that it was of good quality."

"All the very best for the future. The Barranbarrach Stud is gaining a master horseman, and I feel you will be able to teach our Celtic friends a few tricks. Farewell and take care, for I think of you as family."

When the Macdonalds finally arrived at the small west coast port of Whithorn, they were met by a ruddy faced individual who proved to be the Harbour Master.

Checking that they really were the Macdonalds, he shook hands with each in turn, then turned to Donald and asked him if he would be good enough to accompany him to the harbour office.

With Mari and Stuart following behind, the Harbour Master suggested that they would have to make a short detour first. He asked Donald if it was true that he had to take delivery of certain goods, had he been advised of this?

Donald assured him that this was indeed the fact, and wondered what all the mystery was about as he trotted along beside his guide.

Behind the office buildings were several warehouses, some cattle pens and a few smaller structures, all of which could be used to store merchandise of all descriptions. With his keen eye, Donald noticed that everything was in good repair. The harbour master obviously ran a tight ship, to coin a phrase.

Donald almost bumped into his guide, who had stopped abruptly at the door of an outhouse, which he threw open with a grand flourish then stepped to the side.

By this time Donald's curiosity was quivering like a tuning fork. Darting past the bulky figure he entered the building, then stopped with a gasp of delight.

A pair of matched Arabs, a colt and a filly, stood within, quietly pulling hay from a net. Donald stepped towards them and, just as he had introduced himself to his first Arab pony, did the same with these two beauties, who had moved forward in unison to greet him.

Donald blew into their nostrils in turn, pulled their ears and soft voiced them. The rapport was immediate. The Harbour Master, a trifle pompously, advised Donald that they were fully trained to saddle and, oh, by the way, each came complete with full tack, saddles, bridles, blankets, sheepskins and so on.

Donald was absolutely transported with delight. He turned at the sound of his parents' voices and said reverently in hushed tones.

"Can you believe it, some merchandise, think you not? Oh look! Are they not the perfect pair? They're lovely, just lovely, I can't believe it. Tell me it's not a dream, please! I couldn't bear that."

"No! No dream, Donald," replied his dad. "Just another manifestation of the kindness of the Laird of Cruachan, I doubt we will find a kinder or more generous man this side of heaven. Do you know, son, that man's heart was breaking at losing you? The truth is, you are a sort of replacement for the only son he had, and lost in the war, and the sad thing is, that like your mother and I, the Cruachans were cruelly denied any more offspring. I do hope that sometime in the future we can somehow return a gift to those good people that will gladden their hearts, for they are more than worthy of it."

Stuart put his arms around his wife and son and hugged them lovingly, then looking out at the patient Harbour Master, gave him a friendly wink and a smile, saying, "I think we have better get organised and see to the loading. Thank heavens it's forecast a quiet crossing, it will be easier for the beasties and us forbye."

Glancing back at his wife he shook his head and smiled indulgently. "Come on Mari," he chuckled, "you can pet them to death once we are aboard."

Reluctantly Mari moved away. Like Donald, she was entranced with the pair of greys, had they not the biggest brownest eyes she had ever seen.

She was country woman enough to see that they had been properly and skilfully trained, evident by their very acceptance of their strange surroundings, without a hint of anxiety or vice. They obviously trusted mankind, and that was important if a horse was to handle correctly. Already she was composing a letter to the Cruachans, but, oh, how she missed the strength of their friendship already, and they hadn't even left the country yet.

The crossing, as forecast, was like the proverbial millpond, and soon they sailed into Larne. As the small ship docked with practised proficiency, Mari spotted her parents standing huddled together, in the lee of the harbour offices, for there was a cold nip in the onshore wind blowing off the Irish Sea. They waved an excited welcome, then gesticulated at a large horse transporter standing nearby. Mari wondered how they had known to bring such a requirement, then smiled as she realised there had been some fine old shenanigans going on between the Cruachans and the Kellys.

Disembarkation was effected speedily and proficiently, and with horses safely secured within the roomy transporter the entire party set off for the Kelly estate.

Barranbarrach Estate is situated in the north west area of Ulster in the county of Antrim, cradled on the sheltered eastern aspect of the green hills of Antrim. The local market town being Ballymena, which, although small, supplied the general needs of the surrounding countryside and its inhabitants.

A good hour of driving from Larne brought them to a long gravel driveway, which led them down to a large manor-type house. To the rear of this magnificent edifice could be found the racing stables and the stud farm. The Barranbarrach Stud was internationally renowned for the quality of its thoroughbreds and hunters, which were bred and trained to supply a demand that never faltered.

To the discerning eye such as the Macdonalds it was readily evident that the surrounds bore testimony to a profitable enterprise well managed, and they were soon to find out that this was indeed the position.

A welcoming party of house servants met them with smiles on their healthy glowing faces. Donald was assured that his Arabs would be in good hands, as they were quickly ushered into the large entrance foyer. Silver trays laden with spirits and wines were offered around in the traditional welcome.

Mari's father cleared his throat officiously, and a silence fell as he started his welcoming speech.

"As far as I am concerned this day has been too long in coming. Nevertheless, it is the happiest day of my life, and my good wife shares my sentiments, be assured of that. A hale and hearty welcome to each of you. This is now your home, please use it as such, I beg you. Would you all lift your glasses and join me in a toast to a long and profitable future together."

Donald's maternal grandmother had him firmly secured in her arms, smiling and weeping at one and the same time. She gave him a loving squeeze and whispered in his ear.

"You will be master of this establishment one day in the future, and that makes me tremendously happy. I hear you are good with horses, so you will quickly settle in and learn the business, and oh! it is so wonderful to have you here, my grandson, a hundred thousand welcomes to Barranbarrach."

The newcomers were shown to their respective rooms by house servants, advised their baths were being drawn and that the evening meal was preceded by drinks in the western day room, generally everyone met at half past seven, if that was in order.

Stuart, Mari and Donald assured the cheery and respectful servants that this was indeed in order. They knew the layout of the large house, having had many holidays with Mari's parents since Donald had been born.

As it was to be their first meal in their new home it would be a quiet family affair, but the following evening there would be a grand dinner party, when they would be introduced to friends, neighbours, and associates of the elder couple, which would ease their entry into the local social structure.

When the evening meal had ended, Donald asked if he might be excused as he wanted to go to the stables to see that the pair of Arab greys had settled into their new quarters. In reality, he just wanted to go and be with them for a while, so that they could establish a good relationship fairly quickly.

His grandfather responded at once, smiling fondly on his only grandchild, as he rose to his feet.

"Let us go together Donald, for I want to have a look at that matched pair. I have been advised that they may look like twins but in fact they are unrelated, so if you wanted to you could breed them, and surely there is room enough to accommodate them here."

"I must confess that your grandmother and I have been in constant communication with the Cruachans. We aided and abetted in this skein of deception, and we were thoroughly delighted so to do."

The colt and filly had been stabled in adjoining looseboxes where they could see each other. The wall that separated them was made of stout, well-seasoned oak, four feet high. The upper portion of the dividing wall was heavy duty steel bars, so allowing the pair to see each other, but keeping them safely apart.

Donald had not decided whether he would mate them or not, and he certainly didn't want any accidental covering, so he was well pleased with the stabling arrangements.

As the two men entered the stables there was a general nicker of welcome from most of the horses, but the source of attraction was the pair of greys.

They crossed to the adjoining looseboxes and stopped at the colt first. He came forward confidently and, in the way of stallions, stuck his head through the bars and nibbled at Donald's chest. Donald caressed the little stallion gently, rubbing his nose and pulling his ears, then magically produced a couple of sugar lumps which he fed to the questing mouth.

The filly was treated with the same attentions, but all the time Donald's eyes were running over the pair, noting that the only difference was that the colt was slightly stronger of build, and that the dished faces were much alike, with the filly's face being of a finer mould. Aye, he thought, they really are a pair of beauties.

Eamonn Kelly watched his grandson evaluating the pair, and waited for a comment. When none came he posed a question, "What familiar names are you going to give them Donald. Their stud names are quite a mouthful I can tell you, for they come from the Llanderawel Stud in West Wales."

"The colt is called Llanderawel Swn y Mor, whatever that means, and the filly is Llanderawel Lleuad ar y Mor, I don't even know if I pronounced them correctly. Now then! Just a minute. If I recall correctly, aye, it comes back to me now. The colt is 'sun of the sea' and the mare is 'moon of the sea'. Nice names, mind you, but a wee bittie long winded. Mind you, they were trained in the English language, so there shouldn't be a problem in that respect."

Donald stood deep in thought. He liked the names, they appealed to his Celtic soul. He was bound to agree that something that rolled off the tongue more easily would be more practical for everyday use.

A fleeting thought passed through his mind but he failed to catch it. A mere whisper in the wind, elusive as a fairy shadow. Wait now! Yes? Well yes! Of course, it was simple! Swn meant Sun, and Lleuad meant Moon. Yes! That was it. Sun and Moon. All at once he could see the reasoning behind their stud names, for they were a matched pair, like the sun and the moon. Yes, the answer was entirely satisfactory, nice and neat and short.

When he advised his grandfather, and later his parents, with the reasons for his choice they applauded his shrewdness and agreed he had selected well. The animals would be referred to by those names from that moment on.

Eamonn Kelly again made reference to the possibility of breeding the pair, but Donald was deliberately non-committal, he felt that there was time enough to consider that possibility. He wanted to ride them and work with them to assess their suitability for such a role. As far as he was concerned, good looks were one thing, but temperament and stamina combined with health and hardiness were better criteria on which to establish a breeding programme.

Yielding a little, he mentioned this to Eamonn, who glanced at him with surprise, then remarked with a new respect in his voice, "You are absolutely right, young man, your thinking does you credit. I can see we have found a worthy successor to take over the management of this long established stud."

"So you understand your part, Donald, your father will be in over-all control of the estate, you however will be manager of the stud and therefore involved only with the horse side of the business."

"I shall be available on a consultancy level if required, that is until the complete handover is accomplished, but I can tell you here and now, I don't foresee any problems."

Stuart and the two ladies joined them, and after the greys had been petted again, they walked round the various stock pens and buildings, viewing the resident stock as they chatted informally to each other. A cold nip in the air turned their footsteps towards the comfort of the manor house, and a welcome mug of hot chocolate.

As they were adjacent to the last loosebox, Eamonn stopped and then motioned Donald to join them. Stuart indicated to the ladies to continue, advising them that the menfolk would not be too long before they joined them.

The loosebox that they entered was sectioned off to leave a clear area from the doorway to the actual enclosure for the animal penned within. This was rather an unusual setting which puzzled Donald. As his eyes adjusted to the dim lighting, he noticed a huge black horse facing them on the other side of a stout wall, the top half of which was steel bars.

The horse was showing the white of its eyes and its ears lay flat on its head, a veritable monster of menace. It opened its mouth and gave a scream of defiance and anger and its tail lashed in fury.

Eamonn stood just inside the door and made no move to go towards the bars, as he had done with every other animal he had visited.

"Donald, I don't know quite what to do with this beast, he absolutely hates

84

men. He will allow a girl to approach him and handle him as far as grooming is concerned, but that's about it. I had decided he was for the knackers yard, but he's really a magnificent beast, so I was loath to do that, so I must admit that, when Laird Cruachan said you were able to establish a special relationship with horses, I decided to keep him until you arrived."

"If you can do nothing with him, then it will have to be the short straw for him, but it would be a pity, don't you think?"

Donald just nodded his head in response to his grandfather's dialogue, his whole attention was on the huge black horse, he reckoned him to stand a good eighteen hands high.

He motioned to his father and grandfather to leave the loosebox, and as the door quietly closed behind them, he remained perfectly still for a few moments further, letting the horse get used to the smell of him.

Confidently he walked over to the bars that separated them, then went statue-still once more. The horse quietened somewhat, the ears came forward and the tail stopped lashing. The nostrils flared as he smelled in Donald's direction, then he moved forward and put his head through the bars.

Donald puckered his lips and gave a plaintive whicker twice in succession. The black responded with a grunting sound lacking in menace. Donald spoke quietly in a crooning cadence. A lullaby, soothing and beguiling. He held out his hand and allowed the horse to inhale the scent, then blew softly on his hand as it closed ever nearer to the black.

Without fear, he lifted his other hand and gently placed it on the black's nose and, light as a feather on a soft breeze, stroked the velvety skin.

This he continued for a few moments, then he pulled the ears that had lost their quiver and soft-voiced as he always was with animals, he chatted away nineteen to the dozen.

"There you go my bonnie lad," he crooned, "now then, how about I visit you properly. Go back and let me join you." Gently he pushed the big head until the doorway was clear. He undid the latch and pushed his way quietly into the loosebox proper.

Once inside he ran his hands over the animal as he talked nonstop. Lips nibbled at him, little plucking movements, indicating that some part of this introduction ceremony was lacking in one small detail. Donald chuckled and murmured indulgently as he put a hand in his pocket and brought out some sugar lumps that he hadn't used around the stables.

Delicately the huge grass-stained teeth picked the morsels off the open palm, and crunched them with evident satisfaction. Donald stayed with the big black for a further ten minutes or so, then, giving him a goodnight pat, opened the door and left, making sure the catch was firmly secured.

He came out of the building and noticed straight away that his elders had been watching what had transpired through the side window of the loosebox.

His grandfather had a smile of pride on his face as he strode over to Donald and gave him a hug.

"You are a gifted horseman, Donald, that is plain to see. I don't mind telling you, I was scared to hell when you opened that door and went in beside that savage bugger. I tell you, he has damaged quite a few of my grooms, who thought they had the answers in how to deal with him. Ah! If they had only been here to see what happened tonight, they may well have learned something. I tell you what, I have no fear of you not holding your own in the yards, for human nature being what it is, there is bound to be a bit of resentment at you coming in as the new horse manager. At twenty three years of age, they are bound to think you are an upstart and don't know your arse from your elbow. My God, they are in for a surprise."

The evening ended with a hot milky drink, or a dram if that was the choice, then it was time for bed. Early rising was as much a way of life on a busy stud as it was on any farm. It is a countryman's belief that an hour in the morning is worth two in the afternoon.

Up in his bedroom Donald had been surprised to find the bed warmed, and his pyjamas neatly folded under the sheets keeping warm as well.

He got into bed and, lying on his back, he reflected once more on the teachings of Chi Li. His eternal lectures of yin and yang were proving correct yet again, for it now appeared that he would enjoy a life in line with what he called the upper class. Servants at hand to provide whatever service was required of them, and they had actually been calling him sir. Well, that was certainly a novelty, good heavens, he was no better than them, he was the son of a tenant farmer.

Second thoughts however clarified things and put them in their proper perspective. He was in fact the next in line to be owner of this establishment, and he had better live up to the expectations that would be required of him from now on.

With a deep sigh, he snuggled down into the warm bed and within minutes he was fast asleep.

Chapter Eight

Donald awakened and his close proximity talent warned him that a presence was near. Neither body posture nor breathing had altered but he was fully awake and very much alert, his brain functioning as he tested his surroundings with his senses.

He opened his eyes and a knock sounded on the door. He sat up and invited the caller to enter. A quick glance at the clock assured him he hadn't overslept, so what on earth was going on?

A rosy cheeked girl entered the room with a tray balanced before her. Neatly she kneed the door close, and Donald quickly removed his gaze as the white of her thigh flashed.

"Top of the morning to you sir," she bade him cheerfully, "I hope you slept well. Och sure now and it's a lovely old morning, and the wee birds singing their little hearts out."

Donald realised he was gaping and quickly clamped his jaws together. It was true to say that his mother had been guilty of a touch of over indulgence from time to time, but he had certainly never had early morning tea brought to his bedroom before, and here was the 'sir' business again.

"G-g-good morning," he stuttered, feeling like a gauche idiot, "er, ah, yes, just put it on the table there, thank you."

"Och indeed not sir," came the dimpled response, "this wee tray has legs do you see, and fits nicely across your legs in bed. Have you it, now and it will give me time to run your bath, and whilst you bathe I'll set out your clothes. Breakfast is in three quarters of an hour, so you have plenty of time for a wee soak if that is your wish."

She deposited the tray across the legs of the dumbfounded Donald, checked to see it was secure, then with a smile of true blue Irish eyes and gleaming white teeth, she departed through the adjoining door to the bathroom. Donald could hear her singing a soft Irish melody as she turned on the taps which drowned out the more pleasant sound.

He sat for a moment shaking his head in amused consternation, it was becoming increasingly evident that he had a lot to learn in his new circumstances, but it was going to take a bit of getting accustomed to.

With a guilty start he realised he was becoming tumescent, and that flash of white thigh kept imposing itself on his mind, even though he squeezed his eyes closed, like the retinal retention one gets after looking into a bright light.

Despite the fact that he had gently spurned the advances of the local girls back at Cruachan, he was still a naturally healthy young man with natural appetites.

He pondered what to do, then thought, forget it lad and drink your tea, you can get out of bed when she departs, she won't see your indiscretion, don't worry.

Shakily he poured his tea, and as he sat enjoying the hot sweet brew, he reflected on the vagaries of life that had placed him in this setting. For goodness sake, he was being treated as if he were someone important, but when he broached the subject with his grandmother her succinct rejoinder was, you are!

The maiden returned from the bathroom and announced that his bath was ready whenever he was and she would return in a jiffy. As soon as she had gone through the door Donald leapt out of bed and virtually charged into the small bathroom.

He was pleased to see his tumescence subside as he voided his bladder in a copious flow. He scrubbed his teeth and shaved, then sank gratefully into the steaming bath. Ah! Is this not the life of Old Riley he thought and then, giggling like a fool, he thought, no, not Riley, Kelly!

He returned to the bedroom with the towel wrapped around his waist, to find a complete new outfit of clothes set out on the bed. The cheery maid was humming away as she buffed a pair of riding boots which were already gleaming like silk. She enquired if he needed assistance to dress, but Donald assured her quite firmly that he did not.

He moved over towards the bed, and in so doing turned his back on the girl. He heard a stricken gasp and, as he turned to face her and saw the horror on her face, he realised he had forgotten the ragged scarring on his back.

Contritely he held his hands up in the air, and walked towards her as she dropped her face into her open hands.

"I am very sorry," Donald tried to comfort, "to be honest, it happened so long ago now that I forget about it. I know it must have been a shock for you, and all I can say is I'm sorry. I didn't mean to frighten you."

The young maid looked up into his face with wonder mixed with compassion on her own.

"You are sorry? My God, it is I who should be sorry, you must have suffered agonies when those scars were open wounds, and all I could do was embarrass you by bringing it all to your attention. Please sir, accept my apologies, it is not my place to make observations or remarks. If it is necessary sir, and you want me to, I'll hand in my notice, but truly I am sorry, and not for myself, but for what you must have suffered."

Donald took hold of the girl by her forearms and remonstrated gently.

"Indeed you will not hand in your notice. Look, this has been blown out of all proportion. Let us just accept that it is old war wounds or something and let us forget it, alright? Now go and let me get dressed, and before you ask again, you can't help"

The girl dared to give him a quick hug and then departed. Donald donned pants and vest, followed by a lightweight wool shirt and, hellsfire!, a tie, ah well, maybe he should have kept the girl back to help him with the infernal damned thing.

He squeezed into the tight fitting jodhpurs and finally those gleaming riding boots. Putting on the Harris Tweed jacket he looked into the full length mirror and longed for his brief grey shorts.

He felt constricted in movement, and a bit like a taylor's dummy, not in the least comfortable, but he felt that his grandparents expected him to dress the part and he wouldn't disappoint them.

He left his room and strode along the passageway, down three steps, along another short corridor to the suite occupied by his parents.

He knocked on the door and entered at the sound of his mother's voice. Stepping over the threshhold, he paused just inside. His mother turned from the window and smiled as she bade him good morning, then laughed her deep rich infectious laugh at his obvious discomfort.

"Oh my bairn," she gurgled, "are they to make a gentleman of you, and you not keen at all, at all."

Quickly she crossed to him, and putting her arms around him, held him close, as she continued soothingly, "I know it is all strange to you, and you must feel uncomfortable, but you will become accustomed to it, believe me."

"The fact of the matter is that now you are a controller of people and affairs on rather a large scale you must conduct yourself accordingly. Dress and deportment are part of the price you must pay for the position you now occupy. Responsibility induces a certain appearance as dictated by social circumstances, which, in a nutshell, means you have to look the part. Remember this though, always, clothes make not the man, you will be judged on your abilities, not the wrappings."

Stuart entered from the bathroom and walked over to them and folded them to his burly chest.

"Are we not a bonny bunch?" he observed with a huge grin, "let us get down to breakfast, and start off our new life as if we meant it, mind, I can't confess to hunger, not having done any work yet, but I dare say I'll manage a wee bite."

"How does that tie feel, son?" he continued with a quizzical look, " I bet it feels like a choke strap."

Donald nodded his head, smiled, then glanced at his mother and burst out laughing.

"I feel like a parish priest," he chortled, "next thing you know, I'll have lily-white hands and a drip at my nose." Stuart and Mari joined in the laughter, then still smiling they left the room to go downstairs to breakfast.

Breakfast took a full hour on this occasion, but it was only so because the family solicitor was due to arrive shortly after eight o'clock.

He arrived in good time and accompanied the three kinsmen to the estate offices where the deeds of the estate were transferred to Stuart to hold in trust for Donald when he reached the age of thirty.

They were both acutely aware of the change of circumstances into which they had been placed so quickly. After a chat with Eamonn and the family solicitor they realised the tremendous responsibility that went with it.

There was a large workforce which included thirty farmworkers, twenty grooms and stablehands, three gamekeepers, six foresters and the house servants had been increased by four, making sixteen in all, then there were three gardeners and two oddjob men, making a total of eighty.

In the local tradition the families of all who worked at Barranbarrach came under the care of the local squire, who would now be Stuart. He was not overawed, however, as he thought to himself, 'I will just emulate my good friend Hamish Cruachan, then I won't go far wrong.'

When the solicitor had fussily concluded the amazing amount of paperwork involved in completing the transfer, he was regaled with a dram, thanked for his contribution and given a friendly farewell.

Now, thought Donald, I'll be able to escape to the stables. He was very wrong. He was to remain in the office, to learn the pedigrees of the breeding stock, by rote if necessary. Further, he had to commit to memory the stages of training of the animals in hand, due dates of mares in foal, dams and studs of same, the list seemed endless. Eamonn insisted he needed to assimilate all this information so that he had a good general appreciation of the overall picture.

During the course of that day, and the days that followed, Donald was glad that Chi Li had taught him the art of concentration.

He astonished his grandfather at the end of the week by his ability to reel off facts and figures with speed and accuracy and, although he chafed at the bit about his enforced immobility, it proved a worthwhile exercise in the end, for he found he used the information he had absorbed time and again in his position as horsemaster.

Donald had given a great deal of thought to his introduction to the stable hands he would now be in charge of. He had considered the possibility of some antipathy from them. After all he was only twenty three years of age, and they were bound to think what the hell does he know.

The horse manager was bound to feel that he should have been the natural successor to the position of horse master, and, of course, the grooms and stable hands were sure to feel animosity to a young upstart giving them orders just because he happened to be the grandson of old Kelly.

These were the thoughts that roiled in Donald's mind as he strolled down to the stud office on what would be his first day in charge. He had noticed that none of his elders had offered advice, so deduced he was expected to resolve whatever problems arose in his own fashion.

They apparently considered him adult enough, so he would demonstrate that he was. He smiled and thought, 'well it's a challenge, so let me face it head on and play the game to the full.'

He entered the stud office, a sudden silence fell on what had evidently been a very animated discussion prior to his entrance.

"Good morning to you all," he quipped brightly, "please carry on with your discussion, I'm sure it is important. When the day to day business is concluded I would like a little chat with everyone so that I can introduce myself properly.

Conal Duggan, the horse manager, gave a curt nod and turning to the head groom, spelt out the duties for the day. The senior jockey was dealt with in like fashion, but also asked some pertinent questions about one or two of the prospective hurdlers being prepared for the season, which was due to commence in a couple of months.

Donald sat quietly through the briefings, and could find no fault with what he heard. Conal stood up, then crossed to the window to look out into the yard. Donald had the feeling that this was a regular habit, and that not much would go unnoticed by this big man. The headboy and the senior jockey headed towards the door, but Donald arrested their progress, as he went behind the office desk and sat down in the chair vacated by the horse manager, thus taking the position of authority.

Taking the bull by the horns, he looked hard and long at each of the three in turn.

"I feel quite sure that I am not a welcome addition to your ranks," he began,

" I would most likely feel the same in your shoes, but I an not here to oust anyone from his rightful place in the scheme of things, rather I am here in addition, to give assistance in any way I can."

"I am the grandson of the previous owner, and the son of the present incumbent. That is a fact of birth, over which I had no control, but I love horses and love working with them, so I ask only that you allow me to prove myself before you judge me. I have to make the final decisions, but I can only arrive at the correct ones with the information you supply me, therefore we are all responsible for the final conclusion and whether it is the right one or not."

Conal was the first to speak, as was his right.

"Sure now," he offered in a voice rich and resonant as fitted a man of such large proportions, "we generally have a cup of tea at this time in the morning. Would you care to join us sir?"

Donald nodded his affirmation and settled back in the huge hide covered throne. It was pitted and scarred with much use, and the strong wooden frame had been reinforced with steel bars. That it was a personal possession of Conal's did not escape the notice of Donald, but he was quietly making his mark of authority, and was quite sure that everyone in the office knew exactly what was being done.

The head lad handed over a mug of scalding hot tea, thick as molasses, and put milk and sugar at hand.

"I am Tim Murphy," he introduced himself, "welcome to the Barranbarrach Stud."

"Aye, welcome indeed," quoth the horse manager, "my name is Conal Duggan, and this wee shrimp here is our senior rider, Eddie O'Flaherty, an ugly wee bugger, but hands like an angel and a mind like a lance when it comes to reading a field and the competition, probably the best hurdling jock in the whole of ould Ireland."

Never were there two men in such a direct contrast to each other as these two. Conal was all of six feet four, with shoulders that would take a fortnight to walk across, so big and heavy that he used a Clydesdale mare as a hack, only a draught horse being able to sustain his weight throughout the course of a day and not be on its knees.

He was the only one who could ride the black fearsome beast that Donald has been quietly making friends with each evening after final rounds had been completed and nobody was around.

Eddie was indeed a shrimp, he resembled a chimpanzee, four feet tall, with long arms that looked as if they would trail on the floor behind him as he walked.

His face was as wrinkled as a prune and the same colour. His smile was cherubic, until he parted his lips, then one looked into a cavern that resembled a derelict graveyard, with black gaps and the remaining teeth lying askew at ridiculous angles.

It flashed through Donald's mind that Eddie's mouth and the rock face of Bhein na Dhubb had much in common, but politeness made him return the smile.

Eddie's lack of vanity was most apparent, and he smelt as if he slept with horses, but Donald was to learn that he was indeed a master of his craft, just as Conal had said when he introduced the wee man. Around the stables he was called the leprechaun, partly because of his size, but also because of his magic touch with the horses whilst in competition.

Donald stood up and shook hands with all three, and what he liked was that they all looked him straight in the eye during the handclasp.

The short break over, the head lad and Eddie departed to their duties, and Conal suggested to Donald that he might like a ride round the training areas and have a look at just what was going on.

"Shall I have one of the Arabs saddled for you sir?" Conal offered, but Donald shook his head in the negative.

"No thank you, Conal, I'll get round to them in due course. If you don't mind, I would like to see how that big black at the end of the yard handles, he looks like he could use a bit of work."

Conal's eyes came out like organ stops, and he gulped a couple of times before saying, "Perhaps sir we could saddle something a wee touch quieter. That black is a hellish beast, if he can't kick you he tries to bite you, he just seems to hate men. I'll get one of the lads to saddle something else for you on your first morning with us."

Donald stood his ground and gently insisted. Conal shrugged his shoulders and bowed to the inevitable.

"Right you are then sir, I'll go and get a couple of lads and have them fetch the humbug, for as sure as hell we'll need it."

"Whatever is a humbug?" queried Donald, "I thought that was a sweet."

Conal looked at him and realised that Donald was in earnest.

"It is a length of wood with a loop of rope passing through one end. The loop is placed over the upper lip of the horse, then the wood is twisted until the rope is tight around the lip. It controls the horse, through pain of course, until he can be saddled and mounted. I don't much care for the practice, but we'll need it for that beast you intend to ride."

Donald listened with ever growing horror. To willingly inflict pain on an animal was alien to his whole character.

"Conal, this is the first direct order you will receive from me. You get hold of that horrendous piece of equipment and you burn it. If I hear of anyone on this stud using such an artifice they will be instantly discharged and without references. Am I making myself clear?"

Conal looked into the steely blue eyes and nodded mutely, realising that his knowledge of such practices inferred that he condoned it.

"I shall attend to that straight away sir," he said apologetically, then added, "I'll still need to get a couple of lads to help get him saddled though."

Donald put out his hand and caught Conal's arm to detain him for a moment.

"Just a minute Conal, why don't I meet you in front of the stud office in ten minutes or so. I don't want anybody to come near where the black is stabled. If I can't manage to saddle him then I will concede and choose another ride."

It was obvious that Conal was unhappy about this suggestion, but respectful manners to his superior's wishes had to be observed, so he nodded acceptance of the situation and strode off down the yard to where the Clydesdale mare patiently awaited him.

Donald entered the black's loosebox and the huge animal came eagerly to meet him, expecting and getting a tidbit from Donald's open palm.

He petted him for a few moments, and then took the saddle and bridle off the rack, all the time chatting amiably as he unhitched the door latch and went in beside the black.

Almost nonchalantly he placed the saddle across the back of the horse, and with a fluid smoothness pulled it tight and cinched it securely. With another tidbit in his hand, he adroitly whipped the bridle over the black's head as the enticement and the bit entered the horse's mouth. He spent another few minutes fussing and caressing, then quietly and firmly led the animal out of the loosebox.

Outside the stable door, he got his foot into the stirrup and was into the saddle in a trice. He nudged the flanks with his heels, and the big horse moved forward without hesitation, ears flickering and swivelling as it surveyed the activity in the yard ahead.

Conal was sitting astride his mount as Donald approached, and Donald smiled broadly at the look on the big man's face. He also noticed on the periphery off his vision, several heads popping over stable doors, and could hear the excited hum that his appearance on the black had generated.

Had Donald rehearsed his first morning, he couldn't have achieved a more electrifying result than this display of supreme horsemanship. 'Aye' he thought with satisfaction, 'here is the wee upstart riding the terror of the stud.'

Conal and Donald spent the entire day riding around the various training areas, but in addition Conal took them round the marches of the estate, and this took some hard riding, for there were three farms on tenancies that were part of the complete holdings.

The next morning Donald decided that he would try out the Arabs, and advised Conal that he would use the colt first. Conal nodded his head and said he would get a lad to saddle him ready, but Donald demurred, saying that he wanted to handle the horse himself.

The colt was now stabled down in the stud area with the other stallions, and as Donald and Conal passed through the middle of the two rows of looseboxes, the stallions hung their heads over the stable half doors whickering and snorting with ears twitching and heads nodding.

The twelve boxes were built in a 'U' shape so that the animals could see each other and anything that occurred in the yard. This was a deliberate innovation, as it helped to prevent boredom setting in with the inevitable accompanying problems that could occur.

The Arab stallion had his head hanging over the half door, watching their approach, his ears flickered and the intelligent head nodded a good morning. He pushed his nose out and forward, and Donald palmed him a lump of sugar.

He stroked the silky head and gently pulled the questing ears as he talked quietly to the nibbling colt. He unlatched the safe lock and entered the loosebox, calmly guiding the colt deeper into the confines of the stable, talking quietly all the time.

Reaching for a hackamore he slipped it across the animal's head, which offered no resistance. He led the colt out into the cobbled hard, and with practised efficiency leapt across the silky back, taking immediate purchase with his legs. The colt stood quietly as his ears flickered backwards awaiting a word of command.

Conal stood watching all this without saying a word, but now he offered a question.

"Are you going to ride him bareback, sir? Surely you will use the first rate tack that arrived with him? I'm sure it has been made to measure. I can easily get a lad to fetch it right away."

Donald shook his head in the negative. "No thanks Conal, I have always found that the best way to get a feel of a beast is to ride him bareback. Another thing is, I don't much like a bit in a horse's mouth, or any of the other trappings that accompany what's termed as civilised riding."

"To haul an animal around by this mouth is not riding, it's driving, and a lump of steel in its mouth, ruins it in a very short time. In my opinion a good horseman should make use of his voice and his legs to guide a horse, and I think you will find that you have a better trained animal in the end."

During this dialogue Conal had signalled a groom to bring his Clydesdale mare and, as he mounted, he addressed Donald, "You certainly have decided opinions and I won't say they are wrong, sir, but they are unusual, and there will be some raised eyebrows as we ride round the estate seeing the young master riding bareback."

"I say further, it is always refreshing to be introduced to new ideas, but of course only time and testing will prove their worth. However, I look forward to this new liaison, and have a gut feeling that it will prove fruitful to both of us, for it is true to say, I have a few wee tricks of my own that may interest you. So then, away we go."

Donald found the young stallion responsive and well mannered, with that lovely free moving gait for which the Arabs are renowned. It was a feeling akin to sitting on a floating angel's wing.

Arabs' legs look delicate and vulnerable, but in fact have supple bones and tendons like high tensile steel. It is rare indeed for an Arab's legs to break down, as it is called. They suffer none of the usual problems, such as heating up of joints, sprains or strains that accompany the training of highly bred animals.

It is due to the superb elasticity of their muscles that such a smooth ride is experienced. The fluted nostrils are capable of tremendous expansion, inhaling oxygen to lung capacity, providing the fuel that allows them to run great distances without impairment.

Donald and Conal covered many miles that morning, watching the hunters being schooled and hurdlers going through their programmes of training.

Many was the eye cast at the young man riding bareback, but he ignored the inquisitive glances and kept up a running barrage of questions to Conal in reference to many aspects of the work being carried out.

One young rider caught his eye who seemed to have an partiality to excessive use of the whip. He made a mental note to keep a close interest on this preponderancy, although he made no comment at the time.

In the afternoon he used the Arab filly and found her to be as satisfactory as the colt in every way.

It became an established practice to use the colt each morning and the filly in the afternoons.

He started to use the made-to-measure tack that had arrived with the matched pair, but always he used a hackamore rather than a bridle, so strong was his aversion to putting steel into a horse's mouth. He initiated this practice throughout the stud, and if there were any objections they never reached his ears.

From time to time owners and buyers would visit the stud, and it was one of Donald's tasks to conduct them around and answer the inevitable questions.

On the first couple of occasions Conal had held himself in readiness to provide answers to the questions that Donald might not be able to. He was quick to realise that Donald was well up to the task, and eventually he absented himself from these visitations with a heartfelt sigh of relief.

Owners can be a pain in the neck at a busy training stable, but Donald could exert such charm and was obviously so knowledgeable, that he soon gained their confidence and allayed any fears they might have entertained at the stables being under the control of such a young horsemaster. When these visitors watched the rapport he enjoyed with their animals they felt reassured and quite happy for their horses to remain and continue training at the Barranbarrach Stud.

Donald gained in confidence in his new role in life. He took a keen interest in all the facets of horse management, and had certainly gained the respect of Conal, who deferred to him time and again, and by this example so did the rest of the workforce.

It is true to say that some found him a wee bit eccentric in ways, but he carried that indefinable aura of confidence and control that was in itself an authority to those around him.

The feature of his character that did perplex them was that he had a disarming humility, and yet there was nothing servile about it, it was just like an overlying cloak that concealed a strength of will that was at times inflexible.

A visiting driver had rough-handled a hunter whilst loading her into a transporter, and when Donald admonished him the driver, not knowing who Donald was, foulmouthed him, telling him to button his lip or have it slapped.

With deceptive nonchalance, Donald was on the loading gate in front of the aggressive driver. With electrifying efficiency that was like sleight of hand, so fast was the action, he buried his extended four fingers in the flabby solar plexus of the driver, delivering a chopping kite to the bridge of the nose in the same instant with the other hand, whilst the driver, ineffectively and much too late, tried to land with a ponderous haymaker on Donald's chin.

Nudging the supine figure with the toe of his immaculate riding boot, Donald advised the foulmouthed driver to conduct himself with courtesy and politeness if ever he called at the Barranbarrach Stud in the future. If he couldn't comply with that request, then please do not come here again.

To ensure that the mare didn't become the butt of the driver's ill humour a groom was despatched with her. A second horse was loaded to give the groom transport back to the stud.

This demonstration of Donald's amazing ability swept through the stud like a bush fire out of control. All the more relished as it resembled the David and Goliath story of bible lore, for had not that driver been a huge brute, and young sir was only a slip of a boy.

Little did the staff know that, pound for pound, Donald had tremendous strength within his apparently slight frame that far outweighed the flaccid ability of a beer sodden hulk that the badly out of condition driver could have offered.

Conal had watched the display, noting the cool efficiency of Donald, and had spotted what the others had missed. The hair prickled on the nape of his neck as he realised he was seeing a highly trained killing machine operating with deadly accuracy and skilled precision. The most chilling aspect of the demonstration was the cool, emotionless manner in which the remonstration had been executed. There had been neither anger nor excitement, or any other emotion shown on the face of the young sir, he could just as easily have been sweeping the yard, for all the concern he had shown.

To Conal it was an insight into Donald's character that had not been apparent heretofore. He had been pretty sure there had been underlying steel, you only had to look into those bright blue eyes that could blaze with searing intensity to be aware of that, but this was the first indication there had been that he had the wherewithal to back it up.

Now that he thought about it, the only weakness that Donald displayed was his inability to see animals in pain. When colts were being castrated he would absent himself to a distant part of the estate until the necessary therapy was competed. Later he would be found trying to give comfort to the recipient of the vet's scalpel. He realised it was a necessary evil but it didn't make him like the practice, and he would have tears of compassion in his eyes as he offered sugar lumps or carrots to the doctored animal.

It was not a foregone conclusion that Donald and Conal would become friends, but that was in fact what did happen. Donald was down to earth, no airs, graces or affectation. He treated everybody as an equal and with a humility that was most disconcerting at times. Despite this he was held in high regard, and nobody tried to take advantage of his apparent easy going nature, and after the incident with the transporter, it was doubtful if anyone would ever try.

After work hours a practice developed of gathering in the large tackroom, all the hands would wander in and join in whatever discussion was taking place. Donald encouraged everyone to have their say, and he found it invaluable, for once the wooden poteen jar had passed around a couple of times anyone with a grievance would air it without embarrassment during this convivial occasion.

This practice allowed Donald to keep his finger on the pulse of the general disposition and morale of his workforce and created a togetherness that could only reflect creditably within the stud.

It was on one such occasion that Conal invited Donald to visit him at his own little croft, where he bred Irish Water Spaniels. Donald accepted with alacrity and rode across one evening later. He was not to know that he would meet someone on that first of many visits who would have a marked effect on the rest of his life.

Mrs Duggan made him very welcome then bade him to sit down and try these scones fresh from the griddle and a nice strong cup of tea. The scones were split through the middle, still steaming, then lashings of home-made jam and fresh cream ladled generously onto each piece. Donald found they were an absolute delight, mouthwateringly delicious, but oh, the temptation to over-indulge, particularly when encouraged so insistently by his motherly hostess.

With reluctance he confessed to being as full as an egg. Indeed you can only fill a bucket until it's full, then you can get no more into it. He thanked Mrs Duggan, threatening her she would never keep him from the door from now on, and laughingly she said she would hold him to his word.

The two men escaped and ambled down through the garden at the rear of the house, then followed the path leading down through a small orchard which screened the kennels from view, and also acted as a sound barrier.

Donald duly admired the small bundles of fluff, amazed that they were already showing signs of the double coat that is an inherent feature of their breed.

It took a good half an hour to inspect the rest of the kennel, and Donald could see that a great deal of time and attention had been spent on ensuring that each animal was in good condition, and was not at all surprised when Conal told him that he kept winning top prizes throughout the province.

They decided to take a stroll along the river bank and try to walk off the intake of food they had recently consumed. They chatted companionably as they ambled along the well worn path, Conal pointing out the best fishing pools, and discussing the best flies to use as lures.

Hazel, rowan, alder and willow tangled amongst each other in wild profusion. Long grass and brambles growing in a confusion of wildness gave sanctuary to a multitude of bank dwellers. Donald could feel the wealth of life that abounded, he heard the lazy plop of a trout feeding, and a flash of iridescent blue of the beautifully coloured kingfisher as it patrolled its reach of the river. An ungainly heron drifted over their heads before landing on a branch as it took up its station for the evening's fishing.

Donald suddenly stopped with an abruptness that made Conal jostle him. When Conal looked at him, Donald held a finger up to his lips indicating silence. His whole posture altered dramatically, resembling the demeanour of a hunting predator. His nose scented the air and the transfixed Conal was sure he saw the ears focus forwards, although he knew that this was not the right word to express what he saw.

Conal thought he heard something, like a muted bleat, but wasn't sure. Donald pressed the arm of Conal and motioned him to stay, then to Conal's amazement, Donald quite literally disappeared, just seemed to melt into the surrounding foliage.

Donald had sensed a presence and his acute hearing had alerted him to a muffled cry of distress. Silently he glided through the woodland, a flitting inconsequential shadow.

Intense concentration combined with rapid soundless progress brought him to a minute grassy glade within the shadow of the trees. Three figures roiled and wrestled in a confusion of movement, violent and explosive as erupting lava.

Two youths were furiously involved with getting the breeches off a tawny haired fury, spitting defiance. Bright crimson blood flowed from the arm of one of the tormentors, evidence of a fine set of teeth being used effectively.

The girl's feet and knees worked like pistons, as the two youths fought desperately to contain the tigerish violence and impose their will on her. So intent on their sordid business were the youths they were totally unprepared for the blows that delivered them from conscious awareness to insensibility.

Donald bent over the girl on the ground to assist her to her feet. Her two heels thudded into his chest and sent him flying backwards as if catapulted. He landed in the breakfall technique and bounded to his feet in a back somersault, then approached the girl again, but this time with a measure of caution.

Disregarding his own slightly ruffled feathers, he inquired with studied politeness if there was anything he could do to be of assistance.

"Aye," came the reply, "you can bugger off!"

Conal had not been able to contain his curiosity or his need to help if there was trouble, and had followed Donald through the wooded area. He arrived in time to see Donald thrown backwards and watched how he automatically broke fall as he landed and how he had achieved his feet so quickly.

'This lad really is an enigma,' he thought, then looking at the girl for the first time properly, he let out a gasp and hurried over.

"God in heaven! It is yourself my darlin'. By the Holy Mary, what has been going on here?" he demanded. "Who are these spalpeens? I'll castrate them with bricks."

He paused for breath, then remembering his manners, he turned to Donald and made belated introductions.

"Donald, this is the monkey man's daughter, Miss Siobahn O'Flaherty, as wild a hell cat as roams the Antrim hills."

Then, in as bad a pun as ever was heard, he ranted on, jabbing a finger the size of a banana at the recumbent figure, "These senseless morons must have had a feast of magic mushrooms to tackle this bundle of trouble."

Donald stood nonplussed till the tirade expended itself, tentatively he offered the hand of assistance, to be brusquely brushed aside.

When the girl came to her feet in a fluid graceful movement, he could see she was of exceptional beauty. A fine boned face with high cheekbones enhanced by a true peaches and cream complexion. The crowning glory, however, had to be the wild tangle of dark rich auburn hair that shone with health and carried dark shadows verging on black.

Her dishevelled appearance failed to hide a full breasted heaving front, which involuntarily drew his eye as honey attracts a bee. Who was it, for God's sake, who had said to him that a jiggling tit draws the wandering eyes, and why, oh why, should it come to mind now of all times?

A nipped in waist and long tapering legs in tight fitting doeskin breeches completed the picture, but that wide legged stance conjured up the most erotic thoughts.

Donald shuddered as a sudden awakening of pure sexual lust suffused his body. He felt the stirring within his trousers and coloured with shame and embarrassment.

"Have you looked your fill, or should I strip and dance?" she spat out contemptuously, "you're as bad as that pair there, but lacking the guts to make your bid. At least they were prepared to fight for a taste of the honeypot."

Donald's face was a picture of mortification.

"I'm sorry miss. I really am sorry for staring. I mean no harm, and would gladly escort to wherever safety lies for you."

"I wouldn't walk with you through a midden," was the spirited reply, "I'm on my way to see Mrs Duggan and Conal shall be my escort. You just bugger off, back whence you came, and may the thistles scratch your arse as you go by."

She went over to Conal and took his arm, "Come, my bonny man," quoth she, with a big smile, albeit a tremor in the making of it, "I'll get a clean up at your place, and Da will be over in a while to take me home."

Conal had stood through the diatribe in shocked silence, but now he awakened from his reverie and exploded in indignant outrage.

"Just a minute, my fine young miss. First of all you will apologise to my good friend Donald. He came to your assistance and by way of thanks you assaulted him, kicking him arse over elbow. Then you proceed to add insult to injury by giving him a tongue lashing that couldn't have been delivered better by a fishwife. You are a damned little ingrate and for two peas, I'd put you across my knee and give you the belting that the monkeyman should have done years ago."

She looked up into the big angry face in total shock. This man, who had been uncle to her and pandered to her every whim, had never ever in all her life spoken a cross word to her.

She gulped a deep shuddering inhalation, and whispered, "Oh dear! Oh dear! Me and this unbridled mouth! Of course I must apologise and then give thanks. I'm sorry Conal. I was so wound up. I was losing the fight with those spalpeens and I guess I just lost control. Yes, I must say I am sorry. I could easily have been raped but for that young man's intervention."

Donald had just lifted the two young lads to their feet and advised them to depart, and quickly. He turned as the lithe figure approached him. Again he felt the blossom of sexual awareness engulf him. Desperately he tried to exercise control, but, for the first time in his life, failed to impose his iron will on the actions of his body.

He knew his breeches were betraying him, and, looking at the approaching beauty, he knew she was aware of her effect on him, and there he was, powerless to do anything about his treacherous body. The primeval need in his groin, beating time with the pulse of his pounding heart.

As she drew close he noticed the beginnings of a knowing smile at the corners of her full red lips, and involuntarily he licked his own, which had suddenly gone dry.

She stopped directly in front of him, mere inches between them. The top of her head reached the height of his nose. Her body scent assaulted him in full force. Had he been experienced in the knowledge of women, he would have recognised the scent of a woman in full arousal. He was aware only of his own discomfiture, and felt awkward and lacking in confidence.

With a full blown smile on those tantalising lips, she placed a hand on Donald's arm. Chemistry reaction exploded in a crackling, breath stopping, flesh searing frenzy. She snatched her hand away as if she had been scalded, and the smile became tremulous and uncertain.

Piercing blue eyes looked deep into green hazel-flecked orbs of puzzlement and astonishment. She had felt totally in control of the situation, only to have that control snatched away by the treachery of her own, hitherto, unawakened emotions.

In a quavering voice, and now a good yard divided them, she whispered, cleared her throat, took a gulp of air, and said, " I hope you will forgive me for my unwarranted outburst, I'm afraid my feelings were running a bit high. Please accept my contrite and sincere apologies. Thank you with all my heart for saving me from the attentions of those two beasts. I know I sounded ungrateful, but the problem is that I've always had to look out for myself and, truth to say, I have become rather a tomboy in the process."

With a pause to subdue the bloodfire that still lingered with teasing persistence, she took another shuddering breath and continued, slightly stronger voiced, "We must get Conal to introduce us and we shall start anew. Do you agree with that, my knight saviour?"

Donald was inarticulate for a second or so, he had never experienced such an erotic jolt to his system as had just happened when Siobahn touched his arm, sapping his strength so completely that his knees trembled and his hands shook like one with palsy.

He knew his face was red with embarrassment, due to the electric charge that pulsated within him with demanding insistence. Manfully he centred his riotous thoughts and applied himself to the disturbing influence in front of him, who waited for his answer.

"I was pleased to be of assistance," he squawked, despising himself for betraying his disconcertion and weakness. He paused, cleared his throat, then continued, "it was my pleasure, please think nothing of it, anyone would have done the same. I am no knight in shining armour, but thank you for the kind words."

His throat closed on him again, mutely his eyes appealed to Conal to extricate him from this quagmire in which he was floundering.

Conal took up the cudgels on Donald's behalf. He strode across the clearing and put an arm around the discomfited pair. With the insight of a true Celt, he was aware that there had been a meeting of great portent. Pure animal attraction quivered around them in an aura that was almost palpable, such was the intensity of the moment that it was frightening to the two young innocents.

Both being of strong wills, they were fighting to retain their individualities and remain uninvolved with each other. Instead of yielding to the age old call, and Mother Nature's dictation, they tried to create a safe distance between themselves, rather than concede to the overpowering emotional storm that engulfed them.

With age and experience on his side, Conal could have told them that they were ensnared, and any attempt to escape their destiny was doomed to failure. He made no comment, knowing that time would resolve the outcome of this decisive meeting, despite any attempts to the contrary.

"Siobahn O'Flaherty, meet Donald McDonald, the new horse master of Barranbarrach Stud, believe me, he is a gentleman extraordinaire. Donald, meet Siobahn O'Flaherty, daughter of Eddie O'Flaherty, our senior jockey at Barranbarrach," he pronounced in his lilting Irish brogue as deep as a bog.

"We shall now wander back to the house and have a nice cup of tea. I'm sure we could all use one." Playing to the occasion, he swept his hand to the side in a grandiose manner and the flair of a circus ringmaster.

Conal was absolutely delighted with the obvious mutual attraction of the young couple. He had a high regard for them both, and to his romantic Celtic mind, they were completely right for each other.

He knew his wife would be tremendously pleased when he got the chance to tell her, but when that time came his wife had already seen the magnetism that flowed in an almost tangible current between the pair, and told him not to state the obvious.

The three wandered back to the cottage, with Conal between the two youngsters, holding the arm of each as if to maintain a conduit through which the magnetism could continue to flow.

For the first time in his life Conal was guilty of inane chatter, burbling happily about beautiful evenings and the heady smell of dog roses and bog myrtle, and wasn't that the evensong of the thrush? So he prattled on, poetic licence being exercised to the ultimate, as he gallantly tried to fill what could have been a strained and awkward silence.

Siobahn and Donald contributed nothing to the conversation, merely nodding their heads and smiling occasionally. Frequently their eyes would meet, then dart away again like startled fawns, only to seek contact again seconds later.

They were both suffering the tingling aftermath of emotional disturbance, and really would have preferred to get away to a solitary haven of their own, there to mull over what had happened and come to terms with it, but they would have to endure the hospitality of Conal's wife in the interests of good manners.

Sitting in the snug cottage, pleasantly warmed by the aromatic peat fire, which was not testimony in itself to the flushed faces of the two youngest members of the group, the conversation eventually turned to the attempted violation of Siobahn.

Conal, of course, knew the two lads, Mick Reilly and Pat O'Malley, and he assured all present that he would be having a strong wee chat with them about the error of their ways.

He told Donald that O'Malley's brother was the rider who was guilty of excessive use of the whip, and he had noticed Donald's particular interest in that worthy during morning exercises.

Donald agreed that he had been keeping a watchful eye on the lad, but of late he appeared to have exercised more control of his temper and the whip; nevertheless, he would still be keeping him under scrutiny.

The crafty Conal now introduced a new theme into the conversation, explaining to Donald that Siobahn sometimes helped out at morning rides, and that he had tried without success to get her to become a full member of the stud. She seemed to have inherited all her father's skills at riding and was it not a shame that she used them so rarely? Donald looked across at Siobahn, who immediately glanced away.

Not to be diverted, he addressed her directly.

"Excuse me, Siobahn, we need all the good riders we can get at the stud. Would you not reconsider and join our team? I know you would be the only girl rider, but that should not, and will not, be allowed to have any bearing on your status. Everyone is judged on merit, as you would be, and by what Conal has just said, you have that in abundance. Personally, I would be most pleased to have you join us."

Siobahn gave an elaborately nonchalant shrug, which to Donald in his starry-eyed state was poetry in motion, and applied her attention to Conal. This was safe ground.

"You know why I don't come often! My Da thinks I am a disturbing influence among the young riders, and I think that is unfair, for I love working with horses but I am penalised because I happen to be female."

Donald intervened before Conal could make any response.

"That is indeed unfair. You have my word that it will change. I will speak to your father and insist that he removes his objections, and grants you permission to be full time employed at the stud. Shall we say, starting next Monday morning?"

As Siobahn was about to thank him, her father arrived as if on cue, so she greeted him with the news that the new horsemaster wanted her to start work at the stud the following Monday, and what did he have to say to that?

Eddie O'Flaherty looked at Donald and remarked that it was alright by him, but Donald had better be prepared to sort out some bonny tussles, for when the lads started the inevitable sexual harassment and horseplay there would be a few broken heads to mend, for his little madam was hell on wheels when she got her dander up.

To seal the agreement the elderflower wine and the poteen jar was broached and a toast to the future and good relationship with the new employee was made.

Donald, who normally found the poteen a trifle harsh to his palate, enthusiasticlly sank the potent draught as if it were nectar, and although his eyes watered and he gasped with a shudder at his indiscretion, he accepted a refill and foolishly repeated his mistake.

He recognised the beginnings of an impromptu party, and would normally have joined in with alacrity but he wanted to get away to think over the consequences of this fateful evening. In a voice that still lacked timbre, he bade them all a very good night, and made his departure before any protest started.

So much for looking at woolly pups, he thought, as he rode homewards. Thank God the mare knew her way home, for his inner thoughts blinded him to all else.

His heart yearned, and his head rebelled at what had happened to him. He wanted no more of getting involved with a girl. Look what had happened when he gave his heart unequivocally to his first love, Mary.

That had ended in disaster. The hurt still lingered on, like a bad dream the morning after, only it was lasting a hell of a sight longer than that.

He was enjoying life as the horsemaster of Barranbarrach, and he needed no complications to upset the quiet tranquility he was becoming accustomed to. No! No fear! He wouldn't get involved.

Just as his head sorted out the problem, his errant body would give a twitch of remembrance, and he would feel the heat infuse his body with insidious duplicity, unprecedented feelings making a mockery of his mental aspiratations.

He was uncomfortable and disconcerted, a cauldron of conflicting, tormenting emotions. In an effort to calm himself he resorted to deep breathing and intoning a well-tried mantra, but he reached home ere he regained any measure of composure.

Chapter Nine

Detective Inspector Tammy Dale from the Glasgow C.I.D., Clydebank Division, was on secondment to Belfast R.U.C. The task imposed upon him had little appeal but, being ambitious, he knew that a refusal would act as a brake on his, up to now, meteoric rise through the ranks.

At thirty years of age he was considered very young to hold such a position but, in all truthfulness, he had earned his advancements through honest endeavour and integrity of purpose.

Tammy was a spare framed individual, carrying as much beef as a well trained whippet. A long, lean, almost cadaverous face with a hook of a nose that gave him the look of a predatory hawk, this was somehow accentuated by strongly pronounced eyebrows, which kept in shadow a pair of dark observant eyes. Those very eyes had been trained to observe and they were a credit to that training, for they missed very little.

That he should have achieved the rank of Detective Inspector, let alone be a policeman, was one of those quirks of fate that occur despite adverse circumstance.

Tammy had begun life in the squalid confines of a street in the Gorbals area of Glasgow. He was the only child of a drunken father and a dispirited, downtrodden, unintelligent mother, who couldn't protect her unfortunate offspring from the drunken rages of her husband.

Tammy quickly developed into a loner, trusting no-one. He fought the inevitable fights, or used his quick wits to extricate himself when the odds were overwhelming.

A contrariness in his character denied him the questionable safety of a gang allegiance, preferring to go his own way.

When a gang caught him and thrashed him for a bit of fun, he would bide his time and eventually catch the leader on his own and exact revenge with telling effect.

This message was delivered on so many occasions that he arrived at a situation where he was by-passed for easier pickings, and a truce of sorts existed between the gangs and himself.

When one considers the dreadful armament that was used on a daily basis by these gangs, it portrays a clearer picture of the type of character that would, and could, face and nullify such a threat.

Razor blades were sewn into the peaks of flat caps so that a lethal amount protruded that would slice the unwary antagonist. Lengths of cycle chain were bound at one end for a hand grip, the other end was sharpened and honed to scalpel keenness and wielded with much industry in the field of fray.

Pointed knuckledusters of all descriptions were part of everyday wear, for who knows, one might need the benefit of them without the courteous respite necessary to put them on.

Tackety soled boots had rusty nails embedded at right angles to the soles which could lay open flesh to the very bone, and wounds from this speciality would inevitably fester, therefore recovery would be long and painful.

In some instances these wounds resulted in a fatality, when the wound became gangrenous through lack of proper medical care. The threat of tetanus was ever-present, and many a youth had died in the horrendous vice of lockjaw.

Open razors were used to inflict the Glasgow kiss. This was a technique of laying the razor against the right ear and slicing down to the corner of the mouth, then the razor was angled upwards to end at the left ear in an obscene continuous gash.

A bunch of Glasgow headers was a forehead butt, several times on the bridge of the nose, which left it a mangled, pulpy mess. Forty five rapid, east and west of the jaws, was a brutal slapping either side of the face, back hand and forehand whilst knuckledusters were being worn.

This was the background in which Tammy had grown to manhood, and the many scars on his face and body bore testimony to the rough passage life had afforded him.

It was this upbringing that had instilled in him a veritable hatred for intimidation and acts of brutal terrorism which cast him into the role of avenging crusader, and this mould was set with ironcast resolve by a catalyst of quite unprepossessing quality.

At the age of fifteen, Tammy had been returning home from one of his meanderings through the city when he chanced upon four youths beating an old Chinaman outside his laundry shop.

Incensed by the mindless brutality, he literally dived into the melee. So ferocious was his attack that the four youths took to their heels, screaming profanities and threats of revenge.

Tammy picked the old man off the ground, trying to brush him down and straighten the rumpled clothing at the same time. The old man, bruised and bleeding, pulled himself erect with pathetic dignity.

"Thank you, thank you," he wheezed, "please you go, chop, chop, quick, quick.

Maybe they come back. Thank you, thank you, please go now. No more trouble."

"Now then, old father," remonstrated Tammy, "I doubt they will come back for second helpings, cowards rarely do, and anyhow, now there are two of us. If I may say so, you are a bonny fighter on your own, they were not having it all their own way, I could see that. It was four against one that was weighing the decision. I only got involved because it was a wee bittie one-sided for my liking, and anyway, I needed the exercise. Now then! Come on and I'll walk with you as far as your home. I'm in no hurry to get to mine."

Gently he took the arm of the old man and, with a tenderness that would have shocked those that knew him as a real hard man, conveyed his ward in the direction of his home.

A twenty minute walk brought him to the Chinaman's house, which stood out from its neighbours by its very cleanliness. The exterior paintwork gleamed, and even from the outside it was obvious that the curtains hanging at the windows were immaculately laundered, not like the tatty rags that were evident in the rest of the street.

As the old man bent to insert his key into the lock, the door was wrenched open from within, and a little withered stick of a woman viewed them with consternation on her face. Backing into the hallway, she bowed graciously as she retreated before them.

A musical ripple of rich harmonious sound escaped from the shrivelled frame, making Tammy indelicately think of the song of the thrush coming from the mouth of a corncrake. Hurriedly he put the indecorous thought from his mind, and found himself bowing to the old lady.

The Chinaman drew Tammy into a well appointed sitting room, which was tastefully decorated, albeit with a distinct Oriental essence, but there was a quiet soothing ambience which Tammy sensed straight away.

Tammy was conducted to a deep comfortable armchair and offered a drink. He was getting used to the unfinished words and the inability of his host to pronounce the letter 'R' or 'L' in the correct places, so that the offer sounded like, 'Yo rike d link prease', but speech difficulty or not, Tammy was being won over by the quiet dignity of the old man.

"No thank you," he declined the offer as he stood up, "there is really no need. I'll just be on my way home now that you are safely in yours. I'm sure your wife will have questions about your little adventure, so I won't disturb you any longer."

The old man laid a thin, fragile looking hand on Tammy's arm. Almost pleadingly, he asked Tammy to remain, unless he was unhappy at being entertained by Chinese people.

Tammy immediately assured him that he was more than comfortable and that he would be delighted to have a drink, and then he dropped down into the confines of the armchair.

The old lady, who had disappeared, returned carrying a silver tray holding cut crystal glasses and a bottle of local malt whisky. She deposited the tray on a nearby occasional table as she spoke to her husband.

She had obviously asked a question, for he turned to Tammy and asked him if he would share the evening meal with them, it would give them great pleasure if he would. Tammy replied that if they were sure it was not too much trouble then he would be delighted.

Wind chimes tinkled delicately in rippling cadence, and an apparition of utter loveliness entered through the door, and Tammy felt as if he had been sucked into a vacuum, so suddenly did he lose the ability to take in oxygen.

In the worst possible display of bad manners he sat and gaped like a man suddenly bereft of his senses, and so he was, he was absolutely stunned.

This vision of exquisite beauty that he was sure had fallen from the heavens, had rendered him speechless and immobile. The stunning smile that was directed towards him was the embodiment of guileless innocence.

The old man, who had observed the remarkable effect his daughter had produced in Tammy, hastily rose and made the introduction. His daughter's name was Ling Tai Mae, and rather belatedly he introduced himself as being Ling Ho Teo, and his wife was called Ling Tai Su. He also had a son, who would be arriving home soon, his name was Ling Mi Chan.

Tammy croaked out his own name, still in a mist of befuddlement, as he sprang to his feet at last. He raised his glass and bowed to Mae, hoping it was the correct thing to do, then thankfully sank into the armchair again as his legs trembled anew.

The son, Chan, arrived home and, after the introduction, the mother guided them through to the dining area, where Tammy enjoyed a meal that seemed like a banquet.

Small portions on each dish, but the platters kept coming with the regularity of a metronome, course after course. His glass was recharged time and again with a delicious rice wine. It was a new taste to his palate, but one that he enjoyed immensely, as he did the piquant dishes that were placed before him.

Whilst the meal was in progress Teo excused himself to Tammy and, in his own language, explained to his family what had transpired on the street, and how Tammy came to be in their midst, and sharing their humble repast.

When the dialogue ended, the son Chan came round the table to stand behind Tammy. He put his hands on Tammy's shoulders, squeezed gently and said,

"It was kind of you to go to my father's assistance and I thank you. The general way of things round here is, if it is a Chink then kick it, it is just the same as kicking a dog out of your path. You are apparently a man of discernment as well as courage, and I say to you on behalf of my family, you are always welcome in this house, and we would all feel great happiness if you would visit us on a regular basis."

Tammy was flabbergasted at the command of English that Chan demonstrated. He had expected a level of proficiency as restricted as Teo but his surprise didn't end there, for suddenly Mae spoke for the first time and she had an equal mastery of the language, and if her mother had a voice of lilting melody, the daughter was a prima donna in comparison.

To Tammy her voice was a mesmeric fluting cadence of rippling tinkling harmony, a Loreleian allurement of utter enchantment, hypnotic and narcotic in its benumbing effect on him.

All too soon her vote of thanks had ended and he felt like a child deprived of a lollipop. Desperately he searched his fuddled mind to ask a question that would stimulate a further measure of the dulcet tones, but nothing matured within his fuddled brain.

In a daze he followed the family back into the sitting room, where Chan had a short discussion with his father. That they were in agreement was evident from the affirmative nods they gave each other at its conclusion.

Chan sat down beside Tammy on the sofa and, turning to face him directly, paused for a moment to give weight to what he was about to offer to this new found friend.

"I have just asked my father if I could invite you to become a member of our judoka, we both go there to practice martial arts three times a week, my sister Mae comes with us, already she is a black belt 1st Dan in two disciplines. It is a means of our being able to protect ourselves, for on the whole we are not too popular in the city and are often picked on, as my father was tonight. They think we are easy targets to have a bit of fun with, just like kicking a tin can around the street."

"My father agrees with me that you have the right kind of character to learn our system of defence, and it is a way of repaying you for your help this evening."

Tammy, to say the least, was most surprised to receive this offer. He was well aware that the Asians in the city had these facilities, but never dreamt that he would one day be invited to join one.

Grasping Chan by the arm, he squeezed gently and said,

"First of all, Chan, nobody is in debt to anybody here. I have enjoyed this evening more than anything I can think of, so I owe your family, if anyone owes. Good God! For the first time in my life I have felt wanted for myself, and been made to feel like a king. Sincerely, I thank you for that. I would be honoured to join your judoka. I have wanted to join such a club for a long time, so thank you, I will be delighted to come and train with you."

"Now! Just one more thing, Chan. I would like to pay court to your sister. Do you think your father would object?"

Chan shared a brief exchange with his father, then turned to Tammy and translated with a smile,

"My father is delighted that you will join us for training at the judoka, as to paying court to Mae, he says she is quite westernised in that respect, but you must make your own arrangements with her, and the best of luck."

Tammy was well enough pleased with the response. At least there was no objection from the parental side. He nodded his head, then looking at the clock on the mantelshelf exclaimed, "Goodness me, is that the time? I must leave you good folks. Once again, a million thanks for your hospitality, it has been a wonderful evening for me, I have enjoyed it tremendously."

Tammy stood up and, with a last torrid look in the direction of the lovely Mae, made his farewells, promising to call the next evening to accompany them to the judoka.

Chan conducted Tammy to the door and when he voiced concern about Tammy's safety on his way home was assured quite firmly that the streets of Glasgow held no fears for his young friend, who always travelled alone.

Four years passed in which Tammy attended the judoka thrice weekly. Such was his attention to detail that he was nicknamed 'the technician' by his fellow judokists. In his promotion battles to achieve higher gradings his superb techniques always won the day. He rapidly reached the status of 2nd Dan in three disciplines, much to the delight of the Ling family. During this period of development in his life, Tammy also joined the Police Cadets and, on his eighteenth birthday, was initiated into the force proper.

His ability to think on his feet, and his specially acquired skills were quickly recognised and utilised, callously sometimes, by his superiors. He invariably found himself patrolling the waterfront dives and night clubs of dubious repute, and was often involved in gangland warfare.

It was only his just rewards, that his integrity and resourcefulness was finally rewarded by promotion to sergeant, followed quite quickly thereafter by advancement to Detective Inspector.

He spent some time with Homicide, then with the Drugs Squad, but his main interest lay in the terrorist field, which was perhaps an extension of his hatred of gangland atrocities.

He was considered to be a bit unorthodox in his methods, but he certainly got results. Providing he did not break the law himself, the police authority turned a blind eye to his eccentricities, as they viewed his unusual methods.

Tammy went through the usual firearms training, but he was never too happy about using them. As he said repeatedly, it was easy to become dependant on this means of controlling a situation, and being mechanical, the damned things had a nasty habit of becoming useless at the very time they were most needed.

He depended more on his martial arts abilities to keep him out of trouble, and these proved more than effective.

The courting of Mae never really got off to a start, for although in the first instance Mae had been graciousness in itself, in the end the cultural gap was too wide to be overcome, despite a determined effort by both parties.

Tammy still trained in the judoka with the Ling family, and would continue to do so for as long as he lived in the area. He always felt happy and comfortable in their company, and Mae now treated him like a brother, and one well loved, but it was not the kind of love Tammy sought, and in the end he bowed his head to the inevitable and gave up the dream of his first love.

The Royal Ulster Constabulary in Belfast made an official request to the Glasgow Constabulary for a secondment of a detective well-versed in terrorism. This detective would be an unknown quantity to carry out undercover duties within Belfast, and Ulster in general. He would be expected to infiltrate an organisation that had developed called the Irish Republican Army.

This I.R.A. faction was without political recognition and, in an attempt to demand recognition, had resorted to the use of the bullet and the bomb. Innocent people were being killed on the streets with total disregard or moral principles.

It had taken the authorities an unforgivable time to come to the realisation that terrorism was fast becoming a way of life. After each atrocity a demand would be forwarded for consideration, each time this demand was ignored a further demonstration of violence would be carried out.

The province of Ulster is peopled by Catholics and Protestants, causing a certain amount of sectarian hatred. Add to this a faction of people who want all of Ireland, including Ulster, to be totally Irish, opposed to another faction who insist they are British, and therefore subject to the laws of the English Parliament. Here is a fine Irish Broth fermenting and bubbling with discontent, a potential powder keg awaiting the lighted taper.

As far as the Glasgow Constabulary were concerned, the choice of detective was obvious, and so the loaded request was put to Tammy, who, although he couldn't refuse, had his own opinions on the politics involved.

Today's terrorists may well be tomorrow's freedom fighters, and the day after that the heroes of the country, who was right and who was wrong, and who determined either? No, he was not too keen on this assignment.

On the good side, it would mean he would get away from Glasgow for a while and away from the disturbing presence of Mae. Perhaps a change of environment would allow him to reappraise the situation and decide where his future lay in regards to finding a prospective wife.

Here he was at thirty years of age and still a virgin, but it was a secret he kept well hidden from his associates for they would have ribbed him unmercifully. It was not that he had set out deliberately to remain chaste, it was just how the path of life had directed him.

The crossing between Port of Glasgow and Larne in Northern Ireland can be wilder and more turbulent than the roughest passage round Cape Horn in South Africa, and such a day was this as Tammy stood on the forward deck of the rusty old cattle boat on which he was making the crossing.

As the old vessel ploughed gallantly through the heaving swells, the tortured screech of the propellers could be heard clearly as they came free of the water when the prow dived deep into a trough, then would come the judder as the screws hit water again.

'Aye,' Tammy thought, 'this is really wonderful, what is the encore going to be?' The answer to his thoughts was soon to materialise. The ferocity of the wind increased, but now it was loaded with rain, cold and penetrating, biting deep into exposed flesh. With a deep sigh, carrying perhaps a hint of despair, Tammy left the deck and took refuge in a covered passenger lounge, where he had previously left his two suitcases which held all his worldly possessions.

The old tub struggled into the small Irish port and tied up alongside. The few passengers were allowed to disembark first, and Tammy stood back until he was the last to take his position on the double width plank that moved up and down alarmingly as progress was made along its length.

Reaching terra firma with a sigh of relief, Tammy paused to take stock of his surroundings. He had been advised that he would be picked up at the port and driven the few miles to Belfast, where he would be given a briefing, and then left to make his own arrangements for accommodation.

He didn't expect a fanfare of trumpets to herald his arrival, but neither did he expect to be picked up like a common criminal and be bundled unceremoniously into a battered old Ford van.

Once clear of the dock area he was allowed to sit up and the driver and his colleague introduced themselves, and apologised for the indignities that had been afforded him, explaining that every point of entry into the province was closely watched by sympathisers of the I.R.A., and the treatment he had just received would give the impression that he was an undesirable being taken into custody.

The preceding three months, rumours had been spread around Belfast that a Glasgow hard man was due to make his appearance, having outstayed his welcome in said fair city.

Very little more was said for the remainder of the short journey, but at the outskirts of the city, Tammy was asked to slide down in his seat and try to remain unobtrusive until they reached their destination.

The old van juddered to a halt at what appeared to be a hole in a high stone wall. With little ceremony, Tammy and his battered old cases were whistled through the gap, into a backyard which could have been a garden at one time, but was now a riot of overgrowth of all descriptions. A wilderness of bramble, convolvulus and rank grass twisted and gnarled together like an Arcadian nightmare.

They followed a twisting path round the side of the building and came to a halt at a pair of steps that gave onto a wooden door badly in need of a lick of paint to say the least.

One of Tammy's companions hammered the door with his foot, then with a nod they left him standing between his suitcases like some useless phallic symbol.

The door was wrenched open on protesting hinges and Tammy was faced with a dressed skeleton, or so the apparition appeared to Tammy's jaundiced eye. A squeaky voice bade him impatiently to enter, as there was no use standing posing for sure as hell nobody was taking photographs.

Taking a deep breath and clenching his teeth, Tammy lifted his cases and stepped into the hallway that stank as if cats and winos had lived in it for a month.

He followed the skeletal frame down a narrow passage, entered a doorway into what looked like the foyer of a hotel. The comparison to what he had just passed through was remarkable.

They entered a small cosy room with a pleasantly fragrant fire sputtering and fluttering cheerily. On either side was a couple of comfortable looking armchairs, even though they looked well worn.

Tammy's guide motioned to one of the seats and muttered something about refreshments, then withdrew from the room. Tammy sank into the nearest armchair and stuck his feet out towards the fire, contemplating for a moment if he should indulge himself by removing his shoes, but a moment of reflection denied him the pleasure.

The door opened quietly and a man of presence stood within, pausing to assess Tammy who had risen through ingrained courtesy. A cultured Oxford accent was perhaps the last thing Tammy expected to hear, and only by unobtrusively biting the inside of his mouth was he able to stop an horrendous gape from embarrassing him.

"Good day to you! I am Commander Denham-Tring. You report to me alone. Here is a file. Read, digest and destroy before you leave this room. Never come back here. I will always find ways of contacting you. Everything clear? Yes?"

Tammy felt the hackles rise on the back of his neck, but clamped down on the effervescence that bubbled furiously within him.

"If you will excuse me, nothing is clear, and further more it is not going to be. Whatever you have in mind, get someone else. You say you are Commander Denham-Tring, but you offered no proof of that, or your authority to command me in the field. From the moment I left Glasgow I have been treated like a fourth class citizen, and then subjected to your stilted upperclass condescension. Well, put it in your armpit, I am on my way out. I should never have volunteered in the first place."

Grabbing his luggage, Tammy made to depart, but found his path blocked by the well dressed Commander.

"Please, please, just a cotton pickin' moment, Inspector," the Commander pleaded, with his hands held up in a supplicating manner, "I could honestly kick my own arse if I could reach it. Please! Let's both sit down and I'll start again."

Tammy dropped his suitcase and sauntered across to the fire, where he turned to face the intent grey eyes of the Commander. For a brief moment or two there was a heavy silence as the two reassessed one another. The Commander looked round, then seeing a tasselled cord gave it a peremptory tug, ostensibly to summon a servant or waiter, but a knock on the door pre-empted the need, when the person who had brought Tammy to the room entered with a tray holding whisky and glasses and two plates of nice looking sandwiches.

He placed the tray on the coffee table then left without uttering a word. As the door closed the Commander crossed to the table, and poured at least a triple into two glasses, came over and proffered one to Tammy.

"God protect us all in this room," he smiled, as he quoted the local saying, "if we are to get anywhere with this task we will need God's help, I can tell you. This is a right can of worms, believe me. You can trust no-one it seems. There are sympathisers to the cause in every government department, and within the police network. This is the reason for all this cloak and dagger business you have been subjected to. I am directly responsible to the British Government and will be your controller. I also will be responsible for finding out who is loyal to the Crown and who is not. Incidentally, the communication from the head of the Ulster Constabulary in fact came directly from me, and, with a little bit of help from proven sources, I was able to intercept the reply, so in fact you are here, and only myself and the three people you have already met know of your existence, and that is the way it has to be for there is a suspicion that someone high in authority within the R.U.C. is also an authority within the I.R.A."

Lifting the file he had alluded to earlier, he continued,

"As much as I know is documented here, but I am rather afraid there is not much to go on. If you would like to go through it now, we can discuss any points that you would like to bring up."

Tammy took the offered file, but his manner was still stiff and unyielding, even though he accepted that the explanation he had just been given was in itself by way of an apology, or as much of one as he was going to get.

"You have been very clever with your line of patter, if I may say so," he exclaimed, threads of controlled anger still evident in his vioce, and the deep brown eyes glittered dangerously.

"You have assumed that by telling me all of this restricted information you make it impossible for me to refuse to take the appointment. Let me assure you that nothing is further from the truth, I could walk away now. Politics is a dirty word as far as I am concerned, and that is what all of this is about, plain and simple. I am not a politician, I am a policeman. Why should I become involved?"

Commander Denham-Tring heaved a sigh of exasperation tinged with despair. Lifting his hands palm upwards, he raised his eyes to the ceiling, as if in supplication to a higher authority.

"Inspector Dale, your brief is to uphold the law. Basically that is what is being asked of you. People are breaking the law of the land here in Ulster, and it is compounded by a conspiracy of silence. This silence is induced through fear, or by sympathy, and the only way we can see to overcome this parochial reluctance to involvement is to infiltrate the system, find the source of supply of arms and bomb-making materials, and stop it!"

"You were chosen as the right man for the job because of your ability to think quickly and effectively; additionally, you have a unique talent in martial arts, which you may well need to protect yourself. Believe me, I have read your personal file with interest, and I know you are the right choice for this appointment. I have no liking for the task either, but it has to be done and I accept that. I prevail upon you to do likewise. There is of course a carrot at the end. You will find that your rapid promotion heretofore pedestrian to what it will be in two years' time. Two years is the allotted time we will be here, unless prejudiced in some way, in which case we would be removed immediately."

Tammy gulped down half his whisky, too late realising it was Irish and not Scotch. The rawness caught at the back of his throat, and threatened his eyes with tears. He suspected the glimmer of a smile at the corner of the Commander's mouth, and the insane thought crossed his mind that if the smile became fully fledged, he'd wipe it off with a damned good smack.

Suddenly he found himself smiling. Hell on wheels, it had been a swine of a day, but in the end it wasn't this poor sod's fault. He put down the offending drink, mentally noting he would be avoiding that in the future, and stalked across to the Commander and held out his hand in capitulation.

"I accept the task, and here is my hand on it," he announced with a teasing formality, "just one thing though. I am buggered if I am going to call you Commander Denham-Tring, that is too much of a gallop around the tonsils, now you give me a name that's nice and neat, even if you have to fabricate something."

The Commander's face lit up with a huge smile as he heaved an exaggerated sigh, although relief was evident in the piercing eyes.

"By God! You know how to make a guy work for it," he congratulated with grudging respect, "no easy push over, you. Yes, here is my hand, welcome aboard, I am pleased you have agreed to help me. My Christian name is Algernon, as true as I stand here. I think my father really wanted me to be the heavy-weight champion of the world. Please do me the kindness of calling me Al. Short and sweet and as you asked, neat."

Rapport had arrived at last. They sat down and discussed how and where meetings would be arranged, and after reading the file, Tammy asked various questions to confirm one or two points. Finally there was nothing more to discuss, and Tammy decided he had better make tracks and get out into the city and find accommodation, and with this they shook hands and parted.

The walking scarecrow guided Tammy back through the route by which he had entered, and at the creaky door bade him to God's safe keeping. Tammy was to find out at a later time that the poor wretch had been subjected to gas warfare, which had affected his vocal chords, and that sandfly fever was responsible for his skeletal frame, but despite these disadvantages he had a razor sharp mind and was totally a Government man.

As Tammy left the shelter of the house the wind tore at him and howled with maniacal fury. Sleet laden and bitingly cold, it spurred Tammy into action. He had to find lodgings or spend the night on the streets.

Head down and the handles of his suitcases firmly clenched in his cold hands, he trudged along the narrow lane and reached what looked like a main thoroughfare. He stopped to take stock of his surroundings and noticed he was in Donegal Street.

He wandered aimlessly for a short time, absorbing the atmosphere of strange surroundings, then noticing a Post Office, he entered and asked a sweetly smiling young colleen if she could direct him to any bed and breakfast accommodation.

As is the way of the Irish, he soon had several people advising him where the best place would be. Eventually he gave himself into the hands of one garrulous old gent, who assured him that his sister in law ran the best place in the business, and the food was a treat from heaven.

It turned out that the accommodation was suitable, the food was eatable and the location was in the heart of the troubled area. Here the local populace of Catholic and Protestant persuasion continued a traditional warfare against each other, often no longer knowing the real reason.

Mrs Moriarty was a motherly type, and Tammy quickly established a good rapport with the friendly soul, who agreed to make him an evening meal whenever he required it, in addition of course to the normal bed and breakfast arrangement.

Yes! indeed! she would attend to his laundry requirements, but of course that would attract an extra payment, as she was sure Tammy would understand. Tammy sealed the bargain by giving the delighted landlady a months rent in advance, plus an additional amount to cover any extras.

Having settled his domestic arrangements and then been treated to a gargantuan meal by his hovering grateful landlady, Tammy decided he would take a stroll around the city and get his bearings.

He set off in the teeth of a raging sleet-laden wind. He pulled up the collar of his woollen coat and hunched his head deep into the warmth, cursing the foul biting north easterly blast. For all the world he looked like a self-effacing tortoise as he crouched over with just the top of his head showing over the coat collar.

It passed his mind that it would soon be Christmas and he wondered where he would enjoy the festivities and just how festive would they be. Perhaps it was the sound of accordion and fiddle music, coming in fitful starts as the wind chased the sound around the street, that had given rise to thoughts of Christmas.

Stopping for a second or so, he determined that the music was emanating from a pub across the road called the Oak and Sloe. With a mental shrug, he dodged the traffic as he crossed over, fully intent on entering the premises that proclaimed on a tattered sign outside that it provided the best porter in town.

As in all cities, Tammy knew that the best way to announce an arrival, was in a social gathering place and to his mind a pub was one of the best.

He entered the pub, straightening up as he cleared the low lintelled doorway. He paused to survey the scene and there was a heart beat of silence as every head in the place turned his way. One had to be careful these days. A stranger could be a hit man for some organisation or other.

Giving a cheery greeting to all, Tammy crossed to the bar, and being asked what his pleasure would be, he said he would try the much publicised porter and would the barman care to join him.

He was aware of the barman giving him the once over as the rich black ale was being drawn, but he affected ignorance of it. He accepted the offered glass of porter, paid the amount asked for and ambled across to a significantly vacant chair by the smouldering peat fire.

Hardly had he sat down when a voice advised him that the seat he had taken was normally reserved for Seamus Rourke, and as he was a stranger in town, there was no need to get away to a bad start, was there.

Tammy courteously thanked the informant, but pointed out that since the gentleman in question was not here, then it was a sin not to make use of such accommodation as was available.

There was a slight edging away from the vicinity around the seat that Tammy had commandeered and he was not unaware of it The atmosphere became electric to an extent that prickly static pulsed in a latent intensity.

'So' he thought, 'I'm about to upset a personality am I. He must be the top dog of this little flea pit. Well I have to make a mark, so this will do for a start', and leaning back, apparently completely at ease, he was soon tapping his foot in rhythm to the beat of the music.

The general flow of people coming and going continued unabated for some time, then suddenly a pair of hands grabbed Tammy on either side of the neck. Huge fingers like mechanical grabs dug brutally into the neck muscles as Tammy was hoisted to his feet.

Tammy let his head drop onto his chest, then, when he was fully erect, he threw his head backwards with explosive force and was rewarded by the sound of a satisfactory crunch as bone was broken.

The hands at his neck went limp. He wheeled within the loose embrace and drove his four extended rigid fingers deep into the solar plexus of the flabby belly of the figure now facing him.

Stepping back as the head came down with a tortured, strangled gasp, Tammy grabbed the thick greasy hair and, placing his other hand on top, slammed the face down onto the brass-covered heavy wooden table.

Letting loose of the now unconscious frame, Tammy looked up to see the barman converging on him, brandishing an ugly looking shillelagh.

Holding up his hands at shoulder height, palms facing forward he gave a polite warning, steely voiced and hard eyed.

"Look friend! I want no trouble! This craven thing attacked me from the back. That was indeed unfair. I only protected myself, and that is the privilege of every freeborn man, is it not?"

"Now, that wee bit stick you are waving about will not prevent me from defending myself again if it is necessary, and since I detest a beating by whatever means, I will try to hurt you and may well damage you. Now come on! Can we not all have a drink like civilised folk and forget this little upset?"

The barman's advance petered to a halt, cold reason, and a deep intuitive feeling, advised him that this was not the time for misplaced heroics. With a shrug of his heavy shoulders he advanced a few more steps, with the shillelagh trailing through the sawdust on the floor behind him.

He stopped and looked down on the unconscious Rourke, and shook his head as if still not believing his eyes.

"I don't know where you learned your fighting," he remarked thoughtfully, "but I'll give you this. You're fast and dirty, but if I were you, I'd grow eyes in the back of my head, for Rourke will be none too pleased by tonight's events, and he'll try for you on a moonless night, and it will be from the back again, believe me.

Tammy waved a hand in dismissal of such a suggestion, and raising his voice slightly, he gave advice to the assembled drinkers.

"Pay heed to what I say! I am a peace loving man. I want no trouble. It will make me angry if I am given trouble. If I am angry, then I can be violent, and this makes me more angry. Does everybody understand? It is better to keep me quiet and happy, then nobody gets hurt. Any friends of this article on the floor here had better tell him that if he decides to give me hassle he will be asking for grief, and he will get it. If he even blinks the wrong way and I don't like it, he will have more trouble than if he'd opened Pandora's box. I shall be staying in this area, using this pub, and he can either live with that or find another city."

Taking the barman by the arm, he drew him towards the bar,

"Let's call a round on me," he offered, "and do you think that wee band could play the Londonderry Air, och no, it's Danny Boy over here, isn't it?"

The barman nodded agreement and shouted to the quartet to do what they were being paid for, and he wanted Danny Boy for his guest. He slipped behind the bar and began to dispense drinks with practised efficiency, as the bar flies pushed forward eagerly for the free drinks that Tammy was paying for.

In a momentary lull the barman remembered the unconscious Rourke, who was still lying bleeding onto the sawdust, his stentorious breathing through his shattered nose was a pitiful sound, yet nobody appeared in the least interested or concerned. So the mighty had fallen.

In a moment of weakness, perhaps, the barman signalled two of the regulars to drag him the hell out of here, and perhaps they had better organise an ambulance. That was the end of any interest in the matter and soon the ould songs were being sung, as Tammy paid for a further couple of rounds.

On the way back to his temporary home, Tammy took no chances. He kept out of the shadowy areas, and was ever alert to the possibility of attack from the rear, but he reached his lodgings with nothing untoward occurring.

He took a nightcap with Mrs Moriarty, then gave her a blithe good night and went to bed, where he slept the sleep of untroubled innocence.

He awakened early in the morning, as was his wont, and going downstairs he started the day off by rifling out the cold ashes from the fire and hunted around until he found kindling wood. Soon he had a good fire going and the chill started to leave the kitchen.

When Mrs Moriarty eventually appeared, she was in a confusion of apologies and perplexity, sure she had no idea his good self wanted an early start, and och, he shouldn't have bothered with that dirty ould fire. Now look! Breakfast would be no time at all, and she would make a cup of tea this instant.

Quietly Tammy tried to soothe the flustered landlady, telling her to take her time and not start the day out of sorts. He was sorry to have upset her, but in truth he had enjoyed tinkering around and getting things started, and would she be a darling and not deny him such a small pleasure.

It was that first morning, and the simple tasks he had performed, that decided Mrs Moriarty that she would be this nice lad's mother, for he was such a gentle creature and, oh, what beautiful manners, with his lovely soft spoken voice. To be sure, the voice of an angel.

To quote the Scottish Bard, Rabbie Burns,

> 'Oh wad some power, the gift tae gie us
> Tae see oursel's as ithers see us.'

Tammy would have found great difficulty in seeing himself as through the eyes of his landlady, and had she witnessed his treatment of Rourke on the previous evening, it is doubtful if her appreciation would have been as it was that breakfast time.

Chapter Ten

The Monday that Siobahn started work at Barranbarrach would be remembered by Donald as a turning point in his life. She came swinging down through the yard, drawing admiring glances from all directions.

Wolf whistles accompanied her until she turned into the stud office, but she ignored it all with the serenity and composure of a queen.

Donald bade her a pleasant good morning, and then excusing himself left the office, determined that she would be treated like any other employee. It was big Conal's authority to direct her to her duties, so that is how it would be.

Life on a training stud requires interaction between all personnel from time to time, therefore within a couple of days or so of Siobahn starting work at the stud, it was inevitable that Donald found himself in a situation where he and Siobahn were committed to a dual task.

Siobahn was no retiring flower, so quite candidly asked Donald if he found her presence embarrassing or upsetting in any way. Donald replied that as far as he was concerned she was fulfilling her role admirably and he had no complaints about her work whatsoever.

When she charged him with always making excuses and disappearing when she arrived at where he happened to be, he haughtily announced that she was assuming something that was nothing, and certainly he was unaware of this questionable fact.

She smiled disarmingly, and as Donald's heart lurched, then thumped within his chest, she put her hand on his arm and told him she wouldn't bite him, for sure he was really quite a nice person, for a man.

Donald jumped back as if he had been scalded, the blood roared in his ears, and he felt the telltale flush of embarrassment suffuse his face. He was further discomposed when Siobahn burst out laughing, a laugh full of joy and uninhibited pleasure.

The hazel flecked green eyes impaled Donald with the age-old magnetism of enraptured enchantment, and as women have drawn men into entrapment since time began, so Donald responded to the lure, to the beguiling charms of this entrancing auburn haired witch.

He returned a tentative smile, and then heard himself giggling like a fool, but nothing could now stop the full flow of laughter from bursting free as a sense of relief flowed through him at not having to hold slightly aloof any longer.

In one of the looseboxes further up the yard, Conal heard the laughter, and smiled contentedly, his little connivances had paid dividends already.

Donald's mind was in full flight. My God, he was thinking, she is such a child of nature. Both innocent and knowing, but without affectation. What you see is what you get. There is no deceit or airs or graces, just a natural down to earth, pleasing and pleasant girl, with an inbuilt code of moral ethics that demanded, and received, respectful consideration.

The shared laughter dissipated the last vestiges of awkwardness and soon they were chatting away without reserve whilst they trace sheared a hunter, which was their morning task.

Conal passed by on his Clydesdale mare, apprised the new circumstances and nodded his head in satisfaction. Yes! Things were working to plan, and he would take great pleasure in telling his wife that evening how he had played matchmaker so successfully.

Although Donald was, in essence, the horsemaster, he nevertheless did a fair share of the work that was necessary to keep the stud running smoothly.

His forte however, was at the breaking of the young colts and fillies. His superiority to any other in the yard was an established fact in this area of training, and it was accepted without rancour by all the other hands.

The most awkward animal was soon brought to gentle obedience under his remarkable talent. If initial training is ineffective it can be the ruination of a possible imminent star in the hunter or hurdler world, it is therefore imperative that the early training is a good solid platform from which the young horse will go forward with confidence and a natural appetite for its work.

Conal had spoken the truth when he said that Siobahn had the hands of an angel and a special skill with horses, and soon she and Donald were dealing primarily with only the early or formative phase of training.

Donald still had to deal with visitors, day to day problems that arose, and keep in touch with all aspects of the overall training within the stud.

He also kept up his practice with the catapult and his throwing clubs. In addition he would disappear into the teeming forestland and stalk the local wild life, and ran morning and evening to keep in good physical shape. His life was full to capacity, each day had insufficient hours to contain all he wanted to pack into it. He was comfortable in his position of authority, and was now held in respectful regard by the people he governed. On the first morning in charge, he had asked to be judged on merit, and now he was.

Close company with Siobahn had created a warm regard for each other, but neither would make the first step towards a more meaningful relationship. Donald, because he had an irrational fear of a repetition of what had happened with his first love, Mary. Siobahn was likewise restrained by her past experience with the male gender, who had either treated her with derision or had subjected her to sexual harassment. So the relationship burbled along in quiet companionship, but, underneath the shield of respectability and serenity there bubbled a wealth of passion awaiting release.

Donald had twice visited the city of Belfast, and since Christmas was only a few weeks off, he decided to get the chauffeur to drive him into the city, drop him off and return at a predetermined time when he had finished his shopping for Christmas gifts. He arranged with Conal to take charge in his absence and the following morning set off as planned.

It was a morning of harsh sleety weather, the cold wind blew in snarling gusty blasts, foretelling the grim reality of the winter to come.

Barranbarrach, on the lee side of the Antrim hills, would be sheltered to a great extent, but bad weather would, as usual, play havoc with the training schedules.

Donald snuggled down into the warm interior of the preheated Daimler, and decided he would have a nice day in spite of the weather. He had dressed in a warm woollen suit and his Burberry raincoat would keep him both warm and dry, so he was content enough to sit back and let his thoughts wrestle with what sort of gift to buy for Siobahn. He wanted it to be a bit special, but would have to be careful that it wasn't something that could be considered condescending as a gift from an owner's son to a member of staff. On the other hand he didn't want it to be a proclamation of intent, or be misconstrued as a promise to anything in their relationship. Siobahn was not the kind of girl that dangled with jewelry, so earrings or bracelets would not be suitable. What could one buy for a girl who lived life with few wants, or needs, other than be accepted as she was.

Yes, he thought, that is the answer perhaps, something that was natural to her everyday life. But what?

The Daimler glided to a smooth controlled halt, and Donald looked out with surprise. The driver had stopped outside the City Hall and was asking if this was suitable. Donald confirmed that it was and, getting out, immediately donned the warm Burberry and was grateful for its added warmth against the icily cold sleet laden wind.

He told the driver to pick him up outside the City Hall, and explained what time he expected to be met, then he headed off into the nearest shopping area, still no nearer in his mind on what to buy for Siobahn.

Turning into Victoria Street, he ambled along slowly, at this stage merely window shopping. He travelled the entire length of the street on one side, then crossing over he sauntered back along the other, pausing now and then as something caught his interest.

He then began a systematic search of side streets off the main thoroughfare, like a hunting dog quartering for scent.

Hearing the city clock strike the hour of noon, he realised that he had been wandering around like a Jew in the desert, and it seemed that some time had elapsed and here he was, still empty handed as far as a gift for Siobahn was concerned. He had been successful as far as gifts for his parents and grandparents, but the one that most concerned him was as elusive as the Scarlet Pimpernel in French folklore. Perhaps if he stopped for lunch, he would become refreshed in mind as well as body and would succeed in his quest. With this in mind he started to look for a likely oasis.

He was unaware of what street he was in, but that was of no consequence, any pub would supply him with a suitable repast. A pie and a pint would more than suffice.

He continued along the narrow cobbled street for a short distance, then his nose led him to a small cosy looking place that proclaimed bar meals and luncheons were available. This would serve admirably, so he entered into a low ceilinged, black beamed bar room with white washed walls. A cheery fire crackled with enticing invitation, and drew Donald towards its warmth, like a moth to a guttering candle. He removed his coat and hung it on a rack of deers antlers just inside the doorway.

Going to the bar he ordered a pint of porter and a bowl of Irish stew, with a side order of crusty white bread.

The momentary silence that had accompanied his entrance had not gone unnoticed by Donald, but he was unconcerned. All he wanted was a brief respite from the chilling wind and a bite to eat. He was not here to give anyone any trouble, and he certainly didn't want any.

He returned to the area of warmth by the fire. As he approached a cadaverous dark-haired man moved accommodatingly to the side. Donald thanked him for his kindness and remarked that it was a lazy old wind outside and it was nice to find shelter out of it for a while.

The hawk faced individual nodded a pleasant agreement and, lounging deeper into his chair, remarked that Ireland should indeed be called the Emerald Isle, for it sure as hell got enough rain to keep the grass green.

Donald had caught the Scottish burr in the pleasantly modulated voice, and looked the owner of it full in the face as he agreed that this was true, but his native glen in Scotland had been blessed by the same attributes from time to time, and since his livelihood depended on a prolific abundance of that commodity, he had become inured to the discomfort that it brought with it.

Leaning forward with outstretched hand he offered "I am Donald Macdonald of the Macdonalds of Sleat, at present horsemaster at the Barranbarrach Stud of Antrim, and I am pleased to make your acquaintance."

The wiry frame came erect. A smile transformed the scarred face, as Donald's hand was gripped firmly, each instantly recognising the fighting hands of warriors.

"I am pleased to meet you Donald. I am Tammy Dale, ex Gorbals of Glasgow, and currently merchant of fortune in this cold city."

He continued as they sat holding each others hands without embarrassment.

"That was a pretty fair wee speech if I may say so, a bit formal and unco stiff perhaps. I take it that you don't often find yourself in the position of having to make your own introductions?"

Donald grinned, then with merriment bubbling through his voice, he apologised as he explained,

"I'm sorry, you're quite right. Part of my job is to meet and greet owners of horses kept at the stud, and Arabs and Americans in particular love that old nonsense. I suppose I have just developed a habit of introducing myself in the way I did."

The ice broken, the two young men continued chatting through the course of their lunch, exchanging views on current topics and the present political scene in Ulster.

Tammy asked if there had ever been any trouble at the stud, seeing as how the ownership was in new hands that were not Irish. Donald, with a question in his voice, said no indeed, but really it was not to be expected, for sure was his mother not as Irish as the Blarney Stone.

Tammy agreed that it was likely they would escape trouble in those auspices, at least he hoped so. They lingered by the fire for a while longer, then Donald remarked that he had better move along as he still had to purchase one more Christmas gift. He explained that it was a special one, and it was giving him trouble, but he had to get it today, whatever it was going to be.

As Donald was putting on his coat Tammy got out of his seat and reached for his coat, remarking that, although he had only been in the city a couple of weeks, he did know of rather a nice little gift shop quite close by, and it would be a pleasure to conduct Donald to it, if that was his wish.

Donald was delighted with the offer and accepted instantly. In truth he was glad that he would have the company of this new acquaintance for a spell longer. He felt a kinship with this reserved but pleasant individual, and for the first time since arriving in Ulster, a sense of brotherhood and companionship.

They left the snug haven and, turning up the collars of their coats against the bitter blast, bowed their heads and ploughed forward as litter whirled like demented confetti around them.

A short distance from the pub where they had eaten lunch they reached their desired destination, and as they entered, Donald could see it was a veritable treasury of gifts and artifacts.

There was an abundance to choose from, handcrafted wares of wood, pottery, crystal, stone and bronze. Donald was delighted. Surely his odyssey was at an end.

Tammy made no move to depart, for which Donald was glad. As his eyes searched, he pondered on how to entice Tammy to come and stay on an extended visit at Barranbarrach over the Christmas holiday.

He noticed Tammy testing the balance of a hand-made throwing knife, then looking at the price tag regretfully, replacing it back on the display shelf with a shake of his head.

Slowly the pair walked around the Aladdin's Cave, taking plenty of time to assess a probable choice, then Donald heard Tammy call him and going round the display case found him looking at bronze figurines.

"Did you not say this person who requires a special gift was a horse queen?" Tammy queried. "What about that?" He was pointing to a bronze figurine of a mare with a suckling foal.

It was a beautifully constructed piece, made by a local craftsman. The bronze colouration seemed to bring the animals alive with hidden fire, as the piece moved around on the revolving turntable, the lights reflected off it creating a sense of movement.

"That's it! That's it!" cried Donald, "by damn, Tammy, it's just perfect. Perfect. Oh I'm sure she'll love it, for she is horse crazy."

Turning to the shop owner, he asked for it to be wrapped as he would like to take it with him.

Tammy noticed that Donald didn't ask how much the figurine cost, and surmised that his new friend had been saving up for the occasion, nevertheless it did go into his mental notebook as being a trifle odd.

Donald had two carrier bags with string handles to carry his purchases, and having paid what Tammy thought was an exorbitant amount for his latest acquisition, they left the little craft shop.

Donald checked the time, then said he had better make his way back towards the City Hall, where he was being picked up.

Tammy thought for a moment, then said he was sure that a little alley up the street a few yards was in fact a short cut, which would save on quite a long walk, and if Donald didn't mind, he would accompany him to his rendezvous as he really hadn't much in the way of pressing business to attend to.

What Donald and Tammy didn't know was that when Tammy had introduced himself to Donald in the pub, one of the habitual barflies had quickly finished his drink and left the bar with indecent haste. He was in fact one of Rourke's informants, and Rourke desperately wanted revenge on the Glasgow hard man who had treated him with disdainful efficiency at their first meeting.

Rourke was delighted with the news, and recruiting eight of his thugs, a trap was laid. Since Donald and Tammy had lingered over their lunch and then spent time in the purchase of Siobahn's gift, sufficient time had elapsed to enable Rourke to lay what he felt was an effective ambush.

A few yards from the giftshop, Donald stopped and slapped his forehead in exasperation.

"Tammy! I've just remembered. I need another item from the shop. Can you just hold these a second and I'll nip back in and get it? I'll only be a tick."

Before Tammy had a chance to demur, Donald pressed the carriers into Tammy's hands and darted back into the shop. Quickly he made his purchase and was out onto the street before Tammy had time to follow or see what the additional item was.

Tammy's interest however had been otherwise engaged. He had observed the gathering of a bunch of hard looking characters at the end of the street some five hundred yards or so along the road.

Instinct and experience warned him that this could be serious trouble, so when Donald re-emerged from the shop, he quite brusquely conducted him to the mouth of the alley that would take them back towards the City Hall.

As he entered the alley, he noticed that the body of men split into two parties, one coming down towards the alley, the other departing at speed down a street running at right angles to the one where they had initially mustered.

The alley they were now in was about six hundred yards long and joined Millstreet and the Avenue. They were half way along when Tammy spotted a group of four enter with menacing intent. Looking behind, his worst fears were realised as another four had entered the alley behind them.

Tammy and Donald were effectively trapped by a hostile pack armed with hurley sticks and three foot lengths of rope which had a turks head knot at every two or three inches, with two-inch nails driven through the knots. These were dreadful weapons, capable of inflicting the most appalling wounds.

Tammy spotted a narrow covered passageway and unceremoniously pushed Donald into it.

"There is going to be a wee bit of trouble Donald," he cried, "just wait in there and keep your head down 'till I sort it out." He whipped off his coat and jacket in one easy flowing movement, flung them aside, and whirled to meet the approaching offensive group.

Donald placed his parcels carefully against the wall. Quickly and efficiently he gathered Tammy's discarded clothing and placed it beside his parcels, removed his own coat and jacket and added them to the little pile against the wall.

His searching hand found the trusty catapult in the waistband of his trousers at the small of his back. He slapped his trouser pocket to check his throwing clubs were available, and left the shelter he had been thrust into.

Loading the catapult, he fired twice in the space of seconds, dropping two of the advancing group nearest to Tammy. Whirling, he fired twice again and two more of the group that had followed them into the alley dropped to the ground.

Tammy was now in full combat, dropping one wild sweep of a hurley stick, a second combatant sliced down on Tammy's head. Only a last minute fractional duck of his head prevented his skull from being fractured, however he didn't escape entirely. The hurley stick sliced down the side of his head and caught his ear, slicing through the gristly mass and leaving it hanging like a spaniel's lug.

Disregarding the searing pain, he drove the heel of his palm into the upper lip of his opponent with such force the front teeth were driven down the throat and the nose was destroyed forever.

He drove his elbow backwards in time to avert a blow from the rear then, whirling like a dancing dervish, he straight kicked the second combatant deeply in the groin. Spinning again, he drove forward and chopped the already stunned figure in front of him, twice rapidly on the neck root.

Donald had made easy work of his two remaining opponents. He could have dropped them both with his war clubs but had coolly decided that he needed some practice, and had confidently gone forward to meet them.

The war thrum he emitted disconcerted them, freezing any action for a few precious seconds. In that heartbeat of time Donald was upon them, like a machine of destruction.

Spinning in an extended cartwheel, his ankles closed and locked on the leading contestant's neck. The flying scissors, closing and gripping in a deadlock. Momentum force spun the confused ruffian through a violent arc that ended with his head crashing on the cobbled ground.

Donald's second adversary had been unable to intervene in the tournament so far, the action had been so electrifyingly furious, but as Donald disengaged from the now unconscious opponent, so he leapt into the fray, hoping for an advantage with Donald still on the ground having completed the scissors throw.

He had however miscalculated the merit of the opposition. Donald came off the ground in a bewildering backwards somersault, and as the foot of the thug came swinging round in a pedestrian haymaker, Donald dropped in a splits, both legs at right angles to his body, and the foot swept over his head, missing by inches.

Donald came erect, as if projected on steel springs, pirouetted and committed himself to the triple kick, with such devastating accuracy that the bully crashed to the ground, hardly knowing what had happened. He had certainly lost all interest in the proceedings.

As Donald turned away from the recumbent figure, his hand darted into his pocket and he took out and threw one of his war clubs with such speed that it appeared a blur of movement.

Tammy, holding a handkerchief to his torn ear, turned to see what had galvanised his fighting friend into such action, in time to see one of the bullies that had been put out of action at the commencement of the fracas, collapse anew as the club hit him between the eyes.

Donald examined each of the recumbent figures in turn and when he was satisfied there would be no further threat, he returned to Tammy and suggested they should make themselves scarce.

He took the headband cum garotte from around his waist and, placing Tammy's ear more or less in the right position, pressed Tammy's handkerchief over it, then bound it in place with the headband.

Nodding with satisfaction he preceded Tammy into the narrow passageway, where they put on their jackets and coats, despite their shirts and trousers being soaked through by the persistent sleet.

Donald checked his armament, clubs and catapult, picked up his precious packages, gave a nod to Tammy that he was ready, and off they set for the end of the alley and the more crowded main streets.

Donald looked at Tammy with a cheeky grin and remarked,

"That is a fine way to work off a lunch meal. I must, in future, not get involved with strange men, they can so easily lead one astray, and me just a simple country boy. Hells teeth, I was scared to death. I mean, eight of them. That surely wasn't fair. Mind, my Dad is always saying that nobody promised that it would be. I think he might be right. I have noticed as I get older he appears to get a wee bit wiser."

Tammy was laughing heartily, till he realised that Donald was doing his part in dissipating post action tension, and he joined willingly into the banter.

"Aye! Aye!" he gurgled, "I noticed how scared you were. I thought I was good, but, my God, you are some mover. As bonny a fighter as it has ever been my pleasure to see, and I have seen what I thought was the best, but sure as hell they would look like novices beside you."

He rubbed his face with both hands and gave a suppressed shudder, as delayed shock from his damaged ear permeated his system. He breathed deeply, shook his head determinedly and continued,

"I'll be honest with you, Donald. I did think you were a nice young farmhand, despite the fancy title. When I felt the hand ridges I wasn't quite sure whether it was through some kind of work done on the farm, or whether it was the cultured hands of a warrior."

"Now it all begs the question, who and what are you really? Can you tell me?"

Donald smiled at his puzzled friend, but there was a thread of anxiety in his voice as he answered. He realised Tammy was needing medical attention and quite rapidly, nevertheless, to keep his friend's mind occupied, he contributed to the conversation willingly.

"I really am the horsemaster of Barranbarrach. Honestly! Where and how I got my training is a long involved story, which I am willing to tell you, but I think we should have that conversation in happier climes. Let us concentrate on getting to where the car will be waiting. We will go round to the casualty department at the hospital and have that ear stitched up, then I can give you a lift to your home and get you off these dangerous streets.

"Here is something to consider in the meantime. How about coming home with me for a few days and let the dust settle. You are obviously on a hit list for whatever reason, so it will ease the pressure if you drop out of circulation for a wee while. At any rate, give it a bit of thought."

Tammy knew he would accept the offer, for he agreed with Donald's assessment of the situation, but he was also greatly intrigued with this compatriot he'd joined forces with. He had never in his life had a true and complete friend. His early years had imbued him with an inability to trust anyone. His liaison with the Chinese family Ling had been the nearest thing he had known to friendship, but always the cultural differences had prevented complete rapport.

With this unassuming young man he found a reluctance to part company with him. He felt, even in the short time he had known him, that he could be relied on. Heavens above, had he not just demonstrated this in the very immediate past?

They turned the corner and there was the Daimler waiting in front of the City Hall, and Donald sighed with relief.

As they approached, the chauffeur got out of the car and opened the rear door, addressing Donald directly,

"It's a snell wind sir," he observed, studiedly ignoring the sight of Tammy with his makeshift dressing on his head, "but the car is nice and warm, and maybe a wee dram will take the edge off. I made sure the decanter was full before I returned for you."

"Thank you, that was kind of you, Sean," answered Donald, as he handed over the parcels to the waiting hands, "I think we shall get in and have a warming tipple before we start off."

Tammy made no comment as he climbed into the opulent interior of the plush car. He accepted the crystal glass with its amber contents.

Donald held up his glass and, clinking it against Tammy's, he offered a toast.

"Here's to a good afternoon's fun, and if you would allow it, a happy and continuing friendship, for I would like us to be friends from now on."

Tammy held up his glass in a hand that trembled slightly, and emotion choked his voice into a husky response.

"I could not better that proposal, but I endorse it wholeheartedly. I have had some surprises today, and somehow I think there are a few more in the offing, so I am just going to sit back and let it all happen. Up until now they have been the nicest bolts from the blue that have ever occurred in my life. Incidentally, I have thought about your invitation, and I would be delighted to accept. Could I just direct the driver to my lodgings and I'll pick up my shaving gear, etcetera."

Donald was delighted with the response to his invitation, and in no time they had called in to the Royal Victoria Hospital casualty department and had repairs effected to Tammy's ear. He told the bossy matron in charge that a tile had blown off a roof.

They diverted to Tammy's lodgings where he advised Mrs Moriarty he would be away for a few day, but yes, please hold his room for him, ah yes, he would be returning and that was definite. He collected such items as he felt he would require and soon they were heading north west to Barranbarrach.

Tammy now had a proper bandage around his head to keep the dressing in place. He was feeling a bit more like a wounded soldier.

During the drive to Barranbarrach, Tammy asked Donald if he would be able to make a phone call, and Donald assured him there would be no problem, even when it was pointed out that the call would be to Glasgow.

The wind had dropped suddenly, and now large, lazylike flakes of snow were falling in a heavy continuous screen, but the Daimler purred along the quiet county lanes like a large contented cat.

When Donald asked the chauffeur if it had been snowing for long, it was confirmed that, indeed, it had been snowing on and off all day, which meant that at the moment it was fairly parochial, for only a few scattered flakes had blown through the wind in the city. Sleet had been the problem there, had they not both received a soaking during the little fracas.

The automatic transmission changed quietly and smoothly into a lower gear as the Daimler braked to turn in through the gates of a driveway, a long avenue with barelimbed trees on either side, pointing witches fingers at the sullen grey sky.

Winter creates wider panoramas and clearer horizons, and as the car rattled across the cattle grid, Tammy could see a large sandstone mansion house in the distance.

Well tended grounds, with an endless variety of trees and shrubs seemed to create a welcoming atmosphere, and Tammy was quite sure in his mind that when foliage bedecked the at present bare limbs and branches, there would be a breathtaking confusion of beauty to enhance the feeling of welcome.

As they progressed along the driveway, Tammy felt that this introduction to Barranbarrach would be a foretaste to a friendly environment within the mansion house itself. He felt that the people who lived within its sturdy walls would be a caring family, with the wellfare of its workers always being considered.

His quiet thoughts and inner composure suffered a severe jolt when the Daimler pulled up at the flight of steps leading up to the huge doors of the mansion. The chauffeur jumped out and opened the door for him, and then speedily went round the car to do the same for Donald.

Donald took hold of Tammy's arm and led him towards the great wooden doors, as the chauffeur collected the parcels.

"Welcome to my home, Tammy. As they say in these parts, use it as your own. I am really glad to have you here, and I hope you will enjoy your stay. Come on,

I'll introduce you to my mother and my grandparents, I doubt if dad is here yet, but you'll meet him at pre-dinner drinks."

Tammy was absolutely speechless. He had truly expected the car to drive round to the rear of the mansion, to a small cottage perhaps. Although a Daimler had picked them up to drive them to Barranbarrach he had just assumed that it was just a case of the car being in the area. The servility of the driver he had imagined was a quiet little joke at his expense. Oh dear! Oh dear! He was beginning to realise that this simple little country boy was a greater enigma than ever.

He pulled back as Donald led him towards the wide marble steps.

"Donald, my friend," he objected gently, and sadness drifted through the muted tones, "this is no place for me. I'm not in this class or status in life. I'll quite rightly feel badly out of place here. Look! Why don't you just ask your driver to run me back to Belfast? I appreciate your invitation, but honestly, I am out of place here."

Donald put his arm around the shoulders of his friend, and gave them an encouraging squeeze as he refuted such a suggestion.

"Nonsense, Tammy! How can you say that when you haven't even met my family? I tell you what! If it will put your mind at rest, when we have had dinner, if you still feel out of place, then I will personally drive you back to Belfast. Now come on, come and meet the family, I know you'll like them."

As they reached the top of the steps, the heavy doors swung open as if in itself a greeting. A quiet modulated voice welcomed them in, and a pair of arms came forward to accept the overcoats.

They were advised that the family awaited them in the evening room, and the door to that room was opened by the butler, who then stepped back and simply vanished, or so it seemed to Tammy.

Sitting within the comfortably appointed evening room were Donald's mother and grandparents. Mari rose in a graceful flowing liquid motion and coming across the room took Donald into her arms and kissed him tenderly and without embarrassment.

"Did you have a successful day in the city?" she asked, as her eyes turned to Tammy with a searching look that left him feeling he had been scrutinised under an x-ray. 'Not much would escape those discerning eyes,' he thought.

"Mother, I would like you to meet a new friend of mine, Tammy Dale. I have asked him to visit with us for a few days."

Mari went over to Tammy and putting her arms round his shoulders kissed him on the cheek.

"I am very pleased to make your acquaintance, Tammy. Please feel welcome to our home and make it yours. You must be a very special person, for my son, apart from being a very perceptive young man, does not give his friendship lightly. For you to be accepted as a friend in the course of a day says much to me. It would please me if you would stay for an extended period and become my friend as well."

The two elder people came forward and greeted Tammy just as warmly, then one on either side, drew him towards the warmth of the fire and got him comfortably esconced.

A decanter tinkled on the side of a crystal glass and Tammy found himself holding a large fistful of the same excellent malt whisky that he had enjoyed previously in the Daimler, before starting the journey to this elegant home.

Mari pulled a tasselled cord that hung close to the large oak slab, the size of a narrow table, that was the mantelshelf. When the summons was answered in seconds, she advised the housekeeper that the blue room adjacent to Donald's was to be prepared for Mr Dale, and could baths be run for him and Donald straight away.

'Well,' thought Tammy, 'it looks as if it has been decided that I have to stay the night, but I'll see how it goes before I commit myself. I have to say though, the welcome seemed genuine enough, and I don't feel unwanted or awkward. Perhaps Donald's father will prove to be the stumbling block.'

It entered his mind that nobody had mentioned the fact that he had a bandaged head, and wondered if it was gentle good manners that had forestalled any questions.

Tammy was asked if he would like a refill, but demurred graciously, and said he would very much appreciate a bath and shave and change of clothing as he was in fact quite damp.

Donald came over and took the empty glass from Tammy, and set it with his own on one of the occasional tables, then taking Tammy's arm said he would show him where to go, as they left the room.

Tammy followed Donald through a hallway the size of a small dance floor and up the wide stairway with intricately carved wooden panels on the walls. The smell of beeswax and lavender gave credence to the loving industry that had produced the deep shine that glowed with a warmth of its own.

It really was a beautiful old house, Tammy reflected, tastefully furnished and decorated to give an ambience of comfortable dignity. Despite the size it felt like a well lived in home, and not the country showpiece it could so easily have been.

The room assigned to Tammy was spacious and comfortable, with two large windows looking out across the grounds. As Tammy stood gazing out for a few moments, trying to settle his equilibrium as he viewed the white blanketed landscape, he noticed what looked like roofs of some buildings in the near distance and guessed that they signified the location of the stud.

A discreet knock at the door interrupted his reverie, and turning from the window he invited the caller to enter. A chambermaid responded to his invitation, and announced that his bath was ready, and was there anything else he required. When he said that he felt he had everything he needed, the maid directed him to the bathroom and withdrew.

He sank into the deeply filled bath and groaned with pleasure as his cold, tired body started to relax. He pampered himself for twenty minutes or so, then got out and shaved, whilst wrapped in the huge bath towel.

When he had completed his toilette he returned to his room and dressed in his one good grey worsted suit.

He sat down in a large easy chair and was contemplating what to do next when Donald knocked and shouted could he come in. When Tammy answered in the affirmative, he entered and walked across to where Tammy was standing by the chair.

"You are all at sixes and sevens, aren't you?" he observed, then with a smile of encouragement he continued, "if it's any consolation to you, I was exactly the same when I arrived here from Scotland. In a way it was worse for me, for I had to learn to wear proper clothes like a normal person, and that was hard. On visits here I was a wee bit boy and didn't really appreciate the fine standard of living that my grandparents were accustomed to. Tammy, you do get used to it. Humans are the most adaptable breed on earth, and you'll see, Tammy, you will feel better as each day goes by."

Donald took a deep breath and plunged on.

"Tammy, I want you to feel at home. Please don't feel strange or unwanted, for that is so untrue. I could see my mother liked you, as did my grandparents, and wait till you meet dad, he's a right man's man, you just won't be able to stop yourself from liking him."

Tammy felt reassured at Donald's earnest entreaty, and smiled as he replied to the lengthy dialogue.

"Donald, if my Gorbals crowd could see me now, it would blow their tiny minds. A raggy arsed kid with the inevitable snotty nose, sitting amongst gentry folk being waited on hand and foot, would be something beyond their wildest imaginings. I should feel out of place, and yet somehow I don't. I won't deny it has been a bit of a culture shock, but the welcome I got from your family couldn't have been more sincere and, despite myself, I feel quite happy, and I look forward to meeting your dad."

Donald put his arm around his friend's shoulders and guided him quietly towards the bedroom door as he explained the forthcoming scenario.

"We shall now go down and have a wee snort before dinner. I guess dad will be there by now, for he really looks forward to his wee dram before dinner. He says it helps his digestion, but I think that is just an excuse that he doesn't need, for although we seem to drink a lot, we are still not anywhere near the alcoholic stage. Let us away down then."

They entered the evening room to find the family comfortably enjoying a pre-dinner drink. Stuart, Donald's father, rose from the sofa as they entered and came across directly to them. He gave his son a friendly punch on the arm, as he turned and spoke directly to Tammy.

"Let me introduce myself," he welcomed Tammy, "I am Stuart the steward, for I am pouring and serving drinks. I think a nice big one is the order of the day, for I want you to feel so welcome here that you will never want to leave. Come and sit down over here with me, for I always get myself the most comfortable place. I am a bit selfish like that."

Mutely Tammy allowed himself to be led across to the large sofa, and as he sank into its comfortable depths, Stuart dropped in beside him. Light, easy conversation used up the time until they were summoned to the dinner table.

The meal to Tammy, used to frugal fare, was a veritable feast. Three full courses, finishing with local cheese with fruit to follow. When the port had made its second round, Stuart announced that the menfolk would try a frame or two of snooker, so they arose in accord and making their excuses to the two ladies, wandered casually down the long hall to the snooker room, which lay to the rear of the house.

Stuart went directly over to a hanging tasselled cord, and gave it a robust tug. When the butler promptly appeared Stuart asked him to fetch the brandy and the Scottish Malt whisky.

When this had been brought, he asked who wanted what, and when the glasses were charged, a coin was spun to see who would play whom in a double partnership.

The coin decided that Stuart and Tammy would play Donald and his grandfather Eamonn, and that Stuart would break off. Having broken the pack, Stuart glanced across at Tammy and asked if his ear was giving him any trouble.

Tammy recognised that this was a polite way of asking what had happened and responded right away by telling Stuart what had occurred, and the reason behind the attack, but he didn't explain his reason for being in Ulster.

He praised Donald's fighting skills, and insisted he would have been in very serious trouble if Donald had not involved himself in the affray, which still begged the question, how had a country lad achieved such a high level of skill?

Donald had removed his jacket and rolled up his shirt sleeves to play snooker. He now unbuttoned his shirt and took it off, turning his back towards Tammy as he did so.

Tammy could not prevent a gasp of amazement and shock, as he took in the horrifying criss crossing effect of scars on the otherwise tanned skin. The cicatrix stood out in ridges, white and stark, and covered the entire back, from nape of neck to the beginning of the coccyx area.

Turning to face Tammy as he replaced his shirt, Donald explained,

"I was subjected to a whipping with barbed wire when I was fifteen years of age, the very day I finished school in fact. So that something the same should never happen again I was virtually banished from my home into the hands of a sensei called Chi Li, who taught me the skills I now have."

"Tammy! That man gave me abilities I never knew existed. He developed my body and my mind, and honed the latent talents that emerged in the duration of the training. Even now I follow a strict regime to ensure I never become rusty or forget the techniques. I am also a bit of a keep fit fanatic I suppose, but I love the physical effort so find it no hardship to maintain a reasonable standard. The only thing that I miss is a daily contest with Chi Li. As you can perhaps imagine, it is difficult to find someone trained in the arts. Perhaps that has changed now, for I recognise that you have been trained, so perhaps we could practise from time to time."

Tammy nodded agreement, then shook his head negatively.

"Donald, much as I would like to, I am nowhere near your standard. If you decide we can, then it would have to be a case of you being the sensei and I the novice. If you can accept that, then we are away with the wind at our backs, and I really look forward to making a start. Do you run every morning?"

Donald confirmed that this was a daily routine of his, and Tammy made the request that he could join him, and did that mean the tomorrow would be the prelude to the overture that would follow."

The two older men had listened quietly while the youngsters had been talking, so when the final arrangements had been made in regards to the training that would follow, Stuart bet a dram that he and Tammy would wipe the floor with

Eamonn and Donald, and so a fiercely contested game of snooker ensued, with no quarter asked to given, but the laughter and ribaldry decried any vestige of rancour.

Tammy stayed at Barranbarrach for a fortnight, by which time his ear had repaired itself, under the careful ministrations of Mari. When he announced that he must return to Belfast to continue his work, as yet unspecified to any at Barranbarrach, he was harangued on all sides until he agreed to return for the Christmas holiday.

When Donald dropped him off at his lodgings, they shook hands with knuckle cracking force and Donald reminded him that he would be outside the lodgings on the afternoon of the 22nd December, and please would Tammy be there.

Tammy assured Donald that the devil of hell could not prevent him from spending Christmas at Barranbarrach, and that he was already looking forward to the pleasure it would be.

Chapter Eleven

A full fortnight before Christmas, Barranbarrach was a veritable hive of activity with preparations for the Christmas Estate Ball. It was an occasion looked forward to by every one of the estate workers and their families.

Each would receive a small gift and as much food and drink as they could manage. Eamonn Kelly had seen it as a time to show appreciation to his workforce for their co-operation and loyalty over the preceding year.

Stuart, protem the owner, wholeheartedly agreed and decided to keep the tradition going. Work would be confined to the basic necessities from Christmas Eve until the 2nd of January ensuring that all the workers had a well earned break.

Donald had told Siobahn about his new friend and she was looking forward to meeting him as on Tammy's initial visit to Barranbarrach she had not met him, having been away at an aunt's funeral in County Athlone.

She had taken that opportunity to purchase a Christmas gift for Donald and had experienced the same difficulty in the choice of something appropriate as he had on his shopping expedition to Belfast on the day he met Tammy.

Siobahn had decided, after lengthy discussions with a cousin, that during the festive season she would somehow get Donald to commit himself. She was certain in her own mind that she was deeply in love with him and was prepared to yield her independence for a lifetime of being Donald's wife. She was sure in the depths of her whole being that Donald loved her and had at times felt a wee bit impatient with his apparent reluctance to become deeper involved in a relationship of more meaning.

She was unaware that Donald had gone through the trauma of losing his first love and that an unreasonable fear kept him from expressing what he felt. In addition, he felt that his badly scarred back would prove to be prohibitive to the loving clasp of any prospective wife.

It is true that this last reason had only developed in his mind after the reaction of the maid who had attended his needs on his first morning at Barranbarrach. Her initial reaction had stuck in his mind like a burr to a saddle blanket and now it was a continuing festering sore that made him loathe to parade his scars to the view of the opposite sex.

On the 22nd as promised, Donald picked up Tammy from his lodgings. On the drive back to Barranbarrach, he informed Tammy that they had an invitation to visit the horse manager, Conal Duggan, that evening in his cottage. This was traditionally the official onset of the Christmas festivities and he hoped that Tammy had a strong head for drink, for by the Holy Moly, that old poteen was a hellish brew, and of course it was the following morning that the penalty was paid, and in full.

Tammy was greeted like the prodigal son on arrival at Barranbarrach, Donald's family making a fuss of him and doing all within their power to make him feel welcome.

Tammy was much more relaxed on this occasion, and had really looked forward to this pleasant break from the hazardous undercover work he was involved in.

He was resolved to enjoy the holiday to the full and his immediate superior, Commander Denham-Tring, had given Tammy his official blessing.

Tammy had been disappointed at not seeing Siobahn on his first visit and looked forward to meeting the wild colleen that had captured the heart of his friend, even though that friend would not admit to it.

At the time of departure to the party at Conal's holding, Donald, with angelic innocence, asked Tammy what kind of steed he would require for his journey across the estate.

Tammy gasped and stepped back from Donald as if he had discovered his friend had developed a nasty infectious disease.

"You mean we have to go there on horseback," he managed to enunciate, a look of horror on a face that had gone ashy white, "oh no! that is definitely a non starter Donald. I don't know one end of a beast from the other. I don't even want to learn. They are great smelly brutes and to be honest Donald, the thought of actually sitting on one scares the hell out of me. I'll just stay here, you go on and enjoy yourself. Tell Conal I developed something or other, but please don't tell him it was fear."

Donal was laughing uproariously by the time Tammy had finished his renunciation of the travelling plans that had been proposed. Water was running from his eyes as he uninhibitedly delighted in the response to his question.

"I got you going there bonny lad," he hooted, pointing a finger at the disconcerted Tammy, "Oh! you should see your own face. What a picture."

Taking pity on the victim of his amusement, he took hold of Tammy by the arm and took him off the hook.

"Don't fret Tammy, I rather thought you couldn't ride, because last time you were here I couldn't get you anywhere near the stables, so I gathered you would have to be introduced gently to the horses. No! no! We are being driven there and we'll be brought back whenever we are ready to return."

He had enjoyed his joke, but now contrition slapped him like a cold wet cloth. He grabbed Tammy with both hands and looked into the face of his friend and tried to smooth the ruffled feathers.

"That wasn't nice. Was it? I was only trying to shake you out of your inbuilt reticence to let yourself go a bit. Life can be fun Tammy, but you must meet it halfway. I want your times at my home to be remembered by you as happy carefree times."

"I can see and I feel it in my bones, that you are carrying a heavy responsibility of some kind or other, and I have never questioned what your profession is, in your time you will tell me, but remember yin and yang as my sensei taught me; life is a complete circle, with good and bad, sadness and happiness integral parts. Each must be experienced to appreciate life to the full."

"If your life has been hard and demanding up to now, then surely you are at the threshold of enjoyable times. I am selfish enough to want that to start here with us, in the bosom of people who care for you, OK? Now will you forgive me for teasing you?"

Care and consideration were attributes that Tammy had rarely experienced prior to meeting Donald and his family, and it left him with a feeling of non control that he wasn't sure he enjoyed. The only time in the past that anyone had been decent to him was when they wanted something from him.

This freely given solicitude and respect were alien in a way he found hard to understand. Only one instance in his past had been similar, when an Asian family had accorded him their deference and friendship.

"Donald, what can I say! The right words are in my brain, but seem lost on my tongue. I love being here! You are right, I should relax. There is none who would do me harm, I know it! I promise I'll try not to be such a stuffy starchy character, I owe you that much, that's for sure."

He slapped Donald on the back, pronouncing grandly,

"Behold the newborn Tammy, the life and soul of any party, talking of which, lead on, and may the girls be willing and the wine free-flowing. Aye! And may the singing pull the heartstrings and reduce us to tears, for our Celtic souls demand we enjoy ourselves unto sufferance. There is no better way to end any party than to sing the old greetin songs."

Mari was like a bantam hen with two chicks as she clucked and fussed them into the spacious rear of the Daimler, which the chauffeur had been told to get nicely warmed.

She dropped them off at the garden gate of the little stone cottage nestling in the trees. The sound of merrymaking was a continual throbbing furore emanating from the open door of welcome.

The knock to announce their arrival went totally unheard, but eyes had been watching for them. Conal and his wife met them with outstretched arms of welcome.

They were ushered in and brimming glasses of poteen pressed upon them. Tammy was introduced all round and had the honour of being offered a seat. This he declined, saying he would rather fill from the bottom upwards. This put him in Conal's good graces straight away, for he liked a man who was not afraid of a good wee tot or so.

Donald's eyes were almost spinning in his head as they searched and searched the crowded room. Conal noticed the almost frantic survey and the anxious face, but said nothing to ease the obvious agitation of his favourite guest. Mischievously he smiled to himself, and winked a ponderous wink at Tammy, meanwhile jerking his head in Donald's direction.

Tammy smiled and entered the tacit conspiracy with enthusiasm. Had not his friend had a wee tease at him? He knew that Donald was getting anxious that perhaps Siobhan had decided not to come to the party.

In his agitation Donald gulped down a deep draught of his drink, and as the fiery liquid retaliated with a burning malevolence, he cursed his indiscretion as he rattled his tongue around his mouth, trying to cool a scalded palate.

With a suspicion of tears in his eyes, he trumpeted into his handkerchief, and removed the evidence of his weakness with an unobtrusive wipe.

Conal immediately filled his glass and casually remarked that he didn't know if Siobhan would manage to attend the party, for sure hadn't she gone to fetch her cousin whose mother had died recently, and sure it was quite a distance away, was it not.

As Donald twitched noticeably at this innocent aside, Conal's wife took pity on him and putting a sympathetic hand on Donald's arm drew him towards the door. She had spotted the two girls coming up the garden path.

As soon as Donald saw Siobhan, he extricated himself gently from Mrs Duggan's hold and melted back into the safety of the crowd. When the two girls entered he turned and waved with friendly nonchalance.

Tammy watched this little charade with a smile on his face. 'Aye, lad! You're a goner there!' he thought, 'and I don't blame you, she's a beauty, if ever I saw one.'

His eyes lighted on the second girl and he nearly dropped his glass, she was like a twin of her cousin. The same tawny hair and flashing eyes, it was only later that the difference between the girls became obvious, that one pair of eyes was a deep disturbing brown, while the other pair was bright green with hazel flecks.

He remembered his jest to Donald, may all the girls be willing. All he wanted at this moment was for this beauty to be willing to even talk to him.

Grabbing Donald by the arm, he started dragging him forcibly across the room in the direction of the girls.

"Donald! By the green grass of Kerry, I need an introduction to a fair colleen. The first of this pair I take to be Siobhan, but I want to meet her companion, badly!"

They reached the two girls and Donald introduced Siobhan to Tammy. She saw straight away that Tammy was lost. Impishly she engaged him in conversation he neither heard or wanted.

"Oh, by the way," she admitted, when she had extracted the maximum from the fraught emotion-charged vibrations, "this is my first cousin, Bridget, she is going to be living with me from now on."

Tammy leapt forward and captured the slim white hand that had been held out in his general direction.

"My beautiful lady," he burst forth with hitherto uncommon verbosity, "come and I will look after you and get you a drink. I am a stranger to these shores, so let us comfort each other and perhaps we may become friends."

Donald and Siobhan looked deep into each other's eyes and smiled, they recognised what had happened between Tammy and Bridget and were happy for them.

Siobhan closed up to Donald in one decisive stride and wrapped her arms around his waist. Deliberately she squeezed her full body length against him, and felt him quiver like an overstrung harp, vibrating as the ancient summons of nature suffused his treacherous body into responses he couldn't control. Firmly she held him as he tried to ease away from her disturbing presence.

She turned her mouth up into the curve of his neck and whispered.

"If you make me chase you, I will! But I'd rather you accept that I love you, and not for you to keep shying away like a startled fawn in the forest. Am I so hard to love? Because, I honestly feel that, despite yourself, you do love me. Something prevents you from committing yourself, can't you tell me what it is, sweetheart?"

Donald gulped as his diaphragm failed to operate correctly. His grip tightened on this entrancing creature within the circle of his arms. Desperately he struggled to become articulate. He coughed, opened his mouth to speak. Closed it again. Taking a deep shuddering breath to steady himself, he began in a voice hoarse with strain, to explain the fears that still held him captive at times.

Somehow as he related the quiet courtship of Mary, and how she had died, he realised he was finding true relief for the first time, and his heart responded by filling with joy, knowing that he could go forward from here and court this lovely, lovely girl.

Finishing his discourse, he astonished everyone in the room, himself and Siobhan included, by taking her more firmly into his arms and kissing her directly on those enticing full red lips.

Disregarding the entire company, he found that Siobhan was returning his kiss with unreserved passion, and the promise of fulfilment in time to come.

The thunderous applause, clapping, shouting and whistling brought them back to the sensibilities of the occasion, and they broke close contact with a final little hug for each other. Still keeping a firm hold on his publicly demonstrated love, Donald led Siobhan deeper into the room where a space on the settee was made available to them. The fact that they had to squeeze together was only an added pleasure, for constant contact was desirous to both of them.

Donald glanced across to where Tammy and Bridget were sitting and noticed that Tammy had certainly made progress in his charming of Siobhan's cousin, for she was gazing up into his eyes as if he was Merlin the wizard performing some special magic for her alone.

The party waxed in vigour and sound, giving testimony that everyone was enjoying themselves to the full. Each conversation was conducted at shouting pitch as poteen loosened tongues and shattered inhibitions.

Mrs Duggan hammered on the side of a galvanised bucket in an attempt to quell the sound so that she could announce that food was available and would everybody get stuck into it and eat their fill.

It was plain, but filling, fare. Irish stew, with suet dumplings light as fairy puffballs floating on top, all this in a container the size of a horse trough, or so it appeared. Great heaped platters of new baked bread stood nearby to help satisfy the young appetites, with whole cheeses and pickles available if required.

For half an hour probably peace reigned as the party goers indulged themselves to repletion, then Conal stood up and announced it was party piece time. This meant that it was expected that you would sing for your supper, more or less.

Each member in attendance had to sing, dance, tell a story or act out a charade. It was no time for shyness, but the amount of drink that had been consumed guaranteed that there would be few refusals.

Without reservation or false modesty, Conal started the entertainment, singing 'The Maid with the Nut Brown Hair', and if he sang it directly to his own sweet little wife, nobody minded, for he had a pleasant basso profundo voice that carried the melody in good measure.

Mrs Duggan responded to his amorous serenade by playing on the Irish Harp, and Donald felt the hair on the nape of his neck prickle, as shivers ran up and down his spine.

The flickering fingers, scampering and capering over the harpstrings, evoked such a sweet, soul-wrenching melodious accomplishment that he felt as though Mrs Duggan was playing on the strings of his heart. He was aware of tears in his eyes as the strains of the old melody seemed to finally wash away the last vestiges of his loss in the past. Unashamedly he let the tears roll as if the salt water was his own baptism into the start of a new life.

Siobhan, clinging close to him, sensed the evaporation of yesteryear's distress and suffering, the cleansing of the poisons, and silently held him until the inner storm passed. In this crucible of tacit sympathy and understanding was their love finally forged into an indestructible force that would stand the test of time.

When Mrs Duggan quietly faced the tune into a final quivering note, Donald rose from his seat and went across to her. Dropping to his knees he put his arms around her and embraced her, somehow knowingly she held his head to her ample bosom as comforting as a mother with a troubled child.

"You are an angel," choked Donald, "and you play like one. You will never know what that melody did for me, but I thank you anyway."

Mrs Duggan kissed his cheek and murmured softly,

"Oh, I think I understand alright, it's why I played it. Now go to that dear girl, and love her in freedom and happiness, go you now."

One of the young riders jumped up and told a story about this minister who stood up in the pulpit and said there was some who're singing, and some who're not, emphasizing the who're as whore. Mrs Duggan was outraged and gave him a smack on the side of the head, telling him to keep his mind and his mouth clean in her house or out he would go.

Conal, biting the insides of his lips to prevent the loud guffaw bubbling deep in his throat from breaking forth, waved an admonishing finger the size of a banana, but was unable to remonstrate verbally or he would have lost control of the bottled up mirth.

There were many stories told and old traditional songs sung, often with more enthusiasm than musical ability, as with the step dancing, but it was not an audition, it was a crowd of people having a happy time.

One young man had brought his buttonkey accordion, and there was utter silence as he played the beloved Danny Boy. The deep mourning and sense of loss could be heard in every throbbing note of the beautiful melody.

Tears were in evidence again in many eyes, but it is to be remembered that a good Celtic gathering needs to evoke the troubles and sufferings of the past. It's as if they have to be aired and dusted and put one more time to rest. A tribute paid willingly to ancestors and the ancient Celtic Gods who were one and the same thing, were they not?

Conal came over to Donald, seemingly absent-mindedly topping up the half empty glass, and asked Donald if he would oblige with a rendering of his choice.

At first Donald demurred, he had never sung a note since the night Mary died, and had vowed that he never ever would again. Siobhan looked deep into his eyes, making no effort to hide the appeal, a raw hunger and desire that banished the reticence in the heart lifting need to please.

Leaning forward, he kissed her lightly on that irresistible mouth, then nodded his acquiescence.

He stood up, cleared his throat that had suddenly gone dry and tight, gave a slight self-conscious cough, then, to gain a few moments to regain composure, he looked across to Mrs Duggan and asked her if she would be willing to accompany him on the harp, as he hadn't sung for quite some time and he might stray from the tune.

Mrs Duggan assured him it would be her pleasure, and strummed her hands across the strings to signify her state of readiness.

Siobhan edged forward on the sofa and took his hand, giving him moral and physical support. Gently he squeezed her hand as his chin lifted and he started to sing.

The clear youthful tenor had lost none of its clarity, as he sang an old Irish love song he had learned at his mother's knee, and which now was more than applicable to the new love of his life. From this night on it would be their song, and be sung on many occasions but never with the poignance of this first time.

"The pale moon was rising, above the green mountain,
The sun was declining beneath the blue sea."

The hush of the audience was reverent. Any Irish gathering recognises good singing, and this was of the finest quality, holding a semi-drunken crowd spellbound, as the notes rippled through the hush of best order.

"that made me love Siobhan, the Rose of Tralee."

Donald had deliberately changed the name of the girl, to include the name of his new love, and hoped that if ever the songwriter heard of the deviation he would forgive the indiscretion in the knowledge that it had been in the cause of love, just as his beautiful song had been.

As the final words died away, the room erupted with shouts of more! more!, but Donald smiled in negation and dropped down onto the sofa beside Siobhan, who was weeping openly.

"Och! Surely it was not that bad," he joked, kissing the salty glistening eyes. "I really gave it my best shot."

Shaking her head, Siobhan clung to him and wailed as she answered,

"Oh, I love you Donald, how I love you! That was so beautiful I couldn't help crying. Don't you know that a woman at her happiest just has to cry, and look you around, there are plenty watery eyes in this company, it was just so beautiful."

Conal and his wife were beside them, Mrs Duggan kissing at him, Conal slapping him on the back and furiously giving frantic futile dabs at his eyes, punctuated by mammoth sniffs.

"Hell boy, you can sing like a bloody lark. In fact, you are a full blown dawn chorus on your own. Here, have another dram. Nobody deserves it more. Hells teeth, we'll have another song out of you tonight before we're finished. You stilled the savage breast here tonight, I'll tell you. You struck the buggers dumb. It's as if my poteen, and it's good stuff, had been water."

Tammy and Bridget managed to squeeze into a space beside Donald and Siobhan, their eyes told the tale of the emotive stress they had undergone.

Tammy hunkered down in front of Donald and took both his hands into his own. Looking up into his friend's face he said,

"Donald, remember our conversation before we left for the party, I said may the women be willing, the wine flowing and finish the evening with the greetin songs? Well I must have been struck with a lucky star, because all these things have happened here tonight. I have never cried in my life since I came out of nappies, for it was considered not the thing to do, but I looked around here tonight and found that each and everyone was as moved as I, and there was no shame in the crying. It is as natural a phenomenon as laughing and it is absolutely wonderful to be able to cry with your friends as it is to laugh."

"Now, I want to say this while it is in my mind. It is not the poteen talking. My life has altered dramatically since I met you, and thank God I ever did. Younger you may be, but you taught me that life can be fun, as you said it could, and I am as happy as I could ever possibly be. What a friend you are."

Giving Donald's hands a final squeeze, Tammy stood up and, putting his arm around Bridget, drew her to the side to let the other members of the company come forward to say a few words to Donald, who was quite taken aback at the sensation he had generated in this happy throng. He was well pleased that he hadn't let his host or hostess down, however, to him that would have been unforgivable.

The party drew to a close with the old traditional songs being sung in chorus, and although not quite the quality of a trained choir, the enthusiasm was paramount, everyone giving of his or her best.

Goodnights were repetitive and vociferous. Conal shouting that morning rides were still the order of the day, and he would personally skin alive any absentees, which was a bit of a contradiction in terms, but everybody got his meaning. There would be a few sore heads, and impromptu stops to be sick, but they would all turn up.

At the garden gate there was a marked reluctance for Donald and Siobhan, Tammy and Bridget to part and so end this magical night. Eros had struck a mighty blow with double effect.

The lovers hovered and touched, kissed and stroked, the lingering enchantment holding them fettered by invisible chains.

With a shuddering, quivering breath, Donald pulled himself free.

"We must say goodnight," he gasped, "it will soon be time for morning rides. We will see you both then. Both of you come over, for I intend to introduce Tammy to the horses today. He must get to know the pleasure of riding and become one of us completely. Now, goodnight, or good morning, or whatever, but a firm goodbye."

One last lingering touch and he whirled around and started off for home, after a few steps Tammy ranged up alongside him.

"What a night this has been," he wondered aloud, "I feel I am walking on cloud nine, if that's the number of paradise. Do you know, Donald? I feel totally intoxicated and yet I went easy on that old poteen that Conal was so liberal with. I tell you, that Bridget is inside my skin, it's the only way to describe the feeling. Donald, I mean to make her my wife, and as soon as I can decently accomplish it. Would you be my best man? Or hey? What about a double wedding? What do you think?"

Tammy in his euphoria was prattling and chattering like an Aberdonian fishwife. Donald grinned at his exuberant friend.

"I hope this cloud nine is easy on the feet," he interjected, politely stopping the verbal twittering, "for we have a fair few miles to travel, in the course of the night I completely forgot to arrange a lift home. I can see that you have enough steam to reach Killarney, so I don't suppose you'll mind a wee daunder of a few miles."

"The answer to your questions is yes to both. I will be delighted to be your best man, and yes, we could think of a double wedding, but don't you think we should ask the girls first if they are in agreement?"

Donald's quick ears picked up the sound of a vehicle and he spotted the flash of headlights some distance off. He wondered if they were about to be offered a lift home.

This proved to be the case. The estate Landrover growled into view. The window was lowered as it pulled up alongside and his mother's dulcet tones were music to Donald's ears.

"Now then, you dirty stop-outs! If you are drunk you can walk, if you are sober, you can ride. Get in here you pair of tomcats, your night on the tiles stops here."

Tammy tumbled into the back and Donald climbed into the front and kissed his mother lovingly.

"You shouldn't have stayed up to come and fetch us," his voice caressed her, "we deserve to walk. You have a full and heavy day ahead of you tomorrow."

Mari ran her hand gently down her son's cheek.

"I'll be fine, don't worry. I wanted to stay up and see you. I have this strange feeling that this night has been of particular importance to you, and I also have the same feeling about Tammy. You know your dad says I have this funny gift, well it has plagued me all night. Now then! Are you going to prove me right, or wrong? At least put my mind at peace."

From the rear came the sound of a loud gasp as Tammy's breath was inhaled in shuddering intensity. The accuracy of this woman's premonition was startling to say the least. He was not naive, he had heard of the gift of second sight, but this was his first encounter with it personally.

Donald turned and soothed his startled friend.

"It's alright, Tammy, she is not a witch. She is a beautiful, loving mother, with this particular little gift. I've grown up with it, so I just tend to accept it, however, I'll grant you it can be a trifle disconcerting when you meet it face to face for the first time."

Impatiently Mari intervened, "Never mind that old nonsense, tell me what happened or I shall drive you round the country till you are dizzy, but I want to know before we reach home." She placed her hand on Donald's thigh and continued, "please, pretty please. Tell your old mother this instant."

The last few words were delivered in an imperious voice, not pleading as the words suggested, and accompanied by a robust shake of Donald's leg.

Donald leaned across and kissed the flushed cheek of his querulous mother, the scent of her eau-de-cologne as reassuring as it had been all through his early years.

Peace my darling," he soothed lovingly, "we will divulge all. You would have been the first to know anyhow."

"I have decided on the girl I want to marry, and coincidentally, so has Tammy. The girl I want to marry is the daughter of our senior rider, Eddie O'Flaherty. She is called Siobhan. She joined the stud staff quite recently. She and I are responsible for the initial training of the starters."

"I tried not to become involved, because of no other reason than fear of a repetition of what happened with Mary. Siobhan has helped me to lay that ghost. I realise it is behind me, and I can go forward in life and not live in the past. Oh, mum! I do love her."

Mari stopped the Landrover, she turned and swept Donald into her arms, tears streaming down her face.

"Oh! Thank God in his mercy," she cried, "oh, Donald! I am so happy for you. I have been so worried. I knew you still had sadness in your heart over Mary."

"We all loved that bonny wee lass, and Donald, she would be happy for you, I know she would. She was such an unselfish person herself. Oh, Donald, this is really the best Christmas present you could give me. When can I meet her? Is she coming to the party on Christmas eve?"

Donald intruded into the spate of questions bubbling from his excited mother's lips.

"Whoa mum, take a breath a minute, all the questions will be answered in time, but don't you think you are being a wee bit rude to Tammy? He also found his dream girl tonight and you haven't even acknowledged it yet."

Mari whirled in utter mortification onto her knees, in a flash she had hold of Tammy across the back of the seat and bodily dragged him forward and kissed him soundly.

"What can you think of me? Tammy, oh Tammy, please forgive me! I'm not used to having two sons, but I'll improve, I promise you. I am happy for you, Tammy, really I am. I want you to promise that you will get married and have the reception at Barranbarrach. Will you promise me that?"

For the second time that night, or was it morning, Tammy was in tears. He clung to the endearing woman who had called him son, stroking the long beautiful auburn tresses with gentle tenderness, he assured her that she would have complete control of all arrangements, for truth to tell he had nobody else in the world, no living kin anywhere.

Taking a deep breath, Mari arranged herself behind the steering wheel and, selecting first gear, eased forward, homeward bound.

"I'd better get you two scallywags home, you will need at least a couple of hours sleep before work starts," she asserted, but the weepiness was still evident in her tremulous voice. "Oh, my boys! I wish you both so much happiness, and if I could, I would cast a spell to invoke all the gods to create you an Eden in which to live for the rest of your lives. That, of course, is wishful thinking, and more than likely you'll have to take your lumps like everyone else."

The morning of the 23rd of December dawned brisk and clear. The green hills of Antrim gave credence to the words of the songs attributed to them. The air was sharp and invigorating, penetrating into the lungs with searing intensity, but the oxygen was pure and clear, which helped to dispel the over indulgence of some of the previous evening's revellers.

The frost had crystallised the snow into a crackling, glittering whiteness that brought pain to the bleary eyes, and intensified the already blinding headaches that the majority suffered.

The exercising was confined to the covered training areas, which eased conditions somewhat for the hapless riders. 'Never again' was the lamentation as the horses were put through their routines. Conal sat on his Clydesdale mare, completely disregarding the remarks, knowing that if he proclaimed another party that very night, all of them would be there in force.

After lunch, Donald took Tammy down to the stud office, where they met the girls as planned. Tammy grabbed Bridget and hung on to her as if she was his only salvation in this venture that he could not escape.

The two girls were dressed in riding breeches and warm woollen thick-knit jumpers. Both wore ski type knitted helmets pulled down over their ears, knee length riding boots completed the outfits. They were as alike as two peas in a pod, they could easily have been identical twins.

Donald decided they would take Tammy round the stallion boxes first of all and when they entered the square courtyard heads were already hanging over the half doors.

Donald went directly to the loosebox that held his Arab stallion. Lovingly he palmed the questing muzzle a sugar lump, then opened the door and pushed the colt deeper into the box as he made his entrance quietly.

"Come in, Tammy," he said invitingly, as he beckoned his friend forward. Tammy hovered uncertainly until Bridget took his hand and gently guided him within.

Four people and the colt filled the loosebox, but the young stallion stood unperturbed by this invasion of his space. He nibbled at Donald, wanting another tidbit. Donald crooned and stroked the silky head, inviting Tammy to do the same.

Hesitantly, Tammy obliged. Gingerly he put his hand on the gleaming coat, and as his hand slid down the silken neck he exclaimed in wonder.

"He feels absolutely wonderful, so soft and smooth and warm. He really is beautiful, Donald, and so gentle. I would never have believed it."

Donald allowed Tammy to continue stroking the colt for a while, then he passed him a sugar lump.

"Hold it in the palm of your open hand," he instructed his friend, "and you will feel how really gentle he is."

As the soft lips picked the sugar lump cleanly from Tammy's hand he experienced a feeling that he never would have thought possible. He was actually liking being here, close to what he's previously termed as big smelly brutes. He decided there and then that he would get Donald, or perhaps Bridget, to teach him how to ride.

They visited each of the stallions in turn, then decided to look at the mares. As they passed the building at the end of the stallion yard, Tammy, who was now asking endless questions, asked what was housed in that particular stable.

"It's not a stable," smiled Donald, knowing where this was leading, "it's a covering shed," and sure enough, the question came.

"What is a covering shed?" asked Tammy, in all innocence.

"It is where we bring the mares to the stallions to be impregnated, or covered as we say in the horse world," Donald explained patiently, with a smile flickering at the corners of his mouth. Tammy had blundered into that one, he thought.

Tammy went bright red and looked down at his feet, which were shuffling in embarrassment.

"Oh, I see!" he whispered weakly. His three companions laughed in amusement at his discomfort. Dear, oh dear, weren't these townies naive at times?

Bridget took hold of Tammy's hand, pressing it compassionately she explained the need for the covering shed.

"Tammy! On a farm or stud everything follows a natural progression, but a good manager has to intervene as he tries to improve his stock by careful selection. In the wilds it is survival of the fittest, and the strongest get to breed with the females. In our sphere we select which are the best qualities for what we want of the males and females, and we breed to those strengths."

Fully into her stride now, she continued,

"There is one thing over which we have no control however, and that is when a mare will come into season, or heat as it is sometimes referred to. Until she does it is no use bringing her to a stallion for she would not accept him, and in all probability, because she wouldn't be giving off the right odour, the stallion would have little interest in her."

"There is no foreplay as such to get the mare ready for mating as there is with humans, so we have to let nature decide the correct time for coupling. Procreation is a wonderful gift, Tammy. There is nothing unclean about natural intercourse. It is a necessary part of our creation. I am well advised that such an act between a man and woman who love each other is unparalleled, the definitive gift to the giving and the receiving."

Donald and Siobhan had stood quietly waiting for Bridget to finish her dialogue, from time to time they had nodded their heads in agreement.

Siobhan, holding Donald's hand, offered an observation.

"Tammy, I feel quite sure that the attraction between yourself and Bridget wants and needs expression by the physical act of love. I know I find it hard not to demand Donald to forget the fetters of propriety and love me as I want him to. There is no point in being secretive or sneaky about it. It is a fact of life. We live within the mandates of propriety because of the demands of society, but the natural thing would be for us to quench the burning flame of natural want, but the ridiculous thing is, we require a marriage licence to allow us to be natural. It really is difficult to comprehend."

Tammy was standing looking completely nonplussed at these simple country folk, and wondered who had dreamt up such a stupid nomenclature to describe people such as these, who were neither simple nor unknowing.

They were disciples of ingenuity and forthright intelligence, with a keen insight into the important facts of life, and their affinity with their environment gave them a solid platform from which to project control of their own destinies. Truth and integrity of purpose guided them along the path of life with a sure and steady hand.

In an effort to lighten the mood slightly, Tammy bowed to his companions, cupping his crotch with both hands.

"I was not aware my randiness was so obvious," he smiled impishly, "but I thank you girls for the short discourses on life and its vagaries. I am not entirely without sophistication, but to have everything out in the open certainly makes life easier to cope with, and I'm glad we had this little discussion. My word! It is like being introduced to some new type of education in the easiest of way. I am a lucky guy."

The group strolled amongst the mares in a casual and easy companionship, and as usual, discussion on the merits or otherwise of each mare dominated the conversation.

When they arrived at the loosebox which held the little Arab mare, and Tammy was introduced to her, he was simply enraptured. He fondled her and gave her as many sugar lumps as Donald would allow him to. They had to physically drag him away in the end.

As they left the mare, Tammy posed the question to Donald as to whether he could be taught to ride. Donald informed him that there was every chance of that happening. It was a common belief at the stud that anyone who couldn't ride was an incomplete person.

It was decided that Tammy's riding lessons would have to be arranged around his visits to Barranbarrach, for, of course, his work was involved in being in Belfast.

No-one knew what Tammy's work or profession was, and none had posed the question. Tammy knew that soon he would have to give them a job description, but was loth to introduce unpleasantness into this idyllic rustic scene.

Chapter Twelve

December the 24th and Barranbarrach was a buzzing hive of activity. Mari ran hither and yon, a whirlwind of furious industry checking everything she could think of.

Cooking smells filled the air with mouthwatering promise, which was all the worse to bear when the family had to make do with a snack lunch when their senses told them better fare was at hand.

Casks of sherry and brandy stood behind the trestle tables that would support the more than ample assortment of food on offer. Flagons of cider, barrels of beer and even a supply of the illicit local poteen would be available to quench the acquired thirsts that would develop in the course of the long night ahead.

The huge Christmas tree in the hall had an ocean of separately wrapped parcels under its gaily festooned branches. There were of course many extras just in case unexpected guests appeared.

Stuart had agreed under pressure from Mari to be Santa Claus and dispense the gifts, but he had insisted that he would not subject himself, or anybody else to the idiotic 'Ho! Ho! Ho!' attributed to that personage.

The chauffeur had received secret instructions from Mari that on pain of death he would not reveal. He had to meet a privately chartered aircraft at the local airport at exactly seven o'clock and bring the passengers he met safely to Barranbarrach at all speed whilst ensuring they were warm and comfortable.

If anyone asked where he was going, he had the Madam's permission to lie and sin his soul, and Madam would personally give him absolution when he had carried out his unprecedented duty.

When Donald and Tammy went up to their rooms to get dressed for the function, Mari boldly accompanied them. Marching into Tammy's room ahead of him, she turned as he entered and watched his face when he spotted what was laid out neatly on the bed. A full evening suit complete with starched stiff fronted shirt, black bow tie with cummerbund to match, heavy gold cufflinks down to black silk socks and patent leather shoes.

Tammy just gaped, struck speechless, he looked at the splendid attire and couldn't believe his eyes.

Mari crossed to him and gathered him into her arms.

"Happy Christmas my dearest boy, I know it's a trifle early, but I thought perhaps you might like to wear it for us tonight? Don't think you will be the only one resplendent, I am going now to see my other son and whip him into shape, for he is the world's worst to get into an evening outfit."

As she was leaving the room she paused and said.

"By the way, if you are experiencing any difficulty getting into any of that apparel, just ring the bell and one of the maids will come and give you assistance."

When Mari entered Donald's room, he was sitting looking out of the window. He glanced round casually and smiled at the look of determination on his mother's face. The smile became fully fledged as he said jokingly.

"Ah! so it's to be 'kilty, kilty cold bum', tonight is it? Well I'm not sure if I can carry the tartan with the same boldness and dignity as my dad, but I have to learn to swing the kilt sometime, so it might as well start tonight."

Looking into his mother's astonished face, he chortled with delight and with shrewd appraisal continued.

"Aha! you thought you had a fight on your hands, which you were determined to win and now I have burst your bubble before it even began to float."

Quickly Mari crossed to him, burying her face in the softness of his neck she admonished him gently.

"You are a bad wee boy at times and it is not at all nice that you disappoint your mother. Yes my darling, I expected one ding dong of a battle. I am pleased that you are going to carry the tartan, after all it is your birthright. I'm sure you will look splendid. Right I'm off! I have a thousand things to do. Look in on Tammy in a minute and see if he is managing to get dressed alright."

At half past six the guests started to arrive. Mari and Stuart resplendent in their Highland evening dress stood in the main hall to greet everyone.

A happy word whilst coats were being removed and taken away. A glass of whatever the choice to each, then they were ushered into the large function hall, which would be full to capacity before long.

Donald and Tammy made a belated appearance and just in time, for Mari had been on the point of sending someone to hasten them.

As they descended the wide stairs they projected a striking exhibition of refined elegance. Mari had assessed the measurements of Tammy with formidable accuracy. His evening suit could have been made to measure, and the dark cloth accentuated his swarthy good looks, even though his face carried the scars of past conflicts.

Donald was a veritable golden boy, with the yellow blond hair, which he had tried to brush into some kind of order, his crowning glory.

Mari noticed that despite his earlier protestations of inability to emulate his father, he wore the tartan with a confident assurance and dignity that was a tribute to his sense of the occasion. Her discerning eyes noticed that instead of the Skean Dhubb, the black knife, in his right hand stocking, he wore the knife that had been presented to him by his sensei, Chi Li.

She smiled a secret smile, then hailed them warmly as she applauded their descent into the hall.

Mari ensured that Tammy was deeply involved with being introduced to those he had not met previously, and those presented to him were left in no doubt that this was someone special. Putting her arm around him from time to time she would give him a slight loving squeeze.

Stuart and Donald were going dizzy trying to keep up with her directives, but they complied willingly and uncomplainingly, long used to her natural administrative abilities and being her loving slaves.

The ornately carved grandfather clock struck the hour of seven and a vision of loveliness in duplicate entered the hall. Siobhan and Bridget had arrived.

Both wore shimmering creations of green, in slightly differently shades. Siobhan had her lustrous auburn hair piled high on her head, accentuating the graceful sweep of her slim flawless neck, with the determined little chin held high, leading in an almost defiant manner. The graceful outline of a superb figure showed through the gossamer like transparency of the magnificent gown.

Donald's breath whistled as he inhaled with a delighted gasp of appreciation of this lovely enchanting creature.

He had only ever seen Siobhan dressed in breeches and blouses with windcheater jackets to fend off the cold, and they had not been too complimentary to her figure. This apparition of loveliness was the thing that dreams were made of, she was no ugly duckling at any time but this transformation was outstanding.

Moving trance-like he went across to her. He saw the nervousness in her eyes and his heart went out to her anew. She was obviously anxious about meeting his parents and in particular the protective Mari, who she was bound to have heard about. He rushed across to her side to give her comfort and support.

Tammy was in a like state as he accompanied Donald across the hall and as he looked at Bridget an unreasoning fear bit deeply into him for a second. How was he ever going to get this beautiful girl to agree to be his wife. By hook or by crook he thought as he went towards her, then his heart lurched tumultuously as he saw the gladsome welcome in her eyes.

Each of the young men unashamedly gathered his sweetheart into his arms and kissed them a greeting, then Donald, his arm firmly around the waist of Siobhan drew her forward to meet his parents, who had deliberately hung back to allow the initial greeting to be carried out by the two young men.

Mari stepped forward and took hold of Siobhan in a warm embrace, kissing her on both cheeks, she held her tightly as she whispered softly.

"You are the most beautiful girl I have ever seen, but then I am biased already. I would never have been afforded the chance of choosing a wife for Donald. He is his own man, but I couldn't have done a better job."

"I hope you will feel at ease with us and I pray you to believe you are more welcome here than I can find words to express. Stay with me for a few moments, for I am loth to be out of your company. I promise you will get time with Donald, I couldn't be that selfish and keep you separate for long."

Stuart came forward and gently prised them apart.

"Hello sweet girl." he welcomed Siobhan, "watch that woman, she'll smother you with love given half the chance. Mind I'm nearly as bad myself," he continued, as he swept her into his brawny arms, kissing her soundly and giving her a squeeze that made her gasp at the raw strength she felt in his embrace.

Mari was now holding Bridget, welcoming her to the party and telling her how beautiful she looked, then, for goodness sake where was a drink for these poor wee girls.

The three men danced attention until Mari was at length appeased, but when Donald suggested that it was time to enter the main hall, Mari seemed somewhat reluctant.

Stuart looked at her in genuine puzzlement. This certainly wasn't the Mari he knew. Normally she would be in there exhorting the music makers to determined efforts to get things buzzing, and here she was procrastinating like a reluctant bride. Gathering the two girls on either side of him, he announced firmly that it was time to join the festivities.

Mari heaved a frustrated sigh, but followed her husband obediently, holding on to Donald and Tammy on each arm. Glancing back at the clock, she checked the time. Almost half past seven. Another quarter of an hour she thought. Ah well! She would engineer a return to the hall at that time come hell or high water.

A great cheer heralded their entrance and the band responded by playing a measure of Scotland the Brave in tribute to the Scottish influence. Stuart held up his hands and announced the party was officially opened and dare any one not to enjoy himself there would be hell to pay.

At quarter to eight Mari had Stuart, Donald, Tammy and the girls back in the main foyer on a pretext without subtlety or deviation. Stuart was to open a bottle of champagne, the girls were to make ready a silver tray with champagne flutes and

Donald and Tammy were directed to go to the open doorway and be ready to meet and greet some late arrivals.

Her timing was precisely accurate, for as the two somewhat reluctant pressganged ushers approached the door, the Daimler glided to a halt at the bottom of the steps.

Donald and Tammy descended the steps to open the door of the car and Tammy heard Donald gasp as if he had received a blow to the midriff. Glancing enquiringly at this friend he saw that Donald had gone very pale, and wondered at the cause.

Donald almost fell down the remaining steps in his haste to wrench open the doors and get at the smiling trio who sat within. He literally dived in amongst them, trying to embrace them all at once, tears streaming down his face as he tried to articulate and kiss and cuddle at the same time.

He was caught in a maelstrom of an emotional storm, crying "oh dear, well well, oh dear, oh dear" in a tormented litany of incredulity.

Desperately he pull a deep steadying breath. Articulation returned to a tongue that had lost its ability.

"I cannot believe it, I just can't!" he choked out. "Oh, this is a feast to my eyes. Oh, please excuse me, whatever am I doing? Please let us go inside, deary me, deary me. When was this arranged? No! No! You don't have to tell me. It was my mother! Oh! What a woman she is!"

By this time , Mari and Stuart and the girls had reached the bottom of the steps to join Tammy, who was standing with a bemused look on his face.

Donald reversed out of the Daimler and, still holding the hand of a smartly dressed dowager, drew her gently from the car. He turned to Tammy and with excitement ringing in his voice, declared with proprietary delight.

"This is Lady Fiona Cruachan and her husband Lord Hamish Cruachan," as he pointed to his old friend stepping out of the Daimler.

They shook hands with Tammy and were introduced to Siobhan and Bridget, meanwhile Donald was busy with the third member of the visitors. He scooped the slight figure out of the car and clung to him with fierce passion. Unreservedly he kissed the wrinkled cheeks and folded his sensei to his chest in a back breaking hug.

Putting a break on his emotions, he let loose and stepped back, and fighting for composure, he bent low in a deep bow.

"I see you master and offer you a hundred thousand welcomes to my home, which is yours, as I am, to command. You are welcome as the freshness of spring and my heart is full of your coming."

Tammy was most intrigued at the formalised greeting, but in a flash of intuition that would have done credit to Mari's wee gift, realised that this was the man who had developed the fighting skills of his friend.

The slight framed figure emanated a composure and dignity, an aura of efficiency and confidence evident in his bearing, that showed in his protege at an equal level. The strong bond that existed between them was evident, a deep respect for each other that no formal exercise could conceal.

Tammy drew near and stood for a moment whilst the keen eyes raked him in an all encompassing appraisal. The dark head nodded a brief acknowledgement, then Chi Li advanced and offered his hand. As Tammy's hand enclosed it, he felt the hard edge of callous along the outer edge that matched his own. He also sensed the steely strength within the grip and knew he was in the presence of a formidable warrior. He understood at last, the source of Donald's complete science in the martial arts.

At last the latecomers reached the main foyer where they were divested of coats and trappings and were well into their first drinks. The party was now in full swing and as midnight approached an added excitement seemed to develop. Everybody likes receiving presents and the skilful distribution of the gifts from the hand of the squire created no feeling of Maundy Money, rather a genuine appreciation of goodwill amongst friends.

Donald required no more gifts than the company of all his favourite people around him. His euphoria was almost tangible. The stimulus of alcohol was unnecessary. He glowed with happiness and was delighted when Chi Li approved of his choice of sweetheart, as did Hamish and Fiona, who were delighted that Donald had found a potential wife of Siobhan's calibre.

It had taken Fiona a very short time to establish that here was a girl of spirit, determination and intelligence, almost cast from the same mould as Mari herself. Well, was it not a known fact that a son looks for a wife with the attributes of his mother?

An hour before midnight was reserved for the singing of Christmas carols led by Mari and Stuart, then Stuart in his role of squire read a relevant passage from the bible.

Lord Cruachan said grace, thanking the Lord for the bountiful feast that was spread before them. He took this occasion to thank the many involved in the preparation of such a splendid evening.

The great hall clock struck the magic hour and with squeals of delight a mass exodus to the main foyer became almost a stampede in the excitement of the guests.

Stuart appeared in his Santa Claus costume and created such merriment with a most exaggerated 'Ho! Ho! Ho!' that he had vowed he would not commit himself to.

He lifted the first present, read out the name on the tag and presented it with a flourish, pointing at his cheek for a kiss from the recipient, who blushed demurely but complied

Conal announced to all that damned if he was going to be doing any kissing of that whiskery old brute, the hooting and laughter that followed this observation indicated the tremendous rapport that held them in harmony.

Each gift was named for an individual, so that those receiving it, knew it had been chosen especially for them alone. It had taken Mari and her mother many hours of diligent selection to amass the amount of presents to accommodate the entire workforce and dependants of the estate.

When all the estate workers had received their gifts and wandered back into the main hall, Mari indicated that her house guests and sons and daughters-in-law-to-be, as she viewed them, were to remain in the outer foyer.

Giving each a glass of champagne, and even Chi Li accepted a glass, she then explained that, as she was the only one who knew that Fiona, Hamish and Chi Li would be attending the party, she had taken it upon herself to get them a little something to mark the occasion.

For the Cruachan's there was a matching pair of beautiful crystal decanters, complete with a set of glasses for every type of drink possible, in splendid Waterford Crystal. That they were of the highest quality was evident, as the facets scintillated with the brilliance of new cut diamonds. The high clear chime as one glass was tapped against another signified only too clearly why the simile to be as clear as crystal, came into use.

Mari crossed to stand in front of Chi Li and smiled fondly at this man she held in high regard. A trifle apprehensively she proffered the gift wrapped package and said, "Chi Li, I hope I have chosen well for you. I especially wanted your gift to be fitting, but also practical, for I know so well how fripperies and foibles offend you. Please accept this gift, this small offering as a token of the esteem in which we all hold you."

Chi Li bowed and took the package from hands that trembled slightly, aware that Mari was concerned and feeling a measure of disquiet. He crossed quickly to the hall table and deftly removed the wrappings with his usual economy of movement and effort. He removed the lid of the cardboard box, went statue still with his eyes fixed on the contents.

The onlookers waited with baited breath. Had Mari committed a faux pas? Was the present unsuitable? Was Chi Li compiling a gracious thankyou for something he neither need nor wanted? Donald, mentally attuned to the feelings of his sensei, knew he was under stress, although no indication was apparent on the wrinkled face, and his heart went out to him.

Chi Li turned from the table, crossed to Mari, and shook everyone to the core, when he lifted her hand and kissed the fragrant skin. He was not normally a demonstrative man.

"Dear lady, I know not how you came by this tribute, but that it gave you great trouble to acquire I am sure. I am unworthy of such indulgence, but I crave your pardon and accept with all my heart such a wonderful gift. Your choice is perfect in every possible way. I thank you for your generosity and the perceptiveness of your choice."

The gift consisted of a set of antique Chinese rice bowls in eggshell porcelain, six in all, with an equal number of serving spoons in the same delicate composition. Additionally there were two sets of carved chopsticks in the purest ivory, the creamy texture indicating a like antiquity to the dishes.

Mari's face flushed with pleasure and relief at Chi Li's words of thanks, and with more aplomb, turned to the four youngsters of the group.

For Siobhan, a Celtic brooch with a Cairngorm stone. For Bridget a Celtic Cross on a heavy gold chain. Tammy became the owner of a gold signet ring. Donald was presented with his great grandfather's crumach, the Celtic walking stick of a gentleman.

Not to be outdone, the Cruachan's produced a crate of ten year old malt whisky for Stuart and a diamond studded necklet for Mari. A little whispered consultation produced a pair of red Macdonald plaids for the girls and a chased silver hip flask for Tammy.

Unfortunately there was no gift available for Donald, as there had been no way to parcel it up and transport it. However, with the flourish of a magician producing a rabbit out of a hat, Hamish brought forth a bulky and important looking set of documents from his inner pocket and handed it to Donald.

With a sense of something dramatic, Donald broke the embossed wax seal, undid the ribbon and opened the sheets of parchment. He realised it was something of great importance couched in legal terms. As his eyes ran down the formal prose, he gasped and read it again in disbelief at the words contained therein.

Wordlessly he handed the document to his father, while his mouth opened and closed like a stranded fish, desperately trying to form words. He looked at the Cruachan's who were quietly watching with self satisfied looks on their faces.

He heard the wind whistle into Stuart's lungs in a shuddering exclamation and he in turn passed the missive to Mari, who had been trying to read over Stuart's shoulder.

Quickly her eyes scanned the elaborate writing and looking up from the document she asked in hushed tones,

"Does this say what I think it does?" Hamish and Fiona were smiling broadly, as they nodded their heads in unison to the affirmative.

"Why should it not be?" queried Hamish, "we have no blood relatives, no sons or daughters of our own and there is no-one in the world we would rather have as our legatee than Donald. It is our considered opinion that he is a fine young man, well balanced and intelligent. He will make a good warder of our estates when we are gone from this world."

"There is a sting in the tail however, a rider that must be observed. He must at all times do everything in his power to keep the estate intact. He must be prepared to take on the responsibility to attend to the welfare of all the estate workers and their dependants, in the same way I have done during my regime."

Turning to Donald, he continued, "I am prepared to carry on for the next two or three years, but then I would like to be released from the burden. Within that time I would like you to return to your native glen and assume the responsibility of it and its people."

"Should you decide that you do not wish to accept this gift and the responsibilities that it is encumbered with, I will be forced to sell the estate and it would be liable to fall into the hands of an absent landlord, or much worse into the ownership of a business consortium, which is probably the more likely outcome. That is the last thing on this earth I would want to happen, for it would inevitably destroy a community that has survived down through the centuries, so I know it is moral and ethical blackmail Donald, but please say you will accept."

Donald looked at his parents, then at the Cruachans. He grasped Siobhan's hand, for a moment he was like a lost child. Good breeding will manifest itself, and most often in the face of crisis. Wetting his lips, he cleared his throat, but his voice was reedy thin as he struggled to express himself.

"This is a shock to my system," he declared, almost in falsetto, "a wonderful surprise, but it would be foolish of me to blurt out an immediate yes! The first reactive thought is to do just that, however I crave your indulgence and ask for a brief spell in which to think over this generous offer and quite honestly there are others whose council I must consider before I give my final verdict."

Hamish nodded his head in satisfaction.

"Donald, I expected no less, it is the thinking of a wise person to weigh up all the relevant facts and never to arrive at a hasty and ill conceived answer. I respect your wishes, with this proviso. I would like an answer before I depart from Barranbarrach on the second of January. Would that be in order? Will that be enough time for you to arrive at a decision?"

Donald agreed that he would provide confirmation one way or another by the due date and shook hands with Hamish to ratify the pact.

Stuart quietly pointed out that they had been in the hall for rather an extended period and it was about time they returned to their duties in respect of their guests, who must be wondering what was happening. With no further delay they returned to the main hall and joined the merry making that was running at fever pitch by now.

In the early hours of the morning, the party gradually wound down and the guests departed. Those that were left with any kind of articulation, thanked their host and hostess for a 'wunnerful' time, and with varying degrees of preambulative powers disappeared into the night.

For many the long walk home would create its own restorative panacea and they would be none the worse for a long evening of over indulgence.

The week preceding the new year, was given to brisk walks in the bracing cold of a winter that was behaving as it should. Sharp crackly mornings, with breath gusting white and feathery when exhalations punctuated the ethereal stillness that the shrouding snow held in thrall.

Returning to the warmth of one of the lounges for the cosy family chats, sometimes the men would play snooker, argue politics, or discuss horses. Expounding personal theories on a variety of subjects brought good natured banter, but also exchanged ideas in an easy informal setting.

Work as such was confined to the minimum necessary to the welfare of the winter housed stock, so it was a pleasant lazy spell for all concerned.

Donald thought long and hard about the decision he would soon have to make in reference to the legacy from the Cruachans. He decided to talk it through with his parents, but resolved to have Siobhan included in the discussion.

Mari had insisted, and as usual got her way, that the two girls remain at Barranbarrach for the duration of the holiday period, so there was no problem as to Siobhan being available at the discussion.

After breakfast on the 30th of December he asked the three of them if they would join him in the library. A cheery log fire burned brightly in the open hearth, and as they entered it created a warm welcoming glow and a pleasant ambience.

They gathered round the source of warmth, drawn like moths to a flame. Settling into the well worn leather chairs, the three faces turned to Donald. What he would have to say would affect all their lives in different ways.

Instead of asking his parents what he should do, as would have been quite normal, Donald began to speak almost as if he was thinking aloud and not really addressing an audience.

"I started out in life as son of a tenant farmer and there was no shame attached to that. It was a good life albeit work was hard and non-ending. Nevertheless, I was cared for in every possible way and never lacked the feeling of being loved. This is as good a platform as any one could ask for from which to project into life. The only criticism, is that perhaps my mother cosseted me a wee bit too much, but the love that lies behind that failing excuses it."

"I arrived at Barranbarrach and within days of being here, was made to understand that I am the inheritor of this large estate when my father decides to hand over full control. Now another factor has entered the equation that must be considered, and believe me I have pondered long and hard."

"What I would like to do is tell you my decision and then we can have a discussion to iron out any demurrals or arguments."

"I would like to take advantage of the offer from our old and dear friends and become the new master of Cruachan."

Turning to Siobhan, he looked deep into her eyes and with sincerity ringing strongly in his voice, he appealed to her.

"This is neither the time nor the place my love, but I am asking you to marry me and come to Cruachan as my wife and partner, and I know that is asking a lot in one breath. You know I love you and it was only going to be a matter of time before we got round to making the arrangements, so, I beg you, please say yes."

Siobhan stood up with feline grace and crossed over to him, where he leant against the mantel shelf as if taking strength from its solid bulk and enduring qualities.

"My darling, that I would have appreciated a more romantic proposal of marriage I won't deny, but, the answer would still have been the same. Yes! I will marry you and I would follow you to the ends of the earth, and if that is Cruachan so let it be; even if we have to lay some ghosts to rest when we get there, for I know you suffered great loss and pain there in the past. Yes! my darling I accept your proposal with all its connotations."

A chair could no longer hold Mari, she sprang to her feet and rushed across to where the young lovers were gazing into each others eyes. Wrapping her arms around them both she desperately tried to kiss them both at the same time.

"Oh! My darlings," she cried, "I am delighted beyond words. I hoped and prayed this is where the liaison was heading, you have made me a happy, happy, old mother."

Stuart came across in two deliberate strides. He kissed Siobhan on the cheek and shook Donald's hand.

"Well done boy," he gruffed, a suspicious glitter in his eyes, "she is the perfect choice. Beautiful and intelligent, spirited and kind, she will make you a wonderful wife, I am happy for you both." He went over to a small cabinet and took out a bottle of sherry and one of his precious bottles of malt whisky. He poured glasses brimful and toasted the betrothed with the suspicious glitter now fully pronounced as two fat pearls rolled down to his chin.

Mari was well water logged in her happiness and as the tears fell unchecked, already her mind was computing and calculating on the arrangements that would now need her expert attention. Oh! Wasn't life wonderful, and then of course was it not natural, that these two fine healthy specimens would soon have children. Oh! Yes! Grandchildren were always spoiled by grandmothers, it was in life's dictation, to be sure!

Stuart let the euphoria settle a little, settling back in the deep armchair, and sipping quietly at the fine drop of malt. Aye! He might just persuade himself to have another. Instead he leant forward and posed a question.

"Donald, you have decided to accept the ownership of Cruachan and that is your right, but what did you have in mind for the potential ownership of your maternal legacy? Each estate is a viable concern, giving employment to many people. True the one here is not as large as Cruachan, but, it has been in your mother's ancestry for hundreds of years and not to be given up lightly."

Donald heaved a deep sigh as he responded to his dad.

"I am very much aware of what you say dad and I have given it much thought, deliberated long and hard. There are so many permutations to consider and each has different aspects and values to reflect on."

"First and foremost was the answer from Siobhan. Had she refused to leave Ireland, then I would have refused the inheritance of Cruachan. I love Siobhan more than anything on this earth, therefore, owning a part of it was no contest."

"I thought of Cruachan being under the rule of a non caring consortium or absent landlord, and I couldn't bear the thought of those friends we left behind being subjected to that kind of tenancy. Slowly and surely they would be forced to leave the land they had given their life to, and this through increased rents, the raping of the land to meet the increases, coupled with uncaring and indifferent maintenance which would become the accepted normal."

"Dad I could not in clear conscience ignore this possibility, I would have felt myself to be a distant traitor. I depended on Siobhan accepting my proposal and I'm glad she did, because now I can prevent an insidious exodus from a way of life that has existed for years. I can prevent a modern system of Highland Enclosure, that is just as treacherous as the one that evicted your forbears from their traditional homes in your recent history. This may sound far fetched, but if you think of it properly, if a tenant farmer cannot meet his quarterly rent, he loses his tenancy."

"Before he will concede to that, he will plunder his own land and stock until he takes the very heart out of it, and is left with an unproductive holding, but the system still beats him, for there is no fat left, and the bare bones cannot provide the necessary. Now, when the land is plundered to the ultimate, his best breeding stock sold, he is destitute, cannot pay the rent, so out he goes."

"Now then! That brings me to the problem of Barranbarrach. I have enjoyed being here, and I have learned much that will stand me in good stead when I take over the administration of Cruachan. You are still a relatively young man, dad, and will, I am sure, be able to carry on running this estate for many years, so the immediate problem is solved. Conal becomes horse master, which he should have been had I not turned up on the scene. He is more than capable of filling the post."

"The long term solution could be a son of mine eventually taking the ownership under your tuition when the time comes. If Siobhan and I are not blessed with children, then we would have to do a reappraisal of the situation some time in the future."

Stuart looked at this son of his, and admired the application that he had brought to resolving the problem of a double Celtic inheritance. He was inclined to agree with Hamish Cruachan, that this young man was indeed the right choice to take over the responsibilities of running a large country estate.

The very fact that he cared for and about people, would make him a landlord that many would envy. He pulled his Hunter fob watch from his pocket, had a quick glance and exclaimed.

"Good heavens it is eleven o'clock. The time has just galloped past. Come on! Let's go and find everybody and tell them the two pieces of news. I know Fiona and Hamish are going to be absolutely delighted. They have always regarded you as their son Donald, and to be honest I should have seen the likelihood of their offer to you long ago, and come to think of it, now I understand the hours of tuition that you were subjected to in estate management, which I thought at the time a bit superfluous. Och there we are though, everything has its reason."

It was to be dinner time in the evening before Donald got the opportunity to advise the Cruachans of his acceptance of their benevolence, and as Stuart had predicted, they were absolutely delighted, even when Donald expressed his wish to stay at Barranbarrach for the next two years.

This was acceptable to Hamish, for in his long term plans it allowed a two year hand over period before he and Fiona would go on a world cruise.

Donald's maternal grandparents had departed on their world cruise on the evening of the 22nd of December and had therefore missed seeing the Cruachans on their first visit to Barranbarrach.

Hamish asked if there were any changes he wanted to put into effect within the two year transitional period, and if so, could he lay the foundations in preparation for Donald's take over. Donald replied that there were would be several new projects that he would like to introduce, but he wanted the pleasure of inaugurating the new concepts himself, and was sure that Hamish would understand this.

Realising that he was being a wee bit selfish, he yielded to his conscience and said there was one small thing that perhaps Hamish would like to do for him.

The request was for Hamish to try to purchase some good quality Arab breeding mares, as he would like to start an Arab Stud, using in the first instance the colt he had received as a gift from Hamish, as the principal stud.

Hamish was delighted. He pointed out that there was no such stud in Scotland that he knew of. There would be a ready market for the small well trained riding horses of the quality that would be turned out of Cruachan. Were they not a beautiful animal with a free flowing movement that was a delight to the eye. Oh yes! They would be much sought after.

He agreed with Donald that ten mares in total would be sufficient to start off with, and already he was thinking of the pleasure of renewing his acquaintance with those lovely people, the Llewellyns from Llanderawel Stud in West Wales.

When Tammy learned that Donald had proposed to Siobhan, he decided to chance his luck and ask Bridget to marry him. He realised that he would have to advise her of his true status in life and his reason for being in Ulster.

After dinner he invited Bridget to take a stroll round the gardens. Since everything was blanketed with snow, there would be little to admire, nevertheless Bridget agreed with alacrity, intuitively knowing that something important was imminent.

A biting wind blowing across the snow drifts drove them to the sanctuary of a summer house in the shelter of some stately yew trees.

They snuggled close, kissing and fondling each other, kindling latent passions never far from the surface. With a mental wrench, Tammy drew apart slightly so that he could look fully into those dark compelling eyes.

He sensed the disappointment of his sweetheart at his seeming withdrawal, but with determination he began to speak.

"Bridget, I have some explaining to do. I have never given a reason as to why I am here in Ulster and to your credit you have never asked. First however I must ask you if you are affiliated in any way to this new I.R.A. faction that is starting to make demands by the use of the bullet and the bomb?"

Bridget's horrified expression was sufficient and convincing without her outraged disclaimer. Tammy was satisfied that he could now continue with his divulging conversation. Had there been any doubt, he would have been duty bound to put Queen and country before his interests and tell Bridget a pack of lies. It would also have put paid to any ideas about having Bridget as his wife.

"What I have to tell you is a highly sensitive and at the moment a national secret. I am a Detective Inspector of Police from the Glasgow Constabulary on secondment to the Royal Ulster Constabulary, although I am governed here by a Commander Denham-Tring, and haven't even been in contact with any of the R.U.C. people."

"Anyhow, my task here is in an undercover capacity and I won't deny that it is hazardous, even dangerous, because it is, very much so. A certain element within the province are determined to oust all non Irish from these shores and will use any means to effect it. There are other reasons which goad them to the madness of killing indiscriminately in an attempt to have their own way, but they are political and sectarian and even radical."

"Armaments of every description, bomb making materials, guns and bullets are being illegally brought into the province, and it is my job to find out who is doing it and where they are being stored. I have to try and neutralise the arsenals and those responsible."

"This poses a great personal problem for me. You see! I am deeply in love with you, as I am sure you are aware. I want to ask you to marry me, dear heart, but I couldn't do that without you knowing what the circumstances are. Now you have the honest facts and knowing how unfair it is to you, I still say, will you marry me?"

Bridget regarded Tammy fondly, gently she stroked the anxious face and with a voice humming with the fullness of her love, replied.

"Dear Tammy, this must have been a difficult proposal for you. Wanting so much, but fretful of the response. Darling, of course I will marry you. I made up my mind I would trap you, before you returned to whence you came, and this I planned a long time ago. Nothing you have said changes anything. No! that's not quite true. I shall worry about you when you return to your duties, but I am not a fool, I knew this idyllic spell could not last forever, life is just not like that. Yes, my darling, I will marry you, with all my heart I will!"

Having plighted their troth, they walked back to the warmth of the manor house where Tammy announced their betrothal to a delighted assembly.

Mari's eyes seemed to go slightly out of focus and Stuart knew that this remarkable wife of his was already completely involved in what would be a double wedding extraordinaire. He smiled as he thought of the bossing around that everyone would be subjected to, and if the event was not perfection in itself, there would be hell to pay.

New Year's Eve arrived and a small family party was held in the main lounge of Barranbarrach House. When the great grandfather clock in the hall struck midnight, they toasted each other to a happy new year, and shortly thereafter drifted away to their respective rooms and so to bed.

As Donald lay composing himself for sleep, his thoughts carried him through the annals of his life and he had to admit, that the theories of Chi Li's yin and yang, certainly applied in his respect.

He had suffered, physically and mentally. He had been heartbroken and depressed and even then with the natural balancing of life's essence, he now enjoyed a comfortable existence, betrothed to a wonderful sweetheart and now also a man of means.

'Yes' he thought, 'yin and yang, I can remember when I thought it was a far fetched hypothesis of Eastern culture. Well it seemed to be applicable to him without a doubt and he would never be sceptical again.'

His last conscious thought before he succumbed to his slumbers was that he must prove himself equal to the responsibilities that would be his alone to carry. There would be a lot to learn, but, he would do it, because he wanted it enough. This last phrase was an adage of his dad's, who always said, if you want to do something badly enough, you can, and, having captured the basics, can make of it an art.

All too soon January the 2nd arrived and the preparations for departure were strongly evident as the entrance foyer filled with luggage waiting to be load into the Daimler.

Tammy was to travel with the Cruachan's and, when they had been dropped off at the airport, the chauffeur would then drop him at his lodgings in Belfast.

Mari would drive the girls over to Siobhan's, where they would have the rest of the day to put their house in order, for it was back to work the following day.

At lunch time, Mari remarked that the house was like a grave, with only her and Stuart and Donald rattling around in it, like three peas in a gallon jar.

Stuart looked at her fondly and mentally sighed with regret. He reminisced how she had wanted many children, and she had been allowed only the one by a decree of fate. She was the most maternal of women and would have gloried in a large family. The way Donald had turned out, she would have made a good job of bringing them up.

Just a pure and natural mother. What a waste to the human race in many ways. Still they had a lot to be thankful for, being blessed with one. Mind that didn't stop her from mothering each and every person that came within her loving reach.

Donald sensed his mother's disquiet and went across to her. He put his arms around her and kissed her lovingly as he chided her gently.

"Come on mum, don't be feeling lonely. Why don't you ask the girls to move in here on a permanent basis, then you can all plan how to relieve dad of much of his ill-gotten gains on the huge reception that I am sure you have in mind for the double wedding. The company will be good for you and you know you will only be happy if you have lots of things to organise."

Mari jumped up from the chair, eyes sparkling as she waltzed her son around the dining room floor. She stopped, a forefinger went to her pursed lips, the other index finger pointed and waved at the ceiling as ideas chased each other through her mind.

"Yes Donald, that is the perfect answer. Och! I should have insisted the girls remain. Yes, yes! Now then! You will finish your lunch for I am away over this minute and see if they will agree."

She paused and turned to her husband, now desperate for assurance from the safe anchorage of her marriage.

"Do you think that would be in order, Stuart? Do you think that her father, Eddie, would object?"

Stuart comforted her as he had never failed to do.

"I am quite sure that Eddie will have no objections," he smiled knowingly, "for I am led to believe there is a willing wee woman who has been keeping him company for the last few days, who will be more than happy to return when the chicks have flown the nest."

Mari required nothing further, with a dazzling smile and a roguish wink she departed, her last words being, "Ach, it's all so simple, why didn't I think of it before."

Neither Donald nor his father pointed out whose idea it had been in the first place, anyhow it is unlikely it would have been heard, for Mari was disappearing out through the door, almost at a run.

Chapter Thirteen

On arrival at his lodgings, Tammy was advised by Mrs Moriarty that there had been several people looking for him whilst he had been on holiday. When he asked her who they were, she said she didn't know as they hadn't introduced themselves.

She hadn't liked the look of them very much. As far as she was concerned, they were a rough looking bunch and up to no good, she was bound to say.

She sought assurance from Tammy that this would not be the sort of people he would be consorting with because, if this were the case, then he had better seek other accommodation. She would not have those kind of folk coming to her door.

Tammy reassured her as best he could, and went up to his room. As he tidied up, he applied his mind to who the callers could have been. The answer jumped immediately into his head, Rourke and his cronies, no room for any doubt.

With the grapevine system that operated within the city of Belfast, and the contacts that were available to Rourke, he had obviously found out where Tammy was lodging and had called round to pay his doubtful respects.

This was a problem that needed urgent attention. It had to be resolved. His work would be greatly hampered if he had to keep ducking and diving to keep out of the way of Rourke and his band of thugs.

He lay down on his bed and applied his mind to possible solutions. He could face Rourke and frighten him to death. He could possibly reason with the man or he could flash his warrant card in his face and tell him to back off.

No! None of those ideas was really viable. Frightening Rourke would make him more vindictive. There was no way he would listen to reason, and the warrant card that Commander Denham-Tring had obtained from the R.U.C. for Tammy would declare his true status, and not the hard man from Glasgow that had been established.

There just had to be a way, but try as he might, nothing came to his mind, then he dozed off.

He awoke with a start and realised the landlady was calling him down for the evening meal. As he descended the rickety narrow stairs the answer to his problem hit him with a clarity that was undeniable. He realised that he had slept on it and the answer had come out of his subconscious mind.

He finished his evening meal and informed his landlady that he was taking a wander round the town. If anyone came looking for him he would be in the Oak and Sloe later on, having a nightcap before bedtime.

The Oak and Sloe was the pub where the trouble had started, so that was the obvious place to sort it out, one way or another. As he entered the pub the usual hush descended, but this time, instead of the hum of voices starting up again, the ugly, deathly silence continued.

Tammy offered a friendly good evening, but received no acknowledgement, only a flicker of the barman's eyes to the area close by the fire, where Tammy had first encountered Rourke.

Glancing across, he saw Rourke firmly ensconced in his favourite chair, the one he had so brutally tried to eject Tammy from on their first meeting. Half a dozen underlings were paying court and Rourke must have felt safe and secure, for he had a self-satisfied smile on his face.

Tammy ambled across and stopped directly facing Rourke, but out of reach of the bully boys.

"Good evening to you, Mr Rourke," Tammy's voice throbbed with a spine chilling menace. "I hear you are having a terrible time finding me. Your messengers seem unable to deliver the message you are trying to send. Deliver that message to me now, yourself. Or are you the kind of man that needs an army of thugs to sort out his problems?"

The silence was oppressive. Rourke stared at Tammy like a mesmerised rabbit faced by a stoat. His face had become ashen, and a tic on his left eyelid tick-tocked with the regularity of a metronome.

The implacable stare of Tammy kept him pinned to his chair. He swallowed and gulped and his breathing pattern was shuddering and shallow. This was the first time he had come face to face with the man who had smashed his nose and left him senseless on the floor. He hadn't actually seen Tammy's face on that occasion for, of course, he had attacked him from the rear.

Rourke forced a smile on his face, fleeting as a snow flake on a river. Brutally he kicked the chair next to him, indicating that he wanted it vacated.

His attempt at nonchalance was destroyed by the shaking hand he waved in its general direction, inviting Tammy to join him. It would be his pleasure to buy Tammy a drink, and sure they could sort out this old problem.

As Tammy moved forward to take the vacated seat, one of the bully boys changed his position to make it difficult for Tammy to reach the chair.

Almost absent mindedly, but with electrifying deceptive speed, Tammy grabbed him by the neck with fingers like steel clamps, cruelly he slammed his head on the table, then, pivoting with tigerish strength, he threw the base born fool across the room. The crash of splintering wood and breaking glasses was accompanied by curses as diving bodies tried to escape injury and splashing ale.

Utterly unruffled, icily calm, Tammy dropped into the vacant chair. His eyes however were doing terrible things to Rourke's composure. 'God in heaven! This was one dangerous bastard and no mistake' he thought, as worms invaded his intestines and he felt a desperate need to go to the toilet.

For a few seconds Tammy kept Rourke skewered by his piercing eyes, then made his offer.

"I have a proposition for you, Mr Rourke. I find myself at a bit of a loose end at the moment, and it is very boring. I have decided to become your partner. I'm sure you will find it to your advantage. There is an alternative. I put you out of business. I drive you out of the city. Please be well advised, your underlings could not protect you. I can give you more trouble than you have ever experienced in your whole life."

Rourke took the pot of ale from the barman and handed it across to Tammy with his own hands, giving himself a moment of time to arrange his thoughts. What was uppermost in his mind was, that this implacable bastard across the table had demonstrated quite clearly his ability to be utterly and ruthlessly effective, and on the occasion when he had sent eight men against him to sort him out, they had all come limping back like beaten whelps.

Looking at Tammy with eyes that glittered with a mixture of hate and fear, he gulped noisily then, almost in a whine, replied,

"What makes you think that a Glasgow hard-man can walk in here and lay down the law? Let me tell you! You can't dictate terms in this neck of the woods. No man is an island. You, dear friend, are marooned. My resources are limitless. No! I think you have the picture wrong. You won't be my partner."

Tammy took a sip of his porter and replied in an offhand manner.

"Well, you surprise me! I thought being the leader of this motley crowd meant that you had a bit of common sense, or native cunning at least. Perhaps that bash on the head you suffered has adjusted your thinking apparatus and it is not ticking over properly."

"I am a man of exceptional talents that would be an asset in your organisation, and you know it! However, I will join a local federation, and once I am firmly established, I will make life for you hell on earth. So much so, you will choose emigration as the only escape from my harassment."

Rourke leaned back in his throne and Tammy could almost see the wheels grinding in the devious mind as it struggled with a reassessment of the situation.

"Tell you what I'll do," Rourke offered, "I'll take you on, but it will be a seventy-thirty agreement, after all, I have all the contacts. You will have to prove your position, and your initiation will be, to say the least, unsavoury, dangerous and outside the law."

Tammy stretched his hand across the table, struggled to keep a smile off his face when Rourke shrank back from the lethal weapon he had seen in action such a short time before.

"Sixty-forty, and it's a deal. What do you say?"

Rourke made no attempt to take the proffered hand, he wasn't quite sure what it would do. He glowered as he contemplated the offered alternative. He was not used to being denied, or dictated to. He knew his underlings were watching and listening to every word and would ruthlessly judge him in weakness and strength.

He was held in the inexorable force of remorseless willpower from across the table. As he looked into those black depths, he found no flaw or obvious weakness to exploit, and at last capitulated.

"Alright! I accept. Hear you this though. Should you be found wanting, you will be executed, I promise you this, if it costs me my life savings. Be warned!"

Tammy's reply was a vee sign with stiff fingers, but inwardly he gave a sigh of relief, he thought for a moment he had pushed too far.

He sat back, a mask of composure stitched on his face, whilst his stomach churned with inner turmoil. He was becoming more sure all the time that Rourke was involved with the faction he was here to investigate, and if he was careful he would gain much information which would enable him to complete his task.

The remainder of the evening he set out quite deliberately to cultivate Rourke and his gang and win a measure of confidence with them.

He told dirty jokes and related hypothetical stories of his exploits in Glasgow, and how he had run rings round the slow thinking dumb-witted cops.

Slyly he inferred he was in sympathy with the I.R.A., after all had not his very mother been a good Irish girl, and she had suffered at the hands of those English pigs, who thought they ruled the world.

Didn't they boast and brag that the sun never sets on the British Empire, well, that day was coming closer all the time, aye, and not before time. The sooner the better. Hopefully there would be a lot of good Englishmen in the changes about to occur, aye, dead ones!

As the evening drew to a close, the regulars started to drift away. Rourke gathered his gang around the table and laid out the plans for that night's work.

It transpired that a wee-bit boat would be landing on the northwest coast shortly after midnight. The gangs job was to pick up the cargo it would offload.

Certain members of impeccable pedigree and loyalty to the cause would then take the cargo to predetermined places of concealment.

The meeting place, when they got there, was ideally suited for the secretive purpose of landing contraband or illegal goods. Tammy took careful note of the location and, in particular, the faces of the men chosen to carry the consignment to its final destination. One of these trusties would eventually divulge the locations of these secret caches through a medium of false friendship, or by exercising unpleasant interrogation.

Feet sank deep into the sand and shingle as the men laboured under the weight of some of the multi-shaped, canvas-wrapped bundles. Tammy was quite sure that heavy artillery pieces were concealed in them.

He tried to see if there were any identifying marks and was disappointed when none were in evidence. He joked and asked the odd casual question, but all were tight lipped and he failed to acquire any worthwhile information.

What did please Tammy was the fact that he had, quite by chance, crossed swords with someone deeply involved with the I.R.A. on his first night in Belfast, and because of that, he now had an inside edge that it might be possible to exploit.

For the next three months Tammy was involved in meeting boats and shifting cargo on a twice weekly basis. Each time the landing place would be some rocky inlet where only an inflatable craft could make entry.

One piece of information became available to Tammy. As the bundles and packages were being brought up from the beach, Rourke would assess them and call out a number, anywhere between one and ten. Tammy realised this was the number of the cache it was destined for. He realised at this time that he was not really getting anywhere very fast. He couldn't find out where the caches were and was, in fact, too close to Rourke and company to be effective. It was all so damned frustrating.

Commander Denham-Tring was putting pressure on for results and kept promising assistance, but it was never forthcoming.

The difficulty was, of course, that even within the ranks of the R.U.C. there were sympathisers to the cause, so application for help in that area was fraught with danger.

He had offered several times to go with the inshore party and give assistance, but each time Rourke had brusquely turned down the offer. He could not afford to offer again without arousing the suspicions of all concerned, and in particular, Rourke.

It was now becoming vitally important to have an ally on whom he could rely but, furthermore, that person must be someone who could handle himself in dangerous situations.

Tammy knew exactly the person who fitted that description, but would he be able to persuade him to accept the assignment, after all, he was a civilian and a busy man in his own right.

The authority invested in Tammy meant he could bring pressure to bear on any person he felt could further his investigations, but he was loth to do that to a man he considered a brother.

Try as he would, he could come up with no alternative to his initial thoughts as to who would fill the bill. He asked Denham-Tring for assistance but it was pointed out that to try to get someone from the R.U.C. was fraught with danger, for there was no way of being sure that they were not sympathesisers with the I.R.A.

At the end of April, Tammy told Rourke that he was taking two weeks holiday and, to cover his tracks in case he was spotted in the wrong place, said he was going to tour around the country and see a bit of it seeing he was on the right side of the water.

Rourke was not too happy but grudgingly conceeded when Tammy insisted that they had managed before he joined them, so a week of absence would be of little consequence.

He managed to hitch a lift as far as Larne, where he spent some time mooching around to make sure he wasn't under surveillance. When he was sure that nobody was interested in his movements, he set off walking towards Barranbarrach.

As he walked along the peaceful country road he heard the sounds of the plovers and larks, and the dulcet cooing of wood pigeons. He watched for a moment the black and gold honey bees as they droned among the clover at the side of the road. The heady scent of the wild woodbine mingled with the starker pungency of the dog rose. As he ambled quietly along, he felt the tensions of the past three months drop off him like a snake sloughing its unwanted skin.

His mind's eye filled with a picture of Bridget, and unconsciously his feet picked up a quicker tattoo on the gravelly road.

Twice he was offered a lift, once by the driver of the indigenous donkey cart as it clip-clopped merrily along, but each time he declined with a smile, spreading his hands and looking round as if the say, what, and miss all this?

The good samaritans smiled their understanding and went on their way, realising that here was someone enjoying nature at its most benevolent, and if he had the time, why not?

He watched well grown spring lambs leaping and gambolling in shoulder-high clover. Suddenly they would stop, then it was heads down under the ewes' flanks, with tails wagging furiously as they refuelled before playing king of the castle on any suitable tussock.

A few mares with foals at foot made Tammy realise that Donald would have been very busy with the foaling programme at the stud, and the next phase would be the covering of the mares when they came into season.

His thoughts paused there for a moment in self appraisal of what he had just thought and he realised that the lore of the stud, and its phraseology, was brushing off on him. Prior to meeting Donald he hadn't had a clue about the cycles of stud work, or anything to do with rural life. Heretofore he had been a total city bird.

He turned into the red gravel drive and picked up speed again, now he was really in a hurry, he felt he was coming home. He would be arriving unannounced but he was sure of his welcome. This family had demonstrated their regard for him often enough for him to have no misgiving as to how he would be received.

He bounded up the wide steps, and was about to use the large wrought iron knocker when the door flew open and his arms were filled with a screaming, tantalising female.

Astonished and speechless, he smothered the upturned face with kisses of delight. Bridget was the last person he had expected to find on this doorstep.

They stood and embraced and kissed until an amused voice bade them show a little decorum, and would they please come in so she could at least pay the compliments of the day to her darling boy.

Bridget and Tammy entered the hallway, which looked even more spacious than the last time Tammy had seen it, with the huge Christmas tree now absent.

Mari hugged Tammy warmly, then stepping back, scrutinised him closely. She remarked that it was time he had a holiday for he looked worn out. They repaired to the day lounge, tea and cakes were brought to stave off hunger until the evening meal. Tammy was brought up to date on the family news and that of the stud.

At six o'clock, Donald, Siobhan and Stuart arrived from their various duties, and after greeting the very welcome visitor, it was time to get bathed and dressed for dinner.

Even on the farm at Craigburn Mari had always made a point of dinner being punctual, and semi formal. She considered it civilised to have divested the grime and smells of the farmyard before sitting down to a meal. No dung-covered wellington boots were allowed under her dinner table. Dirty nails were an abomination not to be tolerated in any circumstances. Thus had the routine of bathing and changing before dinner become an established custom, which everybody adhered to with strict discipline.

After dinner was finished, everyone repaired to the evening lounge, where Stuart, in his customary role, offered drinks all round and poured for those who accepted.

Mari, in her usual perceptive fashion, had noticed that Tammy was somewhat on edge. Unusually he had not joined in the general conversation during dinner.

Moved by concern, she nestled down beside him on the settee, snuggling close as she took his arm and whispered softly,

"What is the trouble, dear boy? Share it with us who care about you. Something is eating at you and if you don't get rid of it, it will become as corrosive as acid and destroy your peace of mind. Is it something to do with your work?"

Tammy squeezed the arm tucked through his, and looked at her with love shining warmly in his eyes.

"As always, you are direct and forthright, and yes, I have a problem, and it is to do with my work. Bridget knows the nature of my profession and she has obviously retained my confidences and not told anyone else. However, the time has come for me to take all of you into the same confidence."

Tammy then went on to tell his family, as he regarded them, what he had divulged to Bridget before he proposed to her.

He turned to face Mari directly and said with a distinct tremor in his voice,

"I find it difficult to make this request, but I feel I must. The last thing I ever want is to cause you grief or anxiety, but perhaps if I explain how I arrived at the decision, you will understand how it seemed to be the solution to my problem."

"The problem that has developed now is that I need to be in two places at once. I know where the incoming sources of the illegal cargoes are, I know what the contents are. What I cannot discover are the final hiding places, of which there are ten."

"The leader of the runners keeps me well away from the cache areas. Our relationship is uneasy, to say the least. He doesn't trust me, and that is why he refuses to allow me to find out the ultimate destination of the goods."

Taking a steadying sip of his whisky, he mentally prepared himself to make his request. As he opened his mouth to begin, he was almost brusquely interrupted by Donald.

"Good heavens, Tammy, I thought you had a real problem. Dear me! The answer is simple as ABC. I am your man. I'll help you with this small inconvenience. In fact, I am going to immodestly announce that there is no-one better qualified to do the job than myself. In truth, I could do with a bit of a diversion, and this sounds the ideal answer."

Mari quickly intervened,

"Just a minute now! Donald, have you even paused to consider that this could be very dangerous? I rather feel that these people would go to any lengths to prevent their nefarious enterprises from being discovered, and might well commit murder in consequence. I think this needs a wee bit more thought before decisions are made."

She flopped back into the settee, her face drained of colour, and weakly signalled Stuart to replenish her glass, which she had emptied in a compulsive gulp.

Dutifully Stuart filled her glass, then squeezed in beside her. Putting his arm around her for comfort and reassurance, he made his first contribution to the conversation.

"When I had to go to the war, my darling, it was not to your liking, and man understands that woman must wait, and there is nothing nice about that part either. However, wars have to be fought for the ultimate good of mankind, or so we are conditioned to believe. This nasty business that Tammy is involved with is an insidious version of war. The very stench of it is being felt here at Barranbarrach, at the moment in small irritating ways, but all the time escalating in seriousness. Now! We either fight it, or allow ourselves to be subjugated by it."

"Tammy is at the front line, so to speak, trying to destroy the supply lines, which are the mainstay of any fighting force. The more successful he is, the easier it is to contain this despicable, self-nominated faction of gangsters who are determined to rid Ulster of all non-Irish."

"Now then! Donald and I are of that classification, and dearly though we love our home here, it makes no difference to that terrorising rabble, who no doubt have us on a hit list somewhere, and I feel sure we will enjoy their attentions in due course."

"What I am saying, in short, is that Donald must go to war if he wishes, because, believe me, this will be a war of attrition, and anything that will prevent it, or hasten its end, must be contemplated, no matter how unsavoury the proceedings."

Stuart gave his despondent wife another loving hug, then rose and went across to the drinks dispenser.

"That little speech has given me quite a thirst," he declared, "will anybody join me in a fresh dram?"

When the glasses had been recharged, there was silence for a few moments, as each pursued their own thoughts. Donald broke the silence, looking at his mother with embarrassment showing on his face, he tried to convince her that his earlier offer to Tammy was not a vagrant or ill-conceived thought.

"These caches are sure to be in isolated rural areas, there is little doubt of that. Now who can move through any type of terrain without detection better than I? Did I not have the finest teacher it is possible to have?"

"I still say I am the obvious choice to ascertain the whereabouts of these hiding places, so if Tammy agrees, I volunteer."

Turning to Tammy, he continued, "How long would we be involved with this assignment, and I ask only because I have promised to take over control of Cruachan in two years time, and, quite frankly, I won't commit myself indefinitely to something that would deviate me from that course. "

"My tour of duty over here was for a period of two years," Tammy answered, then continued, "at the end of that time I shall return to Glasgow with a promotion to Chief Inspector and with it a safe desk job. I still have twenty months, so that would coincide with your departure for Scotland. However, if we are identified at any time by the factions we are in opposition to, then our usefulness will be at an end, and we should be instantly withdrawn. It is not a task without end, nor should it be. We will be operating in a high stress situation, and nobody can take that indefinitely."

With a distressed whimper, Mari rose from the settee. The futility of argument had penetrated fully. She took Donald and Tammy by the hands, and pulled them close to her. Enfolding them in hungry arms, she admonished them with a timbre of new found strength in her voice.

"I demand of both of you to be extremely careful. No taking silly chances. I demand further, that you both return to this house in good health and sound mind. I exhort you to remember your loved ones and come back to us safely."

Her strength then failed her, as she turned from her boys to her girls.

"Come, my darlings," she whispered in a broken voice, the pain of parting already vibrating and throbbing, "let the men make their battle plans, and us poor women will weep."

"I am sure they will conspire and intrigue better in our absence," she continued in a subdued whisper, then like a mother hen with her wings protectively round her chicks, she swept them from the room, with her arms around them.

Feeling as if they had been deserted somehow, the men looked at each other a little sheepishly, like small boys caught with their hands in the sweetie jar.

Stuart spread his hands and looked skywards as if for divine guidance at the ways of women. He opined that they would all have a good cry and that would help them come to terms with the current events.

The truth of the matter was that the job had to be done. Sure it wasn't pleasant for anyone, but having said that, he appreciated that waiting at home was not easy and this time that was what he was confined to do.

Tammy broached a question about a remark that Stuart had made earlier in reference to trouble around the homefarm and the stud. Donald explained that there were unusual and annoying little things happening. They had at first seemed inexplicable, but now they were getting to grips with it.

When Tammy asked him to explain further, Donald continued with the catalogue of incidents. The first indication of trouble was a fire in the tack room, reason unknown.

Next was a lung infection in two of the senior stallions, but this time it was discovered they had been fed mouldy hay, something that was just not tolerated at the stud, so where had it come from?

On a morning inspection Conal had found a single strand of barbed wire strung across one of the practice jumps, placed a foot above the top of the flight. This could have caused terrible damage to any horse hitting it at full stretch. Being a single strand it would have been next to invisible to the approaching horse or rider.

Gates into paddocks were mysteriously being found open, despite the double locking system that was in use throughout the entire estate. Tyres on vehicles were found slashed, or distributor caps smashed.

All of these misdemeanours were time consuming to put right and some of them were extremely dangerous. The perpetrators had to be found and neutralised, or, as Conal had suggested, castrated with a pair of bricks.

A satisfied timbre entered Donald's voice as he continued,

"Last week my Arab mare came into season, so I decided to have her covered by the stallion that came with her from Llanderawel. I was handling the colt myself, and, as Siobhan was busy with something else, I had Tim O'Malley hold the mare. As a precaution, and particularly with a maiden mare, when she is being covered for the first time, a rope is placed around the nearside foreleg, then, when the stallion rears to cover her, the rope is jerked upwards, lifting her foot off the ground. She cannot lash out with her back legs and so this stops her from kicking the stallion in the chest and smashing his ribs."

"Just as the colt rose to cover the mare I saw O'Malley deliberately drop the mare's foot, and by God, she did lash out. Luckily I saw what was happening and was able to pivot the colt on his back legs away from danger, so no harm was done. Needless to say, if my reactions had been a whit slower, I would have had a stallion out of action for the rest of the season."

"I told O'Malley to put the mare in her loosebox and took the colt back to his quarters, and that was a tussle, for he sorely wanted to finish the job and was most reluctant to be led away. When I shouted to O'Malley that I wanted a word with him in the stud office he took off like a startled hare. I caught him, though, and took him into the feed room, where I did some rather nasty things to him until he told me all I wanted to know."

"He and his brother, who I had met previously in unpleasant circumstances, in company with a crony called Mick O'Reilly, are the ones who have been carrying out the campaign of sabotage on the estate. They belong to an organisation called the Irish Freedom Fighters, and are apparently closely associated with the I.R.A."

Tammy listened with close attention to Donald's story, and suggested he must release Donald from his offer of help, had he not enough to contend with here.

Donald wouldn't hear of it, saying that now they were aware of what was going on, arrangements had been made to neutralise any further trouble.

O'Malley had been sacked on the spot, without references, and advised that any further incidents would be attributed to him and his brother and they would be found and dealt with in a very unpleasant manner.

No! He was quite satisfied that O'Malley would want no more of the attention he had received in the feed room, and his brother was no hero, having experienced a touch of Donald's specialities on a previous occasion he would be reluctant to have a return match arranged.

Now the three men got down to the serious business of planning how they could best find out the location of the arms caches. Stuart, of course, would only be involved in the planning phase, but as the discussion went on, it became patently obvious that he would dearly love to participate in all aspects of the operation, nevertheless his army experiences were very helpful to the discussion.

Finally it was decided that Tammy would continue to assist at the offloading points in the hope of gaining some more snippets of information.

Donald would try to get lodgings at the Oak and Sloe, where Rourke had an office at the rear of the building. Perhaps when Rourke was out meeting incoming goods at some lonely shore, Donald would be able to gain access to the office and see if he could find anything to indicate the whereabouts of the elusive depositories.

Rourke always carried a notebook in his pocket to which he referred time and again. Tammy could easily have picked his pocket but that would have been a useless exercise for he was sure that if ever Rourke lost that book the planned schedules would be changed immediately. No! The information had to be acquired in a circumspect manner. Most circumspect indeed, for Rourke was one very suspicious character, and anything out of the ordinary would be sure to alert him and make things even more difficult.

To avoid suspicion of complicity, a further duplicity would be engineered at the Oak and Sloe. Tammy and Donald would aggravate each other until a fight ensued, with Tammy being the victor, to further enhance his hard man image. Thereafter there would be a continual bickering, followed by Donald backing down at the last minute to avoid another thrashing. However, it would be during these tussles that they would give each other information.

If, or when, the information they sought came to light, then they would both be involved in the disposal of the armament caches. This would prove to be the most dangerous part of the mission, as it was highly likely that the caches would be strongly guarded and any attempt to destroy the depositories would be vigorously opposed.

Tammy now felt that, with Donald's assistance, he must surely make progress, but he was determined to keep giving Denham-Tring as much hassle as he could, to get somebody of authority within the province to give back up support when it was needed.

During the next few days Donald taught Tammy the basics of manoeuvring through terrain of varying conditions. How to use the minimum of cover to advantage, to look for shadows to melt into, or small indentations in the ground that would provide temporary havens.

It was all new to Tammy, who could compete with the best in the city but the countryside was a different kind of operation. The training was necessary for they both felt that the sources they sought would be in isolated areas. Tammy also believed that the caches they sought were not too far from the inlets where they were unloaded. The reason for this was that the parties that transported the cargoes to their final destinations generally returned within a very short time to the Oak and Sloe for an illegal after hours drink. It was here also that payment for the night's work was doled out.

Five days later Tammy returned to his Belfast lodgings, and a week after that Donald entered the Oak and Sloe, where he was almost grudgingly given accommodation in keeping with his general appearance. He had deliberately dressed as a tatty down-at-heel vagabond, and his demeanour was unappealing.

His gift of mimicry enabled him to talk in the local dialect. He pretended to be a fed up fisherman, and was on the lookout for work less dangerous, and better paying, than he had been doing recently.

The barman looked at him scathingly, and pointed out that when he stopped paying his way he would be out on his ear, and damned quick. This was not a home for idlers or freeloaders, and, in fact, it would be better for him to look for something more permanent anyhow.

Donald shrugged his shoulders and said he had no intention of staying long, not at the price he was having to pay for that dog kennel that had been called a room.

The barman slapped his greasy cloth on the bar and told Donald he could like it or lump it, it made no difference to him.

That evening Donald was sitting at a corner table eating his unappetising food when Tammy entered with the Rourke gang. He got up from his seat and went over towards the bar, seemingly to get another drink.

As he was passing Tammy, he shouldered roughly into him, knocking him into a nearby table. Tammy cursed a foul-mouthed epithet and swung round in simulated rage. He pistoned four cruel blows to Donald's midriff, and then a two-handed blow to the bent shoulders that had bowed conveniently from the effects of the punches in the stomach.

Donald dropped to the floor and, as he rolled over, he kicked ineffectually at Tammy's legs, who immediately retaliated with a resounding kick in the ribs of Donald. Tammy then bent and picked Donald up by the front of his fisherman's jersey and threw him back towards the corner from whence he had started.

"You don't come in here and rough me up wee man," snarled Tammy, as he wandered over to join Rourke, who had sat smiling through the disturbance, "and what the hell are you laughing at, what the hell is so funny?" he ranted on, continuing the charade of being out of humour.

Rourke held up his hand in a placatory manner, and in a smarmy insincere voice soothed his apparently outraged partner.

"Now then! Don't start on me. We're on the same side, remember? That poor wee spalpeen only stumbled against you, I don't think he meant any harm really."

"I can do without your placations," Tammy growled, and turning in the direction of Donald, shouted further abuse.

"You'll do well to keep out of my way from now on, you half grown runt, and mind your manners while you're at it."

With the point made to his apparent satisfaction, he lifted his glass of porter and taking a deep draught, showed his appreciation by belching loudly and blowing the nauseous gasses over his table companion.

Donald kept up the appearance of being servile and grovelling, always apologising and giving ground at any danger of confrontation, but from time to time making niggling little remarks that afforded him a clout on the ear from his tormentor.

So well did he act the part that the other regulars in the bar treated him with contemptuous amusement, using him as the butt of their crude, and often cruel, jokes. When they asked him when he was going to get a job, he tapped the side of his head and rolled his eyes like an idiot.

One day he rolled up outside the pub in a nondescript battered old car of indeterminate age or make. It was filthy inside and out, with dents and scrapes all over the bodywork.

When he told an enquirer how much he had paid for the relic, the bar resounded to guffaws of incredulous merriment. What a dope! The seller must have run all the way to the bank, laughing fit to burst, and then gone directly to church to thank God, and could he find it in his heart to send him another idiot.

Donald smiled benignly and accepted all the banter and chaffing without a word in his defence. He now had the means to get around the country. He disappeared for long spells during the day, followed by nocturnal excursions that produced the odd brace of pheasants, or hares, always rabbits and sometimes the occasional salmon, which he would sell in the pub. It was soon accepted that he was in to poaching in a big way.

He contributed to the pub kitchen, often free of charge. It must have been appreciated although the barman never actually said so, but there was no more mention of him having to find other accommodation. He had now become established as a harmless halfwit.

It was only Tammy who kept up his persecution, a continual scathing assault on him. When he was asked why, he nearly choked on the piece of jugged hare he was eating.

"I'll tell you why," he spluttered, meat flying in all directions, "he's a little creep, he gets under my skin just looking at him, and further he keeps directing sly little comments at me. That is going to lead him to an early grave, for I've just about had enough of the skinny, smelly, little rat."

Donald, having set the scene of his 'modus operandi', now decided it was time to get down to the serious side of the task he was here to perform.

His absences were now taken as a matter of course, he could come and go without anyone being in the slightest bit interested. He had even stayed away for a complete night and a day which had elicited no questions whatever from anyone, so that part of his plan was secure.

He carried out a quick appraisal as to the means of a covert entry into Rourke's office, and was sure he would find little difficulty in effecting an entry.

He waited until he got a discreet nod from Tammy indicating that the coast would be clear that night, or the other way round to be exact. Rourke would be at the coast, and the city would be clear of his presence.

Just before the party left for the coast, Donald walked through the pub in his dark coloured poaching apparel. Waving an exaggerated farewell, with heavy bravado he made his exit. He was aware of loud sniggers of amusement that followed his going, but was content in the knowledge that they thought he was off on a poaching expedition.

He drove his car to a derelict site and parked it amongst the abandoned scrap cars that cluttered the area. A transformation occurred, his car disappeared, or seemed to. It was just another old wreck that had been dumped, lost amid others of its kind. This of course was another reason why he had purchased such a decrepit, worthless looking means of transport, nobody in their right minds would dream of stealing it. Further to this, if it was seen parked off the road in a lonely area, it would be assumed that someone had dumped it.

Sitting in the car, he removed his poacher's coat, pulled on a black woollen polo necked jersey. He removed his heavy soled boots and replaced them with a pair of black rubber-soled shoes, which had been well dubbined to prevent any squeaking.

He checked that he had his catapult, his throwing clubs and his knife in the leg sheath. His garotted was around his waist, where he wore it continually. It had become a habit with him to always carry his warriors accoutrements, but he never entered any potential arena without checking that they were easily to hand.

Donald took a circuitous route back to the Oak and Sloe, and as he neared his destination, he kept to darkened areas. Furtively he flitted from shadow to shadow in his clandestine approach.

He arrived at the rear of the pub, where he paused to survey the surroundings. Satisfied that all was quiet, he crept stealthily forward until he arrived at the window from where he would effect entry. The casement window presented no problem. He slid the blade of his knife up between the wooden cross members and eased the levered catch to the side effortlessly.

He pushed up the lower half of the window and slithered over the sill. He paused, reduced breathing sound as he listened to see if his entry had been noticed. Nothing stirred. Gently he closed the window and, as he turned his back to it, closed his eyes for a span of three deep breaths, when he opened them again he could see more clearly in the darkened room.

He glanced quickly around and in that quick appraisal knew exactly where everything was, thanks again to the early training of Chi Li. The room was sparsely furnished. Half a dozen straight backed chairs, a two drawer desk and a bookshelf littered with trivia.

Carefully Donald went through each piece of paper that lay in disarray on the shelf, desperately looking for vital clues. Everything had to be taken to the window to be scrutinised as it was the only source of light. He didn't dare make use of the oil lamp that stood on the end of the desk.

The two drawers in the desk which were unlocked produced a disappointing conglomeration of rubbish. The only thing of consequence being a half empty bottle of Irish whisky and two dirty tumblers.

Despairingly, Donald realised there was nothing of value in this dingy office. His labours were in vain. With a quiet sigh of frustration he turned to leave, but, with a hair prickling sensation, he sensed a presence.

He wheeled in an instant and darted behind the door that was opening with infinite slowness. A burly figure entered the room, then turned to close the door.

His eyes bulged at the sight of Donald, but it was doubtful if he actually saw who it was, as the hard edge of Donald's hand slammed into the bridge of his nose. At the same instant, powerful fingers closed on his throat, preventing any outcry, then almost casually, Donald found the nerve deep in the neckroot and rendered the unfortunate intruder senseless.

Donald allowed the figure to drop quietly to the floor, and turned once more to make his escape. He slid the window open, and whirled as his senses warned him of more danger. A gun appeared in the hand of this new menace. With an automatic reflex action, he spun and with a scything movement of his left foot diverted the threat.

Using the momentum of his spin, the extended fingers of his right hand drove deeply into the larynx of his assailant, and as the head dropped forward in outraged astonishment at such treatment, Donald chopped him to the floor with an emphatic kick to the point of the chin.

Not stopping to check the results, he dived through the open window. Quickly he pulled it down and melted into the welcome shadows. He rapidly increased distance away from the scene of his indiscretions. From time to time he doubled back and crossed his escape route to ensure that he was not being followed.

He reached his hidden car and as he sat inside changing out of the tell-tale clothing, he reflected on the unsatisfactory results of his investigation. Perhaps it had been too much to expect for Rourke to have incriminating evidence lying around his office, but it had been necessary to check it out.

Donald heaved a sigh and decided to drive out to Barranbarrach and spend the remainder of the night and a further day with his parents and Siobhan. They would all have a little chat and see if they could come up with some fresh ideas.

Chapter Fourteen

Donald reached Barranbarrach around two o'clock in the morning and crept quietly up to his room. He conditioned his mind to wake at seven o'clock, then calmly slid into bed and was asleep instantly. He had emptied his mind of the evening's events and would awaken refreshed and ready to discuss with his family new plans that might help his adopted brother, Tammy.

Mari and Stuart welcomed their son when he joined them at breakfast, showing no surprise at his appearance. Donald held his peace for a while and then enquired why Siobhan was late, for it wasn't like her to be tardy in the mornings, she was normally a lark.

Imperiously Stuart held up his hand as Mari's mouth opened to speak. Mari's mouth closed, almost with a snap. Stuart smiled at her and addressed her soothingly.

"I think I had better do the talking here, sweet girl, for you are a wee bit wound up about things."

He leant across and gently stroked her hand, then, still holding it, he turned to Donald, heaved a mighty sigh and started to explain the reason for Siobhan's absence.

When Donald had left for Belfast Siobhan had been a little bit piqued at not being able to do anything of value to help. Spirited and strong willed, she had decided that, as she knew the northern coastline in quite some detail, she would go and do some investigating in her own way. Perhaps she would be able to discover something of value to Donald and Tammy.

She had given herself leave of absence and departed on that rig colt of hers. Stuart believed that she was to stay with an old aunt that had a croft not far from the coast where Tammy had said the shipments were coming in.

Siobhan left Barranbarrach on her jet black rig colt, a huge beast that was reminiscent of a destrier, the huge warhorse of yesteryear.

A rig colt is a colt who, when he was castrated, was found to have only one teste in the sac. In this case, that one had been removed, leaving him in the state of being half stallion or half gelding.

The brutal treatment he had received during this castration attempt had left him with a savage hatred of men. He never missed a chance to exact revenge at any given opportunity, biting and kicking in violent manifestation of his displeasure at their company. This was the horse Donald had ridden on his first morning in the yards, and truthfully he never had any problems with him, but let any other man go near him and he went berserk.

With Siobhan he was well mannered, even gentle, so she had taken to using him in her daily work. He would come to her call and allow her to attend to his needs with good grace.

Because of his huge size she had taught him to kneel on hocks and knees to assist her to mount, something like a circus horse.

Siobhan well knew that her rapport with this huge animal was a source of annoyance to all the male riders in the stud. She was human enough to feel a tremendous satisfaction that, apart from Donald, she was the only one that had any success with the Black Beast, as he was called.

She rode north on her warhorse, heading for her aunt's croft that lay between Coleraine and Ballycastle, two miles inland from the coast and quite near to the old castle remains of Dunluce.

The rig colt covered the distance easily in his unusual gait. The Americans call it sidewinding, which means that at the canter both legs on the same side move forward together in unison. It is a gracious flowing movement, elegant and fluid, the rider hardly moving in the saddle, so it is less tiring, so smooth is the carriage.

Having left early in the morning Siobhan arrived at her aunt's croft around the middle of the evening. Her aunt greeted her warmly, even if she did seem a trifle surprised, but pointed out a building that she was sure would suffice as a stable.

When the horse had cooled sufficiently, Siobhan gave him a drink from a bucket, she wanted to know exactly how much fluid he took in. Siobhan's aunt was making idle chatter whilst Siobhan was attending to her horse's needs, then the old woman advised Siobhan to make sure she locked the outhouse before she came in.

Siobhan asked why this was, the usual practice in the past having been free and easy and nothing ever locked. Her aunt replied that there were some strange goings on around these parts of late, people moving about in the black of night when all good God fearing people should be in their beds.

Siobhan was instantly alerted at this revelation, it indicated she was indeed in the right area to perhaps make some discoveries for Tammy and Donald. Quietly and gently she probed for more information at greater length, and as she did she became convinced that she was on the verge of success in her quest.

Although it is not always apparent, country folk are very much in tune with what happens in their immediate surroundings. If anything out of the ordinary occurs they are instantly aware of it. They are generally not too happy about strangers invading their locale, and will watch very carefully what these invaders get up to.

When Siobhan's aunt realised the depth of interest her niece was showing in the nocturnal activities that were a twice weekly occurrence along the coast, she said she would invite the local gamekeeper friend over for tea and he would be able to give her more detailed information.

The gamekeeper proved to have a wealth of information of the kind Siobhan was seeking. As part of his responsibilities he had to make various checks during the hours of darkness, after all poaching was a problem, and he had to be seen doing his job. During these times he had seen strange goings-on, as he expressed it. Small craft coming in from the sea, offloading God knows what, but more than likely contraband goods.

As a good citizen he had mentioned these sightings to his Customs and Excise friends, but they had been unable to apprehend the nocturnal busybodies, so it was an unexplained mystery to the present time. He pointed out that there were many little coves and inlets along this stretch of coastline, and the runners, if that is what they were, never used the same site twice running.

Giving her aunt the least possible explanation, that would satisfy her, Siobhan decided to become an owl. She would sleep during the days, and hunt her prey through the hours of darkness.

She was fully aware that she would have many fruitless and frustrating nights ahead of her, but she was firmly resolved to discover what she could. At the back of her mind was the thought that her self-imposed task could be dangerous, but she didn't let that vagrant thought deflect her from her purpose.

Many nights passed as Siobhan ghosted through the countryside on her powerful black horse. Dressed entirely in black herself, they were like an elusive shadow flitting through the rustic coastal scene. The hours of darkness during the summer solstice are desperately short for anyone whose work has to be contained within that time span.

Siobhan had many miles to travel each night trying to cover as large an area as possible, but her charger proved to be well capable of it, in fact he seemed to revel in the long distances that were required of him each night.

Each evening Siobhan went out to prepare him for the night's work. He would dance around in excited anticipation and nibble impatiently at her sleeve, flickering his ears and lashing his tail in pleasure at the thought of running free as the wind, and almost as fast.

Siobhan kept her horse within the confines of the stable during the hours of daylight. This was a deliberate attempt to avoid exciting the curiosity of the local populace. She was not particularly keen to broadcast her nocturnal activities, or be dubbed Lady of the Night.

Knowing the tendency for country folk to gossip, she accepted that she would not be able to completely avoid being discussed, and to that end she fabricated a story about special training of her horse that would shortly be going overseas to be used in a particular type of work that would necessitate a lot of night riding.

The end of the second week was fast approaching, and the nights of searching had revealed nothing of importance, then at last her vigil was rewarded.

Oilskins prevented a thorough soaking from the continuous drizzle that had plagued her all night. It hadn't done much for her morale, or vision, then suddenly her pulse began to race when she thought she heard the sound of a labouring vehicle engine. Instinctively she kneed her Black Beast in the direction of the muffled engine noises sounding through the shrouding sea mist that was part of the drizzle. The misery of the inclement weather now forgotten.

In a short time she heard muted shouts of swearing, getting louder as she neared the source. Ground haltering her steed, she crept forward to get a sight of what was happening.

The engine coughed into life again and she could see a dark coloured van start to move off. Quickly she returned to her horse and, having mounted with a running leap, set off to follow the sound of the engine. Now she was thankful for the veiling effect of the drizzling rain and sea mist which she had cursed previously. Conditions couldn't be better, in fact, for now she could follow the sound of the van without the danger of being seen, and providing she didn't become careless she stood a good chance of being led to one of the hiding places of the questionable cargo.

Roughly half an hour passed as she followed the van like a dog at its master's heels. They entered a dirt track through deciduous woodland. The driving conditions were proving difficult on the rain-soaked ground.

She heard gears being changed up and down, and the sudden whine when traction was lost on the greasy surface and the wheels spun uselessly.

Eventually the van turned off onto an even more desolate track, still within the cover of woodland, and after ten minutes or so, slid to a halt.

She dismounted and led the horse away from the track, and when she was satisfied that he was obscured from sight, tied him to a sapling and made her way back to the van.

Two men were scraping leaves and decomposed matter from an area close to the trunk of a large beech tree. Next, they lifted clear a wooden frame covered with wire netting, followed by a length of tarpaulin. Setting them to one side, they began to add the contents of the van to the deep pit in the ground.

As they cursed and laboured, Siobhan took particular note of the site. The large beech tree that marked the location was a neighbour to a tall fir that had been subjected to a lightening strike, a large whitened scar running virtually the entire length of the trunk. In addition to this, a silver birch stood at a crazy angle, almost as if it was pointing to the scene of the labouring men.

Luckily these worthies had left the van headlights on to give them illumination whilst they laboured, this served Siobhan with a perfect floodlit scene that she much appreciated.

Quietly she removed herself from the scene, and returned to her patient mount. As he went to nicker a greeting she grabbed him quickly by the nose and rubbed it lightly as she whispered softly to him.

She waited beside the horse until she heard the engine sound increase, this was followed by shouts and curses as one of the men tried to turn the van and the other gave directions. After a short time she heard the van pass her hiding place as it started its return journey.

Siobhan now set about the task of marking the area so that she would be able to pick it out and return with confidence. The marks would have to be skilfully laid, unobtrusive yet visible to the eye that knew what to look for.

A white blaze mark as used by foresters would be too obvious, but something along those lines was necessary.

Siobhan stood lost in thought for a moment. The Black Beast nibbled impatiently at her, and then, as if in exasperation, tore a mouthful from a nearby shrub and started to eat it.

'Thank you, my bonny boy,' she thought, as she patted him gratefully, 'that is the answer.' Small branches broken off near the ground would be accepted as being the damage of the passing van. Properly done, it would not create the slightest suspicion.

All the way down the track she emulated a wild animal scent marking its territory. When she was finished she was sure that she would have no difficulty in finding the location again.

Glancing upwards, she realised that daybreak was imminent. It was time to get away from this locality. It would be most unsatisfactory, even dangerous, to be found anywhere near this place of secrets.

Siobhan was now able to disregard the offloading point that had been used on the night she first made contact. She felt sure it would not be used for some time to come. This meant she could concentrate her attention on other areas that she felt were likely spots.

With this initial success she extended her leave of absence from Barranbarrach by writing and advising them that she was being successful, but it would obviously require more time to establish all the locations she sought.

So skilfully did she write her letter that, should it have fallen into wrong hands, it would have been indecipherable as to the information it contained.

She was well versed in the intricacies of the political situation in Ulster to know many of its inhabitants were sympathetic to the liberation forces, as they called themselves, and that all correspondence was liable to illegal censorship, so she had taken what precautions she could.

One Saturday night Siobhan attended a small tea party in honour of her aunt's birthday. She met the gamekeeper again, who was inquisitive to say the least, but she fobbed him off by saying she was too busy training her horse to have looked into the affair, but yes, she was still interested and if he found out anything else would he please let her know.

On Sunday she was up and about very early. Dawn was on the point of breaking with the promise of a good day. On the spur of the moment she decided she would go for a long ride along the coast, heading westward. This would give her a chance to survey that area, but also enable her to bypass and check the location she already knew, just to keep it fresh in her memory. She had no intention of actually going to the cache, but she could pass close enough to check her initial marker point.

The morning, as promised, broke clear and warm. High above the larks sang their morning chorus. Down on the beach she heard the piping of the oystercatchers, and the moorland resounding to the mournful cry of the curlew. Clouds of herring gulls screamed abuse at everything that moved, whilst a few of them stood marching on the spot, tramping the close cropped grass to make the worms come to the surface, providing them with a welcome change of diet.

Siobhan let her mount have his head as he ran off the early morning steam. This exuberance he always displayed at the start of any ride. When he had settled down to his mile-eating canter, she surveyed the passing countryside, trying to imagine where the best places for concealment lay. Always she came up with the same answer, it had to be desolate and deserted, similar to the hiding place she already knew.

With this in mind she took interest in any copse she passed, particularly if there was a track running into it.

Lunchtime found her quite close to Lough Foyle. She sat in the shade of a gnarled old oak tree and ate the picnic lunch she had brought with her, but she lost her red juicy apple to her companion.

She was looking down on the lough from a vantage point of perhaps a thousand feet. She decided she would travel no further westwards, for the county to the west of the lough was part of Eire.

The border between Ulster and Eire would create a problem to gunrunners. Getting through the patrol points would be a hazard they would wish to avoid. No! The illegal cargoes would definitely be brought ashore only in Ulster.

Resting for a while longer, immersed in the hypnotic lullaby of a summer's day in the country, her thoughts turned to Donald, and how nice it would be to have him sitting here beside her. Her nipples quivered and jumped out like quivering rosebuds and she felt the familiar warmth flooding her yearning, unfulfilled virginal emptiness.

Her hand sought and found her aching mound, and the moistened softness within, a declaration of the desperate need for her lover, and the soothing intimacy he could provide. Her virgin soul screamed for surcease from this terrible aching need that rolled deep within her, but it was a futile cry of longing, that made her clutch in wanton abandon at her aching portal.

She sat up, mentally berated herself, jumped quickly to her feet and made ready to travel.

Her Black Beast dropped his head and sniffed at the core of her femininity. Gently she pushed his questing head to one side, 'my God,' she thought, 'I am in a bad way, but I'm afraid, my handsome big fellow, you are not the answer to this problem.' As she settled in the saddle she could feel the vaginal wetness and berated herself again, 'look where your thoughts have got you, the unpleasantness of sitting in a puddle all the way home.'

It was some time before the tingling in her blood subsided, for the continual rubbing of the pommel of the saddle was much akin to masturbation. With an effort of will she brought her mind back to the business in hand.

For the return journey she decided to stay further inland, perhaps a couple of miles from the coast as she progressed eastwards and home.

Reaching the top of a rounded hill and looking seawards, she spotted derelict farm buildings in a dip of land that had been hidden from her view on the outward journey.

The deep hollow in which the steading lay was partially surrounded by trees. An outstanding feature that would require closer investigation was the three strands of looped, barbed wire that were strung across the perimeter wall that went completely round the buildings.

'What was the need for security such as that on broken down old farm buildings?' she wondered idly.

'Curiouser and curiouser,' she thought, then the answer screamed into her mind in a searing flash.

This is where all the heavy armament is stored, it was the perfect place. Out of public view, but with a reasonable country lane leading directly to it.

For a moment longer she scrutinised the buildings, trying to imprint the geography of it in her mind. A figure emerged from what seemed to be the farmhouse, the only building with a good roof on it. He was closely followed by two vicious-looking Doberman Pinscher guard dogs.

That was the decider; she knew with deep certainty that this was not some innocent derelict old farm.

With rising excitement she urged her mount down the slope, intending to circle round the entire compound. The windswept trees gave her good cover as she proceeded along a narrow track heading towards the steading.

She reached a level area about half a mile short of the buildings and two men leapt out from a tangle of bramble and wild woodbine, draped from scraggy saplings, at the side of the path she was following.

The first of the two grabbed the bridle, hurling abuse at her. The Black Beast went berserk. Like a striking hawk, and with a petrifying scream of demented rage, his teeth clamped on the assailants shoulder, and he shook the man as a terrier shakes a rat.

Siobhan heard the bones crunch and the dreadful screech of pain that escaped from the mouth that was a rictus of agony. Her mighty warhorse dropped the offending bundle at his feet and lifting his ironclad forefoot, smashed it down on the ribcage beneath him. Next he whirled in a dance of death and grabbed the second assailant, who was trying to pull Siobhan from the saddle as she valiantly tried to fend him off.

In a frenzy of anger the rig colt got purchase on his rider's adversary, and again the dreadful teeth sank deep into human flesh.

The arm, upraised to strike Siobhan, never landed. It was caught in the powerful jaws of the maddened horse. The recipient, in crazy fear, lashed out with his other fist at the horse's head, but it was only fuel to the flame.

The great neck muscles bulged as the horse lifted the idiot clear of the track, shook him and then threw him back onto the ground. As he tried to scramble clear, two front feet crashed into his unprotected shoulders, smashing him onto the ground.

The Black Beast rose on his powerful hind quarters, preparing to drop those heavy front feet onto the recumbent figure, but Siobhan took control and pirouetted the fighting horse on his hind legs so that, when the feet landed, it was on the track and facing away from the steading.

With a sense of urgency she pressed the horse into a gallop and kept him going at quite a furious pace for a couple of miles. One reason was to burn off any residue of rage in her mount, the other was to get as far away from the farmhouse as possible. She didn't want the occupants of the farmhouse to think anything other than it had been a wayfaring rider who had stumbled on the hideout by accident.

What would be made of the attack by her horse she couldn't imagine but of one thing she was sure, anyone from that isolated farmstead would in future approach any other rider with a great deal more caution.

Delayed reaction took hold, and she dismounted shakily. With retching heaves she evacuated the entire contents of her stomach in the lee of a craggy, moss-covered boulder. Her lathered mount looked on with a benign calmness that decried his previous exhibition of demonic rage.

Feeling stronger and more in charge of herself, Siobhan slapped his neck fondly and pulled his ears as she thanked him for being her saviour. She had no idea what might have resulted in her chance meeting with those two men, but she had a nasty feeling inside that it would not have been something she would have enjoyed. She was eternally grateful for the intervention of her powerful ally. 'Damn, but he was the bonny fighter.'

She made him kneel and climbed into the saddle, now with fresh purpose in mind. She decided to head directly to the coast. When she reached the shoreline she ran the colt along the edge of the incoming tide. He seemed to enjoy the splashing of the salt water and, after a good gallop, he frisked about in a happy and playful fashion. Thoroughly cheerful, he seemed free of any traces of latent illfeeling.

If anyone had the thought of tracking them, they would soon lose the trail, for the incoming tide would wash away any hoofprints.

Travelling in and out of the many inlets and small coves that created the jagged coastline of that area meant that the time factor for the return journey exceeded greatly the time taken on the outward leg, so it was with a sigh of relief that Siobhan brought her weary mount to a halt outside her aunt's steading.

She washed the tired horse, getting rid of any traces of seawater, then she groomed and leathered him till he represented a burnished perfection. She fed him a measure of oats and made sure his bedding was dry.

She knew she had used him long and hard, and was grateful that he was such a robust character with a tremendous depth and staying power as he had displayed this very day.

Siobhan continued her nightly vigils and soon determined that she had discovered eight country locations, plus of course the derelict farmhouse, which were being used to store illegal merchandise.

It was a couple of weeks before she found the ninth and final source, and she knew it was the final one, for thereafter she was led to ones she already knew.

Now was the time to return to civilisation. Home to Barranbarrach and her loved ones. She had received a letter from her father, and from Mari, pleading with her to forget her self-imposed exile, and come home. She conceded now, but only because it fitted in with her plans.

Both horse and rider made a leisurely journey south. Both were tough as whipcord after the recent months of hard riding and continual exercise.

It was a good full day's ride to reach their destination of Barranbarrach, but Siobhan kept the pace slow, making a holiday of the journey. It gave her time to absorb what was happening in the countryside around her, and she realised that summer was virtually at an end. The tell-tale signs were readily evident.

Lapwings and starlings had gathered in flocks, as had the swallows and house martins, making ready for their migratory flights to warmer climes.

Half wild native Irish ponies had started to thicken their coats, and a couple of stoats she glimpsed briefly were betwixt and between summer brown and winter camouflage white, like raggy taggy piebalds.

But it was the leaves turning to autumn colours that convinced her that summer was over and that autumn had arrived.

The outrageous colours of reds, brown, yellows, and deep greens vied with each other as if in defiance of the threat of bitter winter weather that would follow this final time of harvest for the pre-winter foragers.

As Siobhan reached the outer perimeters of the Barranbarrach estate, she felt a sense of sheer joy at being back in her own neighbourhood. A place of security and happiness. Only now did she realise the enormous pressure that she had exposed herself to.

She breathed a great sigh of relief and with a whoop of sheer happiness she sent her charger racing the last few miles home.

Busy though a hard working stud may be, she was nevertheless observed whilst still a mile out from the stud buildings, and as was usual, the news swept like wildfire, resulting in a welcoming party awaiting when she finally pulled up at the door of the Black Beast's loosebox.

Dutifully they held back, allowing her to unsaddle him. She led him inside and allowed him a short drink only. She left him then, but it would not be for long, as he needed walking around until he cooled off, then he would be groomed and fed, but oh, she just had to feel Mari's arms around her for a moment, and have a kiss from Stuart.

It was a moment or two before she could reach Mari, for everybody was crowding around to touch her and welcome her home. Tears in her eyes, she at last reached the haven of Mari's arms. She was scooped up by Mari, who folded her deep into her bosom as if she would never let loose.

Stuart was forced to accept second best as he put his arms around them both, and kissed whatever he could, noses, cheeks or fragrant hair.

When Donald left home to return to Belfast he had with him two brace of rabbits he had killed that morning in the dawn mists. He called in at a fishmongers in Ballymena and bought a pair of good sized salmon, which he would produce in the Oak and Sloe as proof of having been away on a successful poaching trip.

He speculated on what the reaction would be to what had occurred in Rourke's office, and wondered idly if any suspicions would be directed his way. He knew of no reason why it should, for he was sure that he had left nothing that would incriminate him, but still, there was always a chance of the unexpected happening.

So well had he played the part of a fawning subservient that nobody gave the slightest thought to him being involved, but a lingering topic of conversation was what had happened in Rourke's office, and wasn't it strange that two R.U.C. constables had been found in there, badly hurt by all accounts.

When Donald was grudgingly told the story, he had to virtually bite his tongue to stop himself shouting out loud that he didn't know they were policeman or he would have made himself known and explained his presence.

For the duration of the summer months Donald and Tammy continued in their efforts to acquire the information that they so desperately needed, but it became increasingly evident that they were chasing a rainbow's end. A radical rethink was needed.

Tammy made one of his special phone calls, and a meeting was convened at which Donald would be included. It would be the first time he was to meet Commander Denham-Tring, but another person had accompanied the Commander. He was the current Deputy Chief Constable of Belfast, and he was here without the knowledge of his immediate superior.

Denham-Tring had been busy in his own way, winkling out the loyal members to the crown of the Ulster Constabulary, and he had discovered that the Chief Constable was in the doubtful category, at the moment nothing concrete, but serious doubts.

The consequence of this meeting was that Tammy was to leave Belfast and go north to the area where the merchandise was being offloaded and carry out investigations in that locality. After further argument, Denham-Tring agreed that Donald could accompany Tammy, but this only after Tammy had explained to the Commander the special skills Donald had and his incredible talent in the field.

Half an hour later Tammy had another meeting, this time in Rourke's office. Bluntly he told Rourke he was dissolving the partnership. It wasn't paying anyhow, so he was leaving Belfast for greener pastures.

Rourke immediately stated that nobody alive left the organisation once they had joined and Tammy had better think again. When Tammy insisted, he was grabbed by the arms by two of the gang, and slammed across the desk as his arms were twisted up his back.

Two others quickly caught his legs and pulled them straight so that he was spreadeagled and helplessly trapped on top of the desk.

Cruelly, Rourke grabbed a handful of hair, and twisting it with malicious enjoyment, lifted Tammy's head until he could look directly into his face.

"Aha! Hard man," he grated through clenched teeth, "not so hard now, eh?" He banged Tammy's face onto the desk, and chortled aloud at the sound of the nose breaking. "How do you like your own treatment?" he gloated, "I've waited a long time for the pleasure of this day. I knew it would come. I know I will remember with great satisfaction this day of days."

"Now then! As a reminder that nasty things can happen, and I can be the provider, I am going to leave you with a little souvenir that you will carry for the rest of your life. Now then, my conquered hero, my itsy bitsy hard man of Glasgow, have you ever heard of knee capping? Oh! It's wonderful sport! A wonderful technique involved, that is the essence of it. A gun is held at the back of the knee and fired. This literally blows the knee cap clean off. Well, I tell a wee lie! Pardon me please, it is not clean off. Oh dear, no! It tends to be quite messy."

"This will be my little gift to you. Only one mind. I don't give too much away for nothing, but this you can willingly have, hard man. Hard man, my arse!"

Tammy screamed in maddened rage. As the muzzle of the gun came to rest in the hollow of his right knee, he exploded, an eruption of adrenaline filled him with maniacal strength.

Leaving a handful of hair in Rourke's grasp, he jerked his head free, and despite the excruciating pain in his arms, he threw his head violently to the right, smashing it into the side of the face nearest to him.

Swinging to the left he made contact with the face that was turned towards him in surprise, the bully on his right fell to the floor completely stunned, the other on the left reared backwards with his nose in ruins and his eyes streaming with tears.

Donald, who had been passing the office door on the way to his own room to pack prior to leaving for Barranbarrach, heard Tammy's initial scream and burst through the door, his warrior's song thrumming deep in his throat, a deadly cadence.

The promise of violence throbbed with spinechilling insistence, paralysing and devastating with horrifying menace.

The torture merchants froze in the face of this appalling chimeral harbinger of destruction as it wheeled and danced a jig of havoc.

Three of the gang were utterly destroyed in as many minutes, with retaliation impossible against this whirling dervish that was like a berserker in full demented action.

As Donald was committing this havoc, Tammy, now free from restraint, dropped to the floor. His questing hand found the throwing knife that Donald had given him at Christmas, in its leg sheath.

As he rose above the level of the desk, Rourke fired the handgun he had grabbed from the desk drawer. The bullet scored a furrow along the side of Tammy's head.

Rourke fired again and this time the bullet passed between Tammy's arm and chest and he felt it burn as it sliced along his armpit area.

He was not to be deterred, despite the burning pain, he threw himself across the desk and plunged the knife into the chest of Rourke. Dragging the blade free, he sliced savagely across the wrist of the hand holding the gun, nerveless fingers let it fall free.

All the fight went out of Rourke as he slid sideways then toppled onto the floor. Tammy whirled now to join the fray behind him, but he was too late. All the gang had now been accounted for and Donald was calmly checking to make sure none of them were playing possum.

The barman came through the door, horror and astonishment fighting for supremacy on his face. With an impatient wave of his hand he dismissed a gathering crowd behind him. His eyes darted around the room as he surveyed the damaged figures lying on the floor.

With new-found respect he addressed himself to Donald.

"So you are not a wee bachle after all. You are in fact the total fighting machine. I watched that performance from the doorway. I am sure I shall never see the likes again. In the name of God, who are you? What is your purpose here? Whatever it is, I hope you are finished, and that you will soon be gone."

Ending this little speech, the barman turned and left the room, still shaking his head at what he had witnessed. When the regulars of the pub heard the story he was going to have a lot of pleasure telling, they would be shaking in their shoes. Not one of them had been anywhere near pleasant to that pseudo little poacher, either treating him with contempt or ignoring him at best.

The fuel of adrenaline had deserted Tammy and he slid to the floor with a groan, even his iron will could sustain him no more. The two bullet wounds were bleeding profusely, particularly the head wound, and this loss of blood was doing peculiar things to his vision and hearing.

With an exclamation of concern, Donald leapt across the littered floor, and kneeling beside his injured friend, gently lowered him into a more comfortable position.

Gritting his teeth, Tammy gestured to the phone and grated out his request. Donald was flabbergasted. Here was his friend, in pain, losing a lot of blood, and he wanted to make a phone call. Tammy was insistent, so Donald handed him the phone and listened in astonishment when Tammy reeled off a string of instructions.

'Agent down. Laundry required. Priority one.'

The phone slid from Tammy's hand and he passed into unconsciousness. Breathing a sigh of relief, Donald checked the wounds. The head wound was still pouring blood. Roughly he tore the shirt front out of one of those available lying around him. Making a wad of it, he placed it over the head wound, then taking his garotte he bound it firmly in place.

The wound under Tammy's arm was superficial but still bleeding copiously. This was not a big problem to Donald. He brought the arm close to the chest wall, then used a wide leather belt, again taken from one of the recumbent figures, crossed the arms and pulled the belt tight around, forcing both arms firmly against the chest wall.

He manoeuvred his friend across his shoulders in the fireman's lift, then almost at a run he made his way through the pub to where his old car was parked on the street. Carefully he lowered Tammy onto the rear seat, made him as comfortable as he could and then set off for the hospital.

Shortly after leaving the pub a black van coming in the opposite direction almost forced him off the road. He cursed the mindless bastard, not knowing that it was the assistance that Tammy had phoned for in his cryptic message, and, had he waited, he would have had help in getting Tammy to medical aid.

He reached the hospital after what seemed an interminable time. He raced inside and quickly got help when he told the receptionist that he had a gunshot victim outside, and he was sure he was bleeding to death, if not already dead.

Brusquely he was brushed aside as a young doctor and a nurse took over. Anxiously he paced the corridor until a nurse took pity on him. She took him to the staff standby room and pressed a cup of coffee into his hands.

She advised him that the initial examination had shown that Tammy was quite lucky in the circumstances. The underarm wound was totally superficial and would heal quickly. The head wound had bled a lot but that was normal and, since the bullet hadn't broken any bones, that wound would also heal without problems. There would be scars, of course, but they would hardly be noticeable amongst the many others his friend carried.

What kind of job was the man involved in, for goodness sake, in many years of nursing she couldn't remember ever having seen such a scarred body.

Donald told her that his friend was an inspector of police, and was she sure he was going to be alright?

She reassured Donald on this point, but suggested that if Donald carried any kind of authority he should insist that his friend be given leave of absence for quite an extended period. "Call it rehabilitation, if you like," she added.

The young doctor came in and more or less repeated what the nurse had told him. Yes, Donald could go in and see him, but he had given Tammy a mild sedative and he recommended that Tammy be allowed to rest.

When the nurse ushered Donald into the cubicle where Tammy was lying, he was confronted by two truculent looking characters, who asked him what the hell he wanted in here.

Donald explained that Tammy was his friend and that he had brought him here and he would like to know who they were and what they were doing in here.

With an obvious effort, Tammy intervened from the bed.

"Peace, gentlemen," he whispered, "we are all friends together," then, seeming to draw strength from inexhaustible reserves, he continued, speaking directly to one of the burly men.

"This is Donald. He has been helping me. Take care of him. Help him to get out of Belfast. There will be a contract on him, now that our cover is blown."

Roughly Donald intervened, pushing forward to the side of the bed and looking down at this friend.

"If you think for a minute that I am leaving you here in that condition on your own, then that head wound is more serious that the doctor has found it to be," he declared, then continuing in the same vein, "I will be here until you are released from hospital. Nobody will get at you while you are incapacitated. We leave here together, and it's not open to discussion."

Tammy was weakly shaking his head and with a weary sigh insisted, "These two guys are policemen Donald, that is why they are here, to make sure we are both looked after. Please! One of them will see you out of Belfast. Please go!"

It was stalemate. The policemen and Tammy argued, but they were pitted against an immovable force.

In the end Tammy was removed to a single side room and an extra bed was supplied for the night to accommodate Donald. The following morning Tammy was discharged with exhortation from the doctor to take things easy for a while.

With beautious innocence that fooled nobody Tammy agreed, then he and Donald were free.

An unmarked police car transported them to Barranbarrach, and Donald's old car was disposed of in a local scrapyard.

Mari and Bridget wept copious tears at the sight of the wounded Tammy and nearly nursed him to a different kind of death. They waited on him hand and foot until, at last, he could take it no longer, and insisted that he had to get up and get out, for there was unfinished business to take care of.

It fell upon Donald now to take an injured person and bring him back to full fighting fitness, and his mentor, Chi Li, would have been pleased at the first class job he did of it.

A month after being wounded Tammy declared himself fit. It was time to make fresh plans for his sojourn to the north of the province to complete the task to which he had been committed.

Both he and Donald had been aware that the mode of transport would have to be horseback, and to that end they had included a lot of riding in Tammy's rehabilitation, and, in fact, Tammy was now at a good standard, providing his mount was well-behaved.

Donald had chosen a big Connemara Grey for Tammy. She was sensible and quiet, but best of all, tolerant with a novice rider and with her help Tammy had gained in confidence every day. Soon he sat with a natural balance and easy familiarity, and could complete the tasks necessary to prepare her for riding. In addition, he was now capable of seeing to her needs by way of feeding, grooming and general care.

Donald chose for himself an ugly, rawboned, hammerheaded gelding. Although he showed none of the finer attributes, by way of looks of his kind, he was strong in wind and limb and could run all day.

Donald had first of all decided he would use the pair of Arabs to go north, but fought the temptation. They would attract attention wherever they went. Since the mission was to be as covert as possible it made sense to use less outstanding mounts.

At last all the preparations were complete. The time had come to make the journey to the northern coast. Autumn was heralding its approach with a crispness in the mornings and the shadows lying longer on the ground.

The two young men were quite happy about this as it would give them longer hours of darkness in which to carry out investigative reconnaissance when they reached their operative area.

The first thing they would have to do would be to try to make contact with Siobhan to see if she had learned anything.

Donald and Tammy had continued practising their warrior skills and were both in good condition physically. Mentally they were determined to achieve a result, and were in fact now eager to get started.

They decided they would leave Barranbarrach on the first of September, which was three days hence, so with the decision made they took a day's holiday and went rough shooting, and thus they were not in the party that welcomed Siobhan home.

Chapter Fifteen

Siobhan composed herself and withdrew from the loving embrace of her 'in-laws-to-be' reluctantly. Gently she pointed out that her trusty steed needed her attentions. Knowing his character, her colleagues made no offer to help but started to drift quietly away to their various tasks.

Patiently Mari and Stuart waited until Siobhan had finished attending to her companion of the past few months. A final loving hug round the glistening, proudly arched neck and she was ready to accompany them to the manor house.

On the short walk Siobhan could contain herself no longer. The questions that had been bubbling on her lips since first she dismounted.

"Is Donald still in Belfast with Tammy? Is he well? Have you heard from him recently?" The words tumbled from trembling lips in a torrent of concern.

Mari glanced over her head at Stuart, and with a conniving wink, replied quite offhandedly,

"Oh yes! He is well. Yes, we saw him not long ago. He has been worried about you. He said he was missing you something terrible. I feel sure he should be coming home quite soon."

Adroitly she changed the subject to other topics, and when they reached the house it was all fuss and bother about having baths and washing hair, with 'goodness gracious, dear girl, have you been sleeping with that horse?' Deliberately the talk went on non-stop, with the name of Donald a stranger to her lips.

Donald and Tammy returned from their day's shooting and an excited Mari met them at the door, a forefinger to her smiling lips.

"She's home, she's home!" she exclaimed in a theatrical whisper, "our darling Siobhan has come home!" Donald began running on the spot and made to dart past his mother, but she placed a hand on his chest and stopped him.

"No, Donald! I know you want to see her, but she is in the bath, and then she will be getting dressed for dinner. She doesn't know you are here, so please, can we surprise her when she comes down for pre-dinner drinks. I managed to get hold of Bridget and warn her not to say a word about you being here. Oh, we are going to have a lovely welcome home party for her. Please say you agree, Donald?"

Donald looked at his excited mother, and couldn't deny the appeal in her sparkling eyes.

"Mum!" he exclaimed, "you really are a devious lady, but alright, let's give

Siobhan a surprise, but in the meantime, just tell me how Tammy and I are going to get washed and changed. We have to go upstairs to accomplish that, as you well know."

Well he might have known, Mari had it all worked out to the last detail. Stuart, Bridget, herself and two house servants acted as lookouts at vantage points. These cloak and dagger methods got the two young men into their rooms, bathed, dressed and back downstairs without Siobhan being alerted to their presence.

The tension in the evening lounge was palpable. Drinks had been poured, but glasses twirled in animated fingers moist with expectancy.

Donald placed his drink on a nearby table, for his trembling fingers had threatened to spill it ever since it had been handed to him.

At last the door opened, Siobhan stepped through and paused. The scream was piercing, rattling and vibrating off the eardrums as she launched herself across the room into the open arms of her true love.

She kissed him. She bit him. She dug her fingers deep into the blond hair, twined her fingers through it and pulled. She was crying and laughing and trying to talk, all at the same time.

Donald held her with a fierceness and passion that matched her own. It was as if there was no-one else in the room. Their reunion was theirs alone, but the burning essence of their love was gloriously luminous, and touched the hearts of the delighted family who were willing spectators.

Holding tightly to each other, they collapsed into the sofa behind them. Stuart brought them drinks and chided gently,

"If you two can get settled down we can have these drinks then maybe we can get round to having a bit of dinner, hm?"

Siobhan took the offered glass, took a sip, kissed Donald, stood up, gave the glass to Stuart, gave him a smeary smoochy kiss and darted across to Mari. Open arms enfolded her again as she taxed Mari about their earlier conversation.

"I thought it was peculiar. I've never known you not be ready to talk about Donald, and there you were, so aggravatingly evasive. Now I understand! Mari, you are truly incorrigible, but what a lovely surprise. Thank you Mari I am truly delirious with happiness."

After dinner they repaired to the evening lounge where Siobhan brought them up to date with what she had managed to achieve during her stay on the northern coast.

There were gasps of consternation and concern when she told them about meeting the two men at the derelict farmhouse. She then explained how her Black

Charger had become involved, and the damage he had done in a mere few moments of time, and said she was sure if he had not attacked she would have been subjected to some very unsavoury attention at the hands of the evil pair.

Donald expressed a desire to go at once and give the big fellow a carrot or something to show his gratitude, but Siobhan dissuaded him, saying that her fourlegged sweetheart deserved a night of peace and quiet after the gruelling routine they had been following just recently.

Donald and Tammy gave what news they had to Siobhan, deliberately making light of the fracas at the Oak and Sloe. Then they told her that in two days time they would be heading for the area she had more or less just left.

The preparations were complete and, apart from a few staples, they would be living off the land, hunting and fishing, sleeping rough, indeed they were quite looking forward to it.

In a voice that brooked no argument Siobhan announced her intention of accompanying them, after all she was the one who knew where all the caches were, including the whereabouts of the isolated farmhouse.

A concerned chorus of voices tried to contradict. She had done enough. She should now rest on her laurels. Siobhan would have none of it, she hadn't spent all that time and effort for nothing. She asked them to see reason. Should Donald and Tammy go without her how could she possible explain where the caches were so that they would be able to find them, and if she couldn't do this, then they would have to spend time, as she had done, in locating the depositories. As far as she was concerned, they were not looking at this in a reasonable way at all.

She applied the coup de grace with all the skill of a master swordsman. If they left without her they would realise that this had gained them nothing, for she would be hard on their heels.

Grudgingly Donald and Tammy agreed, but now they had another problem. They would have to find the equivalent of a safe house. Winter would be showing its face before long and it was inconceivable that Siobhan should rough it out in the open as the two men were prepared to do.

Siobhan couldn't really return to her aunt's croft because explanations would be almost impossible. They didn't want to take lodgings anywhere in the area, for again questions would be asked.

For a while nothing was said, as each wrestled with the problem in their own minds. How could they be in that sensitive area and be accepted in a disinterested fashion. To be seen, but to be ignored as common place and unworthy of note. Aye, it was a puzzler!

Stuart recharged the glasses as the hall clock struck the hour of midnight, and was about to say that this was a wee doch and doris before bed, when Siobhan jumped to her feet with an excited squeal, splashing good malt all over Donald's knees.

"I've got it! I've got it!", she trilled, excitement rippling through the rich dulcet voice, "Oh, it's so simple it's perfect. You know that tinker's caravan that Conal keeps down on his croft? Well, I'm sure he would let us use that. We can check it out and ensure it is habitable, as I'm sure it is, for he goes on holiday in it, we'll even give it a lick of paint if need be. Oh yes! We will travel as gypsies. Everybody ignores gypsies. We can travel around to our hearts' content. Who will care? It's just the very thing."

By this time Donald was standing beside his excited sweetheart, arms around her, he kissed her flushed cheek.

"What a brain? And beautiful with it! You are truly well blessed my darling. I couldn't agree more, it's just the very thing, as you say. It even has a wood burning stove in it. We'll be as snug as a nest of fleas."

"Ah, just a minute! We're going to need another horse to pull the damned great thing. I wonder if we could borrow Conal's Clydesdale mare as well. She'd be strong enough, I guess."

"No need for that," Siobhan butted in, "my big fellow will pull it easily."

"But he hasn't been trained to harness, has he?" Donald asked doubtfully, "and knowing what he is like, he's probably kick it to pieces."

"No he wouldn't," Siobhan retorted defensively, "while you two are fixing up the caravan, I will train him using an old dray. I bet you he'll be ready before you have got the caravan organised."

The delay for these extra preparations cost them two full weeks. Siobhan trained her Black Beast by getting him to pull the trunks of saplings on either side of the riding saddle to begin with. When he was happy with this, she then harnessed him into an old haywagon to get him used to the rumbling noise behind him. Gradually she worked her way behind him, instead of leading him, and the final glory was her sitting at the front of the haywain as he plodded along and took directions from afar.

The majority of the time was spent on the complete refurbishing of the caravan that Conal had given without demur. Mari took charge of this phase, determined that her 'children' would have as good accommodation as possible under the circumstances, even though she was unhappy at losing them again, for whatever reason.

Stuart attended to the mechanical side of things. Checking harness connection points for soundness, removing all the wheels and having new steel rims fitted. He greased the hub assemblies, and oiled all the metal parts. At last he announced himself satisfied.

On the 15th September the three adventurers set off on their journey north. Bridget stood in forlorn frustration. Tammy had flatly refused to allow her to accompany them. She had promised to stay in the caravan and act as housewife, cooking the meals and doing the laundering as was required, and in general being a factotum in making life somewhat easier for them but Tammy had been adamant. She was to remain at Barranbarrach. Mari held her, although swamped in her own misery, but more than willing to give comfort where it was needed.

Tammy looked every part the gypsy, with his swarthy complexion and bell-bottomed trousers. He had a gaudy cummerbund round his waist with the ragged ends hanging to his knees, a spotted bandanna round his neck and tied under his chin, the only thing lacking was a ring in his ear.

Siobhan was a Romany delight, wearing a dirndl type skirt, Victorian lace blouse and a heavy wool plaid round her shoulders. Bright red ribbons tied around the rich, thick, tawny hair completed her 'tout ensemble'. The perfect sultry, sexy-eyed wanton gypsy woman, siren and enchantress of the innocent husbands and sons of the general public. Merrily she laughed at the look on Donald's face when first he saw her in her disguise.

Donald had proved to be a challenge to the inventiveness of Mari to effect a satisfactory appearance. His blond hair was not going to be readily accepted as of true Romany extraction. In the end he had to wear a disgusting old woollen granny bonnet with a pompom bouncing around on the top.

Since all three were well suntanned there was no problem of looking dark skinned. Mari declared she had done what she could, but it is doubtful if the three youngsters would have suffered much more titivating, for they were eager to be away.

Harness brasses gleamed and tiny bells tinkled as the big black horse took them along at a steady pace. Donald rode on one side, Tammy on the other, in line with Siobhan, sitting high up on the driving seat of the caravan.

From time to time they had to pull over and allow other wayfarers to pass. A couple of times they heard 'damned tinkers' shouted in their direction. Far from being displeased they were happy to hear the invective, for it confirmed that they looked the part.

Donald's rapport with Siobhan's horse made it easier for the team as a whole.

All they had to do now was get the big fellow to at least tolerate Tammy. It was something they would work on as the days went by. In some ways it was essential that they could interchange if the necessity arose, including changing horses.

The three mounts that had been chosen for the journey had been held in a separate paddock to allow them to get used to each other and sort out the natural pecking order, which would make them a viable working team.

Siobhan and Donald made a point of always going down to the paddock to feed the three of them with tidbits and give them a light groom. It was only a handling and rapport building exercise which allowed Donald to keep up the harmony he had previously established with the big horse, but it also got them used to coming when they were called.

One morning when they arrived at the paddock Donald gave an exclamation of surprise. He had thought for a couple of days that the Connemara Grey was coming into season, even though it was a bit late in the year. Well, here was the evidence that she certainly had.

The Black Beast was standing behind her and had obviously just finished covering her. His large black and pink mottled penis hung limply beneath his belly, shining with the lubricant oils of the mare.

The mare was standing with her tail in the air, the damp pink vulva flashing and blinking spasmodically. The male horse nuzzled at this enticing pulsing softness, and as the erotic scent assailed his nostrils, the great penis came erect in a convulsive throbbing shaft as he mounted her again.

The vibrating instrument of creation slid into the moist depths of the mare as she seemed to press herself rearwards, seeking the ultimate penetration.

The male horse reached forward and gently grabbed her behind the crest of the mane. The strong buttocks worked vigorously in and out for approximately two minutes and, with a final convulsive lunge forward, his head reached high into the air, then the pumping action ceased. He stayed deeply inserted for a moment, as if to extend the pleasure of the coupling a little longer.

Reluctantly, it seemed, he slipped quietly off the acquiescent mare, to stand behind her in a satisfied demeanour, then moving up alongside her, he rubbed his head against her neck.

Watching this basic primal act of procreation affected Donald as it never had before when he had assisted at the covering of mares. He was aware that his own needs were manifestly prominent, and made as if to turn away slightly from Siobhan, but she had obviously been affected too.

She grabbed him with the roughness of raw need. Pressing herself full length against him as a sob burst from her throat.

"Oh, Donald, wasn't that beautiful? I wonder if he has impregnated her. He has got one teste, remember. Oh! I hope he has, they would produce a wonderful foal."

She pressed tighter against him, moaning as she ground her mound of venus against the hardness she felt at his groin. Her mouth searched feverishly for his as her pulses raced in tumultuous discord.

A wild raging torrent of desperate need engulfed her as she raged in despair at the confining restrictions of material that separated them.

"Donald, Donald! Oh! Please, Donald! I have an awful need of you my darling," she keened into his mouth through lips swollen raw with desire.

Donald stood rooted to the spot, his own desires more than matching the urgency of this seductive temptress in his arms. His swollen penis throbbed with the exquisite pain of need, then denial caused his testes to complain with a savage ache that was breathtaking.

A Calvanistic streak deep within his soul would not let him yield to temptation. It was neither the time nor the place, but additionally, he felt that Siobhan would deeply regret not coming to wedlock a virgin.

He held her and caressed her until he felt the storm subside and the trembling ease. He felt sure she would know that he was not rejecting her and would in fact be glad he had used his strength to avoid what both so desperately wanted. To succumb.

Quietly he turned her away from the horses and slowly walked towards the house until they were out of sight of the paddock.

He turned Siobhan to face him and said with desperate intensity.

"Siobhan my darling, I'll get mother to arrange the wedding for as soon as we return from the north, for honest to God I am near to bursting from need of you. I doubt if I would have the strength to withstand another such storm as we both experienced just then. I love you dear heart, believe me. It would have been easy to let nature take its course, but I feel you would regret it in years to come, wishing that you had married virgo intacta."

He kissed her, and she clung to him, still flushed and now feeling weak at the knees in the aftermath of the emotional storm that had raged through her with such devastating passion.

"Oh! I know you are right, my darling," she murmured tremulously, "but it is so difficult to comply with the requirements of society. I say it again without shame, I do have this compelling need for you, but I will try to help you by not losing control again. I love you, my dearest love."

Now at last they were on their way north. The small gypsy troop slowly wound their way through country lanes. Donald displayed his unerring accuracy with the catapult, bagging rabbits for the pot with consummate ease.

Siobhan teased him about being a wee boy at heart, but Donald just smiled his enigmatic smile, and hoped she would never see the uses such a simple device could be put to.

Tammy smiled in sympathy with his friend, knowing in fact it was a deadly instrument in the hands of Donald, and that it had got them out of trouble on the day the friends had first met.

Two days of travel brought them to a site that they agreed would make a good base camp, it nestled in a river valley of the Bann, slightly south of Coleraine and Limvady.

They had turned off the country road into a little used track that took them into a mixed deciduous and coniferous copse. This was ideal in two main respects, first it would help to protect them against the elements, but also it would be a place of concealment.

A stream of clear water flowed through the copse which would provide for their needs, but additionally there was quite a good grassy area on either side of the stream to provide a bit of rough grazing for the horses.

Once the horses had been unsaddled they were put on a lunging rein and allowed to have a good roll. First the ugly gelding waved his feet in the air, then the mare took her turn. The Black Beast stood quietly watching, and when the mare was satisfied he went over and rolled in exactly the same place. He was showing one of the latent instincts of a wild stallion, for this is something they do in the wild to leave their mark in the roll hollow. Their scent is the last one, therefore the one that lingers.

He went across to the Connemara Grey and checked her out, nuzzling at her tail head. He was unlucky, she was definitely past her acceptance period, and kicked out at him in warning. He gave an exaggerated sigh then left her to go and graze. He was probably thinking it was better to have loved and lost, than never to have loved at all.

Donald and Siobhan watched this byplay of approach and rejection, looked at each other and smiled with shared memories. Donald turned away quickly and became exceedingly busy, acutely aware that he was in a state of erection, accompanied by the now familiar grinding ache in that area.

He ended up by going upstream until he was well out of sight, where finding a deep pool, he stripped off and jumped into the icy water. Five minutes of this treatment brought his temperature and his erection under control. He looked down at himself whilst his teeth chattered and shivers racked his body, and burst out laughing at the sorry sight that met his gaze.

His scrotum was a shrunken prune of a thing, a wrinkled, empty sac. His testes had taken refuge deep in the warmth of his lower body. The once proud staff of his manhood hung like a wizened blue plum.

Hurriedly he dressed, the late autumn wind had little caress in it, rather a trail of icy fingers. He jigged around to get the circulation going, then trotted back to the camp side. It was time to get the evening meal started, and he particularly wanted to show Siobhan and Tammy his piece de resistance, rabbit baked in clay, having been stuffed with brambles and hazelnuts.

As he approached the campside, he heard the sound of raised voices. This was a surprise to say the least. He just couldn't imagine Siobhan and Tammy arguing at any time! Still, without doubt, it was definitely male and female voices raised in dispute.

Quickening his pace he soon entered the base camp and stopped in astonishment as he saw the reason for the quarrel.

When the three wanderers left Barranbarrach, Bridget had become unapproachable and decidedly indisposed to general conversation. She stamped off in high dudgeon, disappearing in the general direction of the paddock that held the rough riding stock. These were the animals that were kept for all purpose duties, and their numbers included ponies, cobs and retired hunters. She looked them over with a discerning eye, checking condition and gait. She wanted something with a bit of depth and durability.

Her trained eye kept coming back to a dun coloured cob, he seemed to have the senior position in the pecking order. He was short coupled and would not be the best of rides, but he looked the most dependable of the bunch.

'Right' she thought, 'you it is, my fine fellow. Have a good night's rest, for tomorrow you have a long way to travel.'

She had decided, Tammy or no, she would be joining the party that had left her behind. She was sure if she left first thing in the morning she was sure to catch up with them, wherever they had gone. Anyway, she would find them if she had to scour the whole of Ulster.

She had no qualms about not finding them, for sure all she had to do was keep asking people if they had seen a bunch of tinkers. They would be able to send her in the right direction, or at least say where they had seen them last, and that would be indication enough.

With a last look at her chosen mount she went back to the manor house to be met by a very concerned Mari. That worthy looked at the determined set of the jaw of Bridget and wailed despairingly.

"Oh no, Bridget, no! You must not even think of it! Tammy asked me to look after you, and I mustn't let him down. Please don't do this to me, please."

With love and kindness choking in her voice Bridget replied, "I must, Mari, I must. Don't you see? Donald has Siobhan with him. But Tammy is alone. I must be with him, to give him backing and support, as Siobhan is doing for Donald. My place is with him, Mari. Why should I sit at home in safety while they face God knows what kinds of danger? I'm sorry, Mari, I just have to go."

Mari looked at the distressed girl and knew she had lost her appeal. She understood how Bridget felt, and couldn't find it in her heart to blame her. Truth to tell, how was she going to stop this determined lass, apart from tying her to a tree or something. Giving Bridget a loving hug, she capitulated totally.

"Well, I suppose we had better go and get some things sorted out for you. Somehow you will have to be a gypsy girl as well. Come on, my darling, let's get started, for I suppose you will want to be away at cockcrow."

Early next morning Bridget caught the dun cob, surprisingly he came without hesitation at her call. The rattle of cow cake in a bucket certainly helped however.

That was the only sort of feed he got for she would be pushing him hard. In addition to the saddle and bridle, she slung a pair of saddle bags across her back behind the saddle, and she was ready for the off.

Happy and excited now, she waved a cheery goodbye to Stuart and Mari and in the pale wash of the morning light she cantered off. When the cob had cleared his pipes she increased the pace, staying just short of a punishing gait.

By late afternoon she had crossed the river Bann at Kilrea, and at the next village where she stopped to give her mount a breather, she asked the question she had asked many times that day.

A bewhiskered old codger sat on a chair made out of a beer tun, in front of the village inn, smoking a clay pipe blackened with age and continual use. Removing the short shank from his mouth, and spitting with sublime accuracy into a nearby flower tub, he nodded his head sagely. "Indeed, to be sure! He had seen a gypsy caravan, it was heading in the direction of Garvagh, and he was sure of that too."

A friend, who was at this moment inside the pub getting a drink, said he had met them as he was coming along the lane to Drumsaragh.

Thanking the garrulous old gent, she leapt into the saddle and took off in the direction the gnarled old finger was pointing.

The westering sun was hovering on the edge of the horizon, increasing the length of the already long autumn shadows. It was now a race against time. She had to find her friends before she lost daylight, or look for a hostelry for the night.

As she passed through Drumsaragh the lanes seemed to squeeze in even more. Gates and fences were obviously not a common feature of this landscape, and the stunted hedgerows were nothing more than demarcation lines.

Anxiously she scanned the ground, hoping against hope that she would notice if the caravan had turned off anywhere. The approach to wooded areas increased her vigilance, which was rewarded when eventually she saw the deep tracks of the iron shod wheels leading towards a copse in the near distance.

She followed the tracks that ran along the edge of a small river, which seemed to flow from the centre of the wood. Worry started to niggle at her, thinking that the wheel tracks were probably those of a farmer's dray, and not those of the caravan.

Then she smelt the unmistakable fragrance of burning wood and peat. Her heart leapt with a sense of pleasure and relief. It was unlikely that a farmer had a fire burning. It had to be the party she sought.

She entered the clearing and noticed at once that it had been well-chosen, even an area of pasture for the horses. She brought her own steaming mount to a halt, dismounted and in two bounds was on a dumbfounded Tammy, almost knocking him to the ground as she threw her arms around him.

His mouth opened and closed, each time his lips came together she kissed them. When his mouth opened and he tried to speak, she darted her tongue inside on a mischievous impulse. This act of intimacy and daring totally discomfited Tammy.

He grabbed her and held her close, and in a futile attempt to gain control, sank a hand into the deep lustrous tresses, to pull her head back so he could look into her eyes. She responded by turning her face into his neck and biting in teasing little nibbles.

Finally he pushed her back so that he could look into her eyes. He put a ferocious look on his face, and demanded to know just what the hell she thought she was doing here. It certainly wasn't a convenient time for a visit, and that was all it was going to be, for tomorrow she would be back off home, and make no mistake about that, my lady.

She retorted that it would be hoped he was fine and strong, because he would have to carry her. She was here because it was her place to be with him, and incidentally, she felt his chauvinistic principles didn't do him much credit.

Did he for one instant think he could drop her then pick her up again when he was ready? Well, she had a different view to that, and it went something like this. For better or worse, and he had better get it into the right rhythm, for she couldn't abide a wrong footer.

This was the scene that made Donald gasp as he re-entered the glade after his therapeutic toilette. He crossed over to where Siobhan was watching and listening with an amused smile on her face and privately taking bets with herself as to who was going to win this little encounter.

Donald put his arm around her waist, marvelling how well it seemed to fit. Gently he drew her away from the pair, faced up to each other like fighting bantam cocks.

"That will run its course," he opined, "and Tammy will lose, even if Bridget has to revert to womanly wiles to achieve it." He continued philosophically, "he is a bonny fighter but he is in there battling with nothing in his favour."

So it turned out to be, before long the combatants were wound round each other in such a fashion it would have taken an operation to separate them, and Tammy conceded that his sweetheart could remain. The proviso was that she remain at camp and be base organiser and that she would never on any account ride out on her own when Tammy was out on a field trip.

Bridget would have promised him the moon just as long as she could remain in camp, and be here each morning when he returned from his nocturnal visitations.

The following morning they awoke to the sound of the dawn chorus. This gift of the rural scene, still rich and abundant despite the smell of bad weather on the wind.

The horses were already grazing but each was given a scoop of bruised oats and half a swede to boost and enrich their diet. It was imperative that the mounts were kept in good shape for they would be worked hard over the next few weeks, being ridden long distances over rough terrain.

Each evening they would leave the secluded copse by a different route. This would avoid developing a well worn trail that would lead to their haven. This would of course mean they would often have to do extra miles to achieve their target for the night. It was an inconvenience that they had unanimously agreed must be accepted.

The four young lovers spent a leisurely day of pastoral peace within the shaded rustic scene. Donald insisted, however, that Siobhan and Tammy had a quick refresher course on stalking through the woods. Although they made a game of it, each knew the seriousness of the exercise, and tried hard to assimilate everything that Donald taught them.

As darkness fell, with sullen black clouds stealing the last of the light from the sky, preparations began for the departure. They had eaten a good sustaining meal and packed some food to take with them, for it would be a long night and hunger was sure to find them before they returned to their rustic haven.

The caravan had proved to be a warm, snug nest, with Mari's refinements truly appreciated. The addition to the sleeping number had proved of little consequence, and each had been able to stretch out comfortably and enjoy a good night's rest.

As they waited for true darkness to descend and allow their eyes to become accustomed to it, they went over the plans one more time. They would ride due west to the first cache in that direction, and work their way eastwards with Siobhan guiding them to the sources she knew.

They would not go to the exact locations, only bypass them on this occasion. Tonight would be a reconnaissance trip only, with no attempt to do anything other than check the locations and the marker points that would lead Tammy and Donald back to them.

Each time Siobhan had discovered a new source, she had drawn a rough plan of the site, with an X marking the spot where the covered hole in the ground would be found. She had added little notes to these plans, such as, mossy side of old oak, or lightening struck fir lies across the path, source is at the root end.

It was to turn out, however, that she would be needed to exactly designate the hiding place personally, for the notes couldn't give enough detail for the men to find it without delay.

This was a blow to Tammy and Donald, for they had decided between themselves that as soon as they knew the locations Siobhan would be excused firmly from the disposal project, as it would be dangerous, to say the least. They had to bow their heads to the inevitable, much as they would have liked Siobhan to be safe at the camp site when they blew up the caches.

They set off from the glade as the rain, which had threatened all day, started with an outburst of demonic fury. Cruelly it lashed with stinging impact. Horses and riders bent their heads against the furious assault, but battled on with unabated determination. The thought consoled them that at least it would keep people indoors, so their passage would go unnoticed.

Two hours of miserable demoralising progress brought them not far from Moss-side, a typical quiet Irish country village. They avoided it cautiously, keeping to the bog and moorland, a muffled indistinct movement, shadows in the night.

In a small copse, lying in a secluded little valley, Siobhan guided them to the hidden repository. The keen country trained eyes of Donald took in the salient features. He spotted the first broken branchlet that Siobhan had used for a marker, and he was the first of the group to see it.

Another long concentrated look and he knew he could return with utter confidence. They wheeled around and set of for the next nearest location. Now they were riding directly east.

At each place pointed out by Siobhan, Donald scrutinised it carefully before being led onto the next. When they had checked the final location, they turned their weary horses homewards to the caravan, which now lay due south of their present position.

They made no attempt to go anywhere near the isolated farmhouse on this occasion. That would be a separate exploit on its own. Tammy felt that this location would require Commander Denham-Tring to come up with some reinforcements to accomplish the removal of armaments located there.

Wet and cold, they slid from the saddles, stripped the horses, let them have a roll, then washed the mud off their legs and checked each hoof carefully. Then it was a scoop of well-earned oats.

Now, and only now, would they attend to their own needs. Bridget ran around doing as much as she could to ease the burden of the weary travellers.

Inside the caravan she had the kettle boiling, and a filling vegetable and rabbit stew cooking gently on the wood burning stove.

At last they were all inside the snug little haven, tired but content. They stripped off their wet clothes, each in turn going behind a blanket stretched across the entire width of the inner walls, where bowls of hot water were ready for them to have a good sluice down. Finally, all had attended to their needs and changed into dry warm clothes. Bridget doled out steaming bowls of broth to each, accompanied by hunks of brown bread.

Each having had their fill, they then arranged themselves around the crackling stove. They threw the blankets on the floor to sit on and used the sides of the bottom bunks as back rests. Donald had Siobhan sitting between his legs and leaning back on his chest, Tammy and Bridget had arranged themselves likewise.

Donald slid his arms around Siobhan and crossed them underneath her bosom, feeling the warm firmness of the twin orbs. He had an almost irresistible urge to turn his hands upwards to fondle the fullness of each.

The old familiar feelings ignited like a bellows-blown fire, and, as the firmness in his groin area developed, he felt Siobhan shudder and quiver like an aspen leaf, then push back against him, obviously aware of what was happening and mutually in harmony to his physical needs.

Donald had to exercise his strength of will to the greatest degree to prevent himself from yielding to the ultimate temptation that can afflict man. Adam and Eve and the forbidden fruit. He was glad that Tammy and Bridget were providing the services of chaperone by their very presence, for his integrity of purpose was being sorely tested; of course he and Siobhan provided a reciprocal service for those two.

With a shuddering sigh he extricated himself from the arms of enticement, albeit with reluctance, and said he would just go and check the horses before they all settled down for a well-earned sleep.

Tammy accompanied him to give the girls privacy in which to get undressed for bed. When they had travelled a fair way from the caravan, Tammy remarked that the hardest part of their assignment at the moment was to stop himself from deflowering his sweetheart. Donald agreed and said he hoped they could get the task completed as soon as possible for he was getting to the stage where he could hardly contain himself.

Changing the subject, they started to discuss how they would go about destroying the contents of the depositories. Tammy already had the means with which to blow up the caches. Commander Denham-Tring had supplied him with a new material called Semtex. It looked and felt exactly like plasticine, and Tammy believed it to be a product of Czechoslovakia, but whatever, he was confident that he would find the same material in the secret caches, for it was so easy to transport.

The farmhouse was a different problem, and Tammy felt that there would have to be a full-scale assault made to have any measure of success. He would ring Denham-Tring in Belfast, give the exact ordnance survey map grid reference, and have assistance sent to help them confiscate whatever was being held there. There was no doubt in his mind that they would find heavy artillery pieces which would be difficult to destroy or carry away.

They decided they would sleep for a few hours, and then, during the afternoon, they would get organised for an assault on maybe three or four caches early the following morning, being in place at the first cache before daylight.

Siobhan would have to accompany them to finger the source precisely, then she could act as lookout and keep an eye on the horses at the same time. Donald would help Tammy to uncover the cache and then act as a sentinel in a roving capacity.

They had an afternoon of rest, and then set off to bed quite early. An hour before break of day found the three within the shelter of the copse that contained the first depository.

Tammy had prepared his explosives and timing devices so that he could achieve a simultaneous explosion at all sites at exactly the same time. During the night he had decided that they would attend all four sites in the one day, even though it meant approaching them during the hours of daylight.

He reasoned that those that filled the depositories did so during the hours of darkness so they stood a good chance of going about their nefarious designs without detection. Therefore the daylight activities of him and Donald had the equal chance of being undiscovered by that faction during the day.

Everything went as planned. They were miles distant when they heard the sound of muffled explosions, each within seconds of the other. Tammy nodded his head in satisfaction, then explained to Donald and Siobhan that the easy part was over. Now, the opposition would know there was competition and be very much on guard.

The next five sites would have to be dealt with individually. Break of day assaults. In position before dawn and the strong possibility of a defence force to neutralise before they could achieve their goal.

For four days they stayed within the shield of the woodland, lying low like foxes in a covert. During the days Donald would continue with fieldcraft tuition, trying to increase Tammy's abilities in that art.

He taught Tammy the silent hand movements, come, go, freeze, be quiet, stay here, abort attempt and return to base. There was, however, another fundamental need of communication in the wilds for hunters who were out of eye contact with each other. This was a system of calls that could be taken for the ordinary sounds of the fauna indigenous to the environment.

Donald had to exercise much patience trying to teach Tammy to sound like a bird or beast that they happened to be practising at the time. His own incredible talent at mimicking local animals was an extraordinary personal ability not easily acquired. He thought back to when he had sat for hours practising until he reached what he felt was a satisfactory level, and in doing so, found he could tolerate a little better Tammy's difficulties.

It was finally decided to keep the repertoire short, and within Tammy's capabilities. The hacking extended maniacal laugh of the cock pheasant was danger. The languorous seductive whoo, whoo, whoo, whoo of the wood pigeon meant come to me. The yap of a lovelorn fox with the pleading howl at the end was an indication that the enemy had been sighted. Finally the harsh screeching protestations of a magpie signalled an attack on a single target.

There were discussions about what would happen if prisoners were taken and what to do with them. At last they decided that when an opponent was neutralised he would be stripped naked and tied with his arms and legs around a tree trunk. If a tree was not available then the victim would be placed face down on the ground, his arms would be pulled behind him and tied to his ankles, leaving the unfortunate bent over backwards like a bow. Either of these methods would keep that particular opponent completely out of circulation, and therefore unable to take any further part in the proceedings.

When Bridget interjected that it would be cold and uncomfortable, Tammy assured her that it was better for them to suffer a little, than for him to find them back in the fray, having recovered from merely being knocked out.

Fight them and forget them was his policy, for it must always be remembered that the second time around the antagonist could easily have learned from the first contest and possibly beat you at his second attempt.

On the third day of their enforced rest, they were sitting outside the caravan enjoying a brief spell of watery sunshine.

Suddenly Donald stiffened and motioned for quietness. He arose and glided away like a stalking lioness, indicating to the others to remain where they were. To their astonishment he just disappeared, vanished, he had merged completely within the woodland.

Then they heard what Donald had tuned into so much in advance of them. Someone was approaching, and there was certainly nothing stealthy about it. After Donald's tuition and their own newly acquired ability to move through woodland quietly, it sounded like a herd of elephants on the move.

A burly redfaced character stepped into the clearing. In the crook of one arm he carried a breech-broken, twelve bore shotgun. The blue sheen of the barrels carried a warning of their own. He glowered at the three tinkers sitting with seeming unconcern a few feet away from him.

"Right, you lot! You have half an hour to be gone from here. Half an hour, and that's too long! This is my land! I don't want you anywhere near it by the time the sun goes down. Got it?"

Tammy rose quietly and stood facing the irate landowner who had stepped back a pace when Tammy stood up. This was going to be a bit tricky. They just had to stay here, but how in hell was he going to convince this truculent character to that effect.

Thinking on his feet was Tammy's forte, hadn't he used it so many times in the past to gain advantage. He smiled at the landowner disarmingly, and making a depreciative motion with his hand, began his appeal.

"I'm sorry we have offended you, sir. We meant no harm. As you can see everything is neat and tidy. We are out of sight of everybody, and we are doing no damage to anything. Would you be good enough to reconsider and allow us to remain?"

A look on the man's face was enough to convince Tammy that this would not even be considered, so he tried a new tack.

"Do you happen to know a Mr Eamonn Kelly of Barranbarrach, the great horse breeder of hunters and hurdlers?" The glower fell from the man's face and a look of interest replace it.

"Yes! I know of him, but what has that got to do with you lot, he doesn't breed bloody tinkers, that's for sure."

Tammy was now sure that this was the correct line of approach, and began to elucidate, hoping to gain the confidence and approval of his interrogator.

"Well! That young man standing behind you, who could have disarmed you in a fraction of a second," at this pronouncement the landowner whirled and gasped in consternation as Tammy continued with apparent nonchalance, "is his grandson, and I feel sure that if you were to ring his grandfather he would make the request of you to let us remain here."

Sorely perplexed and with a myriad of emotions chasing across his face, the landowner made to lift the gun, clicking the barrels into place as he jerked the gun up.

Donald hardly seemed to move. His fingers found the radial nerve and the gun fell from paralysed fingers onto the ground. Casually he bent and picked it up, broke it open and ejected the cartridges, which he courteously placed in the open hand that was being surveyed in amazement.

With a pleasant smile at the man, he extended his hand and said in a soothing voice,

"I am pleased to meet you. My name is Donald and, if you like, I will accompany you to your home and when you telephone my grandfather, I can speak to him and you will be able to verify that what we have said is true. He has arranged this proving exercise to determine our ability to survive without the cossetting we receive at home. I should hate to fail the test. Please help us."

A less hostile demeanour became evident and the choleric hue faded to a more normal colour. He scratched his nose, then holding the peak of his flat cap between the forefinger and thumb, he scratched his head with the three remaining fingers. He cleared his throat, racking, hacking, gurgling and he expectorated with great satisfaction, but came up with his decision.

"Well, my name is Patrick Mulwhinney, and I farm two hundred acres of grudging land. It gives little for the slavery it imposes on me. Be that as it may, it is nevertheless my land and I must protect it from any who may try to use any part of it. Now! This phone call - ye-e-e-s. Now I couldn't be expected to bear the cost of it, could I?"

Donald shook his head in the negative, thinking 'God, but he is a disgusting character.' Mulwhinney smiled for the first time, showing large, predatory beaver like teeth that were a stomach wrenching hue of green and black, and Donald made note not to get too near the breath that passed them.

Mulwhinney became expansive. The telephone call was going to be an expensive one, Donald was convinced of this.

"My steading is a couple of miles away down the road, so why don't we all go down and sort out this little bit of business. I shall kindly lead the way. Yes?"

When the horses were brought into the clearing, Mulwhinney looked them over with a keen horseman's eye.

"I like the grey mare," he offered, pointing with an authoritative air, "and that black is a big bugger, he must be a cross Irish Draught and Thoroughbred, aye, maybe a bit o' Clydesdale. He looks to be about eighteen hands or thereabouts. That's big!"

His lip curled when he saw Donald's hammer headed gelding, then, as he took a closer look, he nodded his head knowingly.

"Aye! He's an ugly bugger, that is for sure. But he's all horse. He's built to last. I'm thinking the cob is not a bad wee beastie, either, aye, aye, they're not a bad bunch."

Having given his uninvited appraisal of the horses, he was about to turn away, expecting to be followed, when he was arrested in mid stride. Siobhan had made her mount kneel so she could get into the saddle, and the black waited quietly for her to mount.

"Mother o' God!" expostulated Mulwhinney in total disbelief, "what the hell is that great beast? A bloody camel, or what? Well! I've never seen the likes in all my days." He started to go across the glade to Siobhan but she anticipated him.

"Please don't come any closer, Mr Mulwhinney," she cried in alarm, "this big beast has a positive hatred of men, and he would savage you without mercy."

Mulwhinney faltered at the urgency in Siobhan's voice, held his ground for an instant, then thinking perhaps she was right, he shrugged his burly shoulders and set off out of the clearing. The mounted party fell in, in single file, and followed obediently.

Chapter Sixteen

Mulwhinney had a tired looking old nag tied to a sapling at the edge of the wood. He gathered the reins and mounted, then like a commander of cavalry, he waved an imperious hand for them to follow.

Heading west into a declining sunset, he maintained a tired walk on his scraggy horse, until they started to drop down into a hollow which sheltered some badly maintained buildings.

Kicking his bony steed into a desultory trot, he managed to pull up with a grandiose flourish, a bit spoiled when his nag instantly dropped its tired head between its knees the instant they stopped. He was obviously a proud man, even though grindingly poor, but the pride of paupers is a well-established fact of life.

The horses were tethered to a ramshackle fence, which was a gesture of security and nothing more. One of the horses on its own could have pulled the fence down, breaking it into pieces without effort. Donald hoped that none of their horses would push against it, or that would be more money to pay Mulwhinney.

They were led into the farmhouse, where introductions were made to his work-worn wife, who offered a hot drink to her visitors. She was a pleasant natured soul, pleased at having visitors for a change. She fussed around trying to make everyone comfortable.

Mulwhinney rang the number he had received from Donald, and after a brief pause, they heard him introduce himself. A short dialogue followed and then Donald was called to the phone.

Eamonn Kelly's voice was full of concern, he asked questions ten to the dozen, which Donald answered in as cryptic a fashion as he could. When Eamonn was satisfied he asked to speak to Mulwhinney again. Donald stood alongside and listened to the one-sided conversation. Mulwhinney kept nodding his head and saying 'yes' at intervals, said a final 'yes' and handed the phone to Donald.

Eamonn checked that it was in fact Donald speaking and then suggested he offer Mulwhinney the hammer headed gelding and the dun cob for services rendered, when they were ready to return to Barranbarrach. To qualify for these gifts Mulwhinney must not tell anyone about Donald's group using the woodland retreat and he must, most definitely, allow them to stay there until they were ready to move on of their own volition.

Eamonn then asked to speak to Tammy, as he had some very disturbing news for him. Tammy passed on the information to Donald later, and it was indeed serious intelligence, which could have an effect on what they were trying to achieve on their present mission.

Eamonn had been advised by Commander Denham-Tring that it had been discovered that the Chief of the Ulster Constabulary was in collusion with the freedom fighters, and passed on any information that he thought would be useful to them.

With this fresh knowledge, Tammy now understood the problems that Denham-Tring had faced in Belfast, and how he had been starved of information and assistance, even when he had badgered his superior.

What was really sickening was the fact that a young, untrained girl, on her own, had achieved more than any of them in obtaining information that was of any value.

A deep slow anger rumbled and growled within Tammy at how his undercover work had been so adroitly negated. A germ of a plan to exercise some sort of redress fermented in his fertile mind. To expose this errant chief would require a well conceived plan which would have to be perfectly executed when the time came. The means to do this had just entered Tammy's mind, the means to deliver the coup de gras to the conniving bastard.

Donald explained to Mulwhinney about the gift of horses, who at first demurred, although not too robustly, then he proclaimed his delight at this more than generous offer, and assured them they could stay till Christmas, longer if necessary. Sure he would not breathe a word to anybody about them being in the area. They were his guests, and that was the end to it.

The four relieved pseudo tinkers returned to the clearing, and after attending to the horses as best they could in the dark, they retired to the warmth of the caravan for a heavy discussion on the events that had occurred, and more importantly, on the recommencement of assaults on the remaining sites that they wanted to make inoperative.

A pallid, fragile looking moon was throwing its last lingering ethereal light on the landscape clad with hoar frost as Donald, Tammy and Siobhan set off to go to number five site.

Donald assured Tammy that the moon would disappear an hour before dawn, so they would be able to make their approach unseen to the wooded area that held the next intended target. This proved to be the case.

Tethering the horses a mile north of the scene, they eased through the woods like wraiths, flitting quietly from cover to cover. Donald's inbuilt compass brought them to the desired spot. Biting disappointment flooded through them. They were looking at an empty, gaping hole.

Forgetting the presence of Siobhan for a moment, Tammy cursed fluently and passionately for a few seconds. Reason took hold. He turned to her and apologised contritely as he kissed her cheek in a plea for forgiveness.

Did this mean that all the caches they knew had been emptied? It was a possibility. He paused and thought for a few moments, rubbing his face with his hands as if it would help him to come up with a sound answer.

He heaved a sigh of frustration, then declared that they should go on to the next site in line, rather than waste the entire journey out, but what did they think?

Donald pointed out that it was the sensible thing to do, so it was decided, on to the next. Dejectedly they retraced their footsteps, and reaching their patient steeds, mounted and headed off eastwards to the next location.

A whirling mist had developed with the true dawn, this quickly dissipated the hoar frost of the night. As the party progressed in single file the mist thickened sufficiently to provide an excellent cover for their stealthy approach and reconnaissance of the intended objective.

Repetition can often induce carelessness, but the three covert figures retained their concentration. They arrived at the cache having circled twice before the final approach, and were delighted to see it remained undisturbed.

Before starting to uncover the cache, Tammy checked to ensure a nasty little calling card, in the guise of a booby trap, had not been left for them.

Satisfied that it was safe to approach, Tammy signalled to Donald and Siobhan to take up their lookout positions. He had decided that under the new circumstances, there had better be two sentries from the start.

Slowly and carefully he uncovered the cache, checking time and again for booby traps. Inside he found that there were rifles and handguns, boxes of ammunition, hand grenades and even sticks of dynamite, some of which were sweating profusely, which meant they were in a very unstable condition. He would have to be very careful he didn't blow himself up.

He thought for a second, then smiled with pleasure. He could use this volatile mixture to his advantage, using it in conjunction with the timing devices he had brought with him. He could blow up the whole depository and its contents, and save his own Semtex.

With everything connected, he was just about to set the timer when the coughing crackle of a startled pheasant ripped through the tranquillity of the woodland.

Calmly, with practised efficiency, Tammy adjusted the timer to activate in five minutes and placed it amongst the armament. Quickly he threw the cover over the hole and scattered some leaves over the area. It would have to do.

He darted into cover and moved well away from the scene. An amorous wood pigeon called an enticing 'come to me' and quietly Tammy made his way towards the sound, to join Donald and Siobhan some distance away from the cache.

The sound of the diesel engine stopped and then they heard voices. Tammy and his compatriots decided there must be at least two men, and there was a moment of silence, followed by excited shouting, which suggested that the disturbance around the cache had been noticed.

The explosion was a desecration of the rustic harmony of the woodland. The shock waves savaged through the undergrowth in mindless brutality.

Birds of the forest were in mute stupefaction for several moments then responded to the outrage with a cacophony of alarm calls.

Tammy raced to the scene and found total desecration. A great gaping emptiness where the arms had been secreted. Two bodies had been hurled several yards away by the blast, and the van was a total wreck of twisted and tangled smoking metal.

Tammy turned about and returned to the couple waiting for him in the woods, they were hanging onto the horses and trying to calm them. Urgently he advised them that they should leave the scene as quickly as possible.

When they were safely on their way he explained what had happened, and said he had left everything as it was. Whoever found the devastated cache might think that the two bodies at the source had inadvertently blown themselves up.

He was convinced that after a certain period of time, when the two men didn't return to their base, somebody would be sent to investigate, and as far as he, Tammy, was concerned, that was the best thing that could happen.

At Barranbarrach, Mari was in a torment of maternal anxiety at the absence of her brood of youngsters. One of life's natural mothers, she should have been blessed with many children, but wasn't. Like a broody hen, she gathered chicks wherever she could, giving her love ungrudgingly. Her concern was greatly increased when she learned of the duplicity of the very man who should have done everything in his power to assist Tammy.

Eamonn Kelly had met Denham-Tring at the local golf club, recognising him from army days of long ago. Chit chat soon established the fact that Tammy was a frequent visitor at Barranbarrach, and it only needed a bit of discreet conversation by both men to realise they could be of assistance to each other.

Eamonn called in favours from many sources and through this discovered that the chief of police was also head of a faction not loyal to the crown.

This man, in the position he held, was involved in treacherous activities, able to exercise great influence on the investigations into the nefarious pursuits of the so-called freedom fighters.

Repeatedly, information had been relayed too late, or misinformation substituted. Files went missing and orders were delayed to such an extent that they were rendered useless in application.

Eamonn was now desperately waiting for Tammy to contact him again, for now he had the name of the Deputy Chief Constable who was loyal to the Government and would act correctly on information supplied. In fact Tammy knew this man, for he had been the fourth member of a meeting that Denham-Tring had arranged when it was decided that Tammy and Donald would come north.

Eamonn invited Denham-Tring and the Deputy Chief Constable to Barranbarrach where a war council took place with Stuart chairing the meeting.

To prevent leakage to outside sources it was decided that Eamonn would now be the contact for Tammy, and would take or give information as necessary. He would then meet either Denham-Tring or the Deputy at the golf course and exchange intelligence in an informal setting where it would be difficult for anyone to overhear their conversation.

In her aching want, her need to see her children, Mari suggested to Stuart that they contact the aunt that Siobhan had stayed with when she had been up north on her own. Perhaps they could visit with her for a few days.

Stuart was against this, saying it would serve no real purpose, and could even cause the aunt to become worried if they let something slip. No! It would be better to wait for Tammy to get in touch, and then if need be they could go north and see if they could render any assistance.

With ill grace Mari conceded, but she frothed and fretted at the enforced inactivity. The emptiness of her life allowed her mind time to again recall losing Mary, Donald's first love. Daily she fell to her knees praying that she would not lose another loved one.

Mari was an efficient administrator and organiser frustrated by circumstances she couldn't control. She bubbled and boiled with the need to be doing something.

Her parents and Stuart tried to console her, but she was unable to find solace in their efforts. Each day was a battle of dragging time and abysmal thoughts. Her mother tried to get her involved with tentative arrangements for the forthcoming double wedding, but it proved no distraction.

Driven by the restless energy of Mari, Eamonn and Stuart at last decided that they would get no peace until they succumbed to her endless pleadings to do something.

Eamonn rang a friend in a little village on the north coast who ran a small pub and did bed and breakfast accommodation and arranged for Stuart and Mari to stay there for a couple of weeks, supposedly to allow Stuart a sea fishing holiday.

Mari was delighted and said she would pretend to go sightseeing each day after dropping Stuart off at a secluded spot. This would give them excuse enough to travel round the local area.

They would ring Barranbarrach each evening, in the hope that Tammy had been in contact, and advised Eamonn where the caravan was situated. Tammy, in turn, would be told where he could contact Stuart and Mari, then if there was any way they could help they would be close at hand to do so.

The night before Stuart and Mari left on their holiday, Tammy rang Barranbarrach. Quickly Eamonn advised Tammy not to say anything of importance but to meet Stuart and Mari at the following address in two days time.

Mari was on the phone in seconds, almost snatching it from her father's hand in her desperate need to talk to one of her brood. She enquired how they all were, then gave Tammy precise instructions where they should meet the following evening. Not in two days, for God's sake!

With a satisfied smile she handed the phone back to her father, who said goodbye to Tammy and hung up, giving Stuart an amused wink with a sideways nod of his head at Mari.

A subdued trio returned to the caravan site. The taking of human life is a tragic and sobering thing. To have been the perpetrators of such a final deed induced a feeling of disgust and self loathing that none of them could throw off.

Wearily they dismounted and attended to the horses in chastened silence. Bridget realised that something serious had happened, but with a diplomacy born of compassion, made no attempt to ask questions. She was sure that a detailed discussion would follow the mid-day meal that was even now waiting to be served. As was her wont on these occasions when the marauding party returned, she helped each of them to divest outwear and boots and get them settled into the warmth of the caravan.

Picking at the tasty stew, Tammy was the first to offer an observation.

"Well! It was just waiting to happen," he began, "this sort of business we are involved in, it promotes the loss of human life. We can console ourselves that it is in the interests of queen and country. For the greater good. The fact remains, that a life or lives have been terminated and that can never be excused. I deliberately set that time on a short fuse. The intention was to blow up the cache before those two got to it. Not to get them as well. To my discredit, I got the timing wrong.

He heaved a sigh as Bridget came across and put her arms around him. Donald took hold of Tammy by the arm and squeezing it gently protested the truth of his friend's assertion.

"Tammy, you take too much guilt upon yourself, and you musn't do that! If there is guilt we all share it. Think on, however, what would happen if those instruments of war and terrorism reached their final destination. What havoc they would cause. On innocent people as well."

"Those two men who were killed perhaps didn't deserve to die, but if you live by the sword then you must surely expect to die by it as well. I say this to you, their lives were terminated because they were there. Had they been law abiding citizens they would still be alive and going about their lawful business."

Tammy wearily shook his head.

"Perhaps you are right, Donald," he commented, "but my professional commitment is to preserve and protect life and property, and it just seems a contradiction in terms when this sort of thing happens. Most important now is that we will be hunted like common vermin. The leaders of those men will search to the gates of hell to find us. They have to, to keep faith with the rank and file of those that blindly follow them. From now on, every minute we stay here we are in great danger, and the truth of the matter is we don't know who is friend and who is foe."

"I think we must give your grandfather a ring and ask if he can suggest someone who is in authority, who might be able to render us assistance. I think we must forget the other caches now and concentrate on the farm, when we have dealt with that we can perhaps get round to the other outlying depositories, but the farm must be next. Do you agree?"

The next day Donald spent hours erasing any tracks that led to the clearing. They had been careful whilst riding to and fro, but they had still left the odd traces that would guide a tracker to their refuge.

Tammy used this time, giving the girls a rudimentary lesson in the use of a hand gun. The two revolvers he had brought with him were light calibre pistols that the girls found easy to handle. They couldn't practice firing them, but mainly Tammy was concerned with the safety aspects of handling weapons. At the worst they would just have to aim as he had demonstrated and squeeze the trigger. Once he was satisfied they were conversant with the safety aspects he insisted they keep one each.

After the evening meal, Tammy decided that he would ride over to Mulwhinney's farm and ask if he could use the phone to call Eamonn at Barranbarrach. Bridget asked if she could accompany him and he readily agreed. She would be able to keep Mulwhinney and his wife occupied in conversation while he got as much information as he could from the only source he trusted at the moment.

When Tammy and Bridget left on their mission, Donald looked across at his sweetheart and knew it was going to be a long, hard evening, in every sense of the word.

It was warm and cosy in the caravan and at the moment gave a sense of security and privacy, the perfect setting for a romantic dalliance.

To still the rising beat of his pulse, and the rhythmic throbbing in his groin area, that would scream its presence despite the effort of will he would exercise to the contrary, he started a conversation on country lore.

For instance, did Siobhan know that the smallest walking bird in Britain was a pied wagtail, all birds smaller than a wagtail hopped.

He had also observed that a travelling rabbit made three short hops, then a long one, so if you were setting snares to catch rabbits the loop of wire should be two thirds of the way along the length of the long jump. These jump patterns were easily seen in the grass, in the form of indentations at measured distances.

Here was something else that was interesting. A fox would find a tree where there were pheasants roosting for the night. It would then urinate on its tail, stand underneath the pheasant and wave its tail in circles. The strong ammoniac smell and the tail waving in circles so mesmerises the watching pheasant that it falls out of the tree and the fox has his dinner.

When a subject is taboo it is sod's law that it will jump into the forefront of any conversation with crystal clarity, and Donald was not immune to such treachery of the slipping tongue.

He continued his interesting tales of the wild woods, unaware that his mouth was starting to refer to the very subject he wished to avoid.

It was an established fact that a cat, even a domestic tabby, was never impregnated by the first tom that mounted her, oh no! and the reason was that the female always stood on her feet through the first coupling, and couldn't conceive in that stance. She had to lie down with her back legs lying straight out behind her when the male mounted her. Another important factor was that the penis of the tom is barbed backwards so that, when he withdraws, he gives the female a sensation of pain which helps her to release the necessary ova for fertilisation, and somehow this doesn't happen if the female is standing up.

Donald's brain caught up with him. Aghast, he looked at Siobhan, who was biting the heel of her thumb to choke back the laughter that convulsed her entire body.

"Oh my God! Did my mouth just say all that?" Donald choked out in mortification.

Siobhan released her teeth from tortured flesh and the rich, deep, throaty laugh filled the caravan. She rolled around in uninhibited delight, whilst Donald sat with his face crimson red in total embarrassment at his gaffe. Crawling over to her discomfited sweetheart she flung her arms around his squirming shoulders.

"Oh my poor wee man," she chortled, "did you ever talk yourself into a corner. I knew what you were trying to do, but you really do make it hard for yourself." Here she was engulfed in uncontrolled mirth one more time, as she gasped out her next words, "no, no, that's not right! It's me that makes it hard for you," and with that little homily she collapsed in utter abandonment.

Laughter is infectious and soothing to injured innocence, and Donald, looking at his fiancee rolling around as the rich contralto of her voice delighted his ears, couldn't help but join in.

It was quite some time before they could sit up and look at each other without bursting out into fresh gales of laughter. Donald remembered an adage of his dad's 'if you can laugh together, you can pull together', and decided this was a good omen for the future.

The merriment eased the sexual overtones, although it would never dampen the grinding need, nevertheless they were able to chat about various commonplace things which kept their minds neutralised from their common hunger.

Siobhan suggested a hot drink, which of course lacked milk. They were getting used to the lack of it, but both agreed it would be lovely to be back at Barranbarrach having one of Mari's chocolate beverages made with hot milk.

Donald grinned and remarked that Stuart would be pleased when they returned home, for he would have been coddled and pampered to distraction by Mari, who just had to have someone to fuss over.

Tammy and Bridget were made welcome by the Mulwhinney's, and sure, Tammy could use the phone, it was a pleasure.

Tammy asked Mulwhinney if he would get through to the exchange for him. This was a deliberate ploy on the part of Tammy in an attempt to deceive anyone eavesdropping at the exchange, then wondering why a stranger was ringing from the Mulwhinney's home number.

The farmer was delighted to do this, for it afforded another chance to speak to the great breeder of horses, and one never knew when this familiarity would come in handy, A contact like this could be invaluable.

When Mulwhinney handed the phone to Tammy, Bridget called the farmer into the kitchen where he would be out of earshot of what Tammy had to say.

She asked questions about the farm, did he raise stock as many did for the market in Scotland? He obviously knew horses, had he ever bred them? What acreage did the farm run to? Did he have any hired help or did he and his wife run the place themselves? Just as she was running out of ideas of what to ask next, Tammy reappeared, and thanking the couple for their hospitality, Tammy paid for the phone call over the slightest possible objections, they bade the couple farewell.

Tammy and Bridget made a wide detour to return to the caravan, enjoying each others company and the clear freshness of a frosty night.

Companionably,they rode side by side, talking quietly but at the same time keeping a careful watch for any other travellers. It was of vital importance not to be seen by anyone as this information could be passed on to those who would be searching for them.

Bridget glanced across at Tammy and caught him with a huge grin on his face.

"Come on, my handsome hero! You must share this one with me. If it makes you smile then it must be good, for you are not one given to smiling too much, come on, what is it?"

Tammy gave a chortle that could have been defined as a dirty laugh, but with the easiness he now felt in this girl's company, he found it quite easy to share his private joke.

His voice throbbed with contained mirth as he chuckled.

"I was just wondering how Donald was coping, being on his own in that snug nest with Siobhan."

Although Bridget knew exactly what Tammy was getting at, she kept him going with a teasing.

"I don't know what you mean, Tammy. Sure they get on like a house on fire in a gale of wind. They are like a pair of magnets, totally drawn to each other." She leaned across the gap, laying her hand on his thigh, deliberately high up, near to his crotch.

"Come on! Explain yourself, light of my life, give me the full thing, for I'm not laughing yet."

Tammy casually lifted the slim questing fingers, turned the hand over as he brought it up to his lips and kissed the fragrantly scented palm, caressing the back of it with a long calloused thumb, he capitulated with good grace.

"Well, Donald is a virgin boy, and I have a feeling that he hasn't even experienced a wet dream, but the sexual awakening he has discovered in his love for Siobhan is just about driving him insane. He wants her with a deep and burning need, but he is so straight and honest he denies her, and him, the physical release they both so desperately need. He is determined that she will attend the wedding altar a virgin, pure and fresh. He fears that if she doesn't she will regret it in the future. So they both struggle along, waiting for that magic piece of paper that makes it all nice and legal, but does it really change anything?"

It was Bridget's turn to smile as she lifted Tammy's long slim hand that was capable of such devastating strength, and yet could be unbelievably tender and gentle. She kissed the hard edge of callous running along the outer edge, and murmured teasingly.

"Oh yes, dear heart! What a foolish boy to be sure! Is it the same fear that holds you in thrall? I haven't been exactly worn out fighting off your sexual attacks. In fact, I'm beginning to think that I don't appeal to you as a woman."

Tammy stopped his mare in half stride, the dun cob automatically stopped in harmony with his equine mate.

"Get off that horse and prepare for the fight of your life, lovely girl," Tammy threatened, but Bridget held her seat and smiled a beauteous satisfied smile, as her lover continued.

"I have acted like a perfect gentleman as far as you are concerned, even though I've gone to bed each night like a three legged wonder, with a pain in the bottom of my belly you couldn't start to imagine. I have never needed a woman like I need you. I'm not denying I've had my share, but you are special, very special, and I intend to keep you that way if it bursts my balls."

He leant across the gap and pulled her against him, kissing her hard, long and deep, until she moaned into his mouth in a torment of need.

Holding hands, they nudged the horses into motion, Bridget swayed in the saddle bathed in the warm glow of a woman in love, and loved in return.

Tammy was back to the usual routine of aching and wanting, just like Donald, suffering self denial. To give himself a bit of relief, he stopped the mare and dismounted. Handing the reins to Bridget he disappeared behind a convenient tree and urinated copiously.

As he remounted, Bridget, in an impish impulsive act, slipped her hand onto the saddle, palm up, and as Tammy went to lower his weight onto the saddle, she gently stroked his scrotum sac.

Had a hot iron been laid across his buttocks, Tammy could not have shot to full leg length in the stirrups quicker, he shuddered and gaped like a stranded salmon, and like retina retention on the eye, he could still feel that silky touch.

His eyes locked on those of his tantalising betrothed as his mouth began to work.

"You brazen hussy! You dreadful, dreadful girl! Oh my God, what am I going to do with you?"

Bridget was almost in hysterics, the laughter pealed out, ringing in the frosty air. Belatedly she placed her hand across her mouth to stifle the sound.

Tammy gingerly lowered himself into the saddle and looked across at Bridget and saw the gleam of tears in her eyes. He knew she was not crying in sorrow, and he shook his head in amazement at the antics this girl could get up to.

When she had quite recovered, Bridget smiled as she remarked that he was a fast mover, and sure did he think that he was going to lose his precious jewels? This little quip sent them both into fits of laughter. As far as Tammy was concerned it was just what the doctor ordered. It gave him a respite from the feeling of self revulsion he felt in the aftermath of the blowing up of the cache and the two terrorists.

Holding hands in quiet companionship, they continued their journey, comfortable and at peace with each other. Their mounts ambled along in harmony, as if double-yoked, keeping close together and allowing the lovers to hold hands and plan for the future.

Tammy asked Bridget if she felt happy about leaving Ulster to go and live in Scotland. Bridget replied that she had no reservations whatever, and in fact was quite looking forward to it.

She pointed out that they would both be able to keep in close touch with Donald and Siobhan when they returned to Scotland to take over the Cruachan Estate and, since Siobhan and her father Eddie were her only living kin, this suited her just fine. She added that she would be glad when Tammy's tour of duty in Ulster was finished, and then they could get married and settle down to a new and safer future.

When they reached the caravan all was quiet and in darkness. At first they thought that Donald and Siobhan had settled down for he night. As they entered the glade a dark clad figure materialised beside them.

Bridget gave a startled screech, and, in a voice trembling with the residue of her fright, gasped out reproachfully.

"Donald! You frightened the life out of me. You just appeared out of the ground. Is everything alright? There hasn't been any trouble, has there? Is Siobhan OK?"

Donald smiled, his teeth a flash of white in the darkness, and patted her hand comfortingly.

"There, there," he soothed, "everything is fine. I was just taking a last look round before settling down for the night. I'm sorry I startled you, but I have to keep in practice in silent approach and it seemed too good an opportunity to miss. You go inside and I'll help Tammy with the horses."

When the chores were finished, Donald and Tammy climbed into the caravan, where Siobhan had a hot drink waiting for them. Tammy passed on the information he had received from Barranbarrach, which was followed by a discussion about whether they should all go to meet Stuart and Mari.

At first Tammy suggested that it would be safer if only one person went to the trysting point, but the obvious disappointment on the faces of the girls, not to mention Donald, who loved his mother deeply, decided him. They would take the chance and all go to the meeting.

The decision made, it was time to settle down for the night, but there was just one more point to settle. Should a guard system be set up each night now? If so, should it commence from this night forth?

Tammy suggested that since the unfortunate occurrence had only happened that very afternoon, it was doubtful if anyone could have located their hideout so soon, therefore they should get a good night's rest while they could.

The following night they set off for the meeting place. Now it was essential that great care was taken not to leave tracks on the ground that would lead unwanted visitors to the hideaway.

The ground, thankfully, was iron hard with the continuing spell of frost, nevertheless, they entered the stream and travelled quite a distance before they made their exit at a rocky hillside, where the scree ended at the water's edge.

The meeting point was on the west bank of the river Bann, at a picnic spot just off the main trunk road, the A45, which leads to Coleraine.

The clear, frosty night had the distinction of being a blessing and a curse. They had good vision in which to travel, but they could also be seen more readily by other nocturnal travellers.

Twice they scurried into shelter, like vagrants evading the law, but eventually they reached their goal, satisfied that they had avoided detection.

Mari's choice for a secret meeting was perfect. A clearing surrounded by fir and larch trees screening the picnic area from road users, and it was doubtful if there would be any picnickers at this time of night, or even at this time of year.

The Landrover sat with the engine purring quietly as the exhaust burbled a bass note in accompaniment.

The four riders dismounted within the confines of the trees, some distance from the clearing. Quietly they approached the occupants of the stationary vehicle.

Donald quietly and quickly opened the passenger side door and almost landed on his back when his mother leapt out and kissed the hell out of him.

He stood quietly, absorbing this demonstration of love from his mother. He knew from past experience there was no way of stopping this loving assault, this need of Mari to show her loss and frustrated motherlove of the past few weeks.

Mari pulled back at last and looked at her son. A quick assessing glance raked over him. Seemingly satisfied, she turned to the other three, who had been greeting Stuart, thereby allowing Mari a moment with her only true born son.

Her arms went wide as she tried to scoop them all under her protective wing, kissing whoever, and whatever, was nearest, in a veritable pandemonium of excited happiness.

The greetings over, they all squeezed into the Landrover. As was to be expected, Mari had packed a picnic hamper with enough food to feed an army. They talked about general topics whilst the food was being consumed, and at last they all sat back, completely sated.

Stuart produced a bottle of malt whisky, and poured a generous measure for the three men. Not to be outdone, Mari poured stiff rations of cream sherry for the girls, and declared the meeting open.

A hush descended for a second or so whilst everyone arranged their thoughts, then Stuart ended the silence.

He began the briefing by confirming that the Chief Constable in Belfast was not to be trusted. The Constabulary contact would now be the Assistant Chief Constable, who had an impeccable pedigree, loyal to the Government who paid him, but he also happened to be a personal friend of Eamonn Kelly.

Mari's parents had returned from their tour just a short time after the youngsters had left Barranbarrach to come to the north of Ulster, and wasn't it a good thing that Eamonn was back on Irish soil, for his help and guidance were priceless.

It had been decided that Stuart would now be acting as liaison and courier. He and Mari were supposed to be on holiday, this gave them freedom of movement, and liberty to rove around the countryside without questions being asked in the wrong places.

Stuart had already arranged an out of the way meeting place with the Constabulary contact for the following evening. His name, by the way, was Peter Mahon, and Tammy and Donald had met him once at a meeting with upper-lip Denham-Tring.

The meeting between Stuart and Peter would take place in a little pub in

Ballymoney in the guise of dry-fly fishermen on vacation, intending to try the streams in the local area, and perhaps they might just try the odd jar of porter to keep things oiled properly.

Tammy now took over the spokesman's chair. He explained to Mari and Stuart about the unfortunate demise of the two men at the last depository they had blown up. He insisted that the whole business would have to be resolved in the very near future, for they would not be able to operate without discovery for very much longer.

With this in mind, he suggested that an assault on the isolated farmhouse must be the next project and it might well prove to be the last.

It was now the end of October, so the first Saturday night in November they should get into position for a dawn attack on the Sunday morning.

Tammy gave Stuart the exact OS grid reference for the desolate farmhouse, and said the assault would commence at first light, which should be around seven thirty, then corrected himself and said the time of the attack would be at precisely seven thirty, regardless of what time dawn broke.

He wanted Peter Mahon to bring three others, which would make a total of six with himself and Donald. This was more than enough. Too many running around caused confusion and was difficult to control.

Here he re-emphasised that he wanted no more personnel than this, as it would increase the chance of the attacking force injuring each other.

One other point he stressed was that each of the assault party was to wear a red arm band on their right sleeve, since he and Donald wouldn't know if they were friend or foe and might inadvertently attack them.

Again there was silence. Tammy went over everything in his mind, trying to see any flaws or if he had missed anything of importance in his brief. He had tried to foresee any problems that might arise, but in the end even the use of a crystal ball would have limited effect. Always round the corner is the unexpected, and one cannot plan for that.

Donald asked Tammy where they were going to get red arm bands, and why had he decided on red? Tammy smiled and pointed a long finger in Siobhan's direction, and announced that they were going to steal her ribbons, and as that was the only colour she had brought with her, then that was the colour it had to be.

Tammy asked Stuart if there was conclusive evidence that would hold up in a court of law, in which to exercise an indictment on the treacherous Chief Constable, but Stuart shook his head in the negative. No, there was nothing concrete! He was going to have to be lured into a trap of some description, which of course would be a tremendous problem.

It would have to be exceptionally well prepared, for he was nobody's fool and, in his position, he had access to resources and information from both sides.

The biggest problem of all in the province was that nobody could be a hundred per cent sure of where loyalties lay with the members of the local populace.

The internal strife of Ulster was like a cancerous growth, insidious and pervading, eating the heart out of the social fabric, and turning neighbour against neighbour, as it did with families. Brothers found themselves on the opposite sides, as did fathers and sons. Mothers grieved at the needless deaths, others rejoiced in the sacrifices their menfolk martyred themselves for.

The rights and wrongs were continually debated, not only by academics and politicians, but by every household.

Strong feelings are not easily disabused. Talking can be inflammatory and it can be a panacea. How can you convince a staunch believer that his beliefs are without significance?

On one side there is a person who insists he is not Irish but British and wants to remain under British jurisdiction. On the other side the voice of opinion is that Ireland is Ireland, and what was taken by force during the building of the Great British Empire was an unlawful deed, and therefore Ulster should be returned to the Eire administration so that the entire island becomes a united Ireland.

Tammy had pondered the political instability and still hadn't reached any satisfactory conclusion. What was a blatant fact in his life was that he was here under duress, really, involved in what he saw as an endless struggle that offered no true resolution.

His contribution was to prevent armament reaching the illegal factions. The feeling of authority being that if these factions had not the wherewithal then they could come to a table and try to settle the differences politically.

He reflected that he was now very close to the end of his secondment, and if the farmhouse assault went off alright he would be free to return to more mundane tasks of normal policing duties in Scotland.

Stuart looked at his watch, and tried to ignore the apprehensive intake of breath from Mari.

"I'm sorry all, good company is the thief of time, and it has certainly done that tonight. We must make our farewells, however unpleasant that may be, but if my reckoning is correct, in five more days this nasty old business should all be finished with"

He kissed the girls soundly, oh, they were well worth kissing! He hugged Tammy and then took hold of his son and kissed him on the cheeks.

"Take care boy," he growled, and made a big fuss starting the engine he had switched off earlier.

Mari's tears lasted until they reached the pub that would be their base on this questionable holiday. Before entering the pub, Stuart observed that Mari needed a bath to repair the ravages of her weeping.

They were made warmly welcome and shown to their room. They were advised that dinner was over, but a late snack could certainly be arranged for them if this was their wish. Stuart and Mari demurred, saying they had stopped off earlier and had a fairly late dinner, but they would both enjoy a hot milky drink, if that was possible.

The quartet of riders filtered their way through the forest with very little in the way of conversation being exchanged. It had been a pleasant interlude to see Mari and Stuart, but a tinge of sadness lingered with them at having to leave the older couple again.

Tammy was lost in thought on how to get the errant Chief of Police into an incriminating situation, for he was sure in his mind that he would always think the job incomplete if he failed to have him indicted. The treacherous bastard deserved to be punished.

Tammy thought that at first he could somehow lure the traitor to a confrontation at the farm, but realised that this just would not work.

The R.U.C. boss would be a director from a safe distance. He would never get his fingers dirty by attending some fracas. Oh no! He would be sure to delegate that responsibility to someone like Rourke, although that particular beauty had already been taken care of. No! There had to be another way to trap him, but for the moment Tammy couldn't think what or how to achieve it.

Donald had been applying his mind to the same problem, but he had started from a different angle to Tammy. At Cruachan a shoot was different to a hunt, and the simple difference was that in a hunt you stalked the animal until you were within positive killing distance, and then you administered the fatal blow; in a shoot, dogs and beaters were used to flush the quarry from cover towards where the guns waited for them in a prepared ambush. Now surely this was the same sort of situation, the only question was which method to employ.

Even as the question arose in his mind, Donald answered it himself. With his skills he could so easily stalk and kill the enemy leader, who lived in isolated splendour in the country, on the outskirts of Belfast. If he did this, however, he placed himself in the same category as the people he was opposed to.

He was trying to prevent further killing so he couldn't justify his motives by carrying out such a final judgement on the party in question. There was also the legal requirement that a man was innocent until proven guilty by his peers in a court of law.

Well, they would just have to flush him out and try to remain within the legal framework while achieving it. Donald pondered for a while and was about to abandon his contemplations when the answer exploded into his brain.

Yes! Yes! By all that's wonderful, that is the answer. He wouldn't flush, he wouldn't draw, he would entice the prey as a tethered goat lures the hunting leopard.

Donald decided he would not blurt out the significance of his brainstorm until he got Tammy by himself, for he knew the girls would strongly oppose what he had in mind.

He wasn't quite sure Tammy would agree, but at least he could bring pressure to bear in that quarter, for he knew that Tammy was determined to see that justice was exercised in relation to the Chief of Constabulary.

The return journey to the caravan was completed with nothing untoward happening. At the caravan the girls were excused from the unsaddling task and entered the van to make ready for bed whilst they had privacy.

As Donald and Tammy were drying off the mounts and putting weather rugs over them, Donald told Tammy of his plan. Tammy was delighted, but wanted to take the part that Donald had planned for himself. Donald said he had better be a bonny fighter to get it, so Tammy grudgingly conceded.

Chapter Seventeen

Donald and Tammy entered the caravan and, in the dim light of the frosty moon peeping through the skylights, prepared for bed. The four of them lay talking quietly for a while and then the drowsy good nights signalled an end to conversation.

Soon the steady, even breathing gave evidence that the inhabitants slumbered in harmony. Tomorrow was still another day unused, and who knew what it would bring by way of diversion.

In the period of waiting for the assault on the farm to be carried out, Donald and Tammy twice approached the location. This was for two main reasons.

First, it was essential to know the lie of the land surrounding the farm, was there cover to make a covert approach, for it would be advisable for Donald and Tammy to be within striking distance at the crucial hour.

Secondly, there was a need to know if there was a guard system and, if so, how it operated, begging the question of how many men were involved and resident at the farmhouse.

On the second visit they saw the ferocious looking Dobermann Pinschers running free within the perimeter fence and noticed that their handler carried what looked like a pickaxe handle. Whether that was for keeping the dogs in line or not, the two watchers couldn't quite fathom. Donald noted that Tammy wasn't too happy about the presence of the dogs.

Apart from these forays out to check the farm, the youngsters kept themselves confined to the clearing and woodland surrounding. It was imperative to keep out of sight of anyone and everyone.

On a couple of occasions Donald had seen what looked like search parties scouring the area. It could only be a matter of time before they were discovered in their little haven that was at this moment an environmental prison.

He and Tammy prowled around the outer periphery of the woodland, keeping out of sight but watching for any approaches to the copse.

At last, the Saturday prior to the attack on the farm arrived. Donald checked and rechecked his armament, throwing clubs, catapult, balanced throwing knife, garotte and shaken, and at last he was satisfied that he could make no more preparations.

Tammy had little to do in the way of making ready, nevertheless he was ready in every possible way. He at last took Donald to one side and admitted that he was a bit concerned about the guard dogs at the farm, he had once seen just what those horrendous teeth could do, and it still gave him the shivers.

Donald understood his concern and took him out into the woodland, where he demonstrated how to deal with savage dogs in attack. Tammy was surprised and delighted at how simple it would be to neutralise the canine menace.

He practised with Donald until he was sure he could carry out the exercise proficiently every time, then he had the cheek to tell Donald that, as a dog, his back legs were useless and bent the wrong way. The fact that he could now joke about it, showed that he had overcome the anxiety he had been feeling.

As evening approached the tension in the caravan was like a stifling blanket of fog. The four occupants dealt with it in different ways.

The girls chattered like fighting squirrels. Donald withdrew into himself, whilst Tammy, taciturn by nature, now became quite garrulous, telling little jokes and amusing anecdotes.

Of them all it was Tammy who had, in the past, gone through this sort of experience, waiting to make raids on criminal establishments during his time as a policeman.

Donald had faced combat when he was tested in multi-confrontation as part of his gaining sensei status, but that had been unexpected, although he had known it was in the offing, but he had never had to wait for a predetermined call to action.

The evening meal was a surprise dish prepared by Donald. He had found a pair of plump hedgehogs, well fleshed in hibernation. He gralloched them, then wrapped them in clay and cooked them slowly in the embers of a smokeless fire he had constructed in the clearing.

He produced the steaming, aromatic platters with the air of a conjurer. He refused to tell the diners what the meat was, until they had eaten.

The two girls and Tammy ate with relish, saying that although the carcases looked like short-legged rabbits the flesh tasted like pork, so come on, what was the flesh they were eating and so thoroughly enjoying?

Donald smiled and conceded to their wishes, telling them that they had just partaken of a delicacy he had often enjoyed whilst dining with the itinerant Romanies that used to come to his father's farm at Craigburn to do seasonal work. What they had eaten was baked hedgehog.

A moment of silence followed this declaration, then exclamations of disbelief. Then they all agreed that it did not matter for it had been delicious, and after all it was no worse than the French eating snails.

They settled down for a few hours sleep. They would have to rise and move out by no later than six o'clock. The girls would remain at the caravan and get things ready to move as soon as Tammy and Donald returned.

There had been quite a heavy discussion about this, as initially the girls had declared their intention of accompanying the two men. They were firmly denied. No coercion on their part could convince Donald or Tammy to the contrary.

They had been asleep for a few hours when Donald suddenly was awake, with alarm bells ringing in his ears. He sat up quickly and silently, but almost cursed aloud when his head hit the roof of the caravan. He sat a moment, trying to work out what had alarmed him. Sliding down onto the floor, his feet searched and found his moccasins.

Pulling on his trousers, he padded towards the doorway, intending to go outside and see if anything was amiss.

Before he could reach the door there was the sound of a double barrelled shotgun being fired, and the door of the caravan exploded inwards from a blast of shot.

Donald froze, as the girls rudely awakened from their slumbers, screamed in terror. Tammy was cursing as he struggled to get into his trousers, in between shouting at the girls to get down on the floor out of harms way.

A raucous imperious voice bellowed outside the van.

"Youse bloody tinkers in there, get your scabby arses outside, and quick about it, or I'll blow up this rat's nest here and now."

Donald nodded to Tammy and they descended the four steps down onto the ground, where they were faced with two roughly dressed characters, each holding a shotgun.

Quickly, the girls got into their clothes, but stayed within the relative safety of the caravan, peering out fearfully from the shattered doorway.

The largest of the two men facing Donald and Tammy appeared to be the leader. He took a pace nearer to Donald and poked him sadistically in the stomach with the gun as he growled through clenched teeth.

"I cannot abide you bloody social parasites, you have no right to be here. This land belongs to Mulwhinney, and I'm damned sure he doesn't know you are here, else he'd have kicked your smelly arses out of here long ago."

His suspicious piggy eyes raked them, poking Donald again he demanded to know how long they had been staying in the clearing. Before Tammy could intervene, Donald replied that they had been here some time, and had been hoping to overwinter within the glade.

Comprehension swept across the interrogators face as he jumped back and lifted the shotgun.

"Aye! By God!" he blasphemed, slavers flying from his slacklipped mouth, "you are the bloody lot we have been looking for. You've been busy little boys haven't you? You are no more tinkers than fly in the bloody air. Just look at the colour of this one's hair, and foreby they are all too bloody clean. Who the hell ever saw a clean tinker?"

"Right you will come with us. There is someone who would dearly love to meet you and have a wee bit chat." Lifting his eyes to the doorway of the van, he shouted to the girls, "come on you sleekit bitches. You are invited to the party too. We'll give you a bit of fun on the side while this pair are singing their wee hearts out to a friend of mine."

Donald looked at Tammy and gave a barely perceptible nod of his head and went into action. An explosion of violence impossible to contain.

The hard calloused edge of Donald's right hand scythed downwards, breaking the wrist of the hand holding the gun. The protruding knuckle of his left hand ploughed deep into the right ear of the intruder, bursting the eardrum and rendering the recipient unconscious.

Tammy dealt with the other man in a more orthodox method. He merely hit him with a straight right, bang on the point of the chin. The scuffle had lasted all of two minutes.

Now there was an unforeseen problem. There was no way these two men could be released. They would have to be held prisoners until they could be picked up by the Constabulary after the farmhouse had been taken.

Cursing with frustration, Donald and Tammy carried the unconscious figures inside the van. They stripped them naked, rolled them onto their faces, pulled their arms behind their backs and tied them to their ankles.

When Siobhan asked why they were being stripped, Tammy replied that it had a psychologically humiliating effect on prisoners, leaving them with a desire not to be found in such embarrassing conditions, therefore being an inducement not to try too hard to escape. Well, that was the theory, anyhow!

The prisoners' socks were tied together at the toes, the knotted ends were stuffed in their mouths and the remainder tied behind their heads, making a perfect gag.

The laces of their boots had been used to lash their wrists to their ankles. Neither Donald nor Tammy noted that the leader of the pair had cotton type laces, whilst the underling had the more common leather-like thongs.

It was time for Donald and Tammy to leave on their mission. As they saddled their horses, Tammy kept up a running dialogue of last minute instructions, on how to guard the prisoners, and for God's sake, if they became a problem, just shoot them.

He pointed out to the girls that the two men they were holding were rough, brutal men, and in their sphere of operations they would be partial to the use of kneecapping of any recalcitrants within their ranks. Just keep it in mind! They wouldn't run far, nor be able to be a problem in that state.

The girls shuddered at this suggestion, and demurred, but Tammy insisted that if for any reason the two men got free, they would be violent and unmerciful in their treatment of the girls.

At any rate, just make sure they don't get loose, or they would be in all sorts of trouble. The girls assured Tammy again that they would take good care, and hadn't he better get going, for time was running short.

The men mounted and with a final wave cantered off to the north west. They were both most unhappy at having to leave the girls looking after the two prisoners, but needs must when the devil drives, and luck is at best perfidious and unfaithful. What they had to do now was clear their minds and tune in to the task in hand.

The girls watched their sweethearts out of sight, and then turned and strolled leisurely back towards the caravan. Bridget excused herself and entered a patch of shrubbery to relieve her bladder.

Absent mindedly Siobhan nodded her head and carried on alone. Her thoughts were with Donald, riding off into God knows what kind of danger. It would have suited her better to be involved at the farmhouse rather than staying in the relative safety of the clearing.

She entered the caravan, her mind still on Donald's departure. It took a couple of seconds for her to realise that she had stepped straight into trouble.

The burly leader of the two men had managed to break the cotton laces that had tied his hands and ankles together. He was already rising to his feet. As Siobhan stepped through the open doorway he leapt forward and grabbed her in a brutal bearhug, trapping her arms between them.

Contrary to what he expected, she gave a little moan and relaxed against him, even though the rank odour of stale sweat made her gag. Involuntary surprise caused him to momentarily slacken his grip slightly, Siobhan slid further down his chest.

Like a striking cobra, her hands leapt forward and grabbed his testes. With a strength born of fear, she locked her fingers around the scrotal sac and crushed with a desperate intensity, mangling the tender fruit within.

As the man's head came forward and down with the excruciating pain, Siobhan crashed her forehead onto the bridge of his nose, at the same time lifting a foot, clad in tough riding boots, she slammed it down onto his naked instep.

Bridget, having heard the commotion, came running in through the door and grabbed a cast iron skillet. She paused a second only to tap the head of the squirming figure on the floor, who had been trying to succour and assist his colleague in some way, then smashed the heavy pan across the head of the unfortunate in the clutches of Siobhan.

Shaking with reaction Siobhan looked down at the recumbent figure on the floor, and although filled with revulsion at the thought of having to touch him, she knew she must secure him once again, it had better be a first class job this time.

Rolling him onto his belly while he was still unconscious, she and Bridget sacrificed a full lunging rein to tether him wrist to ankle, binding and binding until they were satisfied that he would have to be a Houdini to escape.

Siobhan now added a personal touch to the restraints of the prisoners. Again with Bridget's help, they pulled the two men into the centre of the van, then she fashioned a hangman's knot on a loop which she placed around the neck of the leader of the men. Taking the end of the rope, she then passed it through a pulley guide fixed in the ceiling, which had been used to raise and lower a clothes airing rack. Pulling the noose taut, she made another loop with a hangman's knot and placed it around the neck of the second prisoner.

The two men were now belly to belly, balanced on their knees with a noose around their necks. Any movement from one would pull the noose tight around the throat of the other and choke him, so it was imperative that they each remain perfectly still. Should the leader decide he could sacrifice his underling, and deliberately choke him, it would be his own death penalty, for the dead weight would now accomplish what he had done to his colleague.

The men still had their gags in place, but again Siobhan added her own refinement. She tore up a linen sheet and blindfolded them. She noticed that the leader of the two, whom she'd fought with, still had blood escaping from his nostrils seeping into the socks that gagged him, but she was unrepentant and decided that the bleeding would soon stop.

When both men recovered consciousness, she outlined to them the arrangements that were now in force, and advised them not to fall asleep on each other, for shame, oh shame, they could easily kill each other and the world would mourn forever.

The girls made themselves a hot drink, hoping it would help to calm their jangling nerves, and it was while they were sitting enjoying the calming beverage that Siobhan had an idea spring into her fertile brain.

Nudging the underling of the two, she asked him if he had heard of the black horse who had savaged a couple of men at an outlying farm. His stiffening posture gave her the answer.

Conversationally she told him that she was the owner of the horse they were talking about. He was called the Black Beast. This was truly a good name for him, he was a beast, well as far as men were concerned. In fact, he actually hated men with a deep and burning hatred, and did her listener know why? Well, the reason was simple. It was men who had made a bodge job of castrating him, causing him a lot of pain that he couldn't seem to forget. Could one really blame the big fellow for being aggressive. Surely not!

The leader of the pair groaned at the mention of castration, pain scythed through him in searing waves of stabbing intensity.

The one that Siobhan was talking to directly was shaking his throbbing head from side to side, gingerly and gently without too much movement. It was as if he had defined the path of Siobhan's thoughts.

Bridget was looking at her cousin with a quizzical furrowed brow, whatever was Siobhan going on about? She felt sure it was leading somewhere but for the moment she didn't know where.

Finishing her drink, Siobhan stood up and taking Bridget by the hand led her outside the van. She kept them walking until they were well clear of the van, and certainly out of earshot of the prisoners within it.

She explained her plan to Bridget, who at first was a bit doubtful, but then her trust in her cousin overcame any objections she felt and she conceded with good grace.

The first tentative chirpings of the dawn chorus began, something like the clearing of throats before a choir breaks into full voice, or the plucking of notes as an orchestra awaits the arrival of the conductor. As if to announce that the time was now, a cock pheasant hacked out his proclamation of territorial rights, and this signalled the commencement of the full ensemble.

The girls strolled back to the van, oblivious to the woodland melodies being played around them. The finer things of life being subjugated to the harsh necessities that dominated their minds.

They entered the caravan. Without explanation Siobhan lifted the noose from around the chosen victim's throat, pushed him aside and firmly anchored the rope leading to the leader's neck so that he was still unable to move. They dragged the unfortunate underling out of the van, across to where the Black Beast and the colt were tethered. Siobhan removed the blindfold and watched as the man's face went ashen. His eyes bulged out and, as heaves racked his body, Siobhan ripped the gag from his mouth. She was just in time to prevent him choking on his own vomit.

When he had emptied his stomach, she casually patted him on the head and told him he would be better now. In an indifferent tone she advised the frightened chap that she had only brought him out to introduce him to her pet.

Raising her voice, she walked over to the horse. She stroked him lovingly and fed him a tidbit, making sure he had to work at it a bit to get it into his mouth.

The sight of the large, grass stained, yellow teeth convulsed the spectator under duress. He squirmed around as he imagined the terrible damage they could inflict on human flesh.

Siobhan returned to the quivering wretch and hunkered down beside him addressing him in a quiet voice.

"We are going to play a wee game, you and I. It's called question and answer. I ask you questions and you provide the answers. To make it tricky, I know some of the answers, you don't know which ones! If you deliberately give me a wrong answer, if you lie, I will know you have lied, so you will have to pay the penalty.

"The penalty is, I will bring my black friend across and let him give you a wee kiss. Maybe let him nibble your ear. He likes ears. In fact, he quite seems to like any man's flesh."

"You see! The rules are quite simple. Shall we start the game? Now I want you to get your chin off your chest and speak clearly. No muttering or murmuring. Good, clear answers!"

Hysterical articulations spewed from the twisting, grimacing mouth and the final humiliation assaulted the quivering wretch. Foul smelling diarrhoea erupted as the sphincter muscle lost control, and at this final treachery of his own body the emaciated figure jerked in convulsive sobbing.

Not hiding her exasperation, Siobhan had Bridget help her to carry the trussed prisoner to a new location up wind of the desecrated area. Panting with exertion they threw him unceremoniously onto the ground, and Siobhan started her interrogation.

"What is your name?"

"Bill Maguire."

"What is your friend's name?"

"Jim Rourke."

"Who is your direct boss?"

"Seamus Rourke in Belfast."

"Are the two Rourke's related."

"Yes, they are cousins."

"What is the farm called where the goods are stores?"

"Drumtoch."

"How many are guarding it at this moment?"

"Eight men and two dogs."

"Are more men expected?"

"Yes! Today, if today is Sunday."

"How many more men are due?"

"Eight."

"When are they due to arrive?"

"Around ten o'clock."

"Who is the senior boss?"

For the first time there was a hesitation and Maguire squirmed uneasily.

"Please," he entreated, "I'll be kneecapped if I tell you, and they are sure to find out, for Jim Rourke will know you are asking me questions, and he'll tell them when he gets the chance."

Siobhan made no comment. Slowly she rose and stretched lazily. Then she casually moved across to where the two horses were grazing. She untethered the black and walked back towards Maguire.

As they approached the black horse started dancing from one foot to the other, snorting and shaking his huge head. He opened his mouth in a cavernous yawn, and Maguire capitulated immediately.

"I'll tell you! I'll tell you! Take him away, in the name of God. I'll tell you what you want to know."

Siobhan turned round and took the black back to join the cob, retethered him and returned to Maguire. She hunkered down in front of him, but didn't repeat the question as she continued to stare him full in the face.

Maguire took a deep, shuddering breath as he looked at her beseechingly, but there was no offer of compassion on the visage in front of him. Tears of self pity welled up in his eyes, as he sobbed now without embarrassment, then he blurted out the answer that Siobhan was waiting for.

"He is the Chief Constable of the R.U.C., as God is my witness that is the truth. He hates the bloody English, or anybody who isn't a true Irish Celt."

The flood gates were open. The voice increased in tempo, as if to spew it all out in a soul clearing confession.

"He has sworn to rid Ireland of all non nationals, and uses his position to that effect. The extra men who are coming today are going to assist in the clearing out of the farm, for he feels it is no longer a safe place to keep the arsenal. The country nests have been discovered by somebody who is systematically destroying them."

Siobhan had heard enough. She got to her feet and nodding to Bridget, they converged on Maguire. They hoisted him up between them and carried him back into the caravan.

When the gag and blindfold had been replaced, Siobhan adjusted the strangle noose around the neck of Maguire. Double checking the two men were thoroughly secured, she jerked her head sideways, indicating to Bridget that they should go outside again.

Siobhan was moving fast now as she strode towards the horses, Bridget almost running to keep pace with her as she asked what was on her cousin's mind. Siobhan explained that she thought they had better get over to the farm and warn Donald and Tammy that reinforcements were arriving for the opposing faction.

Quickly they saddled their horses, a sense of urgency giving speed to their nimble fingers. A final check to make sure they had the .38 Smith and Wesson revolvers that Tammy had schooled them in and they were off at a gallop heading for Drumtoch farm.

As they raced along Siobhan outlined the plan she had in mind. They would reduce speed a mile out from the farm and advance with caution to within a quarter of a mile. At this point the horses would be tethered and they would go forward on foot.

What happened next would be in the lap of the Gods, they would just have to assess the situation to see how best they could help their menfolk.

Siobhan and Bridget had no way of knowing that the reinforcement party for the farm residents were roughly two hours behind them, but an hour ahead of them was the Assistant Chief Constable with three loyal colleagues he had chosen specially. That the three were ex paratroopers well versed in small arms and assault techniques was an added advantage to their leader, as was their unswerving loyalty to the Crown.

Seamus Rourke was the front seat passenger in the lead vehicle that was on its way to clear the stored armaments out from the farm. He had recovered from the chest wound inflicted by Tammy. Although one lung would never be quite the same, he was still able to keep his position as second in command to the head of the organisation.

It was a quiet Sunday morning, a weak sun shining on the frost clad hedges and skeletal trees made it seem quite bright despite the biting cold.

The party expected little if any trouble and progressed north west at a comfortable moderate pace. Rourke supped repeatedly at a bottle of Irish whisky. He seldom travelled far without such a comfort, like a baby with a dummy stuck in its mouth all the time. Now and again as an afterthought he would pour a thimbleful into the cap of the bottle and pass it over to the driver, but mostly he drank in selfish isolation.

Rourke had already planned where he would relocate the weaponry held at Drumtoch farm, so this was a simple relocation job and then back to civilisation and the comforts of the Oak and Sloe in Belfast.

Despite the lack of one lung he managed to fill the car with thick acrid smoke from the foul smelling black cigars he affected. When the driver went to open the window he was brutally cursed for his attempted indiscretion and consigned to passive smoking.

Peter Mahon, the Assistant Chief of Police, kept glancing at his watch and the sky alternately as he approached the designated area on the OS map, which he had spread across his knees. Now and again he would give a quiet directive to the driver, who complied with a brief nod, but instant obedience to the precise commands.

It was a credit to the four occupants of the car that no sense of tension existed. They were four hardened professionals on their way to complete an assignment and they conducted themselves as such. Just another day at the office. No fuss. Just earn the bread.

Roughly a mile from the farm they sought and found an ideal hiding place for the car. The driver bulldozed his way deep into a large patch of wild brambles and stunted willows. With practised efficiency, they effectively camouflaged any part of the vehicle that had been left uncovered.

Each member of the group now checked each other out. Camouflage cream applied to their faces. Personal arms examined then magazines loaded. Satisfied that they were prepared, the next task was to eradicate any signs of their entry into the patch as they backtracked out to the roadway.

A double march pace they headed for the not visible, but not too distant, farmhouse. Such was the timing that dawn was making every effort to get the day started.

The sky had turned heavy and sullen, the grey clouds hanging heavy, like a woman deep in pregnancy waiting to ease the load. The promise of precipitation of some description sooner or later was of little consequence to Peter and his party as they force marched along the country lane.

When the farmhouse came into view the party stopped. A few minutes elapsed as final instructions were given. Peter checked that all were wearing a red ribbon on their right arm. The group of four split up, two going each side of the road, where they divided again.

They had synchronised their watches and would attack precisely on the stroke of half past seven. Their first requirement was to get into position from which to launch the offensive.

The last hundred yards or so from the perimeter wall of the farm was devoid of anything that would provide cover, but the four attackers were well practised in the art of silent covert approach, and were soon nestled close to the root of the wall in the natural shadow area.

Siobhan and Bridget had stopped on the hill overlooking the farm. It was at this self same spot from which Siobhan had first discovered its existence.

It all seemed peaceful and quiet, and then the sound of gunfire erupted in staccato bursts. A sharp flat crack denoted the use of a sniper type rifle being used. That would mean an extra threat to Donald and Tammy.

A good sniper is a highly competent single shot expert, and can often inflict more telling damage than infantrymen with multi-shot or machine pistols.

Totally disregarding personal safety, the girls careered downhill towards the farm, huge strides in overrun as the steepness of the incline gave them added momentum.

It would take ten minutes or thereabout to reach their destination, and then they would have to find their menfolk and warn them of the reinforcements that were on the way, an added threat to the one they already faced.

It never entered their heads that their very presence anywhere near the conflict would be an unwanted complication that Donald and Tammy could well have done without.

When Donald and Tammy had left the clearing in the woods, they had pushed their mounts hard to reach the farm well before dawn. They wanted to take out any sentries that might be posted around the perimeters prior to the arrival of the party led by Peter Mahon.

Half a mile from the farm, they pulled up in a tree-lined hollow, where they knee-hobbled the horses. Moving stealthily through the sparsely wooded area, they paused at the edge to survey the cleared stretch between them and the farm walls.

This was the danger zone. Sentries would be able to detect any movement with the coming of daylight. Being armed, they would have a clear field of fire within which to pick out a target and neutralise it.

Donald knew the cover of darkness would not hold out for much longer. It was imperative that they disposed of any guards that were between them and the farm. He and Tammy lay scrutinising the ground they had to cover, trying desperately to detect any movement.

A tiny flicker of light showed for an instant, if they had not been concentrating they would have missed it. A sentry was committing the cardinal sin of lighting a cigarette whilst on watch.

Donald silently thanked the thoughtless fool, then nudged Tammy as he spotted the second watchman who was about ten yards the other side of the gate to his colleague. He had been sitting with his back leaning against the wall. Now he got to his feet and was fumbling at the front of his trousers, obviously intent on emptying his bladder against his former backrest.

Donald pointed at him with his chin, then drew his hand spade shaped across his throat. Tammy nodded his understanding, knowing this was his immediate target, and that Donald would take out the smoker.

The darkness held as they ghosted rapidly forward, every tussock or slightest hollow in the ground used to advantage, promoting the unsuspected covert approach.

The guard with his back to them had just finished voiding his bladder and was still standing with his penis in his hand, wistfully dreaming of a girlfriend perhaps, when a strangling band of steel, which was Tammy's hand, gripped his throat, choking off any attempt to scream. A fist hammered a severe rabbit punch to the back of his neck and he collapsed without a murmur.

Quickly Tammy stripped him, pulled his arms behind him and tied them to his ankles, which were bent back from the knees to meet his wrists.

It was not the most comfortable position in which to be left for any length of time, but it gave Tammy no qualms whatever, as he stuffed the knotted toes of the man's own socks deep into his mouth and tied the loose ends firmly behind his head. Using the thug's shirt, he tied one sleeve around his neck, the other to his wrists and ankles. Giving a satisfied nod, he left the trussed prisoner and moved towards the farm gate.

The gate was constructed of galvanised metal, with a heavy duty steel mesh guard attached. It was not the usual sort of entrance to an innocent country farm by any means, coupled with the triple strands of barbed wire running along the top of the wall, it actually drew attention to the farm as being out of the ordinary.

Tammy marvelled at the stupidity of humanity at times, and in particular the sort of people he was in opposition to. Their purpose would have been better suited to have let the old run-down farm continue to look like that. At the moment it looked like a fortress, and it had been that very feature that had drawn Siobhan's attention to it in the first place.

When Donald separated from Tammy he snaked along the ground in a fluid ripple of undulating wizardry. Ten yards from his quarry, he saw him stiffen as if in disbelief.

The mouth opened in a rictus of surprise about to give a call of alarm, as he raised his rifle to the horizontal position.

With blinding speed Donald threw one of his clubs, hoping against hope for accuracy in the doubtful light. The club was a blur of movement, it is doubtful whether the intended target was even aware of its approach until it entered his mouth like an obscene lollipop and smashed its way through to the larynx, preventing the scream of alarm that died in a choking fit.

Donald reached the victim, whose eyes were standing out like organ stops, as he struggled to get air through his mangled throat, and seized the wrist of the hand that was furiously trying to pull the trigger, at the same time the other was fighting to remove the obstruction to his breathing.

Donald got both hands on the rifle and smashed it upwards, catching the guard directly under the chin with sufficient force to break the lower jawbone and knock his adversary unconscious.

Removing his club from the shattered mouth, Donald callously wiped it clean on the guard's jacket and replaced it, ready for use again.

Quickly he did the strip and tether routine and rolled the unfortunate into the darker shadow of the wall, then raced towards the gate a few yards further along the wall.

He found Tammy quietly surveying the area from the gateway up to the farmhouse and adjacent buildings. All seemed quiet and serene, as the birth of the new day brought a first glimmer of light to the scene, they tacitly started to climb the gate. There was no barbed wire across the top of the gate so it was the obvious place to breach the perimeter, additionally it was comparatively easier to scale than the wall, providing sufficient toe and finger holds to get up and over.

They quickly reached the ground inside the gate, then heard the sound that would have made Tammy's blood run cold, previous to his training from Donald. The Dobermann Pinschers appeared from the gloom, hackles raised, and snarling their aggression with bared slavering fangs, as they raced towards the intruders into their territory.

Suddenly they stopped. A sound more terrifying, more heart stopping, erupted into the peace of the morning. The battle thrum of Donald filled the air with a coldly menacing promise that was a violence in its very existence.

One of the dogs slid to a standstill, gave a frightened yelp, and turning, raced away as if the devil of hell was at its heels.

The other one, made of sterner stuff, decided that attack was the best defence, and sprang at Donald who had raced to meet it. The dog had not been trained properly in the art of disablement, and made the mistake of leaping for Donald's throat. With immaculate timing, half way through the leap, Donald's hands flashed forward and caught the front legs, just below the elbows.

Savagely he jerked them wide apart as his knee drove up into the dog's chest, caving in the ribcage. The dog gave a convulsive shudder and, as Donald released it, fell to the ground and was motionless.

In an act of kindness, after his brutal handling, Donald drew a club and smashed it into the base of the dog's skull in the medulla area, which is the nerve centre of the brain. The dog was instantly dead and would suffer no more.

Donald turned to speak to Tammy. In that instant he felt a scalding impact in the centre of his right cheek, and almost in the same instant, felt a similar effect in his left cheek.

Such was the force of this double impact that it threw him sideways. A blessing indeed, for a fusillade of shots filled the space he had just vacated.

He had never experienced such excruciating pain in his life. Searing waves of agony sheeted through his face and head. He felt consciousness ebb and flow and a red mist seemed to dominate his sight.

He tried to look for a safe haven in which to take stock but his blurred vision gave little help, and his thinking processes were badly impaired.

Desperately he pumped oxygen into his lungs, great steadying draughts to settle his equilibrium. He rose and leapt a six foot length, ending in a forward rolling breakfall. This manoeuvre found him refuge behind a horsetrough, thankfully still holding water.

Gingerly he explored his face with questing fingers. He discovered that he had been hit by a sniper's bullet. When he had turned to speak to Tammy the bullet would have hit him below the nose, had instead passed through one cheek and out the other.

The bullet had taken out two of his back teeth on the exit side and, as he spat out a mouthful of blood, he knew he must stop the flow of blood or it would impede his ability to carry on in combat.

Mari had always insisted he carry a handkerchief, no thumb against one nostril and an explosive blow out the other for her son. With a silent thank you to his caring mum, he took out the sissy rag as he called it, and tearing it in half, he folded each to make a small square pad.

Carefully he pressed these into position on the inside of his cheeks, and although he looked like a chipmunk, he felt the benefit straight away.

Something moved in the periphery of his vision. He turned to see Tammy slam the butt of the man's own rifle onto his head. The fight and the life seemed to drain away in an instant as the figure went limp and dropped to the ground.

Tammy looked across to Donald and signalled that he was going for the main building. He pointed urgently at a doorway of a hayloft above the stable, mimicking a man shooting a rifle. He pointed at the door and Donald alternatively. He then turned his hand upwards and nodded his head affirmatively.

Donald received and understood the message. Tammy wanted him to take care of that damned sniper, and that suited Donald right down to the ground.

The sniper had hurt him, could have killed him. Never mind if he was a specialist, it was a cowardly way of disposing of enemies, from a long, safe distance. He signalled to Tammy that he was on his way, and keeping to whatever cover he could use, he streaked for the barn.

Silently he entered the barn and as he slid round the door he prepared to listen. He heard the sniper moving from one side of the loft to the other. Using the sounds to cover any he might make he reached the old wooden rickety ladder that was the access to the loft. He was sure it would creak and squeak like a cave full of bats as soon as he put weight on it.

His eyes raked the gloomy interior of the musty smelling stable, searching for an alternative way to gain access to the loft.

As his eyes became more accustomed to the darkened, shadowy scene, his pulse quickened as he found a possible avenue which was worth exploring.

At the front of each stall, just above the mangers, was a gap in the loft floor through which hay could be thrown down into the mangers.

Silently on the edges of his moccasin covered feet, he darted across the intervening space. He took his first purchase on the rust encrusted cast iron hay manger. Infinitely cautiously he clambered up onto the structure.

Standing now with his feet balanced on the top edge he was able to take his first careful peek into the loft, but not before he had placed a handful of hay on his head, which would at least break the outline if the sniper happened to be looking towards Donald as his head cleared the floor of the loft.

The sniper, however, was again standing at the open doorway of the loft, looking down into the cobbled yard below. Twice he brought the rifle into the firing position, and twice he lowered it again.

'Probably waiting for a clear shot,' thought Donald, hoping the interest would continue in that direction until he himself could get into a position to attack.

With infinite patience, Donald got his hands over the edge of the floor. It now needed sheer muscular power to pull himself up and over. Bending his knees, and using the top of the hay manger as a bouncing board, he erupted like exploding lava through the opening, and as his feet found purchase on the loft floor, he threw himself at the figure by the doorway.

The sniper turned as Donald was halfway across the twelve foot gap that separated them. The rifle rose as the sniper took an involuntary step backwards.

The battle thrum tore from Donald's throat as the primeval lust to kill enveloped him with mindless fury. Chi Li would have been horrified at this loss of control in a confrontational situation.

To Donald, this man had hurt him, more than he had ever been hurt in his life, including his maltreatment at the hands of the Macmillans in his boyhood years. He was intent on retribution.

Never had a sniper faced such an implacable foe. The sheer power of determination that opposed him was like a physical onslaught. Desperately he fired the rifle as he retreated from the advancing menace. He stepped backwards through the open doorway behind him. His scream lasted a mere second before his head hit the cobbles in the yard below, silencing him forever.

Donald was knocked backwards as the bullet tore a furrow across his cheek and along the right side of his head. He would carry a scar from the point of his chin to the crown of his head for the rest of his life.

He lay in an inert heap, the pain engulfing him in spasmodic waves of increasing intensity. He rolled over and was violently sick. The movement of the retching heaves incurred a crescendo of mind-numbing intense agony.

He was bereft of the benefit of clenching his teeth against the pain. His whole head was a sheet of white hot flame that devoured sense and reason. He felt as if it had been turned inside out by a sadist's malevolence.

The words of his mentor forced their way into his tortured mind, and desperately he intoned the soothing mantra.

Pain is physical! The mind can control it. Isolate the pain. Think beyond the pain! Release your inbuilt anaesthetic. You are in control. Decide you have no pain!

The process of thinking through the mantra, divorced his mind from the intense pain. He forced himself into the lotus position and continued the mantra. He took deep breaths and held each within his lungs for a few seconds before releasing through his open mouth.

Gradually the waves of pain subsided, he rose to his feet, and swayed as dizziness enveloped him. With a shuddering gasp he forced himself to stay erect, until the red mist cleared from his vision.

Post shock reaction made him tremble uncontrollably, but his iron will came to his rescue and he held his position. Now he forced his legs to move, and although they felt rubbery and disjointed he walked with the deliberation of a robot around the loft floor until he had mastered the art and regained complete control.

Recovery of all his faculties made him realise he had lost touch with events. He had to find out how the assault was progressing. Tammy could be in serious trouble. He had heard the sound of gunfire but it had been no more than a background clamour that had filtered into his troubled mind.

He walked across to the loft doorway and looked out. It was a moment of carelessness which was rewarded accordingly. One of Peter Mahon's men had a glimpse of a shadowy figure and, thinking it was a sniper, fired off a short burst.

Two bullets tore their way into Donald. One lacerated the deltoid muscle of his right shoulder, the other passing through the meaty part of his inner thigh, just missing the femur bone and the femoral artery.

The impact threw Donald to the floor as fresh pain screamed through his already tortured body. His head hit the floor, an explosion of agony, followed by the gift of unconsciousness.

Chapter Eighteen

Peter Mahon gave the signal to attack. One of his men produced a pair of bolt cutters and cut through the chain that locked the gates. There was no need now for secrecy as gunfire could be heard within the compound.

To Peter this meant that Donald and Tammy were already involved in combat and would need the assistance of his party urgently.

The four men dispersed to lessen the chance of being mown down in a group, and raced towards the main building of the farm complex. Each realised that their approach to the farm had been made a lot easier by Donald and Tammy having taken out the two sentries before the assault party arrived.

Unknown to them, the sniper was out of commission, plus the one Tammy had dealt with. The two sentries were trussed like turkeys for the oven and out of the fight. That left four more to be accounted for.

Two of the assault team raced off to the side to go round to the rear of the building. The one who had to traverse the cobbled yard, saw a figure appear at the loft door and got off a short burst. He nodded with satisfaction when the threat disappeared, obviously hit.

Then he spotted the inert body lying on the cobbles, and a sniper's rifle a few yards away. He slid to a halt. Realisation struck him with chilling certainty. He had taken out one of his own side.

He abandoned his plan to reach the rear of the farmhouse, and raced instead towards the stable door. His whole mind was set on reaching the person he had shot and rendering assistance.

His pounding hasty feet knocked out several of the rungs of the rickety ladder as he climbed in a frantic fury. As his head cleared the gap he saw Donald lying like a rag doll carelessly thrown aside. His face was a mask of blood, and he lay in an ever-widening pool as blood escaped from the fleshy wounds of leg and shoulder.

Desperately Donald tried to come erect, he had just regained consciousness when a figure hurtled towards him. He tried to adopt the defensive posture although still on his knees. He gasped with relief and relaxed when he saw the red armband.

Gratefully he submitted to the administrations of the man who had wounded him with friendly fire. This is a feature of combat that does occur despite the best laid plans

Deftly, the first-aider plugged the wounds, stopping the loss of more blood. Checking Donald's face, he noticed the entry and exit holes of a bullet through the cheeks and, as Donald indicated inside his mouth, he peered inside and saw the temporary pads Donald had placed there.

He advised Donald that he had done everything just right, and to hang on in there and he would be back in a tick. Giving Donald a friendly pat, he got up and then disappeared down through the gap in the loft floor.

Choking with self anger, he raced across the cobbled yard, hearing the growling crump of a hand grenade exploding, as a reeling figure arose almost under his feet. A quick check showed no red armband, and he let loose a quick burst from his machine pistol. The target dissolved in a crumpled heap, this time he wouldn't rise again. He was the one that Tammy had felled with his rifle butt, and for him, he had regained consciousness at entirely the wrong time.

The farmhouse was in the hands of Peter Mahon's party. The special reported Donald's plight and was detailed to take another member and recover him from the loft, and for God's sake, take a first aid pack with field combat morphine shots to administer to Donald before they attempted to bring him down from the loft.

When the first aid team entered the stable they found Donald had somehow reached the bottom of the ladder and was standing swaying like a reed in the wind, his face ashen and sweat standing out on his face like obscene blisters. Quickly they lowered him to the floor and jabbed the syringe into the fleshy muscle of his thigh. The anaesthetic fluid would soon relieve the worst of the terrible pain that coursed through him.

Again Donald pointed to his mouth. Probing fingers gently removed the make-shift pads and he managed to mumble that the bleeding had stopped and he didn't want anything else put into his mouth.

As the two specials assisted Donald to the main farm building, a new charge of cavalry arrived, red-faced and panting, waving two handguns menacingly, albeit uselessly.

They came to a confused halt in the middle of the cobbled yard, then Siobhan caught sight of Donald. In an instant she was beside him in a flurry of concern. Quickly she assessed the damage to her loved one, and as his eyes suddenly lost focus and his head began to flop to the side, she gathered him into her arms as she crooned softly into the blood matted hair.

Suddenly she remembered why she and Bridget were at the farm, and quickly explained to the two specials who had assisted Donald. They left at a run to advise Peter Mahon of this new threat.

Bridget found Tammy sitting looking at his broken leg, and holding his wounded shoulder. She sank to her knees and threw her arms around him as if to protect him from the savage world, and when he asked about Donald, she was able to put his mind at rest, saying he was safe in the arms of Siobhan.

There was the sound of a single shot, then Peter came running round the corner, followed by his men. He arranged for Donald and Tammy to be taken inside the farmhouse, where the girls were to look after them. On no account were any of them to come out of the building, was that clear?

When Tammy asked what the shot had been, Peter shrugged indifferently and said that a bloody great dog had tried to sink its teeth into him so he shot it.

Outside, Peter closed the farmyard gates and stationed two men just inside the wall on either side. The two sentries who had been taken out of commission by Donald and Tammy, were unceremoniously dumped out of sight in some nearby bushes.

Peter set up his ambuscade efficiently and quickly. He was determined that not one of the approaching party would escape, and he was none too fussy whether he took them dead or alive. He was only too well aware of the deviations in the dispensing of justice within the province. Strange judgements were often the case, with out-and-out criminals walking free because of some doubtful legal loophole in the structure of the law, or the interpretation that had been applied to it.

The growl of vehicle engines pronounced the arrival of the awaited party and shortly a car came into view, followed by a heavy goods vehicle.

They stopped at the farm gates and Rourke dismounted from the car and started shouting orders. He stopped. Native cunning registered that something was amiss. Where the hell were the dogs? Why hadn't somebody appeared at the sound of the vehicles?

He whirled and dived for the safety of the car as Peter fired and brought him down. Peter roared in a high clear voice that they were the police and everyone was to put their hands on top of their heads and then stand perfectly still.

Peter rose from concealment at the roadside. One of the men from the truck brought his rifle to bear. A single shot from within the compound hit him full in the chest, throwing him backwards into the ditch at the side of the road.

Peter now organised a head count. The toll was eleven dead and seven prisoners, including Rourke, who had just been wounded. There is a saying that the devil looks after his own, and in Rourke's case he was working overtime.

Only one of the specials had received a wound. It was Donald and Tammy who had borne the brunt of the assault, and as they needed quite urgent attention, Peter already had it in mind that they would be taken with all haste to the nearest hospital with a casualty department which was Londonderry.

Rourke kept screaming that he was in severe pain, and that the Geneva Conventions were quite clear as to the treatment of injured prisoners. He was totally ignored. Finally his continual whining penetrated Peter's tolerance and twanged the nerve ends raw. He wheeled on Rourke and told him that he was lucky, yes, very lucky to be alive, and why did he not shut the hell up before his luck deserted him! This advice proved to be the antidote to Rourke's complaints, and silence reigned.

All the machinery of war was placed in the barn at the edge of the farm, with the prisoners being made to do the humping and grunting. After a couple of hours work the task was completed, and would be blown up by the explosives expert in Peter's party.

Donald and Tammy were placed on mattresses in the body of the lorry to convey them to hospital. The two girls would accompany them and encourage the two horses tied to the tailgate to follow the truck. Speed would be kept to a minimum to ease the conditions for the two wounded young men, so the horses could keep pace without being cruelly extended.

Peter called the local police in Londonderry to arrange for the prisoners and the dead to be recovered but he left two of his men on guard, one of whom would be the explosives expert, who would blow up the arsenal as soon as the rest of the party were clear.

It was a strange sight that entered the town of Londonderry on a quiet Sunday morning, when the local populace were returning from church and chapel, already anticipating lunch.

Peter tried to keep everything low key, but he was sure that the gossip would soon come to the ears of those he would most want not to hear. He knew he would have to make special arrangements to protect Donald and Tammy while they were in hospital.

The two wounded young men were quickly assigned to a quiet side room in the hospital and receiving the attention they needed, and Peter arranged a guard system in case the local sympathisers of the I.R.A. tried to exact some sort of revenge.

The girls saddled their trusty steeds once more and raced back to the Drumtoch farm area to pick up the horses Donald and Tammy had used. They found them grazing contentedly close to the area where they had been abandoned.

The Connemara Grey welcomed the big black by nipping him on the neck when he went over to greet her, but she ran alongside him quietly enough on the way back to the caravan site.

On their way the girls called in at the Mulwhinney steading, and left him the proud owner of the hammerheaded gelding and the cob that Donald had used. When the tack was included, Mulwhinney professed undying friendship with that good man of Barranbarrach.

The girls approached the caravan carefully, but the trussed up prisoners were gone. Quickly they harnessed the big black and were soon bowling along towards Londonderry.

When they reached the hospital they found Stuart and Mari had arrived, having received a telephone call from Peter Mahon. Mari had, of course, taken complete control.

It had already been decided that Donald and Tammy would return to Barranbarrach in the gypsy caravan with Siobhan and Bridget sharing the driving. Mari would sit in the body of the caravan and attend to any nursing that was required on the way home.

The following morning, at the crack of dawn, they set off heading south west, and Mari was convinced they would reach Barranbarrach late the same day. Stuart was heard to remark that the Gods whoever they were had better make sure they paid attention, or there would be hell to pay.

Mari ignored this homily, she was in her element, mothering her chicks with untiring resolve. She sat between them in the centre aisle and holding the hand of each she regaled them with a fund of stories that kept their minds off any discomfort that they might feel during the journey.

She was an excellent raconteur, and once or twice Donald had to point out that it was painful to laugh, and could she tell them less funny stories.

Mari looked at her son's swollen face and resolved to take that stupid helmet bandage off the minute they reached home. Time without number her throat closed in anguish as she thought how scarred her son would be. There would be a puckered scar on each cheek, and then there would be that dreadful scar along the side of his head. Oh! Oh! What had happened to her lovely, handsome, golden boy?

With suspiciously bright eyes, she smiled bravely and launched into stories of ancient folklore which she knew Donald loved and was sure Tammy would find interesting.

The daylight had given way to murky darkness as the small convoy of caravan and two cars filled with Peter Mahon and his men, including Stuart, turned into the drive leading to the big manor house of Barranbarrach. Stuart had phoned ahead, so they were met by a veritable army, who helped in every way they could to get the wounded warriors carried into the house, and settled down comfortably.

Conal took charge of the caravan and horses, and after seeing to their needs, returned to see if there was anything further that he could do.

Young men heal quickly, and soon Donald and Tammy were up and about and starting exercising in the makeshift gymnasium that Donald had constructed when he took Tammy's instruction in hand, but now he insisted that the two girls must have formal training in the martial arts, although he sincerely hoped there would never ever be a time when the girls needed to use the arts.

As Mari had foreseen, the handsome face of Donald sported a dimpled white cicatrice on each cheek, and a long white scar ran the entire length of his right cheek continuing up along the side of his head, where the bullet had gouged out a ragged furrow.

The thing that concerned Donald the most, however, was that for some reason or another, his entire head of hair was no longer blond. It was completely white. This phenomena had occurred within a fortnight of returning home from the Drumtoch farm area.

To make light of it Tammy had teased him gently, saying he would get him a shaky stick, then if he could learn to pee himself he could apply for a place in an old people's home.

This sort of remark would end in Tammy being chased until he collapsed in hysterical mirth. Donald would pretend to rough him up, but the horseplay had the desired effect and soon Donald was able to forget or disregard his new mature looks.

Mari and the girls threw themselves wholeheartedly into preparations for the double wedding. It was arranged to coincide with the Barranbarrach Christmas function. In this way the entire working force would be able to attend.

Mari was determined that it would be the grandest affair Ulster had ever known. The Cruachans and Chi Li would be invited, of course, also the local tradesmen and dignitaries, whoever they were.

Stuart and old Kelly smiled and assured each other that the cost would be horrendous, but there! Mari would be happy, and were not those two girls the perfect partners for the lads who had chosen them, or was it the other way round? Had the girls chosen the lads. Well, whatever, it didn't really matter.

Donald and Tammy had unfinished business to attend to. They planned in secret how to accomplish it, knowing they would face total opposition from all at Barranbarrach.

What they had already accomplished was to eventually prove wasted effort, for Northern Ireland was committed to internecine warfare for the next twenty or so years, with a heavy involvement of British troops being brought in to try and keep the peace. This, of course, had the opposite effect and escalated the war of attrition by the very presence of what was seen by many as the jackboot answer.

Tammy received his authorisation to return to Glasgow on the 1st of February. This coincided with Donald's decision to take up ownership of Cruachan on the 1st of March, which meant that their friendship would not be affected by distance, they would be able to visit each other without restriction.

They looked forward to returning to Scotland, but before they left the shores of Ireland they were determined that the Chief of the R.U.C. would not go unpunished for his traitorous dealings, especially when they heard from Eamonn Kelly that the R.U.C. Chief had travelled to Londonderry and had Rourke released through lack of conclusive proof of involvement with the Drumtoch farm affair.

He stated categorically that Rourke had been at the farm on police authority to confiscate illegal armaments, and had in fact been accosted whilst carrying out his legal duties.

Peter Mahon, the Assistant Chief, was reprimanded for not keeping his superior briefed, which could have avoided people being killed needlessly when they were all on the same side. Law and Order.

The terrorist who had divulged information to Siobhan, with the help of her Black Beast, telling her that the Chief of Constabulary was the overall head of the I.R.A., had somehow managed to commit suicide while being held in jail.

Pat O'Malley, the thug who had tried to rape Siobhan, was now a newly recruited member of Rourke's band at the Oak and Sloe in Belfast, with his brother another new member.

It was Donald's idea to use this fine pair as bait to lure Rourke to an isolated location and then use Rourke to draw the I.R.A. cum R.U.C. Chief into an incriminating situation, from which, hopefully, he would be unable to wriggle out.

Donald and Tammy secretly met with Peter Mahon and Commander Denham-Tring, where the final details were ironed out.

Peter would apprehend the brothers O'Malley, then summon Donald and Tammy to Belfast. This would be the start of the plan going into action.

Donald and Tammy mentioned to sweethearts and family that they would shortly be having a Christmas shopping day in Larne. No! They wouldn't go near

Belfast if you paid them! They further suggested that, as they felt a bit in the way, they might stop with a friend in Larne and have a couple of days sea fishing.

This was subterfuge, plain and simple. Oh yes! White lies to prevent worry of their loved ones, or so they salved their consciences.

The awaited phone call resulted in the two warriors declaring that tomorrow was their shopping day, and they had the grace to blush when everybody wished them good fortune in their hunt for Christmas presents.

Donald had already bought Siobhan's gift. It was a Connemara Grey, sister to the one in foal to the Black Beast, and would be delivered on Christmas morning.

At Belfast, Peter Mahon was holding the O'Malley brothers in a disused warehouse on the outskirts of the city. He had installed a temporary telephone, a necessary piece of equipment to ensure the success of what they had planned so carefully.

Peter left the scene and returned to his office in the city. He would assemble the same trustworthy team he had used on the assault on Drumtoch farm. This team would take up observation positions and give assistance if, and when, required.

Donald and Tammy committed themselves to their task, forgetting any niceties or introductions. Roughly the two prisoners were hoisted to their feet. Their shackled hands were brought over their heads where a rope was secured around them. The loose end of the rope was thrown over a beam and the pair were pulled up until their toes only were in contact with the ground.

Wasting no time on explanations, the interrogators pulled down the trousers and underpants of the hanging duo, who being gagged could make no outcry.

Taking his knife out of his leg sheaf, Tammy grabbed the flaccid penis of Pat. He pulled the foreskin forward with finger and thumb, then placed the blade in a position to slice off the length he had drawn clear of the head of the penis. He looked into the bulging eyes of his victim and observed thoughtfully, "I am sure a good Catholic boy like yourself would hate to become a circumcised Jew. Do you agree?"

There was a frantic nodding of agreement from Pat, whose face had blanched to an ashy grey whilst the sweat rolled freely.

"Well! It is really quite easy to avoid. To prevent any little mishaps, all you've got to do is this, ring Mr Rourke, your boss, and tell him you have caught Donald and me and are holding us prisoners. It is too difficult for you to bring us to him so could he come here. You can then persuade him to come alone, pointing out that the least number of people who know about our disappearance the safer it will be for all concerned."

"Is all that quite clear? Will you do this small thing for me?" The gagged head nodded furiously in a definite affirmative.

Tammy removed the gag and continued, as Donald brought the phone across, "Right you are then, I'll dial the number, and you will do the talking. Could I point out at this stage that your poor wee brother is still in an awkward position, so if you inadvertently make a mistake, there will be two Catholic Jews running around Belfast. No! No! That's not quite right, there will be no running! It will be hobbling around the city, for I will quite frankly kneecap you both, then ring Rourke myself and tell him you gave me all the information I required, that you sang like a lark."

"Now then! Are we all quite clear on what has to be said? Don't be shy, ask as many questions as you like, but just be sure you have it all off pat, Pat."

Tammy deliberately sniggered at his terrible pun, as Pat O'Malley gave a croak of profound anguish, a groan that came from the very depths of his tortured soul. He was being forced to betray the very organisation that he had freely joined, being in total sympathy with what they were trying to achieve.

The implacable look on the face of his interrogator confirmed that the punishment for non compliance would be carried out with no mercy. He would just have to follow the dictates of this bastard who held him in thrall.

Donald stood nearby watching what was going on, brought his own knife out, and casually pulling a hair from his head, cut it in half with a deft flick of his wrist.

The two prisoners watched with the horrified fascination of rabbits mesmerised by a stoat.

Going over to Pat's brother Tim, Donald, with casual indifference, lifted the scrotum sac that seemed as if it tried to shrink itself even further into an unobtrusive nonentity.

He looked into the face of Tim with eyes of steely intent, but his voice was almost gentle as he remarked.

"My speciality is castration. I have perhaps done the operation a thousand times. Of course, it was on lambs or pigs, but there again, the porcine family is not far removed from yours, is it?"

The gagged prisoner nodded furiously, not knowing that Donald had sinned in his soul, having always refused to be involved in castration of the farm animals.

Tim looked across at his sibling, mutely beseeching him to comply with any request these demons from hell put to him.

Tammy dialled the number of the Oak and Sloe and handed the phone to Donald who using his gift of mimicry, said he was Pat O'Malley, and could he talk to Rourke.

When Rourke's voice came through, Donald stuck the mouthpiece up to Pat's face and gave him a nod to start talking.

Pat complied with the instructions he had been given, and if his voice sounded a wee bit strained, Tammy was sure that Rourke would put it down to excitement.

Quickly the scene was set for Rourke's arrival. He wouldn't barge in like a bull in a china shop. His native cunning and naturally suspicious mind would make him very cautious.

The brothers were lowered to the floor and allowed to dress. Donald and Tammy sat on the floor with their backs to the wall, but facing the entrance to the warehouse. They put their hands behind their backs hoping it would appear as if they were bound.

Pat and Tim stood over them, as if guarding them, with their backs to the conveniently open door through which it was hoped that Rourke would come.

When Rourke entered, Pat was to turn round and wave him forward with the empty handgun he would be holding, shouting in excitement to complete the charade.

Tammy assured Pat that if he deviated from the plan in the slightest way, he would gut shoot him, then convey him to the moors and leave him lying on the ground, tethered. In time the hoodie crows would find him, for were they not the bonny scavengers.

The look on Pat's face said it all. How could anybody dream up such a horrible thing to do, it was totally barbaric.

A car could be heard approaching. The ratch of the hand brake, then the engine stopped. A bulky shadow fell across the corrugated door. A hand appeared on its surface and the hinges creaked as the door was pushed all the way back against the wall.

The shadow thickened then held its shape for a second or so. Rourke's head came cautiously into view, body still out of sight.

On cue, Pat whirled and waved with the gun, shouting that for God's sake he was beginning to think that Rourke wasn't coming, but wasn't this a bonny pair of trussed chickens.

Confidently now, Rourke came through the door and marched arrogantly across the warehouse to where the prisoners sat facing him with their backs to the wall.

Striding to within a pace of Tammy, he drew back his foot to deliver a kick to the head of his hated enemy.

Tammy brought the gun from behind his back. Pointing it at the flabby belly three feet away, he advised conversationally, "Please! I beg you! Please give me the pleasure of gut shooting you, Mr Rourke. It would appear that you have more lives than the proverbial pussy cat. This time, dear friend, you have reached number ten. It is a case of come in number ten, your time is up! Now I suggest you sit down while I advise you what you are going to do for my friend and I. It is not an onerous task, and should well suit your conniving twisted mind."

Rourke's mouth fell open, as his hands instinctively went to his heavy beer belly, as if that would protect it. He blanched to an ugly shade of putty, and a tic in the corner of his right eye went tic a tac like a demented metronome.

Tammy seemed to float free of the ground as he rose and motioned Rourke to get over by the wall, where Donald by this time had taken the brothers.

Whilst Tammy kept guard with the gun ready for use, Donald tied up the three prisoners. Satisfied with the security of his handiwork, he nodded to Tammy and immediately herded the brothers out of earshot and bound their wrist to their ankles, thinking, 'ah yes, the old routine.'

Meanwhile Tammy was telling Rourke what he was going to do to him if he refused to comply with the instructions he would be given. First though, there would be a question and answer routine to go through.

Rourke found his voice and told Tammy to perform a physically impossible feat. Tammy was the epitome of cultured politeness. He patted Rourke genially on his back, then advised him that he had two further minutes to expunge his bile and then they would have to get down to serious business. Rourke replied with expletives that would have made a regimental sergeant major blush for shame. Again Tammy seemed to take no offence.

The onslaught was a brutal bombshell that exploded with mind blowing speed. Rourke was standing with his back to the wall, his shoulders touching the bare cement, when Tammy's extended fingers hit directly below the arrowhead of the sternum bone. Deliberately he drove upwards into the bottom of the diaphragm, but careful not to penetrate sufficiently to rupture the heart, which he could have done.

He was not of a mind to dispatch Rourke, but he had to be brutal in this softening up process if he was to get Rourke to do as he was directed.

Rourke tried to bend forward, but the hard outer edge of Tammy's hand hit him beneath the nose. The impact broke the front upper teeth straight out of the gums, as the head was driven back against the wall with a terrible crack.

Tammy stepped back slightly, and measuring the distance, kicked Rourke below the kneecap, a slicing motion that tore the ligaments on either side and nearly ripped the kneecap off.

Rourke gave a strangled scream, blood spraying from his battered mouth. He slumped to the floor in a shapeless heap and curled into the foetal position as if seeking the protection of his mother's womb.

He writhed and moaned in a continuous dirge of ruptured dignity and humiliation, but surcease from the persecution was not to be.

Prodding him with a contemptuous foot, Tammy asked if they could now get down to business for real. He had much to do, and a long way to go before he had completed his tasks for the day. When Rourke painfully nodded his throbbing head, Tammy callously kicked him on the offended knee and said he hadn't heard a reply.

A strangled scream. Rourke screeched the required response through loose lips that slavered like the ugly mouth of a hyena at the kill. Roughly, Tammy dragged the distraught Rourke into a sitting position and threw him against the wall. In short acidic sentences he explained what was required.

Tammy was sick in his stomach at the brutal abuse he was heaping upon the hapless Rourke, but he knew that the only way to get compliance from a character like this was to completely dominate him with apparently mindless violence. It was the creed that Rourke lived by, and could understand, nevertheless Tammy was still using methods he would have preferred not to.

The ploy to bring the Chief to the warehouse was a replica of the one used to bring Rourke to the scene. Set a sprat to catch a mackerel. Simple but effective.

The brothers could not have brought the big fish, so they had been used to catch the better bait.

As Tammy explained what Rourke was to do, and what would happen if he didn't, he could see there was more resistance in Rourke than there had been in the brothers.

Tammy had used the whip, now he decided to use the carrot.

"By the way, should this little scheme work out all right, you, your wife and two little daughters will be transported far from here and given a new identity to start a new life. If it doesn't succeed, you will die. It will be arranged that your family will know only hardship and poverty for the rest of their lives. Truthfully, I don't much care either way. I want the big Chief. The top man. He has betrayed his position of trust and loyalty to the Crown. He is guilty of treason and must face the consequences."

"You, on the other hand, are a native of these parts, not employed by the Crown, and applying yourself to something you believe in. That is acceptable. You didn't serve two masters, and to my mind that is quite honourable, even if I don't agree with your politics or principles."

Tammy could almost see the devious mind working. If the top dog was disposed of, perhaps Rourke would be in the position to step in and fill the void, never mind a new identity, he would be ideally placed to dictate and dominate.

Rourke looked at Tammy for the first time since the start of the dialogue.

"You will stand by what you have just said?" he queried, hope threading through his pain-racked voice.

"I give you my word," replied Tammy firmly, then added, "but I would never accept yours!"

The phone call was made and the Chief Constable vowed to be with Rourke in a short time. Now for Donald and Tammy it was a case of sweating it out again, waiting for the man they wanted to bring to justice. Tammy had given the prearranged signal to Peter Mahon, and knew he was in position and ready to act if necessary.

A car approached at speed, then screeched to a halt. An instant of quiet and then the slamming of the car door could be heard as it was closed robustly.

The screech of the corrugated door was followed by the footsteps of a very confident man as he strode into the warehouse. Inside the door he paused for a moment to allow his eyes to adjust to the gloominess of the interior.

Rourke turned to face him. The Chief brought his right arm up to waist level and coldbloodedly shot Rourke through the heart. With casual disregard, he turned the gun in Tammy's direction, finger tightening on the trigger as he calmly announced that Rourke would have been impossible to live with after his little coup. So let it all be finished here.

Before he could complete the act of pulling the trigger, he staggered back with a shocked expression on his face that turned to bewilderment, then a vacuous visage that pronounced that death had claimed him. He would double deal no more.

Two of Peter Mahon's marksmen had trained their guns on him the moment he entered the warehouse. They had been well hidden behind a central corrugated wall, riddled with rust-eaten holes, which bisected the storage area of the warehouse, but had been able to position themselves with a clear view of the scenario being enacted before them.

Their orders had been most specific. Donald and Tammy were to be protected at all costs. The two marksmen had fired simultaneously, aiming for the heart of the Chief, and like all good professionals, they had been dead on target, and the pun was not lost on them.

With a sigh of relief Tammy lowered his own firearm. He would have shot the Chief before he could have squeezed the trigger a second time, but he was glad he had not been compelled to.

He was gratified that justice had been done. It was perhaps the best way for the double dealing Chief to be terminated. Had he been brought to court there was every chance he could have been exonerated, and then reinstated into his position of authority.

Peter Mahon came through the door of the warehouse with several of his men in attendance. They would tidy up all the loose ends, and remove any evidence of foul play or non authorised practices.

Peter advised the O'Malley brothers quite bluntly that whatever promises Tammy had made to them had no value at all. Tammy had no authority in Ulster as from a week ago. They would go to jail as confirmed terrorists, and remain there for a long, long time. No! There was no use squealing here. Keep it for the police cells, and they could sing like canaries there if they wanted to.

Peter took Donald and Tammy back to where they had hidden the Landrover. He assured Tammy that, in his capacity of Acting Chief of Police of Ulster, he would forward his formal thanks and recommendations to his counterparts in Glasgow.

He felt sure that Tammy would now be in line for a promotion which would be well merited. He also advised Tammy that he would be contacting the Prime Minister in England to advise him of the exceptional qualities of Donald and Tammy. They had been battle wounded and subjected to much suffering but had still carried out their duties in exemplary fashion.

Donald and Tammy thanked Peter for his kind words, but said there was no need to go to all that trouble, for sure it was all finished with and they would soon be on their way to Scotland and a quiet peaceful life.

They were not to know that the very commendations that Peter and Commander Denham-Tring would make to the government would be entered on a very, most secret file that would, one day, be resurrected when the need arose and the government required special skills for some new task.

The cold December day was conceding to a dreary darkness with flurries of snow that added to the chaos of slush already underfoot.

Donald and Tammy wound their way slowly through the streets, their journey being a tour of farewell, although they didn't realise it at the time.

They were chatting idly, trying to unwind from the business of the day. Donald suggested that they make use of the house in Larne and actually have a couple of days fishing. It would blow some freshness into their minds, and really let them unwind before returning to their loved ones in Barranbarrach.

When they reached the secluded cottage on the western shore, they were surprised and delighted to find big Jim Patrick returned from Africa. He made them most welcome, and being a determined bachelor, he had plenty of room to accommodate them. He suggested they stay for a week, for goodness sake, he would ring Eamonn and tell him what was happening, now what about it?

The two warriors thanked Jim profusely but insisted that two days were enough. No! Best make it three, for Tammy had to buy his sweetheart a Christmas gift and that would probably take a bit of time, for he hadn't the vaguest notion what to get.

The weather turned kind, with watery sun trying to lift the ambient temperature. It didn't succeed, but at least it made the fishing pleasurable.

Donald and Tammy thoroughly enjoyed themselves during the two days and were rewarded with catches that did them proud. The sea breezes produced the elixir of life that had been needed as the Irish Sea rollercoasted them around with carefree abandon.

On the morning of the third day they went into the shopping area of Larne and there they both purchased engagement rings for their sweethearts, but not before Donald had rung Eamonn Kelly to stand surety for the amount of money that would be owing to the jeweller.

Such was the standing of the previous owner of the Barranbarrach Stud that the transactions were speedily concluded. The only thing now outstanding was to get Bridget a suitable Christmas gift.

They scoured the small town without success, and Tammy was beginning to despair of ever finding something that would be just right for the treasure of his heart.

They returned to the cottage to have a farewell lunch with big Jim, and during the excellent meal, prepared by Jim, Tammy mentioned that he was not having a great deal of success in purchasing something for Bridget.

Jim held up a finger, then tapped his nose with it, gave a little cough and rubbed his chin with a big gnarled fist. Yes, by God, he was sure he had the very thing! He rose from the table and disappeared through the doorway to his bedroom. When he returned he had a huge grin on his face, even if it was a bit shamefaced. He brought up his hand and opened it, saying, with a touch of embarrassment, that he bought this little foible in Johannesburg one night when he had been well into his cups, and sure what the hell was he going to do with it now?

Lying in the centre of his palm was a brooch of exquisite beauty. It was in the shape of a Zulu warrior in full fighting regalia. The filigree silver and gold was studded with amethysts, rubies and diamonds, and so cleverly had it been contrived, it seemed as if the Zulu was doing a war dance when the piece was moved.

Reverently Tammy lifted the piece out of Jim's hand. He had never ever seen anything so beautiful, he was absolutely awestruck. Donald was nodding his head affirmatively. Yes, this had to be the answer. All that had to be done now was to make sure that Jim didn't short change himself.

For half an hour it was like an Arab haggling stall in a role reversal. Jim insisting, what in the name of God was he going to do with the damned thing. He should never have bought it anyhow, and so on. Tammy wanted the brooch but insisted that he at least pay what he had been prepared to spend when he set off that morning. He pointed out that he was still getting the best bargain in the world.

At last the two of them beat Jim into submission, and he accepted the figure they pressed on him with reluctance. Tammy was satisfied, but had he known the truth he had only paid a fraction of the true value of the brooch.

They arrived at Barranbarrach in the late afternoon and found the Kelly's, Mari and the girls waiting for them in a ferment of excitement.

Peter Mahon had rung and told Eamonn about the dispatch of the R.U.C. Chief. He had said he was temporarily in charge, awaiting confirmation of appointment to the position, and all he was doing was making a courteous call to thank Eamonn for all his help.

Peter added that Donald and Tammy had rendered a special kind of service to the province, for which he was most grateful. He assured Eamonn that he was going to bring their contribution to the notice of those who controlled the political situation.

The duplicity of the two warriors had been discovered. Mari demanded that they should never be so deceitful again. The young men apologised and said of course they wouldn't.

Siobhan looked at her husband-to-be, and said in a tremulous voice that she would be glad when they were married and on their way to Scotland, for if they stayed here much longer she was sure that Donald would become more and more involved with the trouble in the province.

After dinner that evening the men went down to the snooker room, ostensibly to play, but when Stuart served them with drinks, they sat down in the comfortable easy chairs and found themselves discussing the events of the past months.

Eamonn first of all thanked Tammy and Donald for taking up the cudgels on behalf of Ulster. Being a complete Irishman, and loving his country dearly, he was horrified at the cancer growing within his beloved homeland.

A polished orator at the best of times, his rhetoric flowed with a passion and conviction, as he explained the differences that pulled the province asunder.

First and foremost the Papist and Protestant conflict. Each creed utterly confident that theirs was the one and only true faith. Would anybody believe he had heard a four year old child scream in anger, 'kill the Papist bastard'. Surely if it was that deeply entrenched and at that age, what hope was there of ever changing these beliefs at a later stage in life.

Of course there was nothing new in religious wars. History was full of it. The biggest irony being, that religion was supposed to make all men brothers. The fact of the matter, from what he could see, was that the reverse was true and religion pulled mankind apart, and in truth, was the reason for more bloody minded killing than anything else he could think of.

Now on top of all this in Ulster was the political battle that had begun recently, internecine, a war of attrition and it was his considered opinion that it would rage for years to come.

There was the faction that believed Ireland should be for the Irish, and no mongrels please. The hated conquerors, with their historic annexation, should be declared unlawful and all rights and privileges returned to the direct control of the Irish.

Then the other side of this tarnished coin, were those that declared themselves British and wanted to remain so. Now then! Who was right and who was wrong? Or were they both right? It was indeed an imponderable.

He had even heard people on the mainland say that the plug should be removed and let the whole damned mess sink to the bottom of the Irish Sea, but of course that was a remark born of stupidity and would resolve nothing.

Sadly Eamonn shook his head, his eyes seemed to refocus and looking around the faces of his family, he smiled wryly as he raised his hands and apologised that he had got carried away on a subject very close to his heart.

He crossed to where his son-in-law had risen and was standing by the large picture window. He laid a hand on Stuart's arm and asked if he felt he would be better off thinking about selling Barranbarrach and returning to Scotland with Donald, rather than stay here and become ensnared within the Ulster problem.

It could well be the best thing and it would remove Mari from danger. She was Irish and Catholic to be sure, but she had married a Scot who was a Protestant, therefore to some minds she would be fair game for harassment.

Stuart looked fondly at this grey haired old man whom he had come to regard with great affection. Gently he squeezed the gnarled old hand lying on his arm, and said it was something that would require a great deal of consideration. It would have to be in consultation with Mari, for the estate was really her birthright, to carry on through her son Donald and thence down through the years to sons of sons ad infinitum. Under the circumstances he would reserve his opinion until everybody had given it a measure of thought, but off the top of his head, he loved it here and did not feel inclined to be harried off.

To ease the tension that had developed in the room, they played a few frames of snooker until Mari called them for bedtime drinks.

Nothing else was mentioned about the political scene or its impact on the stud, but the menfolk knew that it was a question that would not go away, and answers would have to be found.

Donald was very concerned that his involvement in the struggle the past few months would not have gone unnoticed by the faction being opposed to the British being in Ireland. He felt that they would have long memories and exact retribution in time to come.

The fact that he would be safe in Cruachan afforded him very little comfort, for the family he would be leaving in Ulster were very important in his life. He certainly didn't want to leave them in what could turn out to be their hour of greatest need.

Chapter Nineteen

Barranbarrach was in the throes of cataclysmic dementia, dominated by an iron willed lady who was determined that everybody within range of her eagle eye would be employed to the ultimate and God help anyone who was foolish enough to stand still for a brief moment to draw breath.

Mari had become a task master who would have been the delight of a galley slave master. Unmercifully she ordered family and friends around in exactly the same manner she used to the house servants. It says much for the regard in which she was held, that nowhere did she find unwillingness to comply with the multitude of directives she issued in a continual flow from the dawn of each new day, until she fell exhausted into her bed late each night.

Two days before Christmas Eve the Gods delivered an unexpected bonus. A heavy snowstorm had turned the surrounding countryside to virginal whiteness, as if to highlight the purity of the imminent double wedding.

Mari accepted this as no more than a natural gift from on high. Nevertheless, she was pleased that there would be a white Christmas, which would harmonise perfectly with the white wedding. Stuart had been heard to mutter, would the great redeemer have dared do anything else but provide the ideal conditions.

On the 23rd of December, the Cruachans and Chi Li arrived with two unexpected guests that Mari welcomed as though long lost friends. Her natural hospitality and friendliness making the couple feel instantly at home.

Hamish introduced the couple as Ieuan and Megan Llewellyn, who were the owners of the Llanderawel Arab Stud in Wales. It was from this couple that Hamish had bought the two Arab Greys that he had presented to Donald when he left Cruachan. Hamish was at present buying Arab mares from them for breeding stock at Cruachan.

When Donald and Siobhan were introduced to them, there was an instant rapport and since horses were a favourite topic of conversation, they were soon involved in serious discussions on breeding and training.

Ieuan became very interested in Donald's initial training methods and when it had been well expounded by Donald and Siobhan, he said he felt he might introduce such a system at his stud when he returned home.

Ieuan started to tell Donald and Siobhan about his stud and his hopes and aspirations. Already he was becoming quite well known in the right circles, but it was a slow affair as he would be judged on the quality of his stock, and no matter what, a mare will normally only have one foal a year, so it takes some time to build up a good breeding stock of mares.

The Llanderawel Arab Stud, he continued, lay to the west of Machynlleth in an area of exceptional natural beauty. The narrow coastal plain surrenders to high uplands that terminate in majestic mountains.

Wales has often been referred to as a dissected plateau and all good geographers will know that this is the case.

Llanderawel Estate was a miniature reflection of this, combining low pasture land towards the coast, giving way to marginal type farming which in turn surrendered to rough upland grazing on the mountain tops, where usually are found the indigenous Welsh Mountain ponies, hardy as heather and frugal by nature.

When all the mares at Llanderawel had foaled and subsequently been covered again, the herd was driven to the Alp-like pastures and left there to fend for themselves. They not only grazed the level tops but also ranged the mountain sides, which developed their inherent sure-footedness.

Endurance and the ability to live and flourish in the most frugal circumstances are qualities attributed to Arabs, who are not really ponies, but small horses.

They epitomise the mental picture that the general public have in mind when they think of a horse. Showing a beautiful dished head tapering to a fine muzzle, with large expressive eyes low down on the skull, with constantly flickering sharply pointed ears, always a sign of intelligence in a horse.

The nostrils are flexible flutes with a tremendous expansion, which allows great draughts of oxygen to be pulled into the lungs. The proudly arched neck and the tail held high give the Arab an extremely majestic and imperious demeanour.

Its liking for the company of man is well recorded. In the infancy of the breed the desert nomads kept their horses in their tents with them, so they were in fact part of the family, and it has often been suggested that they were more highly prized then the wives or daughters.

The prepotency of the Arab is also well documented. This is the ability to pass on its finer attributes to other breeds. The Arab has been used extensively world wide to improve local stock.

Ieuan had made every effort to keep his breeding herd in as natural conditions as possible, and the quality of his herd gave credence to his skills.

As Donald and Siobhan listened to him talking about his beloved Arabs and the estate he so obviously enjoyed owning, Siobhan in all innocence could not help but exclaiming that it must be a sight to see. Arabs running free in beautiful surroundings.

Straight away, Ieuan and Megan said in the same instant, "That is easy, come back with us for a month, have your honeymoon at our home. You can see at first hand how we run the stud and look at some of the finest scenery in Wales at the same time."

Siobhan was a bit embarrassed, feeling that she had somehow forced an invitation from the Llewellyns, and demurred saying she couldn't put them to all that trouble, gallantly Donald gave her backing although he desperately did want to visit the Welsh stud.

The Llewellyns kept up the pressure unmercifully and so sincerely that in the end the youngsters agreed saying it would be a privilege and a pleasure. Ieuan and Megan were delighted and a round of kisses and handshakes sealed the agreement.

Now the Welsh couple turned their natural charm on Tammy and Bridget trying to entice them to have their honeymoon at Llanderawel at the same time, but Tammy with honest regret had to refuse since his duties in Glasgow would deny him the pleasure.

Unselfishly he tried to encourage Bridget to go on the offered visit, but she would have none of it, she was adamant she would stay with Tammy and sort out where they were going to live.

The Glasgow Police Authority had arranged temporary accommodation for them, but Bridget wanted to get a place of their own as soon as possible.

Perhaps the most true reason of all was her feminine want of her man. She had waited patiently for the wedding to take place, but my word she was going to wear out that man of hers when all the social requirements had been fulfilled.

If Tammy put a pea in a jar each time he fulfilled his conjugal duties in the first year and took one out each time thereafter he would never live to see the jar empty. That was a promise she had made to herself.

Her vagrant thoughts caused her to press against Tammy as a hot flush of delicious feelings pervaded her ripe body. Heavy moistness developed at her core and she shivered and pressed ever harder against her man.

The day of the wedding, Mari was up long before the barnyard roosters got a chance to crow and it wasn't long before the rest of the household were winkled out with scant ceremony.

The breakfast rules were simple, if you wanted food, then get it quickly, for even the snug breakfast room had a function to perform during the wedding reception.

The wedding ceremony would be held in the main recreational hall, as would the reception which would continue until the following dawn. As the reception was being combined with the Barranbarrach Christmas Eve Party, the catering facilities would be stretched to the limits, but Mari was confident that not one person would suffer hunger or thirst, and the entertainment would be supplied from the widest possible spectrum on offer in the whole of Ireland.

The day progressed in a furious bustle until midday, then a light luncheon was served and everyone was allowed to relax for a moment. Then it was time to spirit the girls away to be bathed and dressed.

Donald remarked to Tammy that it must be some dress to take two hours to get into, and was chastened by a glowering look from his highly excited mother. Stuart who had heard the quip chuckled in amusement and winked encouragingly.

The men were left with strict instructions as to when they should be getting their preparations under way. They all obediently nodded their accord with madam's wishes as she departed with wings spread around her chicks.

Stuart poured a forbidden glass of malt whisky for himself and then shamefacedly realising what he had done, poured one for each of the men. There was a sort of anti climax, a feeling of being in a vacuum

Silently they raised their glasses to each other and threw the contents down their throats, as if in defiance of Mari's exhortations to abstain completely from alcohol before the ceremony. Afterwards the older men would remember and think what a terrible thing they had done to a first class whisky.

Finally the young men climbed the stairs to start their own preparations. Stuart followed shortly afterwards, for he had been tasked by Mari to check the two young men when they dressed to see that everything was present and correct.

They would both be in splendid Highland Regalia and God help Stuart if a button was out of line, or any item not at regimental perfection.

Donald had no problem getting dressed in his national costume, but Tammy had a couple of hiccups before he passed muster. He had Donald in stitches of laughter when he first put on the kilt. He deliberately put it on, back to front, saying that the flat part without pleats was obviously for sitting on.

At last they were as ready as they were ever going to be and Stuart was giving them the final going over when Mari arrived at the open door.

She paused in the doorway, looking them over with the critical eye of an inspecting general. She nodded her satisfaction, then jerked her head to someone standing behind her in the passageway to enter the room.

It was one of the housemaids, carrying a silver tray, which held three glasses full to the brim with an ancient malt whisky and one small glass containing the amber excellence of good sherry.

Mari gave each of the men a glass and lifted her own sherry from the tray to hold it high in the air. The maid disappeared and Mari gave the toast.

"May this union you enter into today, give you all the happiness that Stuart and I have experienced over the years together. You have both been lucky and done exceedingly well in your choice and will have wives who will stand by you for the rest of your lives."

"This is the final cutting of the apron strings and I am well aware that I have been guilty of over protective practices, nevertheless, I will miss having you all to fuss over."

Although her voice had thickened during the last few words, Mari would not allow the tears to flow on this special day. Lifting her glass she took a huge unladylike gulp. Possibly hoping it would wash the hard lump from her throat.

The men gathered round her, surrounding her with their love. Not one of them would dare risk the sound of his own voice, but their actions told the woman whose very heart was breaking, all she needed to know, that she was dearly loved by her menfolk.

Kissing them all she turned and fled from the room, saying she hadn't time to stand around here all day with kissing and cuddling. The three of them distinctly heard the deep gasping sob that escaped the iron control as she walked away down the corridor.

The Civil Registrar had arrived and been duly fed and watered by Eamonn, and when the two young men entered the great hall he came over to join them.

Scotland and Ireland are steeped in old religion, so it was perhaps unusual, or at least out of the ordinary, that on this splendid social, as well as private occasion, that there would be neither priest nor minister officiating to join the young couples in matrimony.

The truth of the matter was that the two girls were Catholics and the men they were marrying were Protestants. When Mari had made presentation to the orders of both, there had been protestations of the need to comply to the religious requirements of either creed.

This had exasperated Mari who, losing patience with the religious dogma, had approached the young couples to ascertain if it was necessary to have a church or a chapel wedding, and had been extremely gratified to find that a civil service was perfectly acceptable by all concerned.

Civil dignitaries, local tradesmen and estate workers joined the family in an excited buzz. Stuart made an aside to Eamonn about, "What! The Queen had decided not to attend." Eamonn laughed and said he guessed that was one stroke Mari couldn't pull or by damn the gracious lady would have been here.

When Donald and Tammy took their appointed places an expectant hush descended on the congregation as they impatiently awaited the entrance of the brides.

Eamonn would conduct Bridget, whilst Siobhan would be on the arm of her father Eddie O'Flaherty. Conal's wife was matron of honour and eight of the estate workers daughters were bridesmaids.

Mari was the mother of the bride, the groom, and the bride and groom. She was just not interested that such a position was without precedence. She was the mother of these children and by God who was going to argue.

Four sets of Irish pipes were heard in the distance as the resonant strains of the wedding march filled the silence. With great dignity and bearing of queens, the two brides made their entrance followed by an entourage that appeared to be a tidal wave of froth and ribbons, lace and flowers.

As one, Donald and Tammy turned to watch the approach of their prospective wives to join them at the front of the gathered multitude. The centre aisle had been automatically adjusted to a width that would accommodate an advancing pair.

This had to be quickly altered to allow the four abreast to advance to the far end of the hall where the young men waited.

Donald's breath whistled in delighted amazement at the vision of loveliness that seemed to drift effortlessly toward him, and he heard on the periphery of his conscious awareness, the same reaction from Tammy.

The brides were indeed beautiful beyond compare, in creations of outstanding artistic achievement. Gasps of wonder and delight from the congregation gave confirmation to Donald and Tammy that they would never see the likes of this again.

The complete ensemble was a tribute to Mari and the wives of the local tradesmen, plus the unparalleled perfection of a local seamstress. Yes! The creations were without equal.

Both girls had opted for half veils, so that they could see clearly and be seen, and indeed why should such large wonderful Irish eyes not be seen?

The nipped in waists accentuated the full bosomed figures of the girls and the curving hips alluded to fecundate promise.

An effervescence of silk and satin, tantalising glimpses of Victorian lace, with shimmering tulle a whisper of enchantment, all seeming to cascade in exquisite teasing delicacy and glamorous perfection, with the bridesmaids a host of angels in like creations flowing behind in peacock tail formation.

The Civil Registrar stood in stunned admiration, mouth slightly open as he surveyed the advancing brides and when they at last stood before him at the sides of their chosen partners, he had to take a deep breath before he could begin the dialogue that would join these beautiful girls to their eager young men.

However he conducted the service in a deeply satisfying clear and resonant voice, eliciting the responses as required, and eventually they were pronounced man and wife, man and wife.

When the newly wedded couples kissed as directed, the hall erupted with a tremendous roar of appreciation and congratulatory approval.

All the menfolk certainly wanted to kiss the brides. They unashamedly pushed and elbowed their way as far to the front as they could to enable them to do just that, and although Stuart announced that the wedding feast was now available, not one man forsook his place till he had kissed both brides.

The food was endless in quantity and diversification. Dishes from the Orient, spicy and hot. Pastas from the Mediterranean. Haute cuisine a la Francaise. Turkish kebabs. Hungarian goulash, the list was endless.

There was every kind of edible fowl, fish and flesh. Whole crabs and lobsters; roasted peacock to tiny snipe. Veal, suckling pig or venison in an assortment of roasts and steaks.

One meat missing from the boards was horse flesh, although eaten by Europeans, and sometimes unbeknownst by British tourists in the guise of Frikadellen, a savoury type of sausage. It would have seemed a profanity to the people of Barranbarrach to devour the flesh of such a noble animal as the one they worked with on a daily basis, and one that was so highly regarded.

At last everybody confided they could eat no more, and moved away from the trestle tables to allow an army of helpers to clear the hall ready for the entertainment to commence.

Now the serious drinking would start. Barrels, bottles, carafes and casks stood around at various points. It was a case of help yourself to whatever tipple took your fancy.

One thing was for sure, there would be no running out of any commodity, for as Stuart had said to Mari when she asked doubtingly if he thought she had covered everything, she had catered for a Napoleon's army.

Chi Li would never be a drinker, although he had toasted the brides and grooms with a flute of champagne, just a sip. Mari kept a close watch over him, she didn't want him to feel out of place.

Her anxiety was eased when she noticed that he seemed to be forming a warm attachment with Siobhan's father, and she was especially pleased about that for they were both loners in a way.

Eddie's live in lover having long deserted him, he now managed for himself after a fashion. Mari had been unable to encourage him to come and live at the manor house, so she worried about him.

Donald enjoyed the odd glass, but was not in any way addicted to strong drink, taking it or leaving it as the social occasion demanded.

He kept a watchful eye on Chi Li, being mindful that this could appear a very alien environment to his sensei, and was gratified to see the developing liaison between Chi Li and Eddie. Siobhan had noticed the companionable way the two men were getting along as she took Donald across to speak to them for a moment.

Siobhan had developed a particular rapport with Chi Li, the man responsible for her husband's remarkable skills, and Chi Li treated her with respect and regard, as he might have done to the daughter he would never have.

He would never be as indelicate as to show her the love he had developed for her, but the future would show that his own life would be forfeit, rather than the wind blow cold on her.

The dawn of the 24th had been long announced by dawn chorus and barnyard fowls. At last the revellers recognised it was time to go home and try to get ready for Christmas Day celebrations.

Hangovers would be part of the price to pay for the previous night's carousing, but nobody was counting the cost. It had been an evening to remember, even if it meant holding heads and saying never ever again.

At the manor house, the New Years Eve was celebrated in a modest way by close friends and family. The evening of the 3rd of January was given over to the preparations for the family guests to return to their homes.

Mari would not appreciate the loss of company, but this time it would be harder to accept, for Donald and Siobhan would be travelling to Wales with the Llewellyns.

Tammy and Bridget would remain at Barranbarrach for a few days more then they would also be off to Scotland.

On the 4th of January, the exodus began. First to leave were the Cruachans and Chi Li, being flown to Scone Aerodrome at Perth, and thence by car that would be waiting to take them to Cruachan House.

The Llewellyns with Donald and Siobhan would fly directly to Cardiff airport at Rhoose and then travel in a chauffeured car to the west of Wales and finally to the Llanderawel Stud.

Although they left a snowy landscape behind them, when they landed at Rhoose there was no evidence of snow, and in fact, due to the kindly influence of the Gulf Stream, the weather was mild and pleasant.

Donald was enchanted with the topography of the area surrounding the Llanderawel Stud, to his mind it was a miniature landscape of his native glen at Cruachan.

The mountains of course by comparison were mere hills, nevertheless they were mountains, with glens. No, that wasn't right, valleys, intersecting the upland areas. An unusual feature that was most notable to Donald was that the mountain seemed to end in flat moorland areas, with rough grazing in abundance.

Siobhan was enthralled for different reasons. She had grown up in the shadow of the rolling sweep of the Antrim Hills, but here there was a distinct diversion of lowland and actual mountains, never mind what Donald said, about them being hills, it was all exceedingly pleasing to the eye, and now she understood the enthusiasm and regard in which the Llewellyns held their property.

Donald and Siobhan were accommodated in the guest suite at the rear of the manor house, which accorded them privacy in their initial role as man and wife. It was perhaps as well, for Siobhan was a keen and vociferous partner in the inevitable sexual interplay between the young couple.

The joyous couplings were earthy and fulfilling, without reservation and with obvious enjoyment to the participants. Being of the country and knowing country ways, their lovemaking was without inhibition and as natural as mother nature intended it to be.

The fourth evening they were there, Donald and Siobhan decided to take an evening constitutional around the stud area, and the Llewellyns decided to accompany them.

Early twilight of the winter solstice cast its eerie spell on the land. Half lights and long, long shadows that waxed and waned in fleeting flirtatious bewilderment to the watching eye.

They strolled along the stud boxes, then looked into the large open courts that sheltered the young stock. These courtyards were a new feature to Donald and were large roofed areas held aloft by pillars, and where there should have been walls there was in fact steel mesh. A central hay manger, was really just a dray holding bales of hay to which the horses helped themselves, and was renewed when necessary by another dray.

The watery looking westering sun still held a tenuous hold, so they decided to take a look at the paddock where the in-foal mares were put out each morning. It had been found they exercised better if they had access to a paddock, and as a consequence seemed to foal easier when the time came.

As they ambled across the grass-bare paddock, facing into the prevailing wind from the west, the hairs on the back of Donald's neck stood out and quivered a primaeval warning as he developed a feeling of foreboding, an inexplicable portent of menace. A subconscious perception pervaded his complete awareness. He felt the adrenaline burst and felt his pulsebeat quicken as his senses increased awareness. He almost quivered like a strung bow.

When the party reached the paddock fence, Donald climbed up onto the top rail and looked over the mares nibbling at the sparse grass. His three companions were content to lean across the top rail and view the mares, as they discussed the merits of each. Donald became detached from the general discussion and his ever questing eyes surveyed the paddock surrounds.

His roving eyes stopped and retracked a few yards. He was sure he had spotted something in his peripheral vision. He raked the area with alerted intent, but nothing out of the usual was in evidence. Still the uneasiness stayed with him, for he was well aware of the value of his presentiments.

From the far side of the paddock, a shadow detached itself from the rails in a gliding fluid motion. Somehow a threat in the very manner of its menacing secretive approach. Black as the shadow from which it had detached itself, the sinuous body approached the herd of mares.

The dominant mare lifted her head form the pasture and snorted in alarm as she danced around in agitation. The rest of the mares responded to the snorting and started to gather closer together in the inherent herd safety instinct.

This was the added stimulant that had Donald jumping down off the fence and running directly towards the ominous, snaking, feline progression.

As he ran on a line of interception he withdrew the 'shaken' from its leather wallet, followed by his other hand automatically drawing his knife from the leg sheath. He never ever went anywhere without his armament and had been thankful for Chi Li's insistence on more than one occasion.

The sinuous body was making a direct approach to the nearest mare, who was snorting in alarm as she watched it come ever nearer. In good time Donald managed to insinuate himself between the two, albeit a good distance still separated them.

With a jolt like an electric shock, he identified the shadowy menace. It was a black panther. Later he would establish that it had escaped from a private collector's menagerie, and since it had become a bit of a liability to feed, he had not reported the loss.

Five days of incessant hunger that growled in its belly like a malignant corruption had brought to the surface the latent killing instincts of its natural characteristics for survival.

Domesticity had deprived it of some of its stalking ability and as the panther had found out, stalking wild animals had proved fruitless, creating the desperate hunger that now drove it forwards with compelling intensity.

Eight yards away from Donald, the panther stopped and snarled a warning. The mouth opening in a dreadful gape of extended yellow incisors, backed up by malevolent reddened eyes that burned with the killing lust.

Donald continued his approach and as the panther sprang high in the air, he sent his 'shaken' into its whirling flight of death. The leaping panther took it directly under the chin and the 'shaken' as it was devised to do, dragged itself through the matted pelt, slicing its way through the jugular artery and continued its trail of destruction as it severed the spinal cord.

Such was the force of the charging cat, that the spring continued, even though the messages ceased to be transmitted from its central nervous system.

Blood flooded its lungs from the severed artery as the grip of death shuddered through its body.

Donald dropped beneath the front extended claws. As the body of the panther passed over his head, he grabbed a handful of the loose belly skin at the same time as he threw his feet backwards and deep into the haunch joints of the cat, preventing the dreadful forward and backwards movement of the back legs and extended claws that could rip open a belly in one slicing movement.

He stabbed the knife deep into the cat's unprotected belly and sliced from back to front in a gutting action, and as the knife hit the rib cage he turned his wrist to deflect the knife blade towards and into the heart.

The fatal thrust was unnecessary, as the panther fell full weight upon him, the 'shaken' having already deprived the panther of life.

Dimly, Donald heard the screams of Siobhan as he struggled to free himself from the weight of the animal. The strong rancid smell was overpowering and reminded him of the ammoniac smell he first encountered when the stag had shown its displeasure at Cruachan, after he had smacked its nether quarters as part of a sensei test.

Ieuan reached the scene and taking hold of the panther's tail heaved it to the side sufficient for Donald to escape. He stood up thankfully and was nearly sent earthwards again as Siobhan literally threw herself into his arms, awash with tears and moans of fear.

Donald soothed her as he held her gently and tried a smile at Ieuan and Megan who was looking at him as if had sprouted horns. Their eyes were prominent and mouths were hanging open in a very ungenteel manner.

Ieuan was shaking his head from side to side in utter amazement, it had been like watching something out of a Tarzan film. Megan was trembling and her face was ashen white.

At last Ieuan managed to articulate, but his voice was strained and quavered slightly as he proclaimed in wonder at what had happened.

"I have never, ever, seen anything like that in my entire life and I doubt that I ever shall again. In the name of God, Donald, what manner of man are you? Where did you learn such skills? That trick with your feet going up into the joints of the beast's back legs to prevent being disembowelled. Well! Surely, there was no way you could have practised that sort of technique. What can I say? Where do I start? Yes! First of all, thank you for saving at least one of my mares from a savage death, and secondly for ridding the country of a menace that would have taken a heavy toll on the local livestock."

"The only gift I can give you Donald, that is worthy of the service you have done for us here, is the choice of any of my Arab stock, and that is without exception."

Donald was already nodding his head in the negative.

"There is no need of that. I am just glad I was here to be of assistance. To answer your first question, I was trained by Chi Li, the personal servant of Lord Cruachan. You will remember meeting him at the wedding at Barranbarrach. I owe that man more than I will ever be able to repay, so where I can, I repay in kind. That is to give freely of my services whenever and wherever I can, if it is in the best interests of mankind in general."

"I do have a request to make however, and that is, may I have the pelt of this beautiful animal. I would like to give it to Chi Li as a present. I am sure he would be delighted with it."

Ieuan made a depreciative movement of his hand.

"Of course you can Donald, although it is not in my gift to give you. It is already yours by virtue of hunter's spoils. Shall we drag it up to the yard where it might be easier for you to work on it?"

Donald agreed, he wanted to recover the pelt before the body heat was lost since the whole operation would be easier and the skin would retain much of its elasticity.

He spent many hours in the days following, working the pelt with salt and olive oil, a labour of love. He knew Chi Li would check the pelt very carefully for any flaws in the preservation technique. He was quite entitled to do this of course, for was it not him who had taught Donald in the first place.

At dinner one Saturday night, Ieuan asked the young couple if they would care to join them at a church service the following morning, Donald and Siobhan readily agreed.

The chapel could accommodate a congregation of a hundred or thereabouts. Donald and Siobhan were surprised to see it was already full to capacity. Neither of them had ever in the past attended a religious service and found seats to be in short supply.

When Donald made this remark to Ieuan, he was answered with a smile as his host casually observed that the Welsh were fond of singing and the chapel gave them a chance to exercise their lungs. He didn't add, that the young couple were in for a pleasant surprise.

Donald had been used all his life to the first hymn of a service being barely audible as the congregation gradually worked up to a full sound as they found their voices.

Not so in this chapel. Perfectly on cue, clear and full, the voices found their key and were instantly in full accord. Bass resonance held the measured beat, as the contraltos provided the fullness. Sopranos scaled to impossible heights with the first tenors fighting for dominance.

Donald felt the short hairs on the back of his neck prickle and stand out quivering like maddened antennae. A quick glance at Siobhan confirmed she was as deeply moved as he was.

He didn't understand the Welsh words, but, he wished with all his heart that the words would jump into his mouth so he could join in this glorious exultation.

What surprised him most of all, was that he had expected all the best singers in the congregation to be in the choir, but this was not the case.

Immediately behind where he and Siobhan stood with Megan, was an old man that Donald considered must be into his late seventies, despite this his voice was as clear as a mountain stream, and as musical.

Such power there was in the basso profundo, that Donald was sure he felt the resonance throb through him as the voice carried the measure with utter carefree abandon.

When the hymn ended, Donald looked at Siobhan and caught the glint of tears in her eyes. He took her hand and squeezed it gently as she whispered to him with her voice choked with emotion.

"I had heard that the Welsh could sing, but I must admit I thought it would only be in trained choirs, but oh! Donald, I feel as if I have heard a host of angels. It was so beautiful, just so beautiful.

Donald agreed wholeheartedly with his sweetheart, as they sat back to listen to the opening sermon. This was to be an eye opener as well, to the young couple.

The youthful minister was a practised orator, with a voice that filled the chapel with his impassioned delivery. Donald thought, they can't only sing those Welsh, they can talk as well. The quality of the rolling cadence was in itself a psalm of praise holding the congregation captive and aware. No nodding heads in this gathering of worshippers. A service full of joy and Glory to God.

No evidence of the fire and brimstone declarations that the two youngsters were used to in their own places of worship, and thinking about it, Donald now knew why the little chapel had been full to capacity. What a pity, in his estimation, that other disciplines didn't follow the pattern of this little chapel in the valley.

At the end of January, Donald and Siobhan reluctantly took their leave of Llanderawel. It had been an idyllic honeymoon, that they would remember possibly to the end of their lives.

At Barranbarrach there was much to do to effect the move to Cruachan. The list seemed endless with veterinary examinations and documentation all part and parcel of seemingly never ending tasks.

There were five horses all told, two Arabs, two Connemara Greys and of course the Black Beast, for he would be essential in the breeding programme that Siobhan had in mind.

Eddie O'Flaherty approached Donald and somewhat apprehensively asked if there was any chances of accompanying Donald and Siobhan to Cruachan.

Donald with a diplomatic flair slapped his forehead in exasperation and apologised, saying he thought he had already asked Eddie if he would come with them.

As he watched Eddie walk off with a new confidence in his step, he was glad that he had been able to convey his sincere happiness to the wee man, and when he remembered how well the jockey had teamed up with Chi Li he knew that a tentative friendship would now take full flower to the benefit of both of them.

The 1st of March dawned clear and bright, and the weather forecast promised that it would remain so for the next couple of days. This couldn't have been better news for Donald, as he was concerned with the crossing from Larne to Stranraer.

It was not a wide stretch of sea to cross, but it had the reputation of being one of the wildest crossings between shores that could be made, and vied with the Bay of Biscay in maelstrom lore.

The iron will of Mari fractured here and there, as she tried to wish them well and kiss them a thousand times. Finally the two travellers were in the bosom of the Daimler instead of Mari, and at Donald's urging to the chauffeur gliding smoothly down the drive away from Barranbarrach.

When they reached the docks, Siobhan led the Black Beauty onto the boat and into the prepared stall for the crossing. She smiled when she overheard one of the dock handlers saying he didn't know what all the fuss had been about the big black horse, for sure! there wasn't an animal alive that he couldn't handle, and that one in particular that had followed the madam aboard was just a big pussycat.

When Donald and Siobhan had taken a walk round the stock and were satisfied all was in order, they climbed up to the top deck and making their way to the prow, faced towards Scotland and their new home. Hopefully to a new and peaceful life.

The Author

The author of 'Golden Boy', Peter Shillan, was born in the Parish of Gatehouse of Fleet in Galloway.

At eleven years of age his parents moved to a remote glen in North Perthshire which quite soon became an environmental prison. Always an avid reader, the lure of faraway places with strange sounding names created a restlessness that could not be denied.

At nineteen years of age he joined the Royal Air Force and served for twentyfour years, travelling extensively the length and breadth of the world, always volunteering for detachments to help satisfy his craving to see new places.

On discharge from the R.A.F. he joined the Emergency Ambulance Service in South Wales. Eight years later he trained as a Chiropodist, which now occupies him three days a week.

His hobbies include water colour paining and marquetry, and caring for five little Llaso Apso dogs which are the delight of his life.

He lives at Bridgend in South Wales with his wife, step daughter and mother-in-law, who encourage him in anything he chooses to do. In this environment he feels at peace and secure, which is a sound platform from which to launch his literary aspirations.

'Golden Boy' is his first full length novel where he has exercised the right to express his deep interest in folklore and country lore with a tongue in cheek application to both.